Copyright

Hardcover design and typography image by: moonpress.co

Paperback cover by: Storywrappers

Edited by: Lisa Nieves-Taylor

Map design done in: Wonderdraft

A Shield of Water

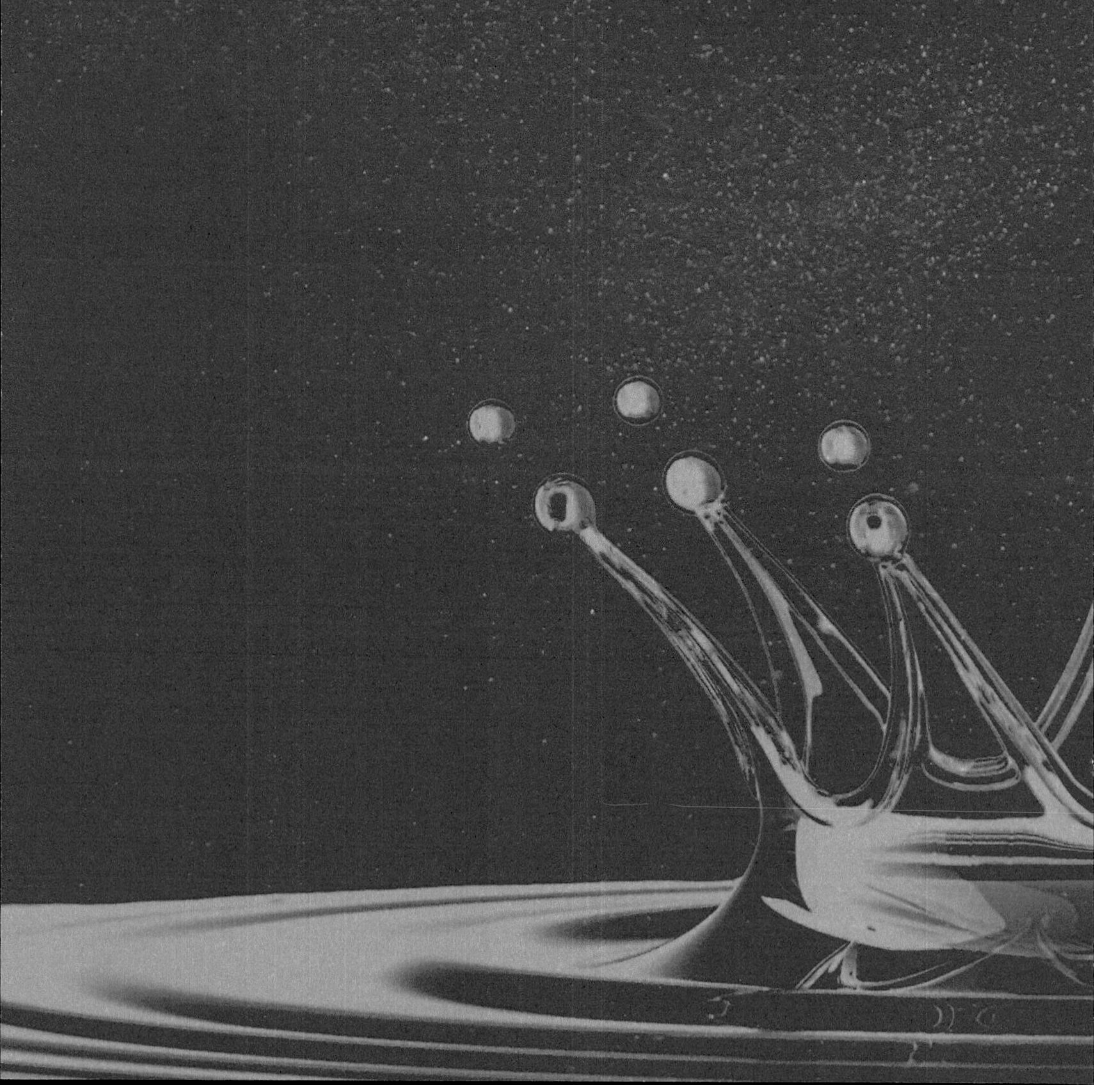

Dedication

To the women who feel trapped.
You are not weak.
You are the bravest of us all.

Fae Elementals Glossary and Pronunciation Guide

Kingdoms, Cities, and Landmarks

Illyk: *Eel-ick*
Tuath: *Two-ahh-th*
Dana: *Day-nuh*
Vellm: *Vey-mm*
Ielwyn: *Eel-win*
Teg: *Teh-gg*
Orknie: *Orc-knee*
Lake Degara: Lake *Dig-are-uh*
The Arcana: *Arc-ay-nuh*
Lywyth River: *Lee-with*
Tir Na Faie (also known as the Feylands): *Tier Nuh Fey*
Ley Line: *Lay Line*
Castle Aileach: *Castle I-lick*
Terrlyn: *Tear-lynn*
Porir: *Pour-rear*
Herria Mountains: *Hair-ree-uh*
Verdt: *Veer-dt*
Ojor: *O-joar*
Wyrshl: *War-shell*
Seirz: *Seer-tz*
Covenglen: *Coven-glenn*

People

Shula Azzarh: *Shoe-luh Uh-zarrh*
Piriguini: *Peer-ee-gween-ee*
Ryker Valda: *Rye-curr Vahl-duh*
Clay Valentino: *Clay Valen-tee-no*
Julius Darah: *Jewel-ee-us Dare-uhh*
Valerio Ashera: *Vahl-eer-rio Ah-sheer-uh*
Weylyn Xanth: *Way-lynn Zanth*

Uric Adriel Nova: *You-ric Ay-dree-el No-vuh*
Orna: *Or-nuh*
King Amos Ashera: *Ay-mose Ah-sheer-uh*
Emperor Robert Laurel: *Robert Lore-rel*
Mairin Valda: *May-rin*
Iona Wylde: *I-oh-nuh Wild*
George Apidae: *George Eh-pihh-day*
Temair Beston: *Tim-mare Best-uhn*
The Kurreen: *The Core-Reen*
Malika: *Muh-lee-kuh*
Veles Riel: *Veh-less Real*
Corvina Rhian: *Core-vee-nuh Ryan*
Terms

Esses: (Pronounced like S. S.) A derogatory term for the Fae. Originally Seelie Scum, later shortened to S.S., then 'Esses'.

Mana: (Pronounced Mah-nuh) The word to describe the Fae entity/deity/god. It is magic, nature, and the elements, as these are holy amongst their race.

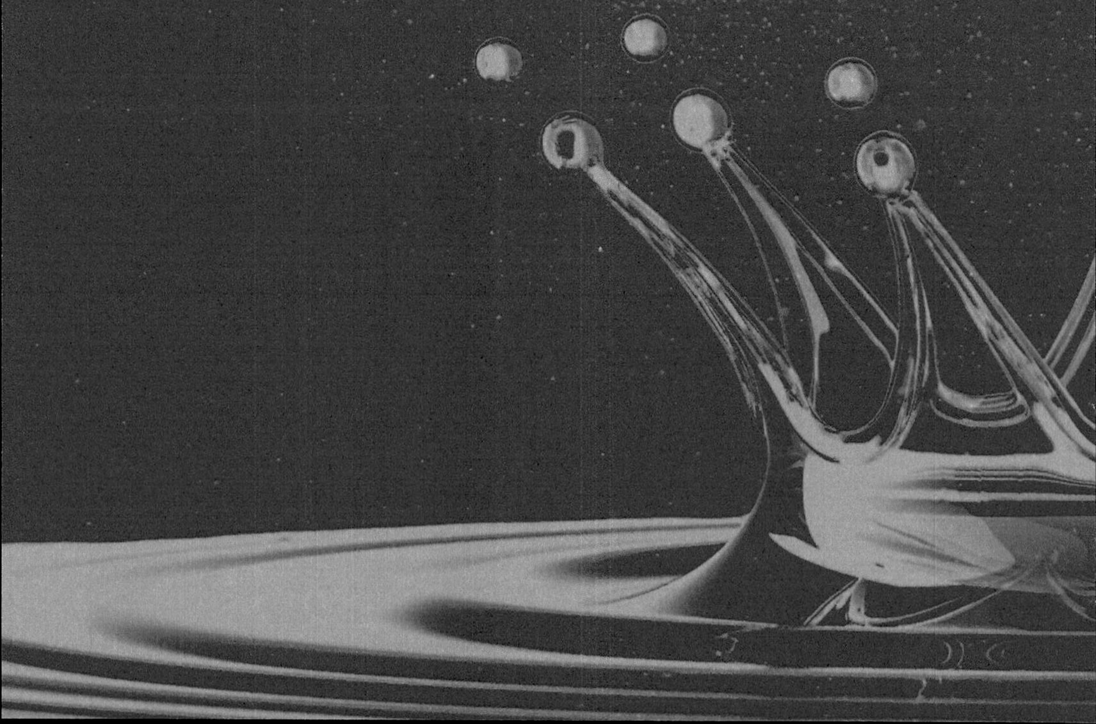

Trigger and Content Warnings

A Shield of Water contains dark and **GRAPHIC** themes such as:

- Sexual themes
- Rape and domestic violence that could be triggering and harmful to some readers. If such material offends you, please be wary of this book, specifically the following chapters: *Chapter 2, Tear-shaped scars; Chapter 7, An iron bride; Chapter 13, Water that burns like fire; Chapter 15, Purification*
- Forced pregnancy of a main character (in relation to the previous trigger)
- Violence
- Gore
- Post traumatic stress and trauma
- Racism towards the Fae and half-Fae in a fantasy setting
- The genocide of the Fae in a fantasy setting
- Slavery of the Fae in a fantasy setting
- Burning/Fire
- Alcohol consumption
- War
- Kidnapping
- Imprisonment of the Fae in a fantasy setting

- Decapitation of a side character

That being said, please proceed with caution and remember that your mental health and well-being always comes first.

If you or someone you know is a victim of domestic violence, please do not suffer in silence. If you need help or assistance, please call the National Domestic Violence Hotline
1.800.799.SAFE (7233)
TTY 1.800.787.3224
Or text "START" to 88788
Video Phone Only for Deaf Callers, 206.518.9361

A Shield of Water is book three of six in the Fae Elementals series. It is in third person point of view and while each book follows a different Elemental, it still contains the points of view from previous characters, including the villains'. It is recommended that this series be read in order and this book contains a very mild cliffhanger.

Illyk
The Lagnh Sea
Gyshapur
Kaym
Vellm
Bazra
Kayron
Valley of the Dead
Barrenhorn
Telshaw
The Arcana
Myrim
Ielwyn
Badfa
Ojor
Mountains
Wintshore
Castle Aileach
Loren
Crystal Forest
Lywyth River
Tuath
Minn
Bridgertown
Seirz
Hiel Lake
Arcancliffe
Covenglen
Vallart
Solle
The Arcana
Dana
Port Bay
Zaen
Teg
Lake Degara
Clyhr
Port Lays
Orknie
Eul
Terrylyn
Porir
Verdt
Wyrshl
The West Isles
Ley Line
Crimson Court
The Iron Mountains
Western Waters
Gold Court
Tir na Faie
The Feylands
Jade Court
Sombhra Mountains
The Seelie Court
The Pool
Elin Ocear
Obsidian Court
Naches Forest
Sapphire Court
The Unseelie Court
N
W
E
Nymph Island

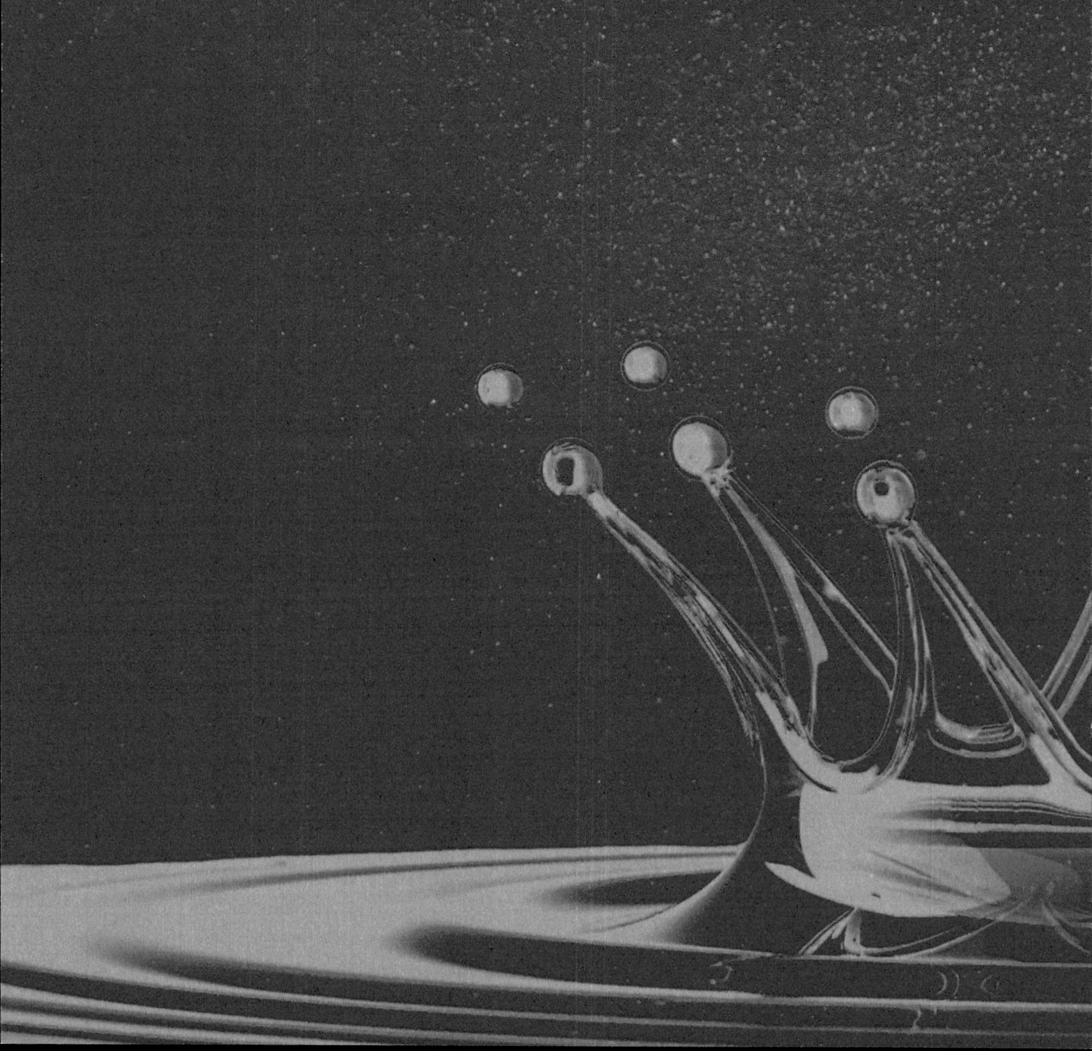

An Advantageous Match

Blood littered the halls.

It pooled down gilded marble like honey, running over bridges and into the waters, where the dark, ominous color of it was washed away as it rushed into the ocean. That did nothing to disguise the smell of it, drifting in through the lace curtains of the opened window.

Death had a very distinguished scent. One even Lady Corvina Rhian could make out past the crisp salt in the humid air, in the pressing sting of iron being welded into new buildings, and in the sweat and body odor of the soldiers come to slaughter her people.

And, quite possibly, herself.

Corvina's hands were clasped delicately in her lap, and she just barely resisted the urge to bunch the pink tulle in her fingers.

"My lady..."

"Silence, Dawn," she interrupted. She did not like using that cutting tone with her lady's companion, or with anyone; however, she needed quiet. She needed to stave off the sharp reminder that soon they would both be dead.

She was aware what course of action Dawn would have them take.

To jump from the windows, take their chances in the water and be swept away by the Lagnh Sea.

Corvina's father did not raise a coward. Even if he'd all but sold her to their enemies beyond the Ley Line for peace between nations—that act seeming cowardly in and of itself—she would not take the easy way out. She was a Rhian, nearly a princess in her own right of the Gold Court, and when her captors burst through that door, she would keep her head high.

No matter what they did to her.

It would be brutal and bloody and it would *hurt*, but she swore to herself she would remain strong. Like her servants had remained strong when the humans had stained the halls of the palace in Fae blood. Everyone who had journeyed with her from their homeland in Tir na Faie all the way to the human lands of Dana had been defeated. She had heard their screams, had tasted the blood in the air, and swore she could feel a rush of magic as their souls were gifted back to Mana.

Only she and Dawn were left. Her companion had ushered her within her lavish rooms and barred the door, begging for them to save themselves, to jump. Corvina refused. Now, the only thing standing between them and death was thick panes of white wood with golden, floral edges and the chair wedged beneath the brass knob. Like that could stop steel or iron.

It wouldn't.

It didn't.

Torn off its hinges, Corvina barely blinked as soldiers rent down the barrier and burst inside, brandishing and pointing their swords in her direction. Dawn shrieked and wept, but Corvina's own cheeks were dry and her heart filled with hatred. She could just make out the whites of their eyes beneath the steel helms that decorated their heads. They were fearful and just as furious as hers.

"Well?" she drawled in her sweet voice—the one she was known for in her court. They blinked slowly as though surprised by the genuine innocence of her tone. "Are you going to kill me or not?"

"*That* is entirely up to you."

Corvina startled inwardly. Outwardly, her gaze lifted to watch the human who'd spoken approach. The soldiers parted for him, an unassuming yet handsome young human. He wore excess finery; a jacket with diaphanous sleeves and too many buttons that glinted against beams of sunlight.

She had met him before in passing, and while their eyes had met from across crowded rooms and dinner tables, they hadn't spoken a word before now.

He stopped in front of her so she had to crane her neck back to look up at him.

"Lady Corvina," he greeted, as if they were old friends and he did not have soldiers pointing weapons in her direction. "I so dislike to come bearing bad news, but your court has fallen. Tir na Faie is being conquered as we speak and your father is dead."

The callous, cold words were a blow.

Discord between the humans and Fae had been toiling over from becoming a mere parry of nations to an outright war. It had been one of the reasons she'd been sent here. To listen, to learn, and to help keep the peace. In that, she had failed. She'd known what the blood in the halls meant, and yet it did not stop the pain of the truth.

Her father... He'd been the High Lord of the Gold Court. With no sons or close male family to take his place, they were lost without a leader. She should have been there to take over as High Lady for what remained of her court until the Seelie King could appoint another in her father's place.

A stinging pain pulsed behind her eyelids, but she refused to let the tears fall. She took a breath and glared up at the man. "What do you want?" Her voice was surprisingly firm, given the circumstances.

"I think the better question here is what do *you* want? You have two options, Lady Corvina; you can choose to live or choose to die. If you want the latter, then I will walk away and let my men have their way with you and your companion. If the former, then I would urge you to accept my proposal."

She blinked slowly, like she would if she was waking from a dream, and took a deep breath, if only to swallow down the words she desperately wanted to spit at him. She was far away from home, her guards and people dead. She did not have the luxury of being impulsive out of spite.

"What is your proposal?"

"Marry me."

There was no preamble, no bending on one knee, no flowers. She was a fool, perhaps, to have hoped that when someone asked it would be in a grand gesture of romance. Preferably from her mate.

He was not her mate.

He was nothing but the man who held her future in his fingertips.

"I am a very powerful man, and you would be protected beneath my influence despite your... afflictions..."

She had the urge to scoff but held back her reactions. She could hear her father's voice in her mind, telling her to be wise. To think.

She must have been silent for quite some time, because he made an impatient noise. "I would urge you to choose wisely and quickly, my lady, for time is running out." He held his hand out, his brows raised in question, in a dare. "Make your decision. Personally, I think we have quite an advantageous match."

She stared at the offending limb in question, her jaw clenched tightly. The desire to turn her nose up at him, to spit at his feet, and tell him to rot in hell was a prominent itch. She had never been overly daring in her life. As the daughter of a High Lord, she had an image to maintain. She had bonds and bridges to build between courts and kingdoms, and above all, she had a duty to her people.

That duty had been ingrained into her since birth. More than that, she loved her home; she loved the Gold Court and the Fae. It was why she'd readily accepted becoming a piece in a game of kings and lords. Now, this human meant to use her as a pawn and threaten her as if she would so easily succumb to fear and bribery.

This meek persona was merely that.

So, when Lady Corvina smiled softly and placed her hand in his, she caught his smile of triumph as if he was a god who controlled the board, as if he had her pieces cornered and his win was inevitable.

Little did the fool know that pawns were not the most important pieces in a game of chess, and Corvina? Well, she was no pawn.

"I accept," she whispered.

She was a queen with tricks up her sleeve.

And the game had only just begun.

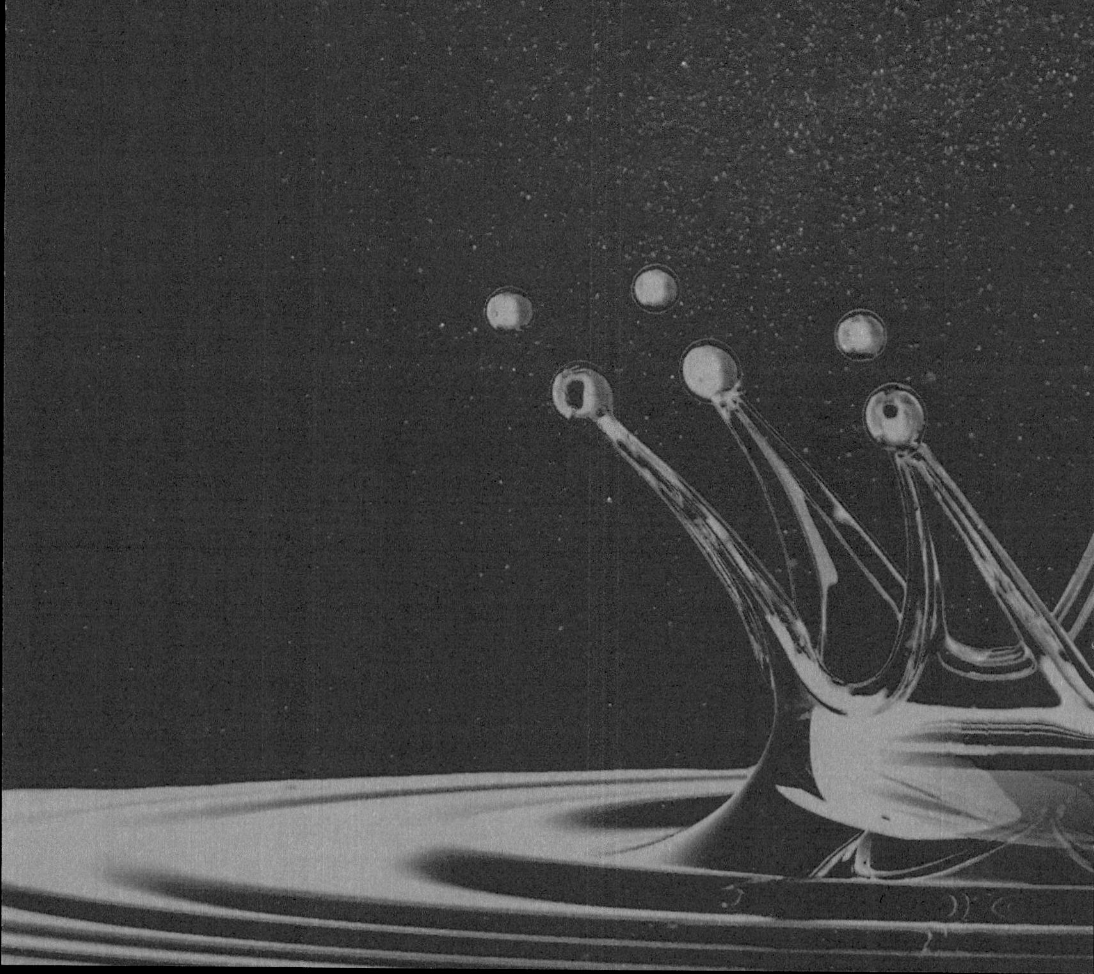

Golden Rivers

4 years later...

The palace was one of three that overlooked the kingdom of Dana. Erected on the sandy cliffs that seemed more like adjacent mountains, each one boasted polished marble and white pillars that held up domed ceilings. Opened archways, stained glass windows in colors of white, blue, and various shades of pink and purple filtered light and a heavy sea breeze through the halls.

Corvina remembered there was once a time when similar halls had been stained in blood.

That was a different time. Years had passed, yet the memory still tasted as bitter and poisonous as iron on her tongue.

Now, she resided within a different castle. The third on those cliffs, and the smallest by far. It overlooked the Lagnh Sea. The bright blue waves lapped up against the shores below, sometimes rising towards the marble bridge that led from the edge of the land where the three castles met and towards the populated city of Port Bay below them.

Corvina always felt god-like when she looked from her balcony to the city below. A cliff and a bridge separated her from the people, and though the distance was but miles she always felt it to be more. One could be separated by more than just a few simple steps, after all.

One could be separated by hearts and souls and emotions that didn't quite measure up.

That was a harsher thing, she thought, to be separated by emotions and sadness and loneliness, rather than a whisper of footsteps. It was a distance far greater. With space, one could easily swallow it up. With emotions, others could go where one could not follow.

Those were her melancholy thoughts as she looked down at the bustling sea-side city. Everyone below had a purpose, a mission, and she could hear the life from her perch. Her hand lifted and reached out. From this position, it looked like she could hold Port Bay in the palm of her small, delicate hand, but it was always just out of reach, never within her grasp.

She sighed and lowered her hand. Even gods became lonely sometimes. Perhaps that was why they created kingdoms. To feel not so alone from their skies. To watch happiness unfold and despair because it was something to be had, yet always so far away.

The cool sea breeze kissed her cheeks, pushing aside her golden strands of hair and the layered pink skirts she wore. Her palms curled against the balcony, her body leaning over to catch the bright blooms of roses below. The thorny vines climbed over trellises and up the side of the palace, overreaching and entwining around pillars with a suffocating force. If she reached out and touched them, she would surely bleed. Like her people had bled.

"Princess, please have a care."

The voice had Corvina pushing against the cool marble and turning to meet the worried stares of her three maids. Juniper, Wren, and Gale. Their eyes darted between her and the balcony. She knew what they were thinking and refused to let them entertain the thought for a moment.

"The city is restless today," Corvina explained.

It was a simple excuse for why she'd been leaning over the balcony and staring off into the distance. Let them not think she had been prepared to jump. She hadn't been, yet she hated how they thought her so weak. She could not blame them for the thoughts, when she had proven at every turn the true nature that she coveted beneath her skin was decrepit.

Her maids relaxed their postures and nodded. Single, tight nods accompanied with terse smiles that did not quite reach their eyes. Though, she did not suppose they had much reason to smile, what with the iron choked around their necks like the vines on the pillars. Only Juniper and Wren wore them, as Gale was human and could roam freely without fear of retribution. She was also her newest maid, and the most talkative.

"Princess, you will be late for dinner..." The words trailed off and Wren chewed at her bottom lip.

"Oh, my, we mustn't dally." Corvina smoothed down the wrinkles in her skirts, straightening her posture, and tucking the errant strands of gold back into place, though the wind tugged at them relentlessly. "Come on, then." She gestured at them to follow with the smallest flick of her fingers.

The maids breathed a collective sigh of relief as Corvina left the freedom of the balcony and slipped back inside the cage of her castle.

Endless lengths of marble, with swirling designs of gilded gold and rose pink, expanded all around her. It sculpted against the walls in sweeping, floral gestures that made the castle look soft and feminine as well as intimidating. Chandeliers swept low from the high ceilings, the wax dripping in slow tendrils against the tapers.

It all felt like something out of a tale, the kind her father had often read to her as a little girl with princesses and princes and monsters, rich and dripping in scintillating finery.

Sometimes, when the light of day poured beams through the windows, the rays of sun catching against the gild of the walls, Corvina was reminded of home. Where the rivers ran golden and the fields swayed with crops in the same wheat colors; where the land seemed bathed in riches, though the real gems were that which the earth gave them. Gifts from Mana that kept the Fae fed and alive.

Not anymore.

Tir na Faie had long since been defeated, and if the rumors were to be believed, it was now little more than a desolate wasteland of iron and the bones of those fallen in battle. The golden rivers she'd waded through in her youth had likely turned to the color of rust, the fields dry and barren, the magic sapped from the earth as if it had never really been there at all.

"Which dress do you fancy wearing tonight, Princess?"

Corvina was torn from her thoughts as her maids pushed open the doors of her chambers and ushered her inside. One of them gently guided her into the seat in front of her vanity mirror, while the others bustled around the room, pulling garments from white wood closets to set them gently upon the bed. An array of fabrics soon found themselves piled onto her blankets, the colors all bright and diaphanous. They tittered around the fabric while Corvina watched with detached emotions.

Traditionally, her maids should have been noble ladies of high birth instead of slaves and servants. Allowing Fae to be near her was a kindness and a privilege as much as a horrible twist of fate. Most of her maids ended up dead.

"However shall I choose?" Corvina's lips pressed together, her eyes tracing the materials in the mirror while Juniper got to work on her hair.

The truth was she did not particularly care what she wore to dinner. Though she'd lived in the human realm for years, she still did not feel accustomed to their strange sense of fashion. Back home, they wore loose skirts that bared the shoulders. Modesty existed, though not in the same sense as it did in the human lands. The clothes were always too tight, with high necklines and long sleeves and heavy skirts despite the heat. And there was a dress code for every occasion. Different garments for breakfast, tea, lunch, and dinner. Not to mention for balls, the theatre, and strolling through the gardens.

Corvina's maids often found reasons to change her attire, making her feel like she had spent half of her day being swathed in and out of tulle, silk, and velvet.

"May I suggest the purple?" Gale asked. In her hands, she held up a dress almost reverently. With a beaded bodice, a neckline that would touch to her throat, and sleeves that would cut at her wrists.

"Excellent choice." The lie tasted like ash against her tongue, yet she had grown used to speaking untruths, for the consequences of being honest were quite severe. She'd long learned to live with wearing and saying things that brought her discomfort.

After her hair was pressed back, away from her heart-shaped face, her maids began to dress her quickly. She was corseted, done up in ribbons and garters until she could scarcely breathe. Once finished, she was escorted from her chambers and into the dining hall, where her husband was already seated.

He stood upon her entry, though he did not bow. Those cold, cutting eyes assessed her from head-to-toe as they often did, searching for anything upon her that would be out of place. Something to use against her, or perhaps the maids, so he could unleash his particular brand of cruelty when he was feeling bored.

Corvina dipped into a curtsey. "Prince Tobias."

When she rose, his handsome smile was all she could see for a moment as he flashed those straight, white teeth. "No need to be so formal, my wife. Please, sit. You are just on time."

The nerves in her stomach did not ease, despite the jovial tone with which he spoke. She took her seat, a butler pushing the high back chair in. Only when she was tucked firmly across from him, did the prince take a seat.

He regarded her curiously, like he did most nights. It took all Corvina had not to fidget beneath his penetrating stare, because she knew he was finding fault within her, and showing the slightest bit of weakness could be catastrophic. This she knew from experience.

Usually, she could gauge the prince's mood based on the placement of his thick, dark brows. Tonight, they arched over his bright eyes, which meant he was not in a particularly angry mood, however that did not mean he could not be cruel even when he was happy. That aspect was ingrained in his personality and she expected nothing less.

"How was your day?" he asked, in a tone that could trick her into believing he actually cared.

"It was fine."

His smile widened. "You look nice tonight."

She was spared having to reply to his compliment as the servants rushed in with trays of food. They set the feast down on the table before them. So many courses, for just the two of them. Artichoke soup, steamed fish and veggies, venison, potatoes and gravy, turkey legs...

Her throat tightened, taking it all in. Human food was vastly different from what she remembered eating in Tir na Faie, where the meat was properly seasoned with a collection of spices infused with magic from the Unseelie Court that all but exploded on the tongue. The food here was bland and tasteless, and it was a battle not to scrunch her nose with every bite she took.

They began eating, the silence interrupted only by their utensils clinking against the porcelain bowls. By the time the third course came around, Prince Tobias began speaking once more.

"How is Reginald?" he asked in between bites of meat.

Corvina forced out a breath, tightening her fingers around her spoon to prevent them from shaking, before she answered, "He is quite well."

"Hmm. Perhaps he is at the age where we should include him at the table now."

She bit the inside of her cheek to avoid replying, staring down at the food on her plate instead. She hated speaking of him with Tobias, if only because it grew harder to keep her mouth shut and be the meek wife he'd turned her into over the years.

"That would be lovely," she merely responded.

Their meal continued in silence. The meat was cut and chewed, wine was poured and sipped, and Prince Tobias stole glances at Corvina from across the table, which she pretended not to notice. In reality, they made her body clench and her stomach tighten. She recognized what the arch over his brows meant, like she recognized the way the corner of his mouth twisted into a smirk.

The food suddenly felt leaden in the pit of her stomach, and she feared it all might rise again if she took another bite. She wanted to escape, to flee and hide from the demands he would make, but she knew just how impossible it was to run from him and come out unscathed.

As the servants cleared away the plates, Corvina reached for the wine and took a healthy swallow, hoping it would blur her senses, though all it did was sour in her throat.

Still, Prince Tobias stared from across the table. He was handsome, though not overly so. Not handsome like Fae men were. Something about him had been unassuming, those first times they'd met. Now, she recognized what lay beneath the gold and riches he drenched himself in. What she had once viewed as plain features she now saw for what it truly was.

Something to be feared.

She finished her wine and made a move to stand. The butler hurried to pull out her chair, and she rose only halfway before the words she knew were coming cut through the space between them.

"Have your maids ready you, wife," Prince Tobias purred. "I will be visiting you in your chambers tonight."

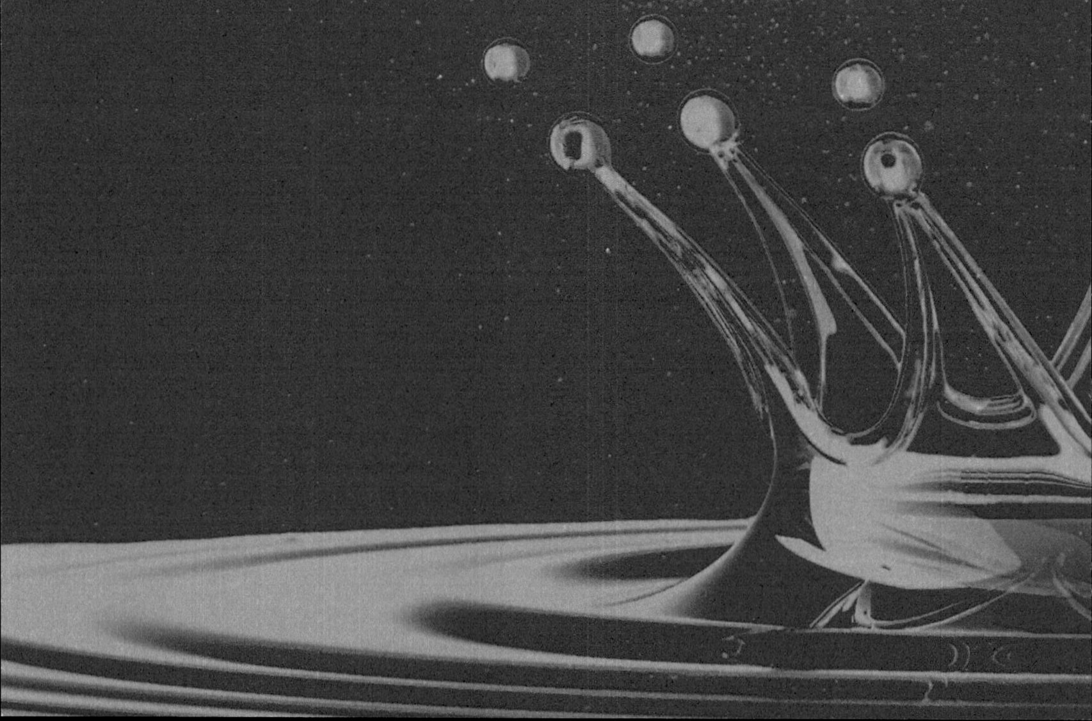

Tear-shaped Scars

The oils felt heavy against her skin and smelled sharply of jasmine. It was a scent that clogged through her nose and lungs, though Tobias seemed to enjoy it. In fact, he insisted she wear it every time he visited her chambers for their coupling.

Which meant Corvina despised it.

It smelled too strong and threatened nausea whenever it pierced her nostrils. As it was, she was attempting not to gag on the pungent odor as it was poured against the surface of her body.

The quiet echoed through her chambers, interrupted by the slick suctioning sounds of her maids' hands on her, rubbing her skin down in its entirety. Juniper kneeled before Corvina, sliding her long fingers up her calves. The hem of her ribbon night dress bunching up to her waist while Juniper's hands slid against her thighs. She paused and pulled away, adding more of the slick substance to her fingers.

Sad hazel eyes met Corvina's blue ones. She knew what came next, and still the humiliation of it never ceased. Juniper looked apologetic, as apologetic as Corvina felt every time she glimpsed the shine of iron from beneath the Fae's neckline, or the twisted mash of flesh where her pointed ears should have been.

While the rest of the kingdoms of Illyk had outlawed the Fae, there were those that lived their lives in Dana as slaves. When they'd been brought over from Tir na Faie, instead of being taken to iron camps, some were sold in auctions. They were branded, their ears, wings, tails, or horns sliced off, and their necks were shackled in iron collars.

It broke her heart to see the restraints against their skin, because Corvina herself knew what they felt like. They burned, singeing flesh and leaving permanent scars behind. She longed to reach between them and yank at the gleaming metal, but stopped herself. It would hurt Juniper more, in the end, for the laws of Dana stated that any Fae caught without a collar would be cut down where they stood.

Her heart broke to think of those in her court, in any court, dealing with a treatment so vile.

But if Juniper and the rest of the Fae slaves that inhabited Dana could handle such torment, then Corvina could handle *this* without complaint.

She gave a single nod and Juniper's fingers slid against her center, rubbing oil along the seam of her womanhood. Her touch was gentle yet invasive as she rubbed it along Corvina's channel, to ease passage of what was to come. Besides, this was more for Corvina's benefit than her husband's.

Oftentimes, he did not care if she was prepared for him or not and would hurt her. Juniper was doing her a kindness. Even if it made Corvina feel raw and exposed.

Once they finished rubbing her down and the hem of her night dress slid back down to her ankles, they took a brush though her hair, letting it fall in curls down her back.

"You make such a pretty sight." Gale sighed wistfully.

Corvina fought back her cringe and instead smiled at her human maid. "That is very kind of you." And very ignorant, though Corvina did not dare say that. She did not want to hurt Gale's feelings, but sometimes her oblivious behavior grated. She could not see past the pretty dresses, the jeweled clips, or ostentatious castle enough to really *see.*

Juniper and Wren shared wary glances that Corvina pretended not to see. Underlying those surface emotions, she caught the pity there. How sad that her maids, who were all slaves, pitied Corvina for what was to come more than they pitied their own dire circumstances.

Just then, the door to her chambers opened and Prince Tobias strode inside. He wore a simple robe in a rich, deep blue, the color of the sea. Rings glittered against his fingers and chains with rubies hung from his neck. The robe parted at the chest, revealing the simple, thin shirt he wore underneath. The lapels of that too parted, showing the coarse, dark hair that curled against his chest.

Her maids stood and curtsied low, though Tobias paid them no attention.

"Leave us," he commanded with a flick of his fingers. The move was imperious and inspired immediate obedience. The maids left in a flutter of skirts, closing the door behind them and disappearing, leaving Corvina and her husband alone.

Bile tasted acrid in the back of her throat, but a deep breath and a hard swallow pushed that aside. For a second, they stared at one another, their eyes connected and unbreakable. Slowly, Tobias began pulling the rings from his fingers, as if by doing so he was somehow heightening the anticipation of his love-making.

Little did he know, the only thing Corvina anticipated was when it would be over.

"Lie back and lift your shift," Tobias said.

It was a barked order, one that made fear and unease trip down Corvina's spine. She ignored it and obeyed, sliding against her mattress and lying back.

Her fingers shook as she gripped the sides of her night dress and pulled it up her thighs, letting the lacey material bunch at her waist.

"Spread your legs."

Her eyes stared up at the ceiling, grazing over the swooping floral designs. She did not dare lift her head to look at him, though she heard the rustling of his robe as he swept it off and tossed it to the side. The clinking of jewelry as he pulled what remained on his person off and set it on a nearby table. Swallowing past the lump in her throat, her knees parted. A cold breeze that could have just been dread blew against her most intimate areas.

"You smell nice."

When his hands came upon her thighs, Corvina did not flinch. She wanted to, but she already memorized the pain of his touch and prided herself in the fact that she was now immune to these moments. It was easy to separate herself from her body, to focus on something else while he took what he needed. She didn't even have to feel it for herself.

Tobias shoved her knees aside, and there was a brief burn in her thighs as he widened them further, wedging himself between her legs. His weight came down upon her, his skin scraping hers. For a moment, he cut into her vision, smiling down. She tried to appear focused on him, to give herself the expression of a besotted wife, but her mind was already wandering to places far away from here.

"Do you want me to fuck you, my dear wife?"

The question barely registered. Corvina blinked and hummed, for she could not think of a suitable reply that was not laced with repulse. It seemed answer enough for him. Whether he believed it to be true or not, he did not care. His hips pressed hers to the mattress, his whole body pinning hers to the bed.

Her back scraped against the lace of her night dress, and she bit the inside of her cheeks as his fingers dove into her channel. The oils guided his fingers inside, though the stretch was still painful.

"Wet for me already." His breath burned against her neck. "I'll ease the ache, wife." A moment later, his fingers were gone, grasping for his member and guiding it to her entrance. He forced his way inside her in a single, painful thrust.

And then the rutting began.

Corvina held her breath through it.

Four years. Four years she had suffered his cock inside her orifices. She'd known the moment she took his hand and watched his smile light up that he would not be a merciful husband. There was no such thing as a merciful human prince.

She had thought herself so clever then. She'd thought herself a queen in a game of chess that those around her were playing. Corvina had meant to strike swiftly and smartly, to call out a check mate. Little had she known that Tobias would take her piece, snap it in half, then sweep everything from the board.

He'd broken her when she'd sworn she was unbreakable.

He'd taken her spirit and crushed it.

Their wedding night had been the worst. She was the daughter of a High Lord. A High Lady in her own right. The moment their vows were said and done, Tobias had dragged her through the halls into a room, where a group of nobles awaited to witness the consummation of their marriage.

Humans and their strange customs.

He'd forced her to her hands and knees like she was little more than a dog and ripped her dress from the back. She'd choked back the tears that threatened to fall, kept her head high and stared at the far wall as if she could somehow be transported elsewhere. Only, Tobias had not allowed her even that.

Hands wrapped around her hair and he thrust into her from behind, rutting wildly, his laughter ringing out in her ears. It had hurt and blood had slid down her thighs, for she'd been a virgin, and he had not been gentle. When he spent himself inside her, their witnesses left. After they did, he readied himself once again only the second time, he took her from behind.

Despite her screams, despite her protests, he entered every piece of her that night, like he could tear into her soul and destroy it with that alone. His body was a weapon meant to punish and break her.

For so long, she tried to mend the pieces he broke. But every night, Tobias took her like that. Forcing her to the ground, to humiliate her and treat her like an animal.

But then *it* happened.

The night everything changed.

He was rutting enthusiastically, his hand wrapped around her throat as if he meant to silence the cries of pain she no longer dared give. He did not need that satisfaction. His chest curved against her back, and as soon as his skin brushed against hers, she felt the pain.

More like agony.

It splintered down her spine like someone was carving a knife into her flesh. For a moment, she feared that was exactly what Tobias was doing. That he was punishing her for some offense she had no clue she'd committed. Her screams came then as fire seared against her back. It was an unimaginable anguish, a blaze that spread through her body, down to her muscles, to tendon, to the bone. It cut through to her very soul until it felt like that would disintegrate and she would disappear.

For a moment, she prayed to Mana that it would be her end. She'd hoped it was, because then the pain would fade.

But it did not.

Tobias pushed against her and cried out in surprise and disgust. He pulled his cock out of her and stumbled away. In the mirror, Corvina had glanced at the blood on his chest, blood that seeped from her back. Her body turned, and the last thing she saw before she fainted from the agony was the single circle carved beneath her neck.

A Fae curse, Tobias had spat when she'd woken later. He'd sneered at her with disgust, like she'd provoked her own pain somehow. She did not contradict him, did not defend herself in her weakness. He would have drawn his own conclusions, regardless of what she said.

And he did.

At least the scars on her back had brought her a reprieve from his nightly visits for a brief time.

At least the scars on her back prevented him from rutting on her while she was on all fours.

He could not look upon them without feeling disgust, so he hadn't taken her like that ever since. Now, he pushed her to her back and loomed over her where she was forced to stare into his face.

Corvina wasn't sure what was worse.

That had been a long time ago, though, and the wounds had long since healed. Now, the scars were raised, silver flesh in the image of a circle with whorls in the shape of tears and waves tearing through the center of it.

The lace scraped against her tear-shaped scar as her husband took his pleasure from her body. His teeth grazed against her; his hands pressed tightly. Tonight, he was tame in his cruelty. Corvina knew this was his version of a kindness. Sometimes, he thought she wanted it this way. That she appreciated his scraps of affection.

Like she should be grateful for them. And maybe, to some extent, she was. It could be worse, after all. He could bind her in iron and chains while he took what he considered were his husbandly rights, tearing apart her body while he did so.

This was a kindness.

His blunt nails digging into her hips cleaved the thought from her mind. Teeth scraped against her collarbone and bit down hard enough to bruise. Hips pumping faster, Tobias spent himself inside her, his groans suddenly becoming all she could hear.

As soon as he finished, he rolled away from her. Heavy breaths echoed around the vast room, breaths that belonged to him alone, just like the pleasure. Corvina listened with growing impatience as he dressed, slipping into his robe and placing the rings on each finger.

If there was one thing she could count on, it was that he never stayed.

Corvina didn't allow the breath to enter her lungs until after he was gone. Until the door to her rooms closed and she no longer felt choked by his presence. Only then did she roll to the side and inhale sharply. The sudden burst scraped against her throat, but that pain was nothing compared to the pulsing ache between her thighs, or the bleeding sting against her collarbone, or the throbbing of her breasts.

Or even the burn behind her eyes that begged her to cry. To let loose the tears of grief and pain, but why would she when she carried that anguish already?

When the image of her heartbreak and loneliness was already etched into the scars on her back.

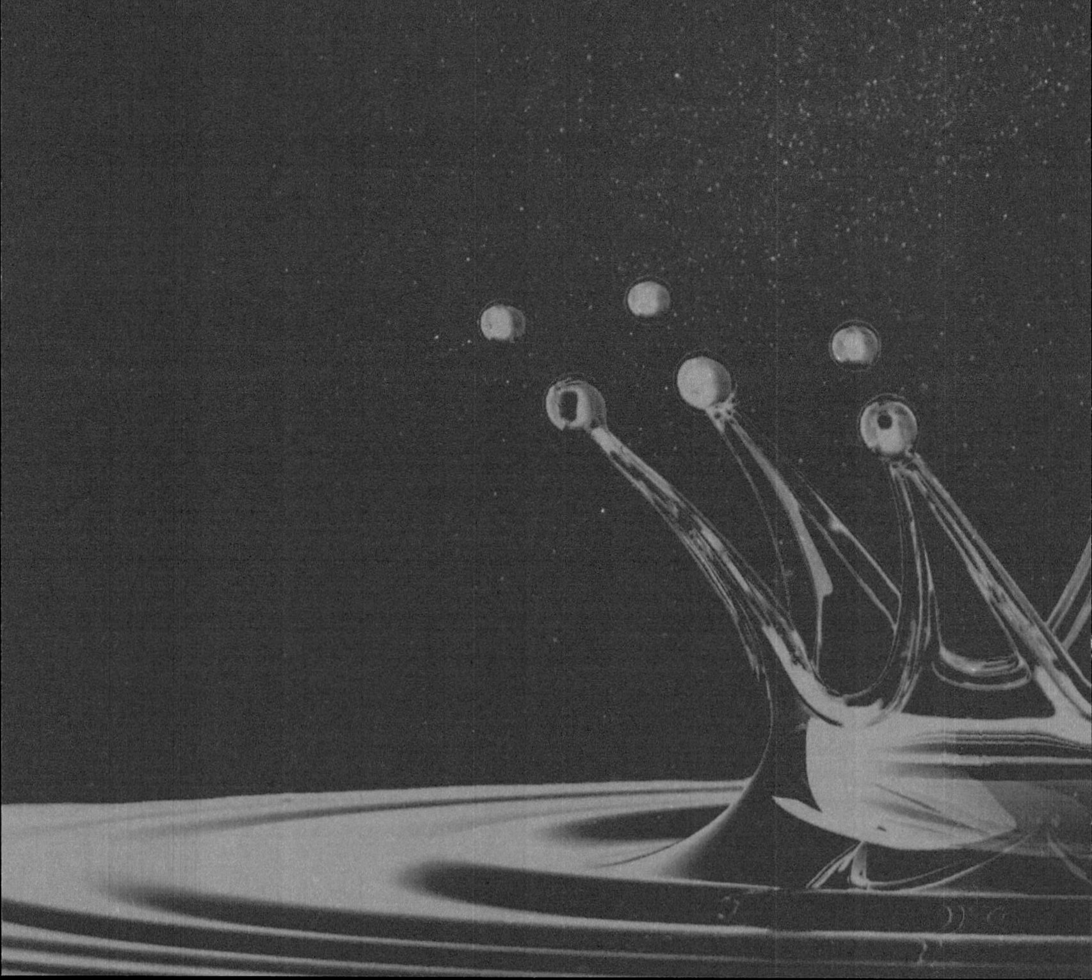

Basil

A wicker basket hung in the crook where her arm met her elbow. It swung back and forth with each bounce of Corvina's steps as she made her way down... down... down the winding stairs. She left marble behind until her heeled shoes touched cold, gray stone. Until the white walls tapered down into crumbling, wet structures where iron bars met brick and curved into small windows where even the sun couldn't reach. The spray of salt from the cresting ocean dripped into the open spaces of the prison that lay deep beneath the castle. Rats scuttled along the ground, their feet loud in the dim quiet.

Usually, the wails of the prisoners could be heard echoing through the cavernous space. Today, there was only the faint dripping of water and her own footfalls—as well as those of the guard who escorted her to a lone cell at the end of the hall.

He did not open the iron cage, as it was forbidden. Yet Corvina wished he would. Not because of her own discomfort—as the proximity of the iron pulsed against her skin and made her itchy—but so she could hug the woman on the other side of the bars.

"Dawn," she greeted, infusing a soft tone of voice without the pity she deeply felt. "Dawn, it is I."

The figure crouched in the corner of the cell unfurled, stretching long, skeletal limbs until she actually resembled a person and not some twisted creature of the Unseelie Court. Dawn crawled along the dirty ground, appearing closer to Corvina beneath a spot where a soft beam of light touched her.

Corvina's lady's companion was filthy. The thought was accompanied with guilt, as Corvina was sure she would be filthy too, had she been the one locked away in a cage. Her heart pounded as she took in her friend and what had become of her.

Golden skin, once the color of blazing dawn like her name, had become sickly and pale. Lush yellow hair was now a dull shade of brown, clunky with soot and dirt that hung across her boney shoulders. The dress she wore was little more than scraps clinging to a broken frame, the hem muddy and torn.

"My lady," Dawn whispered, her voice cracking and hoarse from disuse. "What have you brought me today?" Her weak fingers reached out to grasp the bars. There was a hiss, and a small plume of smoke emerged from where Dawn's palm met the iron.

Corvina forced a smile to her lips, though it wobbled. She set the basket down on the ground and bent next to it despite the impropriety of it. Not that she cared to be a picture of a proper princess, but she knew the guard watching over them would have words with Tobias, who would have *words* with her.

"I brought cheese and sweet meats and..." She grabbed the neck of the bottle and pulled it out. "Wine."

She'd also brought water, which Dawn seemed to desperately need. But her maid reached in between the bars and tore the bottle from Corvina's grasp. Her fingers fumbled with the cork, but eventually she opened it and tipped the contents back to her dry lips.

"I brought enough to last you the week," Corvina continued. The basket would not fit between the bars so she had wrapped everything in cloth and she began pushing them into Dawn's hands. "I should be back next week to bring you more."

If Tobias allows it.

Those words went unsaid, but Dawn was cunning and picked up the silences as if they were screams. Her dull gaze suddenly sharpened, and when she smiled, there was something feral about the way she did it.

"You must have pleased him greatly last night, if he allowed you to bring me such a feast today." The words had the desired effect.

They cut through Corvina's chest and left her head spinning. Her nose tingled, and the familiar tears pricked behind her eyes. "Mind your words," Corvina warned, an unwanted flush crawling up her skin. It would do no one any good if the guard took this conversation back to the prince. Then they would both be punished.

Dawn laughed, a broken, manic sound that was nothing at all like the friend Corvina remembered. She'd been locked up so long that she'd started losing herself. She wasn't the only one who suffered, and yet she often acted as though she was.

It was there in the hatred that burned in her eyes. Like she blamed Corvina for this. For her imprisonment. For being in Dana. For the fall of the Fae.

Corvina could not take credit for it all, but it still fell, a heavy weight on her shoulders that pressed her smaller and smaller to the ground. More than her husband's fists ever could.

"We should have jumped," Dawn spat. Spittle flew and the waft of her sour breath made Corvina's stomach churn. "I wanted to jump. Then I would not be here, chained like a damn animal, and you would not be spreading your legs for human filth."

"Dawn!" Corvina snapped, though her words rang true.

Every day, the same thing haunted Corvina. If she had not taken Tobias' hand. If she had not agreed to marriage. If she had not tried to play a game she did not understand the rules to, she would not have lost everything in the process.

If she had not...

But she *had.*

She had agreed to marriage, believing it would gain leniency for her people who would have been lost without a High Lord or Lady. It had broken her body and spirit until she knew she was unrecognizable now. It had ended with Dawn locked up here as leverage against Corvina, so she'd never dare disobey her husband or his wishes again.

And she hadn't. She didn't have the will to do such a thing anymore. He knew it, yet her friend was still incarcerated and hated her for it.

Even then, Corvina could not find it within her to regret what she'd done that day.

Regret was a betrayal.

She knew that, but every time she wanted to say those words, she felt her throat constrict and her tongue press to the roof of her mouth. How ironic that it felt like a betrayal to tell her own truth. Like maybe she *should* regret what had happened. And such emotions warred from within her, making her silent in the face of that question.

"I have to go," she whispered. Before Dawn could spew more hatred, Corvina was already standing, taking with her the wicker basket. "I shall come next week if I can. If not, then forgive me that, if you cannot forgive the rest."

Laughter greeted Corvina when she opened the doors to her chambers. Not the cruel, malicious kind that skittered across her nerves and made her want to shed her skin. This was the kind that lifted her heart and put a true smile to her face. The kind of smile that was reserved for one person only.

"Mommy!" Basil flew from the bed he was jumping on, landing on his feet in a crouch. He rushed towards Corvina, throwing his arms around her legs in a fierce hug. He momentarily disappeared between the tulle of her skirts before he emerged with a sputter and a laugh.

There was a tightness in Corvina's chest as she stared down at her son's face. A sensation that was undoubtedly the unshakeable love she felt for him. Big, bright blue eyes stared up at her from beneath thick, dark lashes. His hair was an unruly mass of curls in a reddish-brown hue, more brown than red, with hinting streaks of gold against the light. His nose was button-like and round, his lips thin and smiling wide, his two front teeth similar to Corvina's, as they were slightly longer than the others and mousey.

Years ago, when she'd first married the prince, Corvina had feared pregnancy. Because Fae had such long lifespans, their fertility rates were low, and even with the scant possibilities of conception, Corvina had been afraid. With the help of Dawn, she'd been able to procure rue, an herb that grew in thistle-like bushes, to prevent Tobias' seed from taking root.

She suffered chewing the bitter green leaves in secret out of pure unadulterated fear. She had not wanted to think how far Tobias' cruelty could extend, and she refused to bring a child into the world to be exposed to such a fate. More than that, she was ashamed to admit, she hadn't wanted a child with Tobias, for she feared she would hate them as much as she hated their father.

Then a guard had caught Dawn procuring the weed for her, and another maid had found remnants of the herb drying within the drawer of her undergarments.

Tobias had been furious when he'd discovered the truth, for all he'd wanted was a son, in the hopes that if his older brother were to die before he wed his own legacy would be secured. By ingesting that herb, Corvina had thwarted his plans. The lack of conception had made the King and Crown Prince of Dana question Tobias' virility.

Corvina had humiliated him.

He'd beaten her within an inch of her life before throwing her into the dungeons to purge the herb from her system. Only when she was healed did he let her out. The moments after that had been the hardest of her life, with him buried between her thighs for what felt like months. He didn't leave her room, didn't let her out of his sight or the guards'. And Dawn? She'd been locked up for her loyalty to Corvina, used as leverage.

"If you do anything like that ever again," Tobias had whispered against her cheek while his hips snapped against her own in vicious agony, "I'll fucking kill her."

She'd conceived soon after.

Knowing another life had taken root inside of her had been shattering. Like the earth had cracked from beneath her and tilted her off balance. How could she possibly bring a half-Fae child into the world where others would hate them? Where they witnessed the cruelty Tobias inflicted upon her? Would he harm her while she was pregnant with his child?

Worse yet, would she hate the sight of her own offspring the way she despised their father?

The thoughts had plagued her as her belly swelled with growing life. Tobias had been gentle with her during that time, at least, but no less savage in his remarks of her.

"After what you have done, you better pray to the gods that you bear me a son," he would spit from across the table at breakfast.

She'd dreaded the possibility that it might be a girl growing within her, fretted what the prince would do both to her and the baby she hadn't yet loved.

But then her son was born, and the nurse placed him against her breast, where he softly suckled his nutrition. Their chests rose and fell rapidly together, and for the first time in her life Corvina thought she might have felt those special, magical bonds that the Fae often talked about. Something that happened similarly when a Fae found their familiar or their mate, though this was different.

It was a bond of family.

She'd taken one look at the soft plumes of brown-red hair, like the feathers on the fragile skin of a baby bird, and loved him fiercely.

As he grew, the worry still clawed at her chest. She feared that one day she would wake up and the love she had would disappear if he ever turned into anything like his father. Those fears quickly abated every time he flashed his smile at her.

A smile that was her own.

And the rest of him? He didn't resemble Tobias at all, except perhaps in those thick lashes. If anything, he resembled the High Lord of the Gold Court. Corvina's father.

He had all the features of a Rhian. Fitting, she supposed, since he would be the High Lord of their court, if the world ever became what it once was. Back when the Fae ruled on their side south of Illyk. When magic reigned supreme.

The kingdom knew her son as Reginald Wes.

She knew him as Thorne Basil Rhian.

"Where did you go, mommy?" Basil inquired, his arms still buried within her skirts. She knew he wouldn't let go, so she bent and lifted him. He immediately wrapped his arms around her shoulders, pressing wet lips to her cheek.

Basil was three years old, nearing four, and was quite intelligent, if a little shy. She supposed it had to do with the violence he heard through the halls, though the maids tried to shield him from the worst of it.

Corvina pushed aside a curly lock of his hair, setting it behind his ear. Her fingers trailed softly against the curve for a moment. His weren't as sharp or as elongated at her own. They didn't pull back and arch upwards like the tips of arrows. They were small and still had a dull tip at the top. Not as curving as a human ear, and not quite Fae either.

His ears were easy to hide beneath his curls, something Tobias insisted on doing until he was old enough to have them surgically altered.

The thought made her chest hurt.

"I went to visit a friend."

Basil didn't know of Dawn's existence. Not because Corvina was afraid to tell him about her or embarrassed. It was because she knew he would ask questions, things she wouldn't be able to answer. Like where she was or why. And if he did, she would be too afraid to lie to him.

His hands, which were sticky with some unknown substance, grasped her neck. He stared deeply into her eyes, and she caught a spark within him that made her wonder, not for the first time, if he would display gifts from Mana.

She was unsure how strong half-Fae were, or if they even had gifts at all, but she always caught a spark of something in him that was just beneath the surface.

"I want friends, mommy."

Corvina's eyes slowly trailed up, where they caught with Juniper's. There was sadness in the air between them, before they both turned back to her son. They were always sequestered within the castle, so Basil did not often get the opportunity to interact with other children his age. All he had were the maids and butlers. Those times they did get to travel between castles on the cliffs, he always seemed to keep to himself while the other children played through ballrooms.

Like he was afraid to approach them.

Like he knew already at his tender age just how different from them he was.

"Juniper's your friend," Corvina told him, smoothing back his hair again. "And I'm your friend, too."

Basil's smile widened like it was the most wonderful thing in the world. She felt sad for him, that his only sense of companionship were the people currently in her chambers. He was growing restless and needed to move.

"How about a walk about the gardens?" she suggested. "We could play ball if you wish."

Basil wriggled in her arms until she was forced to slide him back to the floor, where he immediately began bouncing on the balls of his feet.

"Juniper will go with you to get your ball while I change into my outdoor dress." She would have been fine with what she was wearing, but Corvina never knew when the prince would appear or what mood he would be in.

It was better to succumb to his wishes than suffer his wrath later.

Juniper and Basil headed out of the room, leaving Corvina alone with an echoing silence. Sighing, she began undressing, slipping into a much more comfortable dress with lighter skirts and shoes that didn't pinch her feet.

When she finished, she met with Juniper, Basil, and Gale, who held a picnic basket in the crook of her arm.

"A fine day for walking, is it not?" Gale swung the basket.

From the corner of her eye, Corvina saw Juniper's lips press together. She knew her two Fae maids were not fond of Gale, though perhaps it was because of her flippant attitude and the freedom being human carried. She was privileged and oblivious to it.

Corvina envied her as well, but could not find it in herself to be rude. She was young and new, but she would learn the ways of the castle and of life soon enough.

"That it is. Shall we?"

The gardens outside were lush with greenery. Due to the harsh heat of the sun and the relentless rise of the waves over the cliffs, it was difficult to keep a garden, yet they managed. Fat blooms of red and pink roses spread from the bottom of the castle. Flowers imported from foreign kingdoms had been planted like jasmine, which climbed up the sides of pillars and whose scent made Corvina nearly gag.

There were also orange trees with hanging branches that birthed fat fruit. They'd tried to bring plants in from the magical, northern kingdom of Vellm as well, but the strange desert plants had not survived the salt-humid air of Dana. The dried husks of palm trees had been dug up long ago, but Corvina could imagine what they would have looked like in their prime.

Once they found a spot shaded by bright wisteria that looped over trellises and far away from the clogging stench of jasmine, they sat. Gale laid a blanket out on the ground where small patches of grass met coarse sand and black rocks. She began pulling the contents out. Cheeses, meats, ham, bread, and pastries.

The sight of them reminded Corvina of Dawn and their earlier discussion.

Considering they were things she did not wish to revisit, she instead turned to Basil, who eagerly held up his ball and gestured to the small patch of open grass where they could play.

They kicked the ball back and forth for a long time, laughing and running circles around one another. It was one of the few times Corvina felt actual happiness. When his laughter rang through the air like soft bells. When the shadows were gone from his eyes for but a moment to reveal the wonderful childhood he was supposed to have.

Taking a break to lounge against the blankets with her maids and son, Corvina lifted a cube of cheese to her mouth and chewed the dry wedge.

"The city was bursting today!" Gale began chattering before she'd even swallowed the first bite of food. Corvina's eyes went to her absently. "You should have seen the colors, Princess. Usually, it's always so busy, but there was a procession of soldiers marching through the streets and the streets were *packed.*" Her voice lowered as she leaned forward. "They wore the colors of the Emperor of Illyk."

The cheese turned to stone in her stomach. Corvina reached for a glass of wine Juniper had poured her and took a small sip, though it did nothing to parch the dryness in her mouth.

The Emperor of Illyk was the one who'd started it all. At least, that's what Corvina's father had told her. She'd been born in the middle of a war, coming out of her mother's womb crying amidst one tragedy after another.

The war had lasted two-hundred years, and Corvina had been born in the one-hundred and thirty-second year of the battling. It had not yet hit her court at the time, but death was bleeding into the lands of gold, as it had already taken out the Crimson Court, and way too close to their home.

Discord had been happening long before the war started. Over territories and magic and things the humans could never understand. On the hundred and twenty-fifth year, they'd taken the Feylands. Among the fighting and bloodshed, a captain rose and led the humans to victory.

As he conquered territories and rallied the once separate kingdoms of Illyk behind him, he built an empire and became its leader on top of the blood and bones of all the Fae he'd slaughtered.

He was famous for the gore. For the mounted heads and ears of Fae he kept in his throne room. She shuddered at the thought of her own body set on display for all to see. And the poor Fae, to be hung with such indignity...

After the emperor had conquered the Feylands and brought together the seven kingdoms of Illyk, he'd created a new era of hatred. His rule was supreme, and yet he'd left for the shadows, not to be seen again. His soldiers were everywhere, though, leaving behind remnants of the emperor in the form of iron camps and new rules and regulations that the kingdoms were expected to follow.

Some of them were negotiated. Like the fact that Fae were meant to be killed or thrown into camps. In Dana, they'd fought against that rule and came to an agreement. Her people were slaves, bought by the dozen like cattle. What reason the emperor's soldiers had for marching into Port Bay, she didn't know. They hadn't been seen here since the treaties were signed by the king.

"There were other men among their ranks as well," Gale continued. "Wearing white robes. I think they were priests from the Brotherhood."

The Brotherhood were a group of humans that preached human superiority over the Fae. Within the recent years, they'd gained a massive following and had started spreading throughout Illyk. Corvina had heard through the courts that their purpose was to purge the magic from the Fae. To literally take the Fae essence from their bodies.

"Oh! I also heard whisperings that the infamous Piriguini's Circus will soon come to Port Bay. Isn't that wonderful? I have heard nothing but amazing things regarding the circus... Though I did hear a rumor about their Fire Dancer, but I cannot be sure..."

"The circus!" Basil interrupted, jumping up and nearly knocking the wine glass from Corvina's hand. Honestly, she was surprised it had taken him this long to interrupt. He was a well-behaved child, too well-behaved and shy. But when he was among those he trusted, he could be hyperactive. "I want to go to the circus! I want to see the animals and the candies!"

Gale swept her thumb across his cheek, wiping away a smudge of dirt and crumbs. "Perhaps your father will bring them to you, little prince."

He is not a prince. The words tried to claw up her throat, begging for release. It was almost instinct, to think those words. That her son was not a prince. Not at all. He was something far greater and far more special than a human prince. But she could not say any of what she wanted to say, for by marrying Tobias, she had all but renounced her Fae ways and embraced human customs, traditions, and beliefs.

They had wanted to wipe all trace of Fae from her, much like the Brotherhood did to others. Her fingers refused to reach for the ears hidden behind her elaborate twisting of hair and what had been done to her there.

Sighing, she bit back the words that she wanted to say with great effort, and instead stared off into the distance.

Though they were there, on the tip of her tongue. In her mind, and in her heart.

He's not a prince.

He's a High Lord.

The King's Ball

Dinners were always an elaborate affair and breathed with all the energy of a funeral. Tonight, however, was different, because Basil had been requested to sit with them instead of with his governess and nursemaid.

It made Corvina nervous. Her whole body was coiled tight, like a bow string ready to snap at the slightest touch. She found herself flinching every time Tobias' spoon hit against the side of his porcelain plate.

Basil was somber tonight. Corvina knew it had to do with his father's presence, whom he feared more than he loved. Tobias had never been cruel to Basil, and yet their son noticed the abhorrent treatment his mother and others received. It kept him relatively quiet as he sipped from his soup. She noticed he kept glancing towards Tobias and opening his mouth then closing it. Like he wanted to say something, but was refraining himself.

Corvina had an idea what he wanted to ask, as he had already asked *her* a thousand times since Gale brought it up.

Her throat cleared and the sound echoed harshly through the room. Tobias looked up, his brows pulling together in a brief moment of annoyance at the interruption.

"We played in the gardens today." Her voice was soft and fearful. It did not tremble, and for those who didn't know her, they would have mistaken her tone for wistfulness rather than the fear that it really was.

"The guards informed me," Tobias dismissed, turning his attention back to his plate.

Of course they had. Even if she couldn't see them, she could always sense their presence, their scents, hear their heartbeats. He kept a close watch on her, and she was so used to the distrust that it no longer unnerved her that he knew her every move.

Corvina cleared her throat again. This time, his spoon dropped against his bowl and he glared. Even that was enough to make her wither in her seat. "Gale told us the circus was coming to Port Bay."

"Who's Gale?"

"M-my new maid."

Tobias' fingers flicked with disinterest, though he'd asked. "Get to the point, Corvina."

"Ba—" She broke off, biting hard on the inside of her cheek until she tasted blood. His gaze sharpened on her, and she could feel her heart rattling in her chest with the nerves. She was always so careful around him, and sometimes she still forgot that she could not call her son by his true name in front of her husband. "Reginald would very much like to see the circus."

He was silent for such a long time, she feared he was going to reprimand her for the slip of tongue. For daring to gift their son with the name of her people, of trying to mold him into anything other than human. Surprisingly, he did not.

"If you behave, I will allow you this," he answered.

Basil vibrated in his chair with excitement that he tried to keep tightly contained, but he failed as a giggle burst past his lips. "I will be good, I swear it!"

Tobias' eyes didn't leave Corvina's, and her throat closed at the threat she read from him. He hadn't been speaking to Basil at all, that she knew for sure. No, he'd been warning her. To be a good, meek wife and do as she was told. The thinly veiled threat hadn't gone past her, and it was one she'd do well to heed. How many times had Basil suffered because Tobias felt Corvina had failed her duties to him?

So she would be perfect. Regardless that she always tried and failed in her husband's eyes, she would do it for Basil. To see that smile light up his eyes. To give him even just a glimmer of happiness in the sad world that was his life.

"There is to be a ball tomorrow," Tobias went on. "My father is hosting it, as the emperor's soldiers arrived in Porir today. He would like to welcome them to Dana, and we are expected to attend and make them feel salubrious." His eyes pierced her like a knife. "Do you understand?"

Do not embarrass me, is what he meant to say.

Because in those events, she always found ways to mortify him. Whether if it was because her mind drifted and she lost track of a conversation, or because she refused to socialize with the dukes and duchesses, lords and ladies of Dana. The fallacy that Corvina tainted the royal Wes name was always along the surface of his accusations. They lived at the end of the whip he would take to her back and in the humiliation she suffered every time he entered her body.

He was an abuser, a rapist, a murderer, an angry blackmailer, and yet it was Corvina who tainted his family name. Because she was Fae. Yet he'd married her. Oftentimes she wondered why, only to come to the same conclusion each time.

It was about conquering. It was about proving to his people that he could take a once-proud Fae and turn her into what he wanted her to be. Human. Or, as human as possible.

The heartache here rested within the fact that he'd succeeded in doing so.

Her cheeks burned and hatred swelled up in her chest. Not for him, but for herself because she had been foolish enough to think she had been worth something when she was nothing. Nothing but a broken Fae chained to the will of humans. Even the fight had died within her, and words she would have said once upon a time in good-natured sarcasm couldn't emerge.

As if that part of her never really lived at all.

Instead, she inclined her head. Meek. Submissive.

Broken.

"Of course, husband."

And she went back to her meal, though it tasted like ashwood against her tongue, and settled like a poison in her stomach. It wasn't due to the food; there wasn't anything wrong with it. The bitter taste was little more than her own disgust.

For the world.

For her husband.

And most of all, for what she'd become.

"You will look breathtaking tonight, Princess." Gale smiled widely as her fingers adjusted the sleeves of her gown, her soft touch grazing Corvina's bare skin.

"I dare say I will." She hadn't looked at the dress yet, except as Juniper had pulled it from her many swaths of fabric. She'd caught the color and little else, her mind working too fast, diving too deep into everything that could possibly go wrong tonight. She couldn't return Gale's enthusiasm—not that she had ever—just like she couldn't return the smile and stuck to noncommittal answers.

"I always had dreams when I was a little girl of ball gowns and parties. You will tell me what the soldiers are like, Princess?" There was such hope in her young eyes that they could be friends. That they could stay up late in the night and whisper secrets to one another. That Corvina would tell her about her life in the courts and Gale would live vicariously through that. This was not new, and neither was the sorrow tightening her throat because this wasn't a joyous occasion.

Besides, if Corvina even muttered another man's name, her husband would hear of it and see to her punishment painfully, slowly.

Juniper clucked, the noise born of annoyance. She did not need to speak to emanate disdain. They all felt it in the air.

Gale's head whipped towards Juniper. "What?" she demanded, ever oblivious. "What is that noise for?"

Juniper's lips pressed together. She seemed to ignore the question at first, brushing down the ball gown as she kneeled before Corvina. Her strokes were firm, methodic, as she straightened the chiffon and smoothed out the ribbons. "Your commentary is tasteless," she bit out. It was a hiss, a quiet one, in case their voices echoed and reached the guards standing watch just outside the rooms.

Gale's nose scrunched and she tucked a strand of dark hair behind her ear. "I do not believe it is. I am not trying to misspeak, I just believe it is like a fairy tale, is all."

Fairy tales were human stories of magic. Legends and history of her homeland that had been twisted for entertainment, celebrated, and read to children at night, just so they could wake up and despise the Fae out in the streets.

It made little sense to her.

"A princess attending a ball..." Gale mused. The envy and wistfulness escaped her voice, and Corvina wanted to tell her newer maid the truth of what her life was, but like hope and happiness, it died in her chest. "It is all very romantic. Will Prince Tobias dance with you?"

He would not.

He never did.

Juniper straightened and whirled, her rage a steady building thing, the press of it seeming to be tempered by the iron band around her throat. Her eyes flashed, and Corvina caught a hint of savagery underneath. "You will learn the truth of things soon enough," she said. "And you will regret your words. For now, tame them in the presence of the princess. She does not need to hear your every thought."

Silence ensued in which the two maids, Fae and human, stared at one another. Gale broke first, turning to look at Corvina with a demure expression. She dipped into a curtsey. "Forgive me if I spoke out of turn," she whispered.

Corvina turned away from her without responding. She looked at herself and the dress that hung against her body in the mirror. It was a sweeping thing of deep blue chiffon, with a neckline that showed the top swells of her breasts and sleeves that hung down her shoulders in dipping ribbons. Diaphanous skirts pooled to the floor, the hem swishing against the sides of her dainty heels.

It was one of the few dresses she owned that showed off a great expanse of skin. She did not feel comfortable in the garment because it would cause eyes to stray towards her breasts and she knew Tobias would notice. And he would not be happy and somehow blame her for seeking attention. It had happened before. He'd been aggravated with his guards for their wandering eyes, so Corvina had tossed all her dresses to the trash and had new ones tailored with higher necklines and longer sleeves despite the heat.

Her comfort mattered little to Tobias. What mattered was her modesty and that others not look upon what was rightfully his.

Yet this dress was one of the few reserved for balls. Anything else would have been deemed inappropriate for the occasion, so she could not change.

"Has Reginald been readied for sleep yet?" she asked as the last of her hair was pinned into place. She tried not to look at her reflection overly long, for she would not recognize the face staring back. As it was, her face was already threatening to heat due to the style her hair had been done in. Golden locks swept away from her timid, heart-shaped face, displaying her ears for all to see.

It was one of her greatest senses of shame.

"He has, Princess," Juniper answered. "I believe they are waiting on you to say goodbye."

To not keep him waiting, Corvina hurried down the hall to her son's room. His nursery was down the hall and to the left of her own chambers. She didn't like being so far away from him, but Danarish royal customs demanded it. Children weren't meant to be near their parents. But even if she didn't like it, she knew it was for the best, lest he hear the things his father did and said to her at night.

Pushing open the wide double-doors of his room, she stepped into the dimness. Moonlight shone through the opened windows, the sea breeze ruffling his thin curtains. Basil lay in his bed, tucked in tightly, with his nursemaid reading a book at his side.

She stood when Corvina walked in, curtseying low. "Princess Corvina," she greeted. "Basil was inquiring about you."

Her son's nursemaid was a kind yet stern human woman with graying hair dusted along the brown strands. They were pulled into a tight chignon, not a single wisp out of place. She started to leave, but Corvina stopped her.

"Please, don't go. I only came to say goodnight. I'll not keep my husband waiting, and I would prefer if you stayed with him."

There were few in the castle that Corvina could trust. Even then, it was a game at the end of a double-edged sword to know who was on her side and who was on her husband's. Yes, the nursemaid answered to Tobias, but Corvina respected her. For her honesty and because she did not look at her with pity or disdain. She treated her like a real person.

"Of course, Princess." She flittered away to a far chair and sat beside the moonlight. Her book was clenched in her lap, and she stared out the window, feigning ignorance.

Corvina slipped beside Basil, taking the seat the nursemaid vacated. "Hello, my love," she whispered.

Basil's smile was shy. "Hello, mommy."

"I'll be going to the ball now. You sleep and be good for Miss Ingrid."

"I'm always good," he answered. There was no bite to the words, but maybe they were the faintest bit chastising.

"Silly me, of course you are." Her hands smoothed over his mass of brown curls, so like her father's that it hurt. "My perfect little boy."

"Will you kiss me good night, mommy?"

"I will always kiss you good night." She leaned down and her lips touched the soft curve of his cheek. Unscarred, not tainted by the harsh realities that lived on the other side of his bedroom doors. It's why she suffered.

So he wouldn't have to.

And to see that content smile as he settled into his pillows and slowly drifted off to sleep made everything worth it. Every scar, every time iron singed her skin or pain blossomed along her body, every time she woke hating herself for what she'd become was worth it.

Once his breathing grew heavy, Corvina stood, smoothing out the skirts of her gown. She nodded at Ingrid and didn't leave until the nursemaid was seated next to Basil again. When she arrived out in the hall, her own maids were waiting for her.

"Prince Tobias is waiting for you," Gale announced with a smile.

And just like that, the peace in her stomach imploded into something more.

Giving them a firm nod, she flicked her fingers, communicating silently with Juniper. Because she'd been with Corvina longer, she knew without words and rushed to fetch a wrap for Corvina's shoulders. Once the sheer material was wrapped around her, she went to meet her husband with her head held high, even if she trembled inside.

She knew it would be a long night ahead.

But whether it would be filled with kindness or violence still had yet to be seen.

The carriage stumbled over sand and rock, even on the paved streets down the hill where three paths met and fractured towards different directions. They took the first, turning sharply, bodies swaying as they traveled uphill towards the king's castle.

The ride was quiet until they reached the top where they lurched to a slow halt. The doors were thrown open and butlers appeared to help them down. Tobias exited first, standing in wait while Corvina followed. She did not allow the servant to hold her hand beyond that first step, because she could tell already that Tobias was scrutinizing every move she made, searching for something to reprimand.

Once her feet touched the ground, Tobias offered his arm which she dutifully took. He was cold to the touch, and it made an involuntary shiver claw down her spine. His hand came over hers as he shot her a side look.

"Cold?" he asked with narrowed eyes.

"No."

They proceeded towards the marble steps of the castle, the white looming greatly above them. Once they made it to the top, they were greeted by tall pillars that held a domed ceiling above the palatial space. A butler was there to greet and announce their presence into the room.

While they were early, they were by no means the first to arrive. Already, the king's castle boasted with hundreds of courtiers of high breed, snacking on oysters, shrimp, and onions and tasting the sharp fizz of spiked cider and the decadent pull of wine. As they were announced, the loud chatter quieted but a fraction and heads swiveled in their direction.

A lump formed in Corvina's throat. It did not matter that she'd lived here a large part of her life, that they knew her and had seen her before. It was always like the first time. She was a curiosity. A slave without a collar. No, that wasn't quite right. Her collars were dresses and jewelry that shone against her throat and neck. They were her shackles like she was an animal in a zoo, and the courtiers were the people on the other side who watched her from between her bars.

Tobias tugged at her arm, pulling her deeper into the room and into the press of people. Overwhelmed by the sudden onslaught of scents, she tried to hold her breath, but the harshness of body odor, fish, and onion permeated her nostrils. Humans brave enough to stop them did so, prolonging their trek across the room and to the throne that sat at the far end against the wall.

The King of Dana lounged against the plush cushions, a goblet of wine dangling lazily from between his fingertips. There was no second throne, no queen he shared the power with, as his wife had died bringing Tobias into the world and he had not remarried. Not even his sons took up place next to him. Corvina knew it was a calculated move on the king's part. He did not wish to show the world who he favored by seating them next to him. A futile thing, considering the whole kingdom knew that it was Arthur whom he truly loved while Tobias received scraps of affection.

The king and Tobias were similar in appearance. Dark, curly hair, cutting jaws and noses, and severe expressions. The king wore his age on withering skin and hair peppered with gray. His rounded belly was hidden beneath the folds of his velvet cloak, but they parted as he sat up straighter once he caught sight of them.

"Father." Tobias released her arm and bowed in greeting to the king.

"King Archibald." Corvina swept into a very low curtsey at the same time.

They didn't rise until the king ordered them to. As soon as they did, the king stepped down from his throne, setting his drink aside. "You are late," he accused, his tone light.

Corvina tensed at the words. It didn't matter how his eyes crinkled as he said them or how playful his tone seemed to be. Tobias took it as the criticism it was.

"You know females and their wardrobes," Tobias clipped back, sending Corvina a long glance. She knew she would pay for this later. The night was not off to a good start.

"Ah, and is she not a vision? Worth the wait, I daresay." The king lifted Corvina's hands and pressed scraping, whiskered kisses to her knuckles. He held firmly, and she knew she could not pull out of his hold even if she wanted to. When he looked back up, his eyes were shining with mirth. "Beautiful, as always, my daughter."

"I thank you, King."

His bear-like hands patted hers. "I have told you before to call me father, dear."

She wouldn't. They all knew she wouldn't. It would be a betrayal to her own father. Which was why the king insisted. He wanted to show his dominion over her. It didn't matter how warm his smiles were or how much kindness he showed both to Basil and Corvina. Beneath it was a venomous viper.

The truth of that shone in his eyes. Eyes that looked similar to Tobias'. Where her husband wore his cruelty on his sleeve, the King of Dana hid it so deeply that sometimes she wanted to believe it wasn't there at all. But it was. She knew it was. Evil wasn't always something one could sense. It was like a sea monster, still and waiting for someone unsuspecting to pass by before it struck.

"And where is your wayward heir?" Tobias asked, pulling the king's attention from Corvina and back to his son. His hands slipped from hers finally, and she let them fall to her skirts. "I did not see him when we came in." There was disdain in Tobias' voice when he spoke of his older brother.

The rivalry between Tobias and Arthur had been going on for as long as Tobias had been alive. Neither brother was adept at hiding their hatred for the other. The evidence of this was ingrained into his words and expression.

"Around. Now, come. There are people I shall have you be acquainted with." The king led the way before Tobias could reply. Corvina didn't miss the tightening of his jaw, a sure sign of his irritation. Even still, he was at a public event, and he managed to tamp it down enough to turn and offer Corvina his arm once again.

"He dares lecture me about my tardiness, but Arthur is nowhere to be seen," he hissed so only she could hear. The anger bled through as his fingers crushed her arm in a tight grip that made her wince.

Fae were vastly stronger than humans. Their eyesight, hearing, and taste far exceeded a humans', and yet being near iron and being so used to Tobias' tirades had made Corvina's pain so much more acute. Before, his touch would have felt like a pinch. Now, she fought not to cry out.

"It is quite unfair," Corvina whispered back at him.

Honestly, though, she did not care for his feelings. She did not care that his father compared him to Arthur and always found Tobias lacking. Perhaps, if he were less cruel to her, she would care. Perhaps she would have grown to look at him with fondness, but only hollow dread lived inside her. An emptiness that couldn't be filled with real compassion, but instead with words that were expected to fall from her lips.

His grip on her eased, and she knew she'd said the right thing. His fingers smoothed against her skin in a touch that she supposed was meant to be comforting. Then he brought her hand to his lips, pressing his cold mouth against her knuckles.

"You're right. It is."

She did not reply because the king stopped before a group of people and turned, gesturing at them. The group bowed low as they approached, and when they straightened, Corvina could make out who—rather, what—they were.

"Prince Tobias and Princess Corvina, these are our guests of honor tonight."

Flashes of robes and steel armor. Iron swords clad at their hips that pulsed waves of discomfort against Corvina's exposed skin. She held her breath, but it didn't stop the drumming of her wild, fearful heart. Beads of sweat trickled against the back of her neck as she stared at the offending weapons, trailing her gaze up to the men to find them staring at her ears.

No surprise there.

When they caught her staring, their eyes widened, and they shuffled from one foot to another almost fearfully. Their hands were discreet, but she caught the slow increments of their fingers going towards the pommels. It was obvious these men were not used to seeing living Fae, and were she not in a castle in Dana next to the kingdom's prince and king, they would have struck her down without thought.

"Extraordinary." Robes rustled like parchment as the priest was the first to move, pointing his glass of sparkling beverage in her direction. "A Fae princess?"

"She is a sight, is she not? Though I am pleased to say that after years of living in Dana, she has left her savage ways behind her." The king smiled at the priest, as if everything that just emerged from his mouth had not been offensive.

"Has she been baptized by the Brotherhood?" the priest asked, as if she were not there and could not answer for herself. As if she did not understand the common tongue he spoke. His drooping eyes were focused solely on the king, and she could just make out a smile beneath sagging, wrinkly skin. "You know it is not a proper cleanse unless she has drunk from the nectar my Brothers can provide, Your Majesty."

"Unnecessary," Tobias cut in. "From what I have heard, the Brotherhood cleanses Fae of magic. My *wife* has no special abilities."

Her back tingled and her blood hummed at the declaration, but she said nothing and gave nothing away.

"We can also cleanse away the taint of Fae blood to make her more normal," the priest continued, eyes straying to where Corvina's ears were on display. She felt that part of her body heat under his scrutiny, and she cursed her pale complexion because she knew her skin was reddening.

"Always speaking of business." The king laughed. "Let us speak of something else. How are you finding our kingdom?"

"Oh, it is very hot."

The king laughed again. "That it is. Hot days and cool, breezy nights. Though I am sure Tuath cannot compare to us, eh, Brother Bastien?"

They fell into senseless chatter until they were interrupted by another soldier's arrival. "Your Majesty," he greeted, sweeping into a stiff bow. When he straightened, Corvina studied his gargantuan form. He was rather tall for a human, and under the armor she could make out the size of his muscles. The intense expression cutting along his sharp features put a sliver of unease in her gut. One she couldn't quite explain.

Save for his size, he seemed a normal enough human soldier. He gripped his helm on the side of his hip, where two swords were strapped in their sheaths.

There was just something intimidating about the man. Black hair shorn short against his scalp, jaw rugged, eyes penetrating. He didn't look to anyone but the king, as if everyone else were beneath his notice. Including Tobias and Corvina.

"Your Majesty, there are urgent matters we must still discuss." His voice was baritone, deep and grave.

"Yes, regarding the rebels, I am aware." The king's tongue clucked and his jovial demeanor changed into one of irritation. It was the same stance Tobias usually found himself in.

"The emperor sent me to help ready your borders against the caravan of Fae rebels—"

"Bah!" the priest interrupted with an annoyed flick of his hands. "You overestimate the danger a few Fae bring, captain. Have you forgotten that the great Emperor of Illyk has placed his trust in the Brotherhood? With us at his side, he would—"

"Forgive me, Brother Bastien," the captain replied coolly. "But I believe some, even the emperor himself, would think that the trust he freely gave was misplaced." The priest sputtered and the captain continued, "Do not underestimate what is coming. Not when the emperor's prized possession has been lost."

"A possession which we will replevin in due time."

Corvina's gaze volleyed back and forth between the two humans. They argued as though unaware that others were near.

"Yes, I see how hard you are working to appease his imperial majesty." His eyes swept over the party. "I thought the Brotherhood had strict rules regarding parties and balls. Though you also have rules regarding ingesting alcohol, so I assume they are for decorum's sake and not because you actually believe—"

"Captain!" King Archibald barked quickly and with annoyance. Even Corvina jolted at the suddenness, knowing he'd only done so because he was growing bored with their banter. "I do not believe you have met my son, Prince Tobias, or his wife, Princess Corvina."

Finally, the captain acknowledged them both. His stoic gaze flicked to her ears before they went to her face, but his expression didn't change. In fact, he was ever polite as he bowed before the both of them. "My pleasure, Prince, Princess." He turned back to the king. "Your Majesty, it is of the utmost importance that we speak."

A silence thundered in the spaces between them all before Tobias slipped his hand from hers. "Perhaps the princess should see to the guests," he suggested coyly.

"What an excellent idea! I believe the Duchess of Port Lays was looking for you."

A lie. One she could smell the moment he uttered it, but there was no reason to argue no matter how badly she wanted to stay and listen in on their conversation. It was not a proper conversation for her ears, and she was no longer a vessel between realms anymore. She was on human lands, was a human's wife, and would conduct herself as such.

"Excuse me, Your Majesty." She curtsied to the king and then to her husband. She acknowledged the rest of the men with a simple nod of the head. "Gentlemen, it was my pleasure to meet you all."

Another lie. This one burned hot on her tongue. She turned away, her skirts swishing against her ankles, and began walking at an unhurried pace.

There was a second silence behind her. Even through the noise of the ball, she could pick apart their voices, though the fact that they all carried iron made it difficult so she only caught snippets of their conversation.

"Caravan... rebels... Azzarh... Prince..."

One name stuck out among the patchy sentences she picked up.

Azzarh.

She rolled it around her mind, mouthed the word to taste it on her tongue. It sounded foreign to her and she was sure it was a name she'd never heard before. But saying it, mouthing it, made something surge in her chest that hadn't been there before.

It was a little burst, like fireworks crackling against a sky or bubbles of fizzy cider popping in the mouth. It was elation, and hinted at a bit of magic.

Taking a breath and tamping it down, Corvina turned about the room. As she did, she could feel the crowds of nobles cringing away from her. They did it in the most discreet manner possible, angling their bodies and watching her with wary eyes. Curious eyes.

She knew what the courtiers whispered about behind their fans. It was no great secret that Princess Corvina's Fae ears were scarred and twisted at the tips. That they were ugly, gnarled flesh that not even her Fae blood could heal because they'd been mutilated with an iron blade. So desperate she'd been to be accepted by the humans, that in a fit of hysteria, she'd reached for a guard's iron knife and made an attempt to saw off the elongated points of her skin. She hadn't succeeded, yet she still wore them on display at these events, scars and all, so they would know that what she wanted more than anything was to be one of them.

They needn't know the truth.

That the wounds had not been self-inflicted, but a product of the prince's outrage at what she was and the many things she'd done to anger him. They needn't know that while he was rutting inside of her, his blade had carved into the tendons at the tips of her ears as if he could cut off all evidence of her heritage.

They needn't know how deep her shame bled. How it pooled into the cracks of her lungs and into her broken heart.

Let them believe what they will, she thought. For the truth was always a harder burden to bear.

So distracted, she startled when a hand grabbed her elbow and whirled her around. She almost tripped against the smooth marble, gasping and cringing away before she schooled her expression and met the eyes of the last person in the world she wanted to see.

Holy Schemes

His grip on the flute tightened by the second the longer he watched Captain Brannon whisper in the king and prince's ears. His face remained stoic as he sipped his cider, listening to his harsh words and command.

Bastard. Captain Brannon was a bastard.

Brother Bastien's anger rose up his chest and curled around his throat, making it all too difficult to swallow back the bubbling liquid. His face was flushed, and if anyone asked him, he would blame it on the drink in hand and not the man he'd been forced to accompany to this sweltering kingdom.

How dare he? How dare Captain Brannon try to tarnish his image among royals and soldiers alike? Foolish man. He did not understand what the Brotherhood stood for. He did not understand that there was power in their sect. That they controlled the rules and laws of the gods. That they could baptize those tainted with Fae blood and make them something other.

Something they desperately wanted to be.

The Brotherhood had been approved by the emperor himself. By his good graces, they were allowed to spread their gospel throughout the empire of cleanliness and the superiority of their own race. But because of that, the Brotherhood had rules to follow. For how could they preach to the world if they did not make their own bodies holy?

And what was power but the ability to manipulate that which others most feared?

It was a law of nature. One Captain Brannon threatened to shit on every time he opened his whoremonger mouth. He was a dangerous man, for he did not put his faith in the tales the Brotherhood weaved. He did not believe in their tonics and baptisms.

He was a man who believed in one thing only.

His own vengeance.

And those were the most dangerous of all, simply because they could not be controlled.

Sure, the captain had given them the fire Elemental at behest of the emperor once she was found. He had decided to give them the benefit of the doubt then and had regretted it once he came down to the catacombs to find blood staining the floors.

He'd blamed the brothers.

As if it had been their fault that little Fae bitch was cleverer than they could have known. And now she and her group of Fae rebels were wreaking havoc across the empire and Captain Brannon was scrambling to get her back and the Resistance under control. And Brother Bastien had been forced to come with the insufferable oaf to right his mistake.

Because the Emperor of Illyk was as unforgiving as he was cruel.

Brother Bastien downplayed the direness of the situation, but inside he was just as eager. Especially now that the captain no longer trusted them and would not be informing him of anything. He was stuck grasping at air, making his own guesses, and following the soldiers around like he was a damn dog and not a mouthpiece of the gods.

He sipped his drink, ears straining to hear every word.

"We will speak more tomorrow." The king waved the captain off and reached for a goblet of wine from a passing servant. "Come here late in the afternoon and we will discuss this further."

Interesting.

Brother Bastien watched Captain Brannon ascent with a nod of his head before he turned his attention, along with the prince, towards the ballroom floor. Their gazes found the princess, the prince staring at his wife with narrowed eyes while Captain Brannon scrutinized her darkly, intently.

Even more interesting.

His attention shifted back to the king. He would need to secure an audience with him before the captain. But for what reason could he claim the king's time? Yes, he was a member of the Brotherhood, but the Danarish king was a self-important ass. He would only meet with Brother Bastien if he had something interesting to offer.

As of yet, he had nothing.

Brother Bastien smirked into his cup.

But by the end of the night, he would.

Hidden Lies, Hidden Scars

"Prince Arthur!"

The crown prince's smile was slow and lazy as he settled his palms against her arms, touching bare skin. She wanted to flinch away from the touch, but his grip was firm, like he worried that if he let go, she would slip against the floor again. Looming over her, his eyes twinkled with something that felt a lot like malice.

Corvina tried to hold her composure, aware of the stares they garnered. Clearing her throat, she took a step back, causing his hands to fall to his sides, and she dipped into a curtsey.

"Forgive me," she whispered, her voice a tad breathless. "You startled me is all."

His eyes brightened and his smile widened at her words, and a sliver of unease crept through her body. She realized her mistake as soon she spoke. Admitting to her fear would do nothing but give him ways to torture her later. Like creeping up on her when she least expected it.

The Wes men were cruel bastards. But none of them more so than her husband's older brother. It wasn't just that he was cruel, he was cunning as well. There was nothing more frightening than someone who was vicious *and* intelligent. A stupid, mean person could be easily bested, but not the prince. There was just something in his eyes that wasn't in the eyes of his father or Tobias. It was knowing. Like he could see through things and pick apart words to find weakness and fragility underneath.

Arthur was infinitely more attractive than Tobias, smarter, and with more power as firstborn. Tobias could have forgiven the first two, but the third filled him with a rage that he often took out on Corvina.

The prince flashed her his charming smile then, taking her stiff fingers in his hand and bowing over her knuckles. He was meant to hover over them only, but his lips pressed to her skin. She could hear the room's intake of breath as he straightened, aware that others were watching, yet not caring.

He was the heir.

He could do whatever he wished.

"My brother is a fool if he has let you wander the room on your own."

Her body stiffened and dread was slow and prevalent in her gut. "I *am* allowed certain freedoms, Prince Arthur."

His laugh was like the tempo of a harp. Beautiful and melodic. "I simply mean that others would look upon you, and I know I would be far too jealous of a husband to want my wife alone."

His words were encased in implications she didn't want to contemplate. They were a warning, one those who did not know him would pass off as nothing more than charming words to his sister by law.

"My husband has nothing to fear in that regard, as my eyes are solely for him."

She didn't want to think what he would ever do to a man she would stare at in passing. Or to her. It was better to lock those urges up like she had so long ago until desire and interest no longer lived within her blood.

"How loyal," Arthur mused just as the tempo of the music changed around them, veering into a slow waltz. He smirked and held out his hand. "Will you do me the honor of dancing?"

The waltz was romantic, meant for spouses, partners, or those who were courting. It would be entirely too inappropriate to dance with him. Especially when she had not yet danced with her husband. Human traditions dictated that she must dance with her husband first before anyone else or it was seen as a sign of disrespect.

Arthur knew it.

The whole court knew it.

Yet he asked her anyway.

"I thank you for the offer, Prince Arthur, but I am afraid I must decline on the grounds that it would be entirely too inappropriate."

That cold smile never fell from place. He looked prepared to strike like a snake snapping at its prey. "More inappropriate may it be that you'd deny a dance from the crown prince." He held his hand higher, a command that she take it. Despite the consequences. Despite what he knew his brother would do to her if he saw them. And he *would* see them. The whispers would reach his ears like a wave cresting a shore. Rumors always did so in that manner.

But she could not take it.

She had to adhere to the rules of human society, whether she believed in them or not. She would not offend her husband, crippled by the fear he'd ingrained within her soul for her wrongdoings. This would enrage him.

But Arthur did not seem to care. His hand slipped into her own and he tugged her forward forcefully, in such a manner that his touch looked gentle, reverent. And when he leaned down, breath fanning against her skin, she wanted to vomit.

"Do not deny me," he whispered, his fingers crushing hers in a grip that made her swallow back a whimper. He straightened, pulling her with him so she was all but in his embrace. Then their feet were moving, turning and twirling about the room in time to the music.

She hated the way his chest pressed against hers, the glittering buttons of his jacket touching her bare skin. It seemed an intimate thing, to have his clothes touching any part of her. Her mind spun along with her vision as he twirled her around and around. It was then she noticed the courtiers had made room for them. A circle around them like they were little more than a spectacle for amusement. And in the sea of faces, Corvina caught sight of Tobias, the nuances of his earlier expression dipping into something low and dark.

She would be paying for this transgression later.

When the song ended, their feet stopped, and yet Prince Arthur didn't let her go. She tugged away from him discreetly, stepping away while his hand still held tightly to hers. To others, it probably looked intimate. Which was likely what he wanted.

The heir of Dana was a wicked man, even while he was not openly violent.

Tobias chose to approach them at that moment, his eyes flashing like lightning across a sky, a sure sign of his violence bursting past the cracks.

"Ah, little brother." Arthur still had not released her hand, no matter how hard she tugged. "I was just telling your wife what an excellent dancer she is. But, of course, you know that."

He didn't because Tobias never danced with her. He figured if he did not, then others would not be brave enough to ask her. He would not worry about other hands roaming over a body that belonged to him, for no one would shirk the customs that had been established long before he'd even been born.

No one would dare dance with another man's wife, if he'd not done so first.

Yet Arthur had.

"Thank you for the riveting conversation," Arthur went on, oblivious to his brother's rage. Or rather, quite aware of it, but he did not care. He thrived on harming him in subtle ways where Tobias could not fight back, lest he look like the weaker, petulant brother. "Enjoy the festivities." He bent over her hand once again, this time making no secret of the way his lips skimmed across her knuckles like he was staking claim to her body. One that Tobias already had.

He walked away. As the strings of music changed, Tobias turned to her, his gaze flicking down her body, like he was memorizing every place his brother had touched.

The silence was as suffocating as the smoke of ashwood in the air. Whatever hope that she could allay the situation died as he leaned towards her. His hand rose towards her face.

Don't flinch, she told herself. *We are in public, he will not strike you, don't flinch.*

His fingers brushed aside an errant lock of gold, tucking it back behind a pointed ear, where his fingers grazed the twisted tips. That alone felt like a warning.

"You dance as beautifully as ever," he complimented.

That, too, was a warning.

A promise.

One she knew he meant to keep.

A throat cleared and they both turned. Immediately, Corvina was greeted by a soft pulse of iron, and her neck craned up to look Captain Brannon in the eye.

"Prince Tobias." He bowed respectfully. "I have come to ask permission to dance with the princess."

Tobias barely blinked before answering, his tone not concealing his bitterness. "Of course. What is one more?" He walked away before Corvina could say anything, and she watched him go a moment before the captain stepped into her vision and offered her his hand. She reluctantly took it.

They began to move, this dance slow. Others around them dispersed and danced now that the spectacle was over. They weaved their way between bodies. It was a long song, one that would last for what felt like forever.

Captain Brannon's hand sat respectfully in hers, while the other was settled lightly against her waist. He kept a respectable distance between their bodies, which she appreciated, but he said nothing for a long time and that made her nervous.

More so because he was observing her closely, his eyes on the tips of her ears. Her face heated under his scrutiny, and the proximity of his iron swords made her feel lightheaded. She had assumed he would be the sort of soldier who did not touch Fae unless it was to end their lives. But here he was, dancing with her.

"It is a rare thing to see a Fae in Dana who is not collared," he said after a few minutes of silence. His grave voice made Corvina shudder, but it was mostly his words, the impertinence behind them and the implacable severity of them. His gaze swept to the exposed flesh of her neck where she figured he imagined the iron collar would go.

Or his big, meaty hands.

She swallowed, and he eyed the delicate movement of her throat before his eyes found hers once more.

I suppose you are accustomed to seeing Fae heads skewered on pikes instead. Those were words she wanted to say. Words she would have said in the past before she became a broken creature who flinched at the hatred in his gaze.

"Then again, Danarish customs are strange to me."

She could not twirl with him in silence. He would expect an answer, of that she was sure, even if she wanted to give none. "They were strange to me at first as well," she whispered. "But I have grown used to their ways."

"Hmm..." His hand inched over her hip, closer towards her lower back. "I have heard your tale. Gifted to the Danarish king as a show of faith from your father. He thought it would spare his court." They twirled and her head became dizzy with his words. "Your court fell regardless, and instead of sending you to the reservations, you became the bride of a prince and studied the human ways from within your marble palace."

There was something particularly off-putting about his recount of her life. Like he was poking at an infected wound for amusement, even if the mirth did not shine within his eyes. Nor did cruelty. He was cold, callous, stating facts of the world instead of using what he knew to hurt her.

That made her more wary of him than even her husband. At least with him, she knew what to expect. At least with the Wes men, she knew cruelty was akin to amusement. What to expect from a man who uttered terrible things and found no joy or any other emotion within them?

"Emperor Laurel rounded together the Fae with magic," Captain Brannon continued. "He let the Brotherhood cleanse them of Fae taint. Were you cleansed?"

He hadn't been there when they spoke of this among the others, so he had not heard. She'd not been baptized by the Brotherhood, but by the King of Dana himself. Their customs were different from the rest of Illyk, and unlike the others, they did not place fortitudes in the hands of the Brotherhood. They believed in their gods, and had baptized Corvina in the elements, in the Lagnh Sea.

Water had enveloped her body and it felt like home at the time.

That had been enough for them.

Besides, they had not wanted to relinquish their toy to the emperor. After all, Corvina had been given to *Dana*, in the hopes that an alliance between the humans and Gold Court could come to fruition. That at least they could have one kingdom as allies, and afterwards, somehow, they could sway the rest as well once the war became unbearable.

It hadn't mattered what the Emperor of Illyk wanted at the time, since the treaties had already been signed. Corvina Rhian belonged to King Archibald Wes and his sons. She was theirs to do with what they pleased.

"I was cleansed according to Danarish customs in the sea, before the gods, as it should be." Her reply was automatic, practiced. Truth be told, that was the only time she had ever felt content. Not because she actually believed she was cleansing her Fae heritage, but because the water was a part of her as much as she was a part of it.

She'd known instinctively it would be the last time she would ever be that close to freedom before everything changed.

His hand inched closer to her lower back, palm resting above the curve of her bottom. Her breath became labored, and while the touch didn't feel sexual or forceful, it was searching. His hand slid up her spine, stopping just below her neck.

Right over her scars that were hidden beneath her dress.

"The Danarish are rather fond of their elements, are they not?" he mused, his hand tracing slow circles. She wanted to tense, to push him away. But in her fear, she froze. "Are you inclined towards any one in particular? The sea?"

"I cannot say I understand what you mean, Captain, as the sea is not an element, as you're implying. If it is an element you mean, then it is the water, not specifically the sea since it is composed of much more than liquid." For a moment, her breath halted in her chest. For a moment, she'd sounded so much like her old self that it hurt. She cleared her throat. "I revere all of the elements and the gods of the Danarish." The music died down, and as soon as the last note strung, she stepped away from him, giving herself much needed space. "Thank you for such an invigorating dance and conversation, Captain."

He bowed low and appropriately. "The pleasure was mine, Princess."

Sweeping past him in a swish of fabric, she marched along towards her husband. She didn't want to be with him, but she did not relish in being alone either. Not among these people, and not where Captain Brannon felt he could question her.

She knew he'd targeted her alone because she was weak. Because he sought to intimidate her. And he had. It grated to admit that she felt more threatened by the Captain of the Emperor's Guard than her own husband. She'd rather face being ostracized by him, than the captain's hands gliding along her back.

Almost as if he were...

Searching.

For her scars or for something else, she wasn't sure. Though how he would know about her scars was a mystery. Only her maids and her husband knew what image marred just below the base of her neck.

And she did not know what it meant.

But when he asked her about the elements, about the sea, she feared that maybe he knew what magic flowed through her veins. A magic she'd discovered as a little girl. A magic her father had helped her hone and perfect, ever the patient teacher. A magic she kept hidden, that no one living knew about.

That only the dead, and the sea, knew she possessed.

Interesting. There were so many things that Brother Bastien was discovering, even through the dim haze of inebriation that clouded him. Like the way Captain Brannon eyed the Fae princess while she danced with Prince Arthur. He studiously followed her around as she twirled around the ballroom.

Brother Bastien would have thought he just wanted to fuck her, but even that seemed odd. They'd been attached for months ever since the fire bitch escaped from the temple in Tuath, and not once had the captain taken any interest in a woman. The rest of the soldiers had rutted their way through nearly every brothel across Illyk and yet the captain had remained within the confines of his tent.

He'd started to believe that the proclivities of the captain leaned towards something... else. The thought certainly had not disgusted him, as many of his brothers had tastes that exceeded the bounds of sex, race, and age.

So when the captain marched towards the princess and requested a dance, Brother Bastien's eyes narrowed on the action. And he watched, taking in the scene with ferocity. He drank in every movement. From the way his hand rested on the curve just above the princess' ass and slid up higher, pausing on the spot just below her neck. His fingers traced a pattern there. Pressing. Searching. They drew a figure, over and over again that made the Fae princess stiffen.

And Brother Bastien chased the figure with his own eyes until it formed in his mind.

And he knew.

He *knew.*

Vibrating with satisfaction, he approached the King of Dana, who was downing his wine with little reservation. "My king." He bowed low, his robes rustling against the floor. When he stood, the king was all but sneering down at him.

"What?" His ruddy cheeks were flushed as the drunkenness began to overtake him. Which meant Brother Bastien had to act fast. Before the king could forget their conversation and dismiss him.

Just as he was about to open his mouth, Prince Arthur appeared beside them, clapping his father on the back in a familiar gesture that had not been extended to Prince Tobias.

"Father," he greeted. He turned to Brother Bastien and his smile held more malice than joy. "Priest."

"Your Majesty." Brother Bastien bowed. "Forgive the interruption, but I have something of the utmost importance—"

"Not this again," the king groaned. "You are worse than the captain. What could you possibly have to say to me that would be more important than the festivities going on around us?" He waved a hand through the air.

Brother Bastien leaned forward, lowering his voice so only the two royals could hear. "Trust me, Your Majesties. You will want to hear this. For it has to do with Princess Corvina... and what I suspect she is hiding."

An Iron Bride

"Let's go."

Tobias' hand encircled her arm in a crushing grip that she knew would bruise. Just like she knew that as soon as the purple formed, she would heal due to her Fae heritage. Fast healing was a trait she was thankful for and also abhorred. If only because Tobias always found ways to make the pain and the scars endure longer against her flesh. Through iron and ashwood.

And tonight would be one of those nights.

He did not wait for her as he all but dragged her from the party. The fringes of Tobias' patience frayed. She could feel his emotions running high, his rage splintering through him and begging for release like it was some magic that lived inside him. Eyes followed as they left.

He had been irritable and cutting for half an hour, and she wondered if it had anything to do with Captain Brannon and the way his hand had trailed against her back. She should have shoved the soldier away, but that would have caused a scene. She could still feel his touch against her body like it was a brand, and she shivered as they burst outside and a warm sea breeze blew against her body.

"Tobias—"

"If you know what's good for you, you will shut your mouth," Tobias gritted out. He fell into silence, all but tossing her into the carriage. She scrambled to a sitting position; the slamming door was proceeded by the roll of the wheels that would take them away from the king's dreadful ball.

The tension in the carriage was stifling; she could almost choke on it. Her heart pounded, and with every passing second, Tobias' silence grew. And when the carriage parked before their own castle, he yanked her down and dragged her through the halls.

"Tobias..." She whimpered as his blunt nails dug harder into her. "Tobias, you're hurting me."

"Not yet," he spat the promise like a curse. "But I will."

"Tobias, please, I have done nothing wrong."

Guards lined the walls, and none made a move to intervene, though she hadn't expected they would. They never did. And all she could do was follow behind him because fighting was useless and futile against the force of his rage. Tears welled up and spilled, already anticipating the pain that was to come. She wanted to be strong, but the strength had left her so long ago.

When he arrived at his chambers, it was when fear truly entered her soul.

"Tobias, please!"

He ignored her, throwing open the doors to his room and pushing her inside. Legs tangling against her skirts, she skidded forward, righting herself and turning...

Just as the slap bounced across her cheek.

Pain splintered up the side of her face, making her head throb. She gasped, the tears stinging. In her mouth, she tasted blood.

"You fucking whore."

His hands pushed her backwards and her feet complied on their own, walking like she'd been trained to do after so long of suffering the same treatment. Every movement was ingrained now. She knew where to go, where he wanted her, and what she would suffer, and her body moved. Even while her mind screamed at her to stop and fight back.

"Tobias," she pleaded. "I've done nothing wrong."

"Shut *up*!" His hand cracked against her face once more just before he dug his knuckles into her sternum and shoved her. She fell against the mattress of his bed, not realizing it had been so close. She bounced on the blankets and he reached for her ankles. Her muscles burned as he forced her legs wide open. She wanted to kick out but couldn't.

Didn't.

She didn't understand why he was doing this. Was it the captain? Because he'd taken liberties?

Cold iron clamped around her ankles, and she felt the burn against her skin immediately. Hissing from between clenched teeth, the tears worsened. She tugged at the bonds, fear clawing up her throat, making her freeze.

"Tobias, please..."

But he wasn't listening. He was too far gone in his rage. Thighs straddling her waist, he leaned up, grabbing her wrists and attaching them to the iron chains he kept tethered to his bed for this precise occasion.

He'd had them installed they day they'd been married to tame his Fae wife. He only brought her in here, subjected her to *this*, when he was deeply unhappy. In her rooms, he was never this cruel. Never this violent. Here, he had complete control over her body.

Over her.

"You fucking *whore.* Did you deliberately seek to embarrass me tonight by dancing with my fucking *brother* before everyone's eyes?"

She blinked at him slowly, tears fogging her vision before they cleared and she could make out every cutting line of his rage. Of course, this wasn't about the captain. The captain was a nobody, beneath her husband's notice. She should have known this was about Arthur.

"I didn't! He *forced* me! I swear—"

"Save your fucking lies!" This time, it was his fist that connected to her face, the iron rings he wore slamming against her flesh and scraping it so she bled. She felt a tooth in her mouth loosen, and the agony was indescribable.

Then it was just his fists and his rage.

His blows didn't cease. They hit wherever he could reach. Her face, her side, her arms. When he wasn't satisfied with that, he wrapped his fingers around her throat, cutting off her airway. She gasped, arms and legs jerking against her bonds.

He was a heavy weight pushing her down against the mattress. And within his eyes, true evil dwelled. She could see it in the clenching of his jaw, even as her vision blurred. He didn't ease his grip. Her lungs shrieked for air that wouldn't come.

He leaned down, his nostrils flaring as he inhaled sharply.

His hands left her throat and she gulped down much needed breaths while his fingers pinched her breasts hard enough to make her cry out.

"You fucking smell like him."

The flash of steel made her flinch, and then she felt air against her bare body as Tobias chopped away the fabric of her clothes, from neckline to waist, to lower. The knife touched her skin, iron singeing and creating wounds that would scar against her pale flesh. He didn't care. He dug it in deeper until she screamed and cried out. Until her magic stirred inside her, wanting to burst but unable to because of the iron. Even through the agony, she tamped it down.

Even as he tossed the bloody knife away and separated the ruined folds of her dress and palmed her breasts, pinching her nipples until the hurt was all she knew.

She cried and sobbed, but knew no help would come.

"Did you like dancing with him, wife? Did you like his filthy hands all over you? Do you wish it was he who was your husband instead of I?" He reached between them, loosening his pants and shoving them down his waist until his erection sprung up, angry and demanding.

"I swear I didn't—"

Her protest ended on a cry as he gripped her hips and forced his way inside her, breaking past her folds to sheathe himself within. He began to move, his hips snapping in short, violent thrusts.

"You are *mine*," he growled, and every word was feral and painful and humiliating. "And I will fuck the smell of him off of you." His fingers pinched her clit, and she cried out in pain as he tore through her. Like he was trying to force pleasure where there was none, where it could never be and never go. Where she'd never had it. He leaned down so his chest brushed hers. Until his lips were a breath away from her own, and there was a glistening, vile promise in his eyes coated in blood, in pain. Making her little more than his iron-clad bride.

"I will fuck the memory of his touch from you completely."

And he did. Until her throat hurt from pleading and her body ached in too many ways. Until he took what he wanted over and over again from between her thighs and broke her spirit all over again.

Blood & Sex

"Oh my gods!"

Corvina jolted awake with a gasp and a grimace, as the movement sent a splinter of agony down her entire being. She cracked open her eyes a fraction, though doing so resulted difficult, due to the black eyes she sported. They should have healed by now, but seeing as how Tobias had beat her with the iron rings around his fingers, her body was too slow to heal them.

Her vision was foggy as she peeked around the room. Through the agony in every bone and surface of her skin, she could sense another presence in the room. Several presences.

The buttery glow of morning sunlight slanted across her exposed body. No longer chained, she still lay sprawled against Tobias' mattress as if she were. He must have unlocked her bonds when he'd awoken, and she'd been so lost to sleep that she hadn't felt it at all. But the evidence of them were still there in the raised flesh around her wrists and ankles, bright red against her pale skin.

It hurt to move, but she did so slowly, lifting her head slightly. Even that fraction of a movement made her neck twinge where Tobias' fingers had wrapped around her throat.

"Princess, don't move!"

She recognized the voice and could make out a blurry figure in the doorway of her husband's chambers.

Juniper.

"Oh my gods..."

And that voice belonged to Gale.

Her face heated with shame as she felt her maids surround her. Their hands were careful, and still it was agony to be touched. They treated her like a newborn, pulling her naked body towards the edge of the bed. The damp press of a cloth across her aching, tender skin made her wince and hiss out a breath. In her mouth, she tasted the coppery tang of blood.

"It will be alright, Princess," Juniper whispered, swiping a cloth across her brow just before the smell of herbs and ointments clogged her nostrils. She'd come prepared. The whole castle must have heard her screams the night before.

Juniper's blatant lie made a smile start to curl on Corvina's lips. But her throat felt too hoarse to chuckle or tell her maid that her lies were just that.

Lies.

It did not matter how sweet or reassuring they tasted leaving the tongue when they were poison either way.

"Why would the prince..." Gale trailed off. Corvina forced her eyes open more so she caught sight of the maid and immediately wished she hadn't, slamming them closed again. She couldn't handle the pitying glance or the tears in her eyes.

It would only break her further.

"I told you," Juniper replied darkly, low enough so only Gale could here. "I told you it would steal your words. The prince is not a kind man."

"Juniper..." Corvina's voice scratched like rocks against marble. Her whole throat felt swollen, her tongue leaden. "Don't," she warned. If the guards outside of the rooms heard, they'd take what her maid said back to Tobias, and Corvina could not live with another maid imprisoned or worse.

There was silence again as they worked at cleaning her body. The mint of the ointment burned as it went on her scrapes and bruises, but it eased to a coolness that settled deep in her bones and started to take the swelling down. It eased the process of her healing, cleaning any traces of iron from her skin. She still didn't move, though.

Not until she heard the footsteps running across the castle and towards the room. Not until she heard Basil's innocent voice.

"Mommy?"

Her hand shot out to grip Gale's wrist. "Please," she begged, tears in her eyes. "Please, he can't see me like this. He can't. It would—" It would hurt him. She was always so careful about her wounds, about not letting him see that his father's cruelty went beyond cutting words.

She did not want to subject him to the truth.

She watched through swollen eyes as Gale swallowed before her maid pulled away, picking up her drab skirts with a fierce determination that Corvina had never seen from of her before.

"Princess." She curtseyed and a moment later she disappeared. Corvina listened with bated breath as she walked and met Basil's footsteps halfway. "Good morning, little prince," she greeted cheerily. "Your mother is feeling a bit under the weather. How about we let her rest and you can show me all your toys? I hear you have a flower collection..." Her voice trailed off as she led Basil away. Only when their footsteps faded could Corvina breathe again.

She slumped back against the bed and Juniper resumed tending to her. The silent swipe of rag and ointment against her body was almost tranquil. The steady, methodic rhythm reminded Corvina of the push and pull of lapping waves. It was gentle and soon, she grew numb to the stinging burn.

When Juniper finished, she helped bring Corvina to a sitting position before slipping a robe over her arms. The smooth silk was cold against her skin and didn't chafe her wounds, something she was immensely grateful for. Standing was another matter entirely. Her weak ankles and knees buckled, nearly sending her toppling to the floor. She would have, if it had not been for Juniper's steady hold against her.

Limping across the room and down the halls, they passed statuesque figures of guards, who's eyes trailed after her. Some eyes flashed with fear, others flashed with pity. But none had offered to help her, to stop the brutality her husband wreaked upon her. She couldn't blame them for it, even if she resented it. What would make her think they would ever put themselves on the line for her?

Dawn had, and look where that had gotten her.

They made it to Corvina's chambers. The bath was set up in the corner of the room behind a screen and she stared at it longingly, wanting to wipe any traces of her husband from her body. Even if the evidence of her beating would remain, she wanted to wipe between her legs, let the water take away any trace of his seed from her body.

But she had to let the ointment settle in first, let the swelling go down before she could cleanse herself. Both she and Juniper knew this, so she wasn't at all surprised that Juniper led her towards her own bed, sitting her among the plush of pink, rose gold, and white pillows and blankets.

She would have healed faster in the waterfalls of the king's castle. Hot springs powered by enslaved Fae, imbued with healing magic. But Tobias would have never allowed it. Not when he liked his wife to feel the pain he left behind. A constant reminder. A constant threat. Constant *suffering*.

Wren was already waiting within her chambers, setting up a tea tray. Chamomile, ginger, and lavender to soothe her nerves. Juniper reached for the dainty tea cup and pressed it into Corvina's shaking hands. As she did, her fingers moved discreetly over the cup, dropping leaves into the substance. Corvina barely had time to blink before her maid was pushing the cup to her mouth and forcing the contents down her throat.

The soothing taste bit against her tongue, but underneath that, as the leaves touched her mouth, she knew what that bitterness was. Her eyes widened in surprise, but she still guzzled the contents down, swallowing the leaves whole. It hurt her tender throat, but she did not care. When she finished, Juniper took the cup and turned away.

Corvina stared at her maid's back, emotion swelling in her chest. She knew what Juniper had discreetly placed there. An herb that her husband had forbidden her from taking to prevent pregnancy. Ever since the first time he'd discovered what Dawn had been helping her do, he had ordered chefs and taste testers to guard everything she ate and drank. He had forbidden the maids from helping.

Yet Juniper had.

She'd risked punishment to help Corvina.

Tears swelled in her eyes all over again, but she refused to let them fall. She felt unworthy of Juniper's help and feared what would happen if Tobias discovered what she'd done. But for now, she'd accept it for what it was.

A gift from a friend.

One she'd never be worthy of, but still appreciated just the same.

An hour later, the swelling and bruises had gone down considerably. There were still fading markings along her face from where his iron rings had kissed her skin, but her maids had quickly covered it with cosmetics so no one would know she'd been beaten the night before.

As she and Basil made their way to breakfast, her son oblivious to why Corvina was walking slower than usual, she noted her husband was already sitting at the table, the spread laying out in front of him. He hadn't served himself, however. And only did so once she and Basil were seated.

Poached eggs, scones, jam, fresh fruit, and thick slices of ham with a side of roasted tomatoes was quickly served before her. She wasn't sure she could swallow the harder foods, as her throat still ached, but Tobias was always ruling over what she put in her mouth. So, she began cutting up her food in silence, too afraid to look up at her husband even though she could feel his gaze on her.

"Corvina."

His voice was like a whip she wanted to flinch away from. It took her a moment of composing her emotions before she slowly turned to him. She wondered if he could make out the fading bruises beneath her high neckline, the mark of his fingerprints on her body.

His gaze did a quick assessment of her wounds, like he could see them beneath the powder. For a moment, something that looked like regret flashed in his eyes but was gone just as quickly. She was familiar with his sporadic emotions and knew it never lasted more than a few hours, so she did not allow herself to feel even the slightest bit of elation at the repent in his eyes.

"Are you well?" he asked, his voice above a whisper.

No.

She was not well.

She wanted to crawl back into bed and stay there. She wanted to avoid looking him in the eye. She wanted the pain in her body to disappear. She wanted her people to still be alive and her presence here in Dana to have been worth it. She wanted a mate who would love and care for her. She wanted so much that she knew she would never have.

So she settled with a quiet, "I am fine, thank you."

His brows pulled together as if he didn't quite believe her, but thankfully he did not reprimand the lie. Instead, he picked up his fork. "After breakfast, I have decided that we will visit the circus."

The announcement was greeted with Basil's fork clattering against his plate. His eyes went wide and hopeful. "Really, papa?"

He indulged Basil with a smile. "Your governess tells me of your intelligence and your nursemaid commends your good behavior." Tobias' eyes went to Corvina. "You've earned it."

Those words had been meant for her.

You've earned it.

With her blood and her sex. Like a common whore, she had earned an outing for her son. It cheapened her and made shame crawl a pathway up her neck in marks of red. He was insulting her, but he knew she'd not say a word about it because it made Basil so happy.

"Finish your breakfast, Reginald," Tobias continued. "We will be leaving soon. Your maids have been informed and so have the guards." He went back to his meal, though his eyes never strayed from her face. Like he was waiting, expectant.

"Thank you," she whispered to him. Because, despite what had happened and why he was doing it, he was making their son happy.

He smirked, and not for the first time, she loathed that he was attractive when only evil lurked beneath his skin. "No need to thank me," he said. "You are my family after all. I would do *anything* for my family."

He kept eating, and Corvina tried, but her mind kept going back to those words and the heavy weight they implied. And for the life of her, she couldn't figure out why they filled her with dread.

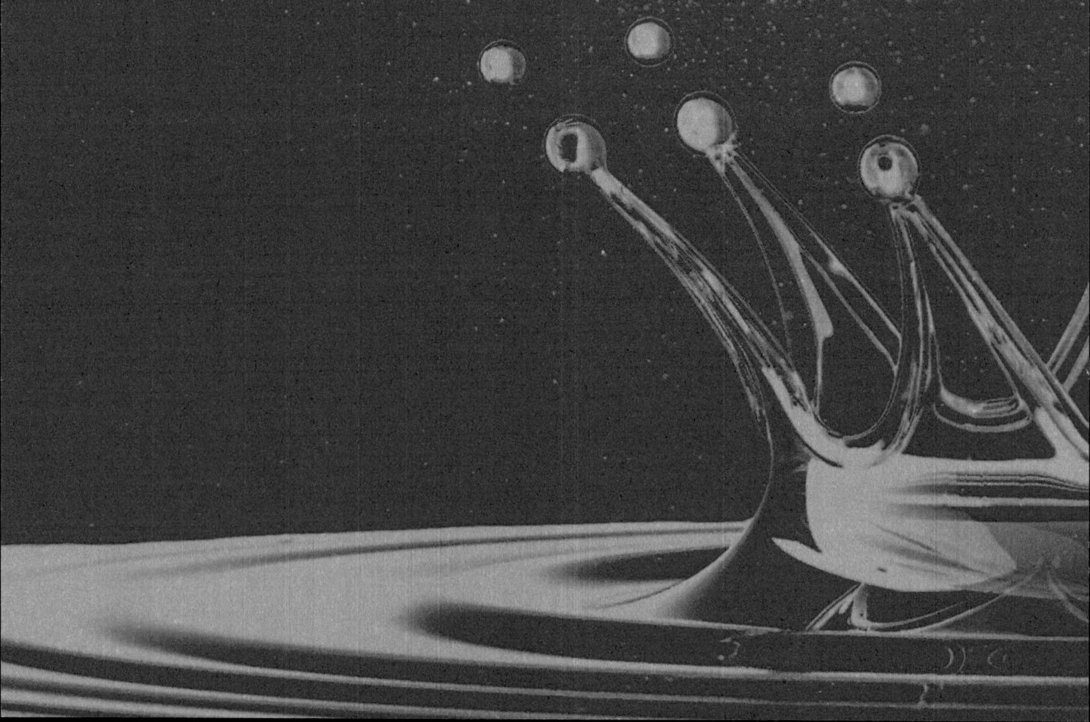

Fanny

The circus must have been informed of the royal family's arrival because it had been empty, as if reserved for them, their servants, and their guards only. They were greeted at the circus' entrance by a man that couldn't have been over three feet tall. He wore a striped red and white jacket tailored to his frame and a top hat taller than his legs.

He welcomed them, bowing low so his head touched the floor. He told them his name was Piriguini, and that this was his circus before he led them deeper into his set up.

It was like being transported into another land entirely. While there were no bodies pressing against them to jostle them out of the awe, there were circus attractions in abundance.

Females walked around with beards that dragged along the ground. Men with skin that appeared reptilian and with split tongues, both sexes with metal protruding from every inch of their skin, twins conjoined at the hips and heads. People tossed fire and knives all around them. Others sold confections like dough covered in chocolate, popped corn dipped in sweet caramel and rolled into balls the size of Corvina's fist; there were drinks as well, in bright colors that fizzled and popped like cider but were brighter and looked like something from the Unseelie Court.

A strange, exotic sort of magic breathed along the ground these humans walked on. In a world where normalcy was revered, to see these humans blatantly defy those societal norms and be the odd, twisted creatures they were was refreshing. It was a fearsome thing to behold to watch them perform with pride. Yet, at the same time, it filled her with a sense of melancholy.

Humans paid to see these weird creatures and within the next breath condemned the Fae for the same things.

Swallowing back her thoughts, Corvina instead decided to focus on Basil. Her son bounced eagerly on his feet, bursting to the brim with barely concealed excitement as he tugged on his nursemaid's skirts towards the vendors of candy.

Tobias did not reprimand his son for being overly familiar with the help. After casting her husband a long side glance, Corvina decided that he was in a better mood today and would give them free rein over the circus, so long as they stayed near him. Testing that theory, she pulled her hand gently from his. He did not force her back, but let her go easily enough so she could step towards her laughing son and bask in the joy of the moment.

Last night had been something of nightmares. Today would be better. She knew that as Basil lifted a kabob skewered with soft confections on the end, waving it in her direction.

"Look, mommy! Candies!"

"Allow me, my prince." Gale appeared and took the candies from him, plucking one off and chewing it for herself without fear. She smacked her lips, tilted her head slightly, then handed the candies back to Basil.

She'd taste tested her son's food. Sometimes she forgot about the necessity of such an action and horror filled her. She was used to having others taste her food first, but for herbs that didn't belong. Not for poisons or malicious intent.

Her grateful smile found Gale's, and her new maid nodded a small gesture of acknowledgment before she stepped away, a presence at their backs, never too far away in case she was needed.

"Papa, do you want candies?" Basil asked shyly, pointing them in his father's direction.

Corvina tensed.

They'd never been out together before. Not on an adventure quite like this one, so she was unsure of how Basil's question would be received among witnesses. But Tobias surprised her by plucking a candy from the kabob and popping it into his mouth.

"Hmm, my favorite." When he smiled at their son, there was no trace of the monster that lived inside him.

Basil smiled bashfully, eating the rest of the candies before he rushed after the small circus owner, who showed them the attractions by pointing at them with his black cane.

"Shall we?" Tobias offered his arm once again. Corvina was reluctant to take it. Not when the memory of his body doing unspeakable things to hers was still fresh. But what other choice did she have, really?

Her arm nestled into place next to his, and using the other hand, she picked up the hem of her skirts and they wandered after Basil.

As the hours passed, Basil's excitement grew with each attraction. "Mommy, I want to see the girl who twists her body!"

After his declaration, Piriguini led them into an enormous striped tent that matched his waistcoat. He hastened them towards a seating arrangement that seemed to have been set specifically for them near the front. Plush pillows and rich blankets along with trays of snacks and food had been set out as if by the royal servants. Corvina wouldn't have been surprised if that was the case.

They sat and Piriguini marched his small legs to the center of the tent, his boots scuffling along the patch of dry ground. He lifted his walking stick, making a series of gestures and an introduction that Corvina barely heard. She was so busy focused on her son's face, her heart warming with each passing moment.

Her attention drew back to the stage, or rather at the top of the tent. Ribbons were tied up there and fluttered to the ground. From the slicing panes of ribbon, a body of a young woman unfurled, twisting and pulling herself up by her arms and legs. Her every movement was dexterous and captivating, as she all but flew between colorful ropes. Her body twined around them like a sinuous snake in a dangerous dance. Many times, Corvina found herself gasping, fearing that the human was about to fall to her death, but she caught herself in time with a smile. Every movement was purposeful, made to look accidental. And when she finished, she slowly glided towards the ground, her feet touching the floor. With a swish of her wrists, the ropes were released, and she gave an extravagant bow.

Corvina clapped alongside Basil and the servants, feeling a breathless sense of awe at the performance.

Tobias must have noticed, because he leaned towards her, his lips touching her skin. Her body flinched, but he pretended not to notice. "Would you like to meet her, wife?"

A sense of familiar dread and fear clogged her throat, making her as unresponsive as ever. It was always more prominent after a session of torture similar to the previous night. Her emotions were heightened and she always felt like she was balancing on the edge of a blade, waiting to be impaled.

Tobias did not wait for her answer. Instead, he lifted his head and called out. "My wife wishes to meet your acrobat, Piriguini." Like always, his words were a command that was immediately obeyed.

Piriguini bustled the young female towards them with a flourish. Once she was close enough, she curtseyed. The movement was shy and awkward, like it wasn't something she was used to doing often. Of course, it wasn't. How often would a poor circus girl meet royalty? Corvina just hoped her husband would not reprimand her for the poor gesture.

"You may rise," Tobias said. He lounged back lazily against the seat, exuding an air of arrogance and power. His arm draped at Corvina's back near her shoulders. She fought back her disgust and schooled her expression.

The young female had blonde hair, a shade a bit dirtier than Corvina's own, cropped short near her scalp. Spandex covered her body like a second skin, the bright material sticking to her crevices and leaving little to the imagination. Her husband's eyes did not linger on her form, but her face.

"It seems you have impressed the Princess of Dana a great deal with your performance." Tobias stroked his chin. "She was quite eager to meet you."

"Thank you, Your Majesty." She curtsied to him and when she turned towards Corvina, she did the same. Her big eyes rose to meet Corvina's face. "Thank you, Pri—" The words froze on her tongue mid-way. She sucked in a breath. It was an audible gasp, one Corvina was sure she hadn't mean to utter, because her cheeks heated a moment later. She'd simply been caught off guard by Corvina's appearance.

Her beauty.

The ears that were on display. Though scarred, so obviously Fae.

Perhaps her blunder would have been forgiven. After all, it wasn't widely known to those outside of Dana that the youngest prince harbored a stolen Fae bride. It would have been forgiven and forgotten, had she not decided to twist her mouth into a quick, disgusted sneer.

One that Tobias had seen, even as she tried to quickly mask it.

"Does my wife disgust you, circus freak?"

The young woman jolted back as if she'd been slapped by the impact of Tobias' words. Her mouth opened, closed, and she visibly trembled as she realized what slight she just committed. "Y-your Majesty..."

Tobias' entire body tensed and he straightened, pulling his arm away from Corvina's shoulders to lean forward. His posture gave the air of a lazy, sardonic feeling. It was anything but. "What is your name?"

Her wide eyes got even wider. "F-F-Fantasia... Though I am called Fanny."

"Fanny." Tobias whirled the name around his tongue. "In some countries, the word 'fanny' also means pussy. Did you know that?"

Corvina tried to avoid looking at him, but cruelty and vulgarity was hypnotizing sometimes. The fall of chaos, though it made her stomach roil and her body tremble and her mind wither, was an addicting force. Once you watched something gravitate towards the ground, all you could do was wait for the crash and the silent aftermath.

And pray you came away unscathed.

"Come closer, Fanny." Tobias beckoned with a flick of his fingers.

Behind Fanny, Piriguini stammered. "Now, my prince, can we just—" He almost swallowed his tongue out of fear of the glare Tobias sent his way.

"Come *here*, Fanny," he demanded again.

This time, she obeyed. Her steps were slow, unsure, as they shuffled in their direction. She did not come close enough so Tobias could touch her, though. But it didn't matter. Distance meant nothing. She stopped, clasping her shaking fingers at her stomach.

"Now, answer me, do you think my wife to be disgusting because she is Fae?"

Fanny's ears reddened. Noncommittal answers stumbled out of her mouth where they couldn't discern the answer from her lips. As if they needed to. It was obvious that she hated Corvina on sight. Was this show really necessary? But she kept her lips closed, knowing that contradicting him in public would earn her a terrible fate.

Even Basil was quiet beside her, sensing the horror of the moment or the shift in the air. Corvina wanted the maids to usher her son away, but she feared breaking contact from the situation. Like tearing eyes away from a predator would make it strike.

"N-no, Your Majesty," Fanny was finally able to push out.

"No?" Tobias mocked. Clearly, he didn't believe her. "Then, if she does not disgust you as you say, get down on your knees and kiss her feet."

"Your Majesty?"

Tobias leaned forward and this time, the cruelty dripped from his words like a slow sliding nectar. "Get down on your fucking knees, wench, and kiss my wife's feet."

Humiliation burned Fanny's cheeks as much as on Corvina's. She wanted to turn to Tobias and plead with him to stop this cruelty, but she knew of what little use it would be. Once he set his mind on an idea, he would see it through until the brutal end.

Breaths were captured in frightened lungs from everyone bearing witness. The air shimmered with fear and the hot sting of the prince's rage. It was suffocating, more so than the sweltering air of Port Bay.

Fanny turned in Corvina's direction. Their eyes met. This time, she did not sneer, but even so, Corvina felt her hatred. She saw it deep in the depths of her round eyes. Just like she saw it every day within the eyes of her husband and the courtiers.

But if she knew her husband, she knew this slight was because he wanted no one else to hate her but himself. He wanted no one to insult her but himself. This was not some royal rage on her behalf, but rage against those he felt judged him for his choice of bride. So he would set it to right by humiliating the poor girl.

Yes, she'd sneered at Corvina, but as she'd endured much worse from the hands of her very own husband, it was not cutting. It did not injure her. She just wanted to get up and leave, but he was prolonging the moment purposefully.

"Well?" he prompted.

Fanny swallowed and slowly sank to her knees and crawled towards Corvina. Her cheeks burned brightly, and it was like the embers of a fire bouncing from one body to the next. Her humiliation was tangible, invading Corvina's body. Her breath came in small bursting pants, but she hid it behind the steady rise and fall of her chest, and her lips compressed into a thin line.

Her eyes stayed on Fanny's crawling form. When the woman reached close to her body, Tobias said, "Present her with your feet, wife."

Oh, how Corvina loathed him. She almost refused. It was on the tip of her tongue to defy him, a taste she swallowed back and past the lump in her throat. She was no hero. Even if she wanted to stick up for this young woman, Tobias would find a way to make them both suffer tenfold.

Corvina would not defy him. She could not. Not without repercussions. Perhaps that made her weak. Perhaps she'd become the one thing she swore she never would be. But it did not matter. This was her fate now.

Her fingers grasped the sides of her gown and she pulled, the hem crawling just above her ankles to present the delicate heeled shoes. She lifted them to Fanny, and she swore her heart stopped beating for a fragment of a second due to the hatred in the human's eyes. She glared up at Corvina while she leaned forward, pursing her lips and pressing them to the tips of one shoe and then the other.

As she pulled away, Tobias stood, smoothing out the lapels of his velvet jacket. With rather cruel force, he shoved Fanny away with his leg and she went sprawling backwards with a cry.

"Next time you feel the need to glare upon the princess, my *wife,* remember this moment, scum." He turned and offered a hand to Corvina, which she was forced to take. Her fingers eased away from her dress, letting the material swish around her feet once more. She took his hand, allowing him to help her stand. She avoided looking at Fanny as she did so.

She'd already seen enough of the girl's humiliation. She didn't need to see any more.

"Remember that you are barely good enough to lick the shit off her shoes."

And with those parting words, their party left.

Elemental Insinuations

Their day had been ruined and the energy as they walked around the circus had shifted. It seemed like word had spread around the circus about what had happened with Fanny. Where once the circus dwellers rushed to accommodate them, now they gazed upon them warily. And when Corvina's eyes met anyone else's, they quickly looked away. To hide their disgust, no doubt. Lest the prince decided to make them do something completely abhorrent.

Corvina never thought she'd be so eager to get away, to go back to her perfectly gilded cage and hide away from others. At least there the only one who looked upon her with disgust was her husband. And perhaps guards from beneath their helms. The benefit of that was that she could not see them, and so it didn't matter.

Here, expressions were out in the open and they made her uncomfortable. Not even Basil seemed to have the same joy he'd previously displayed.

"You are upset with me," Tobias said.

Corvina froze, unsure of what to say. He would know if she were lying and would punish her for it as much as for the truth. It was only a matter of choosing the lesser of two evils.

"Why?" His fingers tightened a fraction on her hand. He pulled her to a stop, turning her so they were facing one another. The servants kept their distance, but Corvina did not doubt they would hear this conversation. Servants heard everything. "I was merely protecting your honor, Corvina."

"I know." The words were whispered. Already, the sting of tears burned behind her eyelids. She felt one slip and Tobias made a noise of impatience, grasping her chin tightly and tilting her face up. Her jaw hurt, and he only held her tighter.

"A slight against you is a slight against me."

The imprint of his iron-clad fingers would be on her skin by morning. She was sure of it.

"You understand that, right?"

"I do, husband." That did not mean she accepted it, though. But what she thought and accepted mattered little. What mattered were his feelings, his anger.

She was nothing but a vessel to sink his cock into, a prize won in the war, a bag to punch, a child to berate. She'd been reduced to so many little things that she no longer knew her own voice.

"Good." His fingers smoothed against her skin, the gesture tender and a contrast to the flashing eyes and angry expression. "I would do it again."

It was a promise. Like cutting out hearts and taking off heads was something meant to impress her. It was a demonstration of his kindness, given in the only way he knew how.

But she didn't want his bloody kindness at the expense of others' lives and dignity.

"Prince Tobias."

Tobias pulled away from her and turned without concealing his twisted expression of annoyance. The clang of metal alerted them to several approaching figures, and the scent of iron had dulled her senses enough that she hadn't noticed them at first.

Corvina's body went cold at the sight of Captain Brannon. He stood between two other soldiers. His massive body cutting an imposing figure, clad in all that leather and armor, the two swords at his waist. He stopped before them, bowing first to Tobias then Corvina, his eyes stopping just long enough for her breath to catch with fear.

"Captain Brannon," her husband all but sneered much in the same manner Fanny had sneered at Corvina. "What do you want? I am busy. Spending time with my family, as you can see."

The captain's eyes pulled away from Corvina to regard her husband. She marveled at how well his chiseled features did not change. He could have easily been speaking to a servant, the emperor, or a pile of dirt. So little expression he showed, but his eyes seemed to burst with dark curiosity.

"I can see that, and forgive the interruption, but I was hoping we could speak on the matter in regards to—"

"Then keep hoping," Tobias interrupted. "For a prince is not called on, and I think you have forgotten who you are speaking to. I am a prince of Dana, not some lowly foot soldier you can order about." Already riding the anger from Fanny's disrespect, he was now directing it towards the captain. Though, unlike Fanny, the captain did not tremble.

As if he didn't fear Tobias at all.

Perhaps because he could crush him with his meaty fists.

What it must be like, she wondered, to not feel fear.

"Unfortunately, my orders come directly from the emperor. The highest authority in all of Illyk." Captain Brannon met Tobias' cold stare with a hard one of his own. The words weren't spoken in any particular tone, but they implied an insult just the same.

"How dare you—"

"Your Majesty, forgive the interruption..." A trembling messenger stepped towards them, holding up a folded and sealed page between his fingers. It tore the men away from the argument for a moment.

"What?" Tobias snapped.

"A missive has arrived. From the king."

With a roll of his eyes, Tobias snatched the page up and walked away, tearing it open with impatience.

He was but a few feet away, and yet it felt like miles. Corvina felt suddenly vastly alone in the captain's presence. And his attention was focused wholly on her, his eyes searching. He made her feel flayed open. Like all of her secrets were out with that single glance. It was a brutish stare. One that threatened to tear her apart if she even breathed.

"How difficult it must be, dear princess, to suffer an iron touch." His gaze pointedly strayed to her neck, like maybe he could see the wounds that had already faded.

She fought away the urge to let her hand go to her throat.

"I am afraid I do not know what you mean, Captain."

His lips pressed together and she realized he was hiding a smirk. He looked to her husband, still reading his missive, then back to her. "I suppose you have the *elements* to soothe the iron touch, do you not?" He put just enough emphasis on the word 'elements' for it to crawl down her spine like a spider.

She blinked at him. "Sorry?"

"Magic is a strange thing, or so I've been told. When it is suppressed for too long it explodes. Sometimes, we see the evidence of it in little things. Like scars..."

The heavy implication, the hint of what he was saying, as if he knew what Corvina was, what was hiding beneath her skin, settled heavily like a stone in her stomach. Those roaming hands, the way they'd glided up her back. She thought he'd been searching. Maybe he had. Maybe he'd felt the scars her dresses hid.

Or maybe he hadn't and was hoping for a reaction. For her to give away a sense of what lived beneath her skin.

Instead, she furrowed her brows in confusion. "I'm afraid I don't know what it is you mean. I am magic-less, and I no longer follow the path of the Fae. I'm Danarish now."

His smile was slow and condescending. "Of course, princess. Forgive me if I implied otherwise."

She offered him her sweetest smile. "You are forgiven."

"Forgiven for what?" Tobias suddenly appeared beside her. She looked up at him, but his expression was more annoyance and distraction than anything else. It let her know that he did not hear their conversation and did not care that she was conversing with another man in the first place. "Captain, I am cutting this visit short. I have other things to see to. Corvina, come." He took her arm and tugged her away. She went, but felt the pressure of Captain Brannon's gaze on her back the entire way.

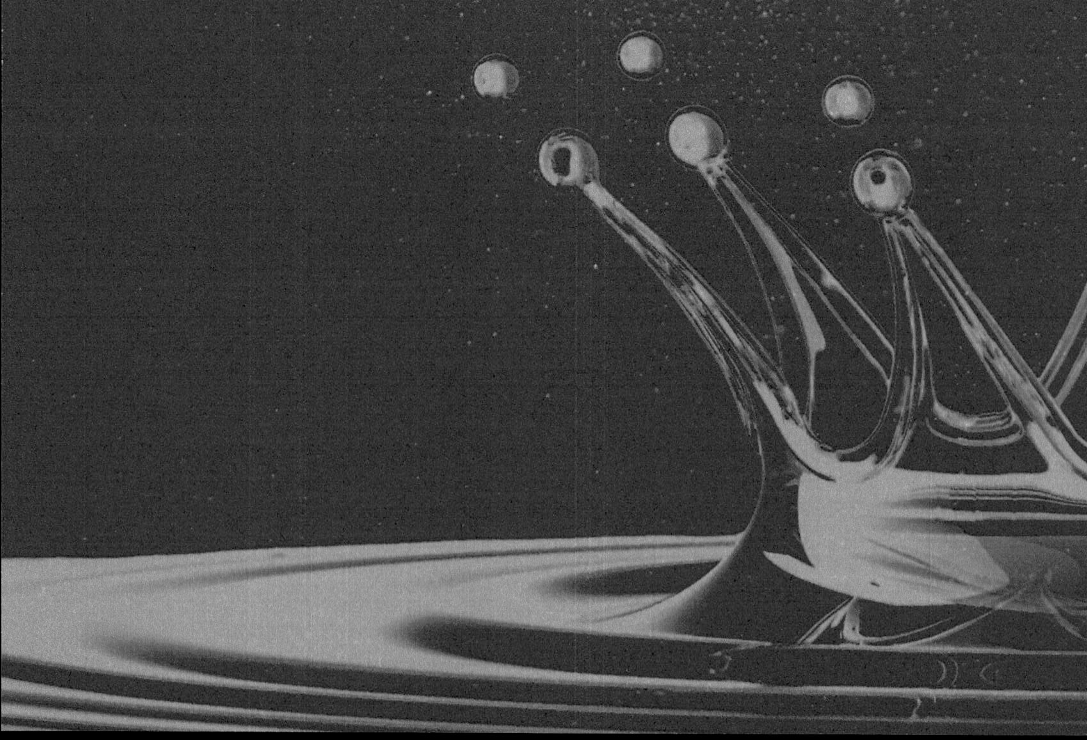

The Touch of Fae

His palms itched to reach for the sword at his side. An impulse, really. One he was acquainted intimately with and could stave off just as quickly as it appeared. He always knew that once he took one life, he always desiderated to take more.

Stealing souls was an addiction. Taking lives in the name of the Emperor of Illyk was his elation. It was a monster, lying in wait to be fed, and patience was his greatest virtue.

Captain Brannon watched the Fae walk away, the temptation to take her and confirm what he suspected building like an ache. It spread, buzzing through his palms and in the center of his chest, akin to eagerness. He tamped it down, just like he tamped everything down. Feeling was a weakness and a distraction, one he could scarcely afford.

His knuckles whitened under the grip he had on the pommel of his sword, grasping it firmly. His emperor was a demanding leader, his desperation becoming evident as he sent his soldiers to search for the Elementals.

Ever since the Fire Dancer had slipped from the Brotherhood's fingers, the emperor had grown impatient to bring in the Elementals and take down the Fae Resistance. Even with the blood of the Seelie Prince tainting the second blade he wore at his hip, the Fae had already amassed an army of their own as they took a portal from kingdom to kingdom, rescuing Fae from prisons and camps.

Their movements had slowed after a while, and the Fae trackers led the captain to believe that the Resistance was slowly making their way here. To Port Bay, Dana. He'd brought his armies here to figure out what they could possibly want from the sea-side kingdom.

When he'd met Princess Corvina, he'd known. His fingers had glided along her back, feeling for what he only guessed would be there.

Markings.

Markings like the ones aligned on Shula Azzarh's back. Markings unique to Elementals alone.

"Request an audience with the king," he ordered to a soldier at his side, while his gaze remained stark on the pathway Princess Corvina Rhian had walked on.

As if she'd carved an invisible trail of magic, one he knew she possessed, in her wake. "I believe it is time to rip the veil from the royal family's eyes."

"Sir?"

Captain Brannon didn't turn. "Do not tell Brother Bastien what you are requesting." Insufferable, sanctimonious fool. It was because of him that they'd lost the Fire Dancer in the first place. Him and his whole sect of idiots who thought they could play gods. Could play at toying with the Fae.

The soldier nodded and hurried away. The captain eased a breath slowly from his lungs, fingers relaxing slowly off his weapon. The tips danced across the pommel instead, tracing the same line he'd traced up the princess' spine. A single touch of Fae gave up so much truth. Like how skittish of a creature she was. Like how frightened she was of her husband. Like how she eased away from the touch of his fingers the closer they smoothed over the scars hidden beneath the material of her gown.

And how she stared at him like Captain Brannon knew a secret no one else did.

Whispers, Elementals, and Azzarh

Parchment hung over every wall they passed. On each, images slashed over the page with furious brush strokes of portraits meant to frighten anyone catching sight of it. Details sprang from the pages, strange faces of monstrous-looking creatures. The kind that parents spoke to their children about. The kind that hid beneath beds and fluttered on wings to steal teeth by wrangling them from gums in the middle of the night.

Corvina's steps faltered near the images. Pictures of Fae, of her brethren, slapped on Illyk's Most Wanted signs. Of a beautiful female Fae, with long flowing hair and an intense expression.

Fire Dancer.

Shula Azzarh.

Wanted: Alive and Intact.

Those words were written in bold lettering, almost as bold as the strokes of her face and hair. The portrait seemed to stare back at her, though she knew that notion was ever ridiculous, as portraits could not stare. Yet when Corvina looked upon the eyes of the painted face of the Fae, something within her stirred. Hummed. Breathed like that first whisper of wind in the mornings. The kind that tugged at strands of hair and pushed aside curtains. The first fresh breath of life. Of a new day.

And that name... something about it...

Then it all fell into place.

She'd heard that name spoken only the night before by Captain Brannon himself to the king and Tobias. It had been a harsh whisper, mingled with other words she could not now remember.

If only she could. Then maybe the feeling in her chest would be explained...

"Come along." Tobias gripped her upper arm and tugged her, as she'd stopped walking to stare. At his insistence, she followed quickly, letting him usher both her and Basil into the awaiting carriage. Once they were seated, their transportation gave a jerk and sped through the streets.

"Is everything alright?" Corvina found herself asking quietly, demurely. They'd left rather suddenly. Granted, she'd been eager to leave, but now she loathed to when she caught sight of the annoyance on her husband's expression.

"My father requests to see me at his castle."

That hadn't answered her question, but Corvina didn't pry. The last time she'd asked questions he hadn't wanted to answer, the back of his hand had connected to her face, his iron rings scraping along her skin and splitting it open. It had taken hours to heal.

Better she not upset him anymore than he already was.

For the next few moments, all they could do was ride in the silence.

"What is so important that you had to take me from the company of my family?" Tobias had barely made it through the doors of his father's throne room before the words left him. He wasn't one to usually speak so disrespectfully to the king, but his anger burned with enough force to rupture from his body.

He knew he shouldn't, but he needed to set those instincts free. Self-control be damned. The ire he held towards his father and brother were always so tightly restrained that, just this once, he needed the relief those words brought. But it wasn't enough.

A part of him knew he craved violence and blood. Those two things could assuage an ache in his chest more than anything else. An ache that never seemed to go away, but only pulse hotter until it seemed like an empty void opened up inside of him. Even as he filled it with what his mind and body demanded, there was still something *missing*.

His father sat upon his throne, resting his elbow leisurely against the armrest. His brows flicked up at Tobias' announcement. "Sorry to interrupt your day of play," the king drawled slowly. "But while you were traipsing through the circus, your brother and I were here doing *royal* work."

That's when Tobias noted they weren't alone. His brother leaned against a far pillar, obscured by slanting shadows. When their eyes met, Tobias' flashed and his jaw clenched while Arthur gave him a mock salute and a smirk. The smirk Tobias wanted to slice right off his brother's mouth with a knife.

Besides the two, there was another person present as well. Tobias forced himself to look away from his jester of a brother and saw the priest. He wore his white robes, the hem dusted with the clinging remnants of sand.

Tobias quickly composed himself, his anger only rising at his fuck-up. He couldn't have entered the throne room with more finesse than the way he had? He was just giving his father more reason to doubt his capabilities as a ruler.

Fuck.

"Brother Bastien," he greeted absently. He turned back to his father, watching as the king dropped his arms onto the tops of his thighs and leaned forward. It was too-casual of a stance to be purely casual. It was calculated, meant for observing. "You requested my presence, Your Majesty?"

"Yes."

He said nothing else, staring at Tobias like he was searching for something. This was a game of his. He liked to think he made Tobias uncomfortable. For the most part, he did, but Tobias would certainly never show it to the old bastard.

Finally, the king snorted and sat back against his cushions. He waved a hand in the priest's direction. "Brother Bastien has brought interesting... information."

"Information regarding what?" He kept the wariness out of his tone as his gaze wandered towards the priest.

He'd been inconsequential the night before, but Tobias studied him now. He was of wide berth, his stomach rounded in the middle. The robes gave no hint of the form beneath, except to flow out stiffly and make him look so much wider that he likely was. His face was ruddy and red, his cheeks bright, his lips puckered naturally.

He looked like an oaf.

"Information regarding your wife, Your Majesty," he answered coolly.

Once the words were out of his lips, Tobias stepped forward, fists clenching. He'd not tolerate *anyone* speaking ill of Corvina. Did they take him for a fool? Did they think him so weak as to allow such a slight? She belonged to him. And, Fae or not, he would not allow any insult.

"Tobias," his father snapped, stopping him in his tracks. "Listen to what the man has to say before you start chopping off tongues. It is very curious."

He barely stopped himself from charging forward. Relaxing his muscles, even as they ticked in his jaw with annoyance, he narrowed his eyes on the priest. "Then speak," he ordered. "And have a care with your words."

"Fear not, Prince Tobias. The Brothers have all taken a vow of celibacy, and I would not dare imply any of what you're thinking in regards to the princess in my words."

A vow of celibacy? That was a load of shit if Tobias had ever heard it. Still, he inclined his head. "Then speak."

"As you know, Emperor Laurel has been doubling his efforts in finding Fae with magic. Specifically, the Fae that are called the Elementals."

"So the captain said."

Brother Bastien scoffed. "Captain Brannon is an oaf. He caught the first Elemental. Her name was Shula Azzarh; she was hiding away at a circus, that one. Then the fool let her *escape*."

Tobias grunted. He couldn't imagine a female Fae slipping past Captain Brannon, what with his wide frame and deathly glares. But any man could fall prey to a pretty face. It was why Tobias himself jerked Corvina around sometimes. Better he establish his dominance than her try to get any ideas about manipulating him. Besides, he'd saved her from death. The least she could do was submit.

"As you can imagine, the emperor has not been happy with the captain. It is why he is being so insistent that the Fae Resistance are marching here as we speak."

"Tell my brother why they are marching here, Bastien," Arthur spoke. The manic glee in his voice was unmistakable. It had Tobias instantly alert. And when his brother peeled himself from the pillar and stepped into the golden sunlight, he hated him.

Hated him with every fiber in his being.

Since they were children, Arthur had been insufferable and jealous of Tobias' arrival. He had done all he could to make him miserable until Tobias had grown enough to fight back. They no longer settled their differences with fisticuffs but with cutting, poisonous words.

Arthur was perfect in every way. At least, according to the king. Arthur was smarter, faster, more cultured, and above all, it wasn't Arthur who had killed their mother during childbirth.

That was Tobias' first slight.

Whatever Brother Bastien had to say next, Tobias knew it would not be well met, given the shine in his brother's eyes.

"We believe they are coming here in search of the next Elemental. The Resistance is trying to find them before Emperor Laurel can. Naturally, we cannot let that happen."

"So what?" Tobias crossed his arms over his chest. "Would you like us to search through our reserves of slaves to find your Elemental? Send the beast off with you and to the emperor? Feel free."

There was silence and Brother Bastien cleared his throat delicately. "See, Your Majesty, I believe I already know who the Elemental is."

Something sour churned in Tobias' stomach and he knew what the priest was going to say before he opened his mouth to say it.

"It is Princess Corvina, Your Majesty."

"No." The word cut out of him like a knife.

The king's brows rose. "No?"

Tobias shook his head and uncrossed his arms. "Not her. My wife has no magical abilities to speak of. You are wrong."

"I do have experience with these things, Your Majesty," Brother Bastien continued. "There is proof enough in appearance that—"

"Just because she's Fae you think she's some Elemental?" he demanded. His voice rose to a shout. He could no longer keep a rein over his temper. He felt it coming unleashed. Like a caged beast bashing itself against its bars.

"It is not because she is Fae. Not all Fae wield magic. But if you are so adamant on believing she is innocent, perhaps simple proof..."

"What *kind* of proof?"

"The Elementals have distinct marks upon their flesh that sets them apart from other Fae, and each Elemental has a mark singular to the powers they wield. The Fire Dancer, for example, had scars."

"Scars," Tobias echoed. His throat closed, his stomach churned, and his chest? It was on fire with rage, a force so great it knocked the breath from his body. He pictured the scars on Corvina's skin. The one situated just below the base of her neck.

The one that sickened him every time he saw it.

A Fae curse, he'd called it.

But what if it was something more?

"Twin flames in adjacent circles. Each Fae is different, but their markings are similar. Five circles with stars, four circles with vines and flower blooms, three circles with whorls of clouds, two with flames, and one circle with a wave of water."

Tobias felt like he'd been stabbed in the heart. His eyes swept over to his father, who regarded him curiously and then to his brother, who's mocking lilt of his smile made Tobias' teeth clench. The fucking bastard. He was taking joy in this.

And Tobias, he felt... he felt betrayed. His wife had that scar on her back.

A Fae curse.

She had looked him in the eye and allowed him to believe that that's what it was. Instead of this... Instead of whatever Brother Bastien was spouting.

An Elemental.

No. She couldn't be. Because if she was, that meant she lied to him. And if she'd lied to him about that, what else had she lied about? She'd taken him for a fool once by attempting to prevent pregnancy. What else was that bitch concealing? Right under his fucking nose.

Magic—

"No," he gritted out adamantly. "She is not." He did not want them to know the truth. But he realized a little too late that his father likely had spies everywhere. He probably already knew of her scar.

"If you require further proof..."

"In shock, brother?" Arthur taunted, interrupting the priest. "Can't imagine why your pretty little wife would keep such a thing from you?"

"Shut your whore mouth, Arthur," Tobias snapped. "She is no Elemental."

"By the gods, has she bewitched you so that you cannot see the truth when it is in front of your face?" The king stood and stepped down from his throne, looking at Tobias with... pity. "Tell me she has not used her magic on you?"

"She has no magic!" Tobias shouted. "And even if she did, she is too weak to use it."

"Yes, well, you made sure of that, didn't you?" His father's eyes shone, and it was one of the few times he saw pride in his depths.

"If you have doubts, Your Majesties, there is a ritual I can perform to test the veracity of my claims. However, I must ask, should we do this, you keep it from Captain Brannon. You understand why, I'm sure. The fool could not be trusted with the Fire Dancer... I would hate to put the safety of your princess in the hands of that ignorant man."

"Rest assured that secret is safe with us," the king replied for them all. "It would do no good for others to discover such a thing."

"The ritual, what does it entail?" Tobias felt his head spin. The priest's smile grew wider.

"It is quite simple. I must let her swallow this nectar." He reached within his robes and pulled out a small glass vial with liquid inside. "It is a nectar of the gods. It will reveal her true self to us. Her magic will have no choice but to come forth, and we will see for ourselves then if Princess Corvina is truly what she appears to be."

He contemplated this, snapping his teeth together so hard, a headache began to form at his temples. His wife. His fucking whore of a lying wife...

She would pay.

He would make her pay for this slight if it were true.

"I agree to the ritual," Tobias whispered as his eyes met Brother Bastien's. There was triumph there, but he ignored it. Couldn't see past the haze of his own anger. "What is it that you need from me?"

Over the course of the next few weeks, Corvina found she could breathe a little easier. If only because her husband was strangely absent from their lives. For days, he'd been coming and going, pausing only long enough to tell her he had business to attend to with his father and would be occupied.

Her curiosity burned. What manner of meetings could be so important that he was called away all day every day? She wasn't complaining about it. The hallways of their own castle breathed freely now that he was gone. The servants had lighter steps and the guards didn't look so morose.

Still, the situation was strange. The king hardly ever had reason to call upon Tobias. Usually, Arthur was the one that was sought after. She wondered if it had something to do with the emperor's soldiers and the Brotherhood.

Neither were an established faction in Dana, much less in Port Bay. She'd heard whispers from the servants that the Emperor of Illyk was settling and cracking down on more Fae than ever before.

"I've heard they're here looking for a group of Fae rebels," Gale whispered. Though, whispered wasn't the appropriate term. When she spoke, she did so with vivacity, so that all those around her could hear.

For a while, after she'd witnessed what Tobias did to Corvina, her new maid had been quiet and timid. Like walking near Corvina was akin to walking on glass. It faded though, like dark colors faded from the sky to make way for daylight until Gale started spreading her blissful, ignorant sunshine once again.

"You've seen the wanted posters around the city," she continued. "I've heard they're searching for magical Fae." Her voice lowered. "Elemental Fae. Specifically, the former Fire Dancer of Piriguini's Circus, Shula Azzarh."

"That's enough, Gale," Corvina snapped. Though her voice was a tremulous whisper, it still held an irritated bite to it. It had her maids looking at her with surprise from where they were, brushing out her dress for the day. "That'll be enough gossip." Then, to soften to the blow, she added, "My head is throbbing."

Juniper stood slowly, setting her brush to the side. "I will bring you some tea."

"No, thank you, Juniper. I think fresh air would do nicely." She needed to get out of the suffocating confines of the castle. Even while every window was open, with the archways of the pillars, the breeze and sunlight filtering through, it wasn't enough. She needed more. She needed air, the smell of the sea breeze.

Her skin felt itchy, her chest felt tight, and the whispers of all those rumors echoed in her mind painfully.

"Shall we change into your outside attire, Princess?" Juniper was watching her closely, and Corvina wondered if the other Fae knew just how close to the edge of insanity her mind was.

"That will not be necessary, Juniper. Please keep an eye on Basil. I will be back momentarily." She stood from her vanity and turned. Her maids hurried to curtsey, maybe object that she not go anywhere alone, but Corvina's quick feet were already carrying her out of the room.

Outside, the guards were aligned along the halls. She ignored them as she walked. Keeping her composure was difficult. Keeping a straight back and her head tilted high was a struggle when all she wanted to do was fall to her knees.

Her skin felt too tight across her frame, the clothes she wore even worse. She itched, and she knew why. It was the magic pulsing beneath her skin, demanding release. Captain Brannon had been right about one thing that day. Magic needed an outlet, or else it festered within the body like an infection. She'd already suppressed it for too long.

She tried to keep that part of herself at bay as often as she could. Her father had demanded it of her right before he'd given her up to Dana.

"Do not tell a soul what it is you can do. No one knows. Not even the courtiers accompanying you. No one can know what you are. What lives inside you."

Magic.

Elemental.

While her father had not forced her to suppress her magic at all, she still kept it a secret. Practiced, trained in secret. And when she'd arrived, she was forced to hide that part of herself away. When it grew to be too much, when her magic begged for release, she gave into it in the only way she knew how.

It was dangerous, but even more so to keep such raw power locked up inside of her for too long.

She stumbled out of the castle and into the gardens. The scent of jasmine choked her, clawing at her lungs fiercely. She tried gasping, her feet breaking into a run. Anyone who looked out of the windows would see her rushing towards the edge of the cliffs. Her hands shot out, palms slamming against the crumbling, marble balcony just along the edge.

She leaned over it, looking down at the drop below. At the sea Dawn had begged her to jump into to save themselves from this hurt. Corvina stared at the water, at the vicious crash of waves. They looked like hands, like fingers, like bodies piling on top of each other to reach the high side of the cliff.

Water was as gentle as it was unforgiving. It soothed aches and drowned people, innocent or not. And it was the element Corvina Rhian wielded. One she let sleep inside her. One who's power she'd nearly forgotten as the days went by.

She used it enough to keep the itch at bay. But other than that, it was like everything that was Fae—Seelie— about her had been squashed to dust.

Corvina watched the waves, wondering for a treacherous second what it would have been like to be taken away by them. To take Dawn's hand and jump from the balcony and into the sea below. Perhaps her magic could have saved them. Perhaps not. Where would they have ended up? Would it have been worse? Better?

Worse. That's what her mind whispered. She suffered, but not like others suffered. She had a son, a home, food. If she gave that up, she would have nothing but a scattered court drenched in iron. Besides, she had Basil to think of. She would not subject him to a life on the run without food, or when they knew nothing of the world beyond Port Bay.

She was trapped.

Yes, Tobias had shoved her into the cage, but she'd been the one to lock the door and toss the key.

Taking a breath, Corvina concentrated on the waters below, letting a discreet sliver of magic loose. The waves responded, her magic pushing the water higher up the cliff side like a storm on the rise. The ache in her chest and beneath her skin abated. Slowly, with each tendril she let out of her body, the waves rose.

"What are you doing?"

Her magic startled, exploded, causing the waters below to rise all the way up to the edge. The spray of salt sloshed against her shoes, drenching her hem. She jumped back with a gasp, the cold water and the voice a shock to her system.

She whirled, facing her husband's stern expression. She felt his anger and fear held her frozen. Her chest rose and fell with every breath, and already she could feel the burning sting of tears threaten to fall because she knew what was to come.

Tobias marched towards her, his stride angry and determined. She couldn't move, not even to flinch when he reached her and pulled her away from the edge.

"Were you thinking of jumping, wife?"

"N-n-no. I wasn't. I swear it!" The tears slipped down the curves of her cheeks. Already she could imagine the pain and tried to brace herself against the onslaught that would come.

He shook her once, rattling her skull. "Don't fucking lie to me."

"I swear! I was just taking a moment to breathe! I wouldn't leave... I wouldn't leave Reginald. I—" She took in a sharp breath that hurt her thought. "I wouldn't leave you."

The most painful part about those words were that they were true. There was no place she could hide that Tobias wouldn't find her. She wouldn't leave, because she would protect Basil. He was her priority. It didn't matter how often he broke her body or her spirit. It didn't matter that she was already lost. All that mattered was her son. That he be safe and fed and away from a world that would see him dead for the blood in his veins.

Here he was a prince and was afforded all the protection of one.

And Tobias must have sensed the truth in her words, because his touch eased. His hand rose and she flinched, but he didn't strike her. Surprisingly, he wiped away a tear from her cheek.

"You should not be alone, wife. Come back inside."

She blinked her wet lashes at him, sure the confusion registered on her face.

"I have been gone for too long," Tobias said, his mouth twisting in a smile. There was no malice behind it, and it made her wary. "I should like to take lunch with my family."

It was a strange thing to say, but she didn't want to question his moods, especially when he seemed to be in a light one today. She offered him a small, trembling smile that didn't reach her eyes and a nod. "Of course, husband."

He pressed her arm into the crook of his own and tugged her gently away. They moved slowly, and when Corvina looked up to gauge whether this was just a dream, she found him looking back. Back to the balcony where she'd been standing. Back at the water on the edge of the cliffs. Back at the waves of the Lagnh Sea.

Which were now still and steady as a pleasant dream.

Something was wrong. Dreadfully so.

It started with the lack of abuse and poured into small acts of kindness that Tobias had never bothered to perform before. Simple things like pulling out her chair, like sitting closer to her, like serving her lunch and pouring her wine. He did not speak, not even to berate her when her hand trembled and she knocked over her glass of wine, smearing the juice on his sleeve. He merely snapped at a servant to clean it up and continued watching her through lowered lids.

"My meetings have gone on longer than I anticipated," he began between bites. "I did not expect to be away from the castle so often. I do not like it, so I have scheduled to take my meetings here."

Her stomach sank to a pit in her body. "M-m-meetings?"

His gaze became sharp like a blade. "With Captain Brannon and his soldiers as well as the Brotherhood. A nuisance. They want to create a plan of attack against mythical Fae rebels. As if Dana would ever let the filthy beggars get past our borders..." He snorted and continued eating, then swallowed and spoke. "They're looking for something called Fae Elementals. Says the emperor wants them."

Her blood ran cold and she tried to keep her breathing even. The emperor wanted the Fae. That was not news, but the bit about the Fae Elementals... She hadn't been sure if it'd been a product of Gale's own enthusiasm, but now she knew it for the truth it was. And it filled her with fear. She shouldn't be afraid, because she knew she was safe here. As long as her secret remained just that.

And the Fae rebels? They were real.

Her mind flashed back to the posters outside of the circus and the Fae painted on them.

Shula Azzarh.

Just thinking the name sent something tingling through her body. It was a strange sensation. Like she'd drunken too much spiked cider and the bubbles lived in her chest and spread through her veins. It was like... like when her magic built up in her chest, but different. Like when she'd first laid eyes on Basil and felt that sense of family, of recognition. Like maybe there was a kinship there.

But of course, that was utterly ridiculous. She had never even laid eyes on the woman beyond her image on parchment. She couldn't possibly feel a kinship. It was probably her magic. It needed to be let loose a little more. She could do that while she was in the bath, since Tobias had interrupted her at the cliff side. She had to make sure no one was near, though. It had been too close, and she didn't want him making the connection about what she was.

"Tell no one," her father had said. *"They cannot know."*

She released a breath and looked up to find Tobias staring at her once again, his gaze intent, deadly. Like he knew her secrets. But before fear could take root inside of her, he schooled his face and smiled, and she'd forgotten he wore the expression at all.

True to his word, the next day, the halls were filled with the emperor's soldiers. They wandered with purpose, as if they'd been in the castle before. It was no surprise when the king's castle boasted the same design as Tobias'.

They went in and out of meetings with her husband. She knew they were there, but they attempted to make themselves as invisible as possible. Still, their presence had every Fae in the castle on edge.

Juniper and Wren jumped at every little noise, spilling Corvina's morning and afternoon tea. Even Corvina herself felt the situation rather like an omen. It reminded her of four years ago. When they'd gone about the halls slaughtering her courtiers. When the war had been won and the emperor needed that final act to establish his rule.

Before the Danarish king sent the soldiers on their way to restore his own order to his kingdom. While he was a subject of the emperor, the kingdom of Dana was still his own by right.

Gale, however, was oblivious to their peril. She tittered around the castle, a flushing maiden when faced with handsome soldiers. It irritated Corvina, Juniper, and Wren to no end. It was obviously hard for Gale to look past beauty and see beneath.

Like the fact that those soldiers had killed people. That they bathed in Fae blood and relished in it.

That they were looking for Corvina.

She tried to avoid leaving her rooms, but knew that her husband's personal guards would report back to him about her odd behavior. So she kept to her regular routine. Visiting Dawn when she could, which wasn't as often as she liked. Playing with Basil out in the gardens, taking tea and lunch with her maids, and wandering about the castle.

She was currently doing that, away from her maids. They were readying her dinner gown, letting Corvina gather her thoughts. Tonight, she would be hosting Captain Brannon and Brother Bastien, and she needed a level head to do so. Mainly, to face the captain.

As she turned a corner, she nearly ran into crinkling robes of white. Skidding to a halt, she startled, flinching at his proximity before attempting to school her face.

But the priest merely bowed low and respectfully in her direction. "Princess Corvina," he greeted. When he stood to his full height, he regarded her in a cold, strange way. "How do you fare?"

"I-I am well, Brother Bastien." Blast. She hated that her voice shook, but it had always been difficult for her to hide her fears. She took a breath, hoping it would help settle her emotions. But all she could think of were those robes and what he represented.

Unease slivered down her as she realized they were alone, with no other guard in sight. It didn't bode well for her, and if Tobias found out she'd been alone with a man—any man, regardless of religious beliefs— he would punish her.

"If you will excuse me, Brother Bastien. There are still many preparations I must make. But I will see you at dinner, of course." She gave him a wobbly smile, which dropped when he didn't return it. She sidestepped and walked past him, but his voice stopped her in her tracks.

"I know what you are, Princess."

Her heart shot up to her throat, but she didn't dare turn around. She couldn't even speak, when her voice was stuck behind the fear and panic of his words.

"I-I—"

"Do not deny it."

"Good day, Brother Bastien." She took a step.

A single step.

It was all she managed before thick arms wrapped around her middle and squeezed. Her mouth opened and she started to cry out, but a cloth covering her mouth and nose stopped her. She inhaled and her throat screamed in agony as ashwood oil coated her tongue. Her body smashed against the priest's chest and too late, she tried to fight.

Too late, because the ashwood took over her system, spreading poison slowly through her body. Her limbs grew weak and she slackened in his hold. A hold that was as firm as it was almost... reverent. And his voice echoed in her ear like a dark lullaby sung by Unseelie Courts in forests. Of death, violence, carnage...

"The emperor has been searching for you."

That was the last she heard before the darkness dragged her under.

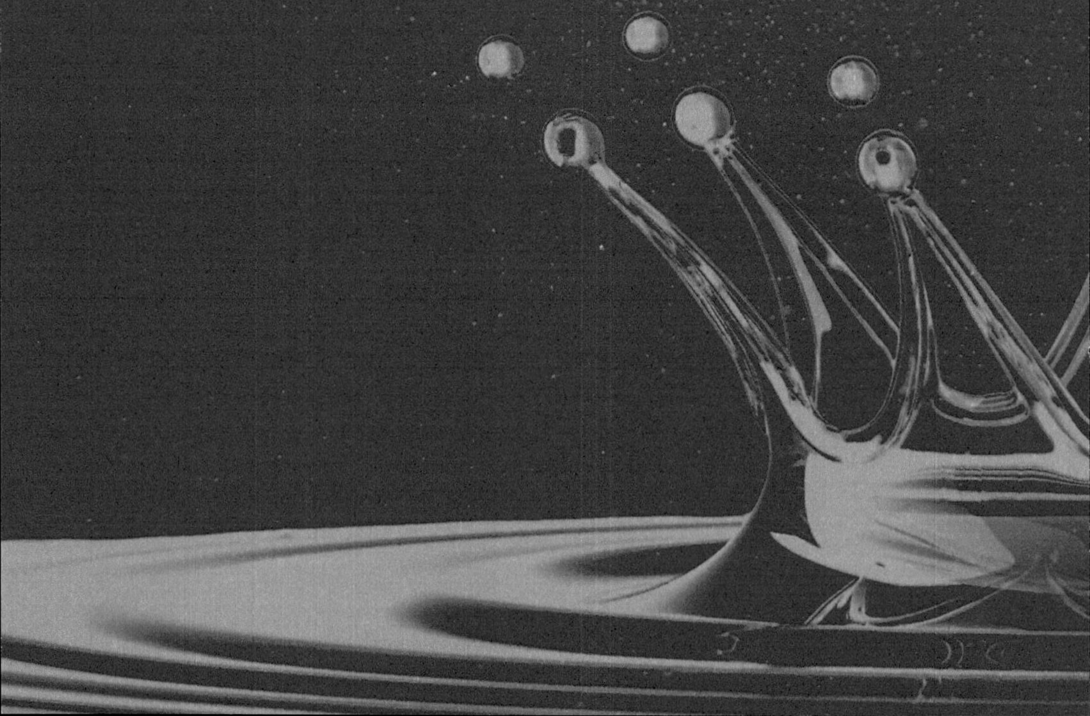

Water That Burns Like Fire

Drip-drip.

Drip-drip.

Drip-drip.

The slow, lulling sound of water both pulled her to wakefulness and threatened to send her back into unconsciousness. She would have welcomed the darkness. There, she wouldn't feel the pain. Not like this. The throbbing of her head was an incessant ache, but the swelling of her throat, the leaden feel of her tongue preventing her from swallowing, it was much worse.

Her eyes slowly blinked open. In darkness, she saw spectral images of flickering lights that floated like souls or will-o'-the-wisps. Her parched lips smacked together and when her vision ceased to be a blur, she noted her surroundings.

The heavy weight of dread settled in her stomach. She sat up, a wave of dizziness making her head spin from the brusque movement. But she came up short, her arms tugging as her wrists were weighted down. Iron manacles clanked like a sea of snakes pooling around her cold body. She trembled. In fear and agony. The iron singed her skin, making her wrists and hands throb. She gave an experimental tug, but the other end of her chains was nailed to the ground.

Panic set in. It was fast and all-consuming, burning through the vestiges of her mind. Memories came back, feeding into the frightening, dire situation. Of hands, clamping around her. Of ashwood choking through her throat. Of darkness and Brother Bastien's voice as he held her close.

Brother Bastien.

He had done this.

She didn't need to wonder why.

She feared she already knew.

A keel burst out of her throat and tears slid down her cheeks. She knew she sounded as weak as a wounded animal, but the comparison was not so far apart from how she felt, from what she probably looked like. Golden curls unwound from their twist, matting against her sweaty cheeks and neck.

Hysteria fractured in her chest as the dripping continued. She knew without looking closely where she was. She recognized the dank, mildew scent of the dungeons. The annoying dripping came from a nearby window, through which soft beams of light shone through, illuminating the dusty floor.

And the fact that she wasn't alone in her cell.

"T-Tobias... What are you—?" Her voice was merely a hoarse rasp. Every word hurt, scraping against her throat until all she tasted in her mouth was the coppery tang of her own blood. Her gaze shifted from the shadows slanting across Tobias' angry face to the white, parchment robes of the priest beside him.

Brother Bastien was looking down at her like she'd poured open the secrets of the gods and he was desperate to consume them all. And her husband? He looked like he meant to murder her.

Her hands trembled as she lifted them. She didn't know why she did so. To show she was harmless? Of course she was. She was chained in iron. Iron was perilous to Fae.

"P-p-please," she beseeched. "I've done nothing wrong..."

"Of course you haven't, my dear." It was the priest who spoke, his voice firm in its reverence. "Do not be alarmed. We merely brought you here to test you."

Her eyes sought Tobias, but he didn't speak. His jaw was clamped tightly closed, set hard and angrily. Her head angled back to the priest. "T-t-test m-me?"

What sorts of tests was the priest talking about? Her senses still felt groggy with the ashwood oil, she couldn't comprehend anything except her fear.

The priest stepped closer to her. His feet were silent against the dungeon floor, but his robes crinkled when he bent. Instead of answering her, he drew his finger along the dusty ground, walking and tracing what seemed to be a circle. But for what purpose?

For a few minutes, the only sound in the dungeon was the steady *drip-dripping* of water from the window and the priest's rustling robes as he went in a circle around her, drawing symbols into the dust on the floor. When he finally finished, he stood before her, a looming, picturesque figure of power and intensity. The shadows slashed across his face and he reached a wrinkled hand towards her.

She flinched away from his touch, but his rough hand clamped around her chin, tilting her face upwards so her eyes were fixated on him and her lips pursed beneath his hold.

"We will test your magic and determine if you are worthy."

It was on her tongue to deny she had magic, but he never gave her a chance. His grip tightened and with the other hand, he reached within his robes to pull out a vial filled with swirling liquid. He uncorked it one-handed and brought the substance towards her lips.

"W-w-wait!"

She started to struggle, trying to pull away from him and whatever it was he meant to give her. He clasped her firmly in his grip. She cried out, her eyes manic as they searched for Tobias in the darkness. Not even the sobs wrenching from her chest made her husband move forward. To protect her. To save her from this.

Though why she'd expected such a thing, she could not be sure.

"Still," the priest ordered.

She found herself obeying and immediately hated herself for being so subservient. But it was all she knew. And then the crystal vial touched her lips and tipped.

Water hit her mouth. He poured it all inside then clamped his wrinkled, calloused hand over her lips and nose to ensure she swallowed it all.

And the water... it burned down her throat like fire.

She tried spitting it out, but with his hand clamped against her, she couldn't manage more than to swallow the contents. It choked her on the way down so that when the priest removed his hand, she coughed. The agony of it seared her throat and bit at her insides. She felt ignited in the worst possible way. It cut through her bones, her muscles, her veins, until every inch of her body was invaded with fire.

A crack sounded and it took a moment to realize it had been from her head hitting the floor. Her forehead throbbed, but it was nothing compared to what wars waged beneath her skin. She cried out for Tobias, peeking her eyes open in a desperate plea for help.

But instead of being met with his face, she was met with light. A brilliant blue light expanding across the floor around the sigils the priest had made. They twined, a latticework of lightning streaking across the ground, coloring through the edges of the symbols. Of stars shattered within five separate circles, of vines curling and twining through four circles, of wisps and swirls like clouds separated in three, of twin circles of flames and...

And one circle, with whorls of tear drops and crashing waves.

Like the very scar that marred her back.

Bile pooled past her lips and nausea roiled in her stomach. She dragged herself away from the image, closing her eyes as if that would shut out what she'd seen from her mind. She wheezed, slipping against dirt and magical light. Her eyes opened and when she turned to look at Tobias again, he was wearing a mask of disgust.

"So you are worthy," the priest whispered. "You are the water Elemental."

A sob pulled out of her chest. No. No! Her secret, the secret she'd kept for years had been ripped from her. And in the worst possible way.

"You lying whore." Tobias stepped towards her, all but shoving the priest aside. A cry tore through her as Tobias yanked on her chains. Her limbs screamed as the movement pulled her upwards, her arms all but suspended. "You fucking lying whore!" His booted foot shot out and connected to her midsection. The air expelled from her lungs and when he let her go, she fell back, gasping for breath.

"Do not mistreat the emperor's property!" the priest interjected breathlessly. "She must be given to Emperor Laurel, alive and intact."

Wanted.

Alive and intact.

Like the posters in the city.

The chains slid from Tobias' palms, pooling to the ground. "What do you mean the emperor's property?" he demanded. "You said you were testing her for magic. You didn't say you were taking *my wife* to the fucking emperor!"

"Watch your tongue, you foolish boy! Do not speak ill of the emperor." His robes rustled, but Corvina could hardly see the movement from behind her watering eyes. "Have you not been listening? The emperor is searching for the Elementals. It is our duty, by law, to send them to him. It matters not if one of them is your wife."

"You can't have her," Tobias argued viciously. "She's mine."

"She is the emperor's!"

"He will have her over my dead body."

Her eyes opened fully to watch the two men face one another off. The priest lifted a brow then released a deep sigh. "Then so be it. But the emperor must know what your wife is and he can take necessary action." He started to walk away, but Tobias yanked him back.

"You will not be telling the emperor anything, priest."

The slide of steel. A grunt. And blood. It splattered against her face, clouding her vision crimson. She blinked it away, her eyes widening in time to see the priest's heavy form slump to the ground.

She didn't need to feel for a pulse to know he was dead. It was in the stillness of his chest, the lack of breaths wheezing past his lips, and the blood blooming across his chest where the sword had entered his heart.

The scream caught in her throat, too afraid to whistle out like she wished it would. She held it tightly inside her, so tightly that the edges of her vision started to blank as unconsciousness threatened her once more.

"Fuck!" Tobias tossed his sword to the ground where it fell with a clang. His boot shot out, kicking the priest's limp body. "As if I did not have enough shit to contend with already." His gaze cut to her and she flinched away from the force of it.

"T-T-Tobias..." Her teeth chattered together and she felt suddenly so cold.

Maybe it was the priest's blood on her face. Maybe it was whatever concoction he gave her to drink. Maybe it was the fact that she felt no remorse that Tobias had killed him. Could one feel fear and remorse in the same breath? All she knew was that he had threatened to take her to the emperor. And while she feared her husband's too-eager, murderous hand, she feared the emperor more.

No. She would not mourn the priest.

"Shut your lying mouth," he snapped. "Magic... How long have you known and kept it from me?" He retrieved a set of keys from his pocket, slipping into the manacles around her wrists. Once she was free of the confines, his hands encircled her wrists and he hauled her up.

Her legs snagged against the folds of her dress, nearly causing her to trip. As it was, she was already standing on shaking knees, but Tobias caught her.

"How fucking long?" His nails dug into her arms. The manic glint in his eyes was unlike any she'd ever seen before. It superseded any anger she'd ever known from him, transcending to madness.

Her chest clenched and the confession poured from her in a stuttering rush. "A-a-all m-my life."

He scoffed and then he was pulling her. Out of this dungeon and out into the hall. She tripped to keep up with him and he all but dragged her across the ground. She recognized where they were. She'd visited it plenty of times. The same hallway where he kept Dawn.

She tried to dig her heels in as he marched down the hall with determination echoing his every footstep. "Lying bitch," he hissed.

The few guards stationed averted their gazes as they passed. Her pathetic whimpers did nothing to entice their help. It never had. She was mere furniture to them. That's how little she meant. How little she felt.

"Fucking lying cunt." His grip tightened, nearly shattering the fragile bones in her wrist. "After all the leniency I've shown you. After sparing your fucking life, this is how you repay me. With your filthy lies. Open it!" He stopped suddenly at the end of the hall, ordering the guard there with a shriek of fury.

The guard rushed to obey, his keys chattering as they slipped into the lock. The barred cage swung open and Tobias wasted no time shoving her inside. Her knees buckled, legs giving out beneath her. She hit the floor, her hands shooting out to try and break her fall. Palms scraping against the stone, she cried out as Tobias fell on top of her, his thighs straddling her waist from behind.

She bucked against him, fingers scrabbling against the dirty ground, cracking and bleeding as he bared down on her. His fingers slipped into her hair, pulling it from its twist. His nails dug into her scalp, yanking her head back.

"I gave you everything, Corvina. And you betrayed me." His fingers wrapped around her throat, the iron from his rings burning against her skin. His touch was gentle, and she held her breath, waiting... His lips brushed against her ear, the heat of his breath making her shiver with dread. "You betrayed me and yet I still killed an emperor's priest for you." His hips bore down on her once, twice, before he lifted and shoved her face against the floor. "And now I have to fix your fucking mess."

She tasted dirt and blood against her teeth, whimpering as he pressed her cheek tighter against the floor. Still, she couldn't stop herself from asking, "W-w-what will you do?"

He paused and for a moment she thought he wouldn't answer, but then his fingers came to her mouth. Too late, she realized he held a vial to her lips. She jerked away but wasn't fast enough as the ashwood oil poured into her mouth. He closed his palm over her nose and mouth, forcing her to gulp it down.

She choked on it. Her throat closed, body trying to reject the poison, but it was too late. The edges of her vision frayed and Tobias' weight eased as he stood up.

"I will cover up his death," he whispered, as unconsciousness started to drag her under. "I will send that meddling captain away. And when I'm finished there, I will come back and you, wife, will go where filth goes."

The echo of his footsteps was the only hint that retreated. The cage closed, trapping her inside, leaving her gasping for breaths that wouldn't come.

The darkness dragged her under the depths. The agony was too much and she couldn't keep it at bay. She let it swallow her whole. She gave in.

And in the distance, she heard Dawn's voice, sad and manic and filled with regret. "Do you wish you would have jumped now, my Lady?"

Power for Dana

"You killed the priest."

"Fuck the priest," Tobias growled at his father. He'd deserved what he got for trying to steal his wife away. And now he was rotting beneath the Lagnh Sea, his body held down with rocks and steel, his existence as inconsequential as it had been before.

The king's eyes narrowed. "Careful how you speak to me, second born. You will not like the consequences."

"Do you know what the Emperor of Illyk will do to us if he discovers what you have done, little brother?" Arthur sneered from his place near the wall. He was always leaning against something. Always relaxed. Always without a fucking care.

"Do you know what he planned on doing with my wife?"

The king waved off his words with a flick of his hand. "You will have doomed Dana for a woman. A Fae woman at that."

"Is her pussy that good, brother? Pray tell us."

"It is not about her. It is about Dana and our power. The emperor has ruled over us for far too long. We know very well how beneficial it is to have slaves. The emperor means to kill them all in his iron camps. Then what are we to do?"

This silenced his brother and father. For once, he felt as though they were actually listening and weighing the severity of his words.

"We alone should reign over *our* kingdom. What has the emperor done except send soldiers through our streets and empty our coffers? Who cares if one fat priest is dead? No one else knew what Corvina was. Let them continue to be oblivious. Get rid of the captain while you're at it. We can fight our own battles."

The king contemplated this a moment while Arthur merely looked irate. "Father—"

The king held up a hand, interrupting his firstborn. "Tobias is right. The emperor's demands have been growing too steep for a long time. While he lets us rule as we wish, there is still a noose around our necks, even if he has not tightened it yet. We all know Dana was the last kingdom conquered. We never wanted a treaty with the emperor in the first place."

"Then send away—"

"I will not send away the captain or his soldiers," he interrupted again. "They are too valuable to us. Especially if what they say is true and a Resistance is coming for your wife. We will need them."

"Father—"

"In chess, what pieces are moved first, my sons?"

It was Tobias who answered. "The pawns."

The king's answering smile was deliberate. "Precisely. Should the Resistance come, then let the emperor's pawns charge forward first. Let them destroy one another. In the meantime, the both of you will keep your mouths shut regarding Corvina and the priest. If you left any witnesses, have them killed to ensure absolute silence. We will bide our time. The captain suspects Corvina is an Elemental." At Tobias' glance, he shrugged. "He requested an audience with me and I granted it. He all but implied so in our meeting. He is hoping we will turn her over to him."

"I won't."

"*We* won't," the king amended. "I feigned offense at the thought and sent him on his way. I am no fool. Corvina is our war prize. The daughter of a High Lord *and* an Elemental? Her existence in Dana is valuable to us, to our kingdom. We can exploit her magic, her power, as we see fit. I don't give a fuck what the emperor wants. She is ours."

This time possessive need didn't rise up in Tobias' chest. It was hope, the strange feeling. It burst inside, making him feel elated. For once, it felt like things were going his way.

"What do we do about the captain's suspicions?" he inquired.

The king paced the floor. "We have two options. We can fake her death or we claim she slipped through our fingers like the fire Elemental did theirs. As for which… I will let you decide, son. She is your wife, after all."

Tobias nodded. "Yes, father."

"In the meantime, I have wine that needs drinking and a whore who needs fucking. Goodbye." With that, the king turned and left the two brothers alone.

They stared at each other but didn't speak. And, without acknowledging the others existence, they both turned in opposite directions and left.

Purification

Corvina drifted in and out of consciousness long enough to realize she'd been chained and collared. Iron wrapped around her already swelling throat. Her breaths wheezed from her lungs. The taste of blood was heavy against her tongue.

In those moments when her body jolted awake, she made feeble attempts to crawl towards the bars of the cage, but her ankle was weighted down by the short length of a chain. Groans were the only sounds of pain she was able to make before the agony dragged her under once more.

She lived in between nightmares and anguish. Her body shut down against the poison Tobias had given her. She sweated, writhing on the ground as her pores tried pushing it out. Her magic dulled into less than a flicker. Her senses and body ached, but she felt weighed down to the floor, unable to move or even open her eyes.

Days passed. It could have been hours or weeks. Within the dimness of the room with nothing but the dripping water or cries of other prisoners, she found it hard to tell time. Her lips cracked and grime covered her eyes in a sheen layer. Soon, her own rankness filled her nostrils. Her hair became a ratted mess against her neck and shoulders, and madness and fear crept in her thoughts.

Her fear only incremented the longer she was awake as thoughts of Basil permeated her mind. Fear for him, of what her husband would do to him, or what he was going through without his mother. She could hardly think of her own fate. Yes, she feared for herself, but it was rooted to what Basil would become without her. She was not ready to leave this world. She was not ready for her soul to join Mana. She was not ready to leave her son.

It was with those thoughts she fell asleep and with those thoughts she awoke again to find Tobias in the cell with her. She pulled in a breath and her fingers trembled as they lifted, pushing aside a ratted lock of hair to see him clearly.

He appeared the perfect princely picture, which made her even more aware of what she looked like.

"Wife," he greeted.

"T-T-T—" She couldn't get his name out past the pain.

Tobias sneered at her a moment before walking deeper into the cell, hauling a small stool with him. He sat it in front of her, his boot connecting softly to her stomach to roll her on her back. Her neck angled sideways to watch as he took a seat.

"The captain suspects what you are," he said conversationally. "I told him you had fallen ill with sickness, but I do not think he believed me. However, medics have been in and out of the castle, so how could he not?" He smoothed his hands down his thighs. "Tonight, this mysterious illness will take your life. Tomorrow, your body will be prepared for your funeral."

A sob rushed out of her at the thought. Her funeral. If he'd told others she was dying, it was because he truly meant to kill her. Tears leaked from her eyes, but Tobias ignored them.

"He was being too meddlesome. I finally convinced him and he's left the castle, though he has not abandoned Dana. At least he is out of my sight for now, and we finally have a moment to ourselves." He bent, lifting one of her hands into his lap. His touch was gentle, thumb circling around her pounding pulse like he meant to offer comfort. "I've missed you, wife." His gaze softened on her into one she could have believed was love. "Especially at night." He pat her hand, his fingers tracing the empty spaces between her own. "Do you miss me?"

She swallowed past the tightness in her throat. "Yes," she rasped.

"Hmm." His fingers kept up their continuous movements against her skin. Each swipe of his thumb was slow and almost sinuous. It lulled Corvina into a state of dream-like ease. "Why did you hide your powers from me?"

Just like that, the state shattered and she sucked in a breath, tensing her body. She tried pulling her hand away but Tobias kept a firm hold on her. His eyes searched hers, still calm, but inquiring.

"M-m-my father told m-me to."

"Hmm." He paused his stroking a moment, then continued. "I do not know much of Fae customs, but here in Dana, once you are married, your husband becomes the only authority in your life."

The words were laced with scorn and something else. Something poisonous.

"I'm-m-m s-s-sorry." She hated that she stuttered. She hated how weak she sounded. But it's what she was. Weak. Biddable. Subservient. She was his to do with as he pleased.

"Too late for apologies now, wife. So tell me, does our son have magic, too?"

"No."

She wasn't expecting the pain that followed. A crack resonated through the cell. Her finger bent at an unnatural angle. Broken.

"Do not fucking lie to me. Does our son have magic?"

She screamed as he pressed against her bent finger. The pain radiated fire up her arm, making her gasp between shouts.

"Answer me!"

"No! He doesn't!"

"Are you fucking lying to me?!"

"No!" She wasn't lying. At least, not entirely. It was quite possible Basil could have developed powers later. He was too young. Her own powers had grown when her first blood hit. Everyone developed abilities at their own pace. She couldn't say for sure if Basil was Mana-gifted or not. Or even if half-humans *could* be gifted.

She would die before she confessed that to him, though. For the sake of her son, she would keep her mouth shut. No matter what he did. He could beat her, rape her, break her, and she would not give Basil up.

She didn't know what he would do to Basil if he knew that fact. She didn't want to find out.

"Are you lying to me?" he repeated, softer this time.

The tears flowed down her dirty cheeks staining a sticky pathway against her skin. A watery breath shook through her. She shook her head. "I swear. I swear. I'm not lying. I swear."

"Ssh." His hand lowered to cradle her cheek. She wanted to cringe from the touch but found herself too weak. "Do not cry, wife. All will be well." He lowered her hand to her chest. She cradled it against her thumping heart and peered up at him, trying to hold back her sounds of pain. "Reginald will not be tainted by you."

The words were so ominous, they sent a lance of fear straight to her heart. She reached for him, but Tobias was already standing. "Tobias!" she called out.

He grabbed his stool and lifted it.

"Tobias! What do you mean by that? Tobias!"

"I mean, wife, that I will not tolerate this tainted lineage any longer. To keep our son safe from it, I have decided to send him to the Brotherhood at the end of the month. They will cleanse him of the Fae taint of your blood. They will purge and purify him until he is born anew. Like we should have done to you long ago."

No.

No!

She pushed herself up, ignoring the bite in her body. "No, Tobias, please! He's just a boy!"

"Precisely. Best to get it out of the way before the age makes him unsalvageable."

The fiery taste of water burned down her throat. The memory of it, at least. She recalled the liquid sloshed down her throat. The agony it put her through. Then, she tried to picture Basil going through it. What they'd do to her son. They'd torture him. They'd hurt him.

"No! You can't!"

He pierced her with a hard stare. "I can and I will. You forget, wife, that he is *my* son. One you reluctantly agreed to give me, if you recall. I will do with him as I see fit. And you will rot in this cell the rest of your pathetic life until I get bored of you. Then, I will kill you myself."

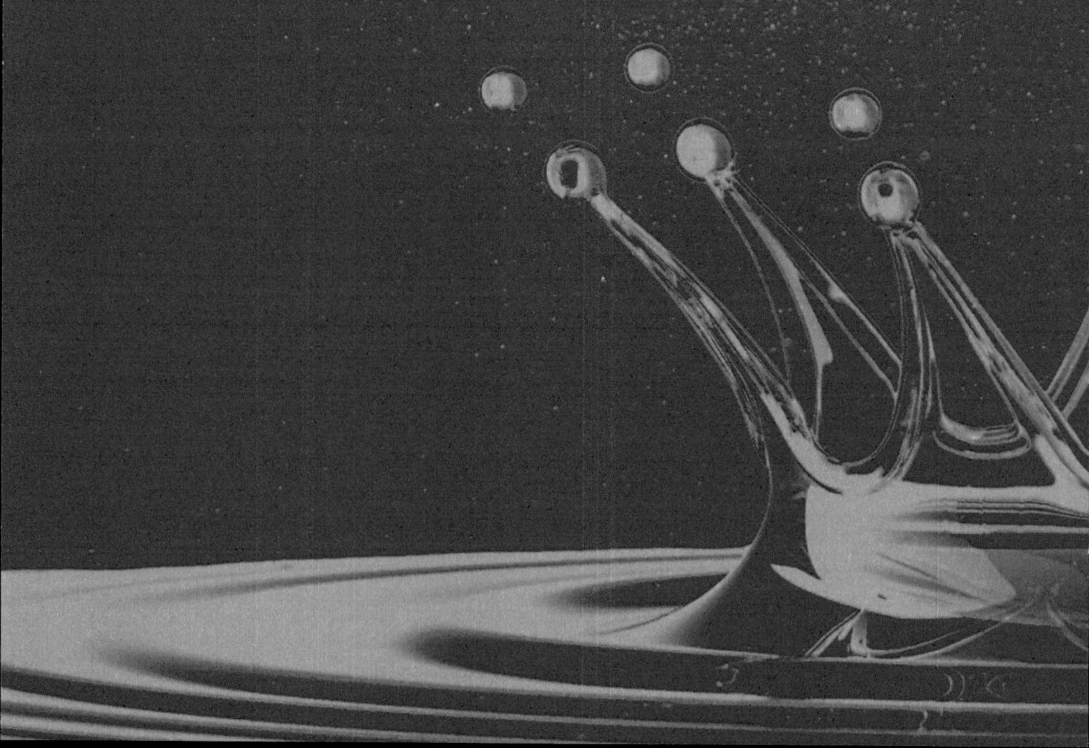

Of Sea and Heartbreak

"I smell the sea."

It drifted through the bars of the single, circular window. Water sprayed through in soft splashes, and dripped onto the stone floor.

Drip-drip.

Drip-drip.

It smelled sharply of salt. Past the smell of her own sweat and grime and blood, she could scent it in the air outside. Her fingers stretched, reaching for a patch of sunlight that slanted through. She missed the soft beams against her face. Missed the grass beneath her feet as she ran with Basil, kicking a ball back and forth.

Most of all, she missed her son.

The end of the month.

Tobias was taking her son away to be tortured by the Brotherhood at the end of the month. After he'd given her the news and left, she'd tried desperately to get herself out of her confines. The iron was all but unbreakable. Even as she reached deep within herself for the spark of magic, the ashwood in her system prevented her from tapping into it.

Usually, it itched beneath the surface of her skin, her soul, begging for release. Now there was nothing. Not even a throb to show that it had been there at all.

She suspected it was the food. Every day without fail, two meals were brought to her. Fruit and fish and rice. Simple meals that she devoured. And every time the last bit of sustenance hit her stomach, her eyes drifted closed and she slept. Waking was agony. Her every bone felt broken, her throat rubbed raw.

She had stopped taking the food, but the guards had come in and forced it down her throat, so she had no choice but to swallow it. Besides, it was better to keep her body nourished, even as poisoned as it was. She needed to try and stay awake.

In case she could escape.

But as the days passed, it was looking less and less likely. Despair was a crushing weight on her. The days flew by, even for her. Soon, it would be the end of the month.

Soon, he would take her son away.

She tugged on her confines with whatever strength she had left in her every night. She called to her magic. She screamed and cried in the hopes that someone, anyone, would come to save her.

It was futile.

No one was going to help her. She was alone. And soon, she would lose the only person she loved. She did not want to think those treacherous thoughts. She wanted to fight. But she was all too aware that her situation wasn't a fairy tale told to human children. This was real life. And in real life, Fae chained with iron, collared, and with ashwood poison coating their blood could accomplish very little.

It still did not stop her from trying until her fingers bled. Until unconsciousness claimed her. She spent her nights dreaming in vivid images. Of golden eyes and a man prowling towards her in a field of wheat.

It was the Gold Court. And this man looked like he belonged there with his coppery skin and long dark braid fluttering against the wind. She imagined the court looked different now, but this was a dream. And in dreams, the world could be whatever she wished it to be.

His fingers rose and trailed over the tops of the stalks. Each one ringed. He was tall and lithe like a lazy panther in his disposition. When her eyes flicked up to his ears, she saw the pointed curves of them.

Fae.

His eyes were the real fascination. They were flickering, only the whites of them visible. She was transfixed on his stillness and on the whites of those eyes. Even though she couldn't see his iris or pupil, it still felt like he was looking inside her. Reaching with phantom hands that she could feel...

Corvina had awoken with the sunlight peeking through, the beams cradled against her outstretched hand, shining down on her broken finger. She'd tried setting it herself, but had only hurt it worse. Now, it was just strange-looking and disjointed.

Keys rattled and footsteps echoed, pulling her out of her thoughts. It had felt like days since she'd last had the company of the guard who brought her food. There were several sets of footsteps. A moment later, her cage was being opened. She watched with trepidation as two guards brought in a tin and set it near her. Then, servants fluttered in. Servants whose names she didn't know and...

Gale.

They carried buckets of steaming water, which they poured into the tin, filling it to the rim.

"The prince has ordered a bath for you," Gale said. Her voice had lost all sense of cheeriness, and she wouldn't meet Corvina's eyes.

Her body shivered. Like, like maybe she was afraid of her. Because she was Fae. Because she had magic.

That hurt. More than she thought it could. And sometimes, the wounds of the heart were more painful than any blow that could ever be inflicted.

"Up you go, Princess." The servants lifted her numb body, and Corvina hissed at the jostling movement. It rattled her skull and made nausea roil. She wanted to turn and vomit but swallowed the bile down.

Instead, she focused on the opened gate, desperately wishing she had enough strength to run through it. But she could barely stand upright, even with the help of her maids as they began to slowly undress her. And besides, the guards stood there facing her, meeting her broken gaze like they knew what she was thinking and meant to stop her with a blade to the heart if she tried.

The ribbon on her back loosened, the bodice slipping down her thinning arms. She whimpered, her gaze fearfully on the guards and the way they took her in as her shoulders were slowly exposed.

"Turn around," Gale ordered them softly. "She is the princess. Prince Tobias would not like your eyes on her like this."

Both soldiers shifted nervously and seemed to reluctantly turn. Their fear of Tobias was greater than their own morality.

She wanted to offer Gale a smile of gratitude, but the servant still did not look at her.

They stripped her down to nothing and helped her inside the water. The warmth of it soothed and stung her body. It was an uncomfortable fit. They did not remove her collar or ankle chain, but scrubbed softly at her body with a scented cloth, wiping off the grime and dirt she'd accumulated over the past few weeks. Her hair was combed through with soap, their hands gentle as they pulled out the tangles.

Corvina didn't move through it all. As they bathed her like they would had she not been locked up. And when she finished, they helped her stand. Water sluiced off her naked body. She breathed in, willing her magic to control it. To do something.

There was nothing but emptiness.

They dried her off, wary of her broken finger, and then helped her slip into one of her more simple, modest dresses. A skirt of white with a brown vest and blue wrap. Her shoulders were bundled in the silk wrap, the material gentle on her aggravated skin. Her hair was left down in waves.

She wanted to say she felt better after that bath, but she didn't.

She wanted Basil. Needed to get out of here and to her son. But her limbs didn't respond. Her throat didn't work. If anything, her eyelids felt heavier with the weight of unconsciousness. The ashwood was working through her veins again, dragging her with spectral fingers.

At this rate, she would die within the week.

"Your meal will be brought to you shortly, miss." While Gale finished brushing her hair, the soldiers and servants began lugging the water and tin out of the cell. For a moment, they were distracted. And in that moment, Gale leaned forward and whispered in Corvina's ear.

Low.

Low enough so no one else heard.

"Be ready."

Corvina's mouth opened but no words came out. She had questions, but her groggy mind couldn't even begin to formulate them. Be ready for what? For death? Yes. Surely that's what she meant.

Gale pulled away and stood. She curtsied quickly before she followed the rest of the servants out and left Corvina alone.

With more questions than answers.

With the dread in her stomach, for the words had felt like a warning. A threat of looming demise.

With the *drip-dripping* of water onto the floor.

With the lonely sensations of heartbreak.

And of the sea.

Of Ice and Fire

Death was slow coming. It did not return for her that day. Or the next. Or the next. Eventually, she wished for it. She wished it would pounce into the light instead of creeping like a leper in the shadows. Let it drag her from her iron prison and chains. Of the maddening drip of water and the howls of cries echoing through the stone walls.

Her own pain mingled with the pain of others, creating a symphony. A song of the dying. She heard her heart shatter like cymbals of an orchestra. Over and over again, the sound burst through her ears until it drowned out everything else.

All she knew was heartbreak. All she knew was approaching death.

Hope had long since disappeared. The hope that she'd somehow manage to escape. She couldn't. Her body had grown weak. Her flesh pulled against bone, her lips cracked, and her veins were stark against her skin as the poison invaded her bloodstream until there seemed to be no magic left inside her.

Or maybe this was her death, she thought, as her lids cracked open a fraction. Maybe this was Tobias' revenge. To slowly feed the ashwood to her body and let it poison her in torturous increments. She opened her mouth, but no words came out. Instead, it was a hackling cough and blood. It sprayed against her chin and the floor. She didn't bother wiping it away. She already knew she looked like hell; what was a little more blood? Her hair was streaked with dirt from where she rested her head in the night, and the dress that had fit her merely a few days ago now hung from her thin frame.

Her palms caked with grime, she pushed herself up to a sitting position with all the strength she had left to muster. Her nails cracked against the stone floors and the small bit of exertion made her pant. Air evaded her lungs, no matter how deep she inhaled. So she breathed in short bursts instead.

Hair slipped over her face and a weak hand trembled to push it away. She wasn't sure why she'd sat up in the first place when all it did was make her dizzy with weakness. It wasn't until the *drip-drip* reached her ears, and the silence thundered like an explosion of solitude that she realized.

Why was no one crying?

Then she heard it. A burst of sound. Like how one found themselves muffled from the surrounding world as they lay beneath the water, and when they emerged, everything was just so much brighter. Louder. Lighter...

She didn't recognize the noises, except to say they were so different from anything she'd grown accustomed to hearing while here. She leaned forward, straining her ears, but lost her balance and fell against the floor again. She couldn't get up a second time. Her body wouldn't allow it.

Instead, Corvina crawled. Using her nails and fingers, she scraped herself along the floor, centimeter by wretched centimeter. Her arms stretched over her weighted head, her eyes blinking rapidly. The sounds grew louder, scraping, like steel on steel. Harsh breaths, and the sound of something else. And through it all she could scent something new and foreign. Something that didn't belong down in the dungeons but in the light of day.

Something like embers and confections and ice and peppermint.

And magic.

Something smelt like magic.

A groan tore from her lips as her body wanted it more than anything. Craved the magic and richness in the air. It coated her tongue, another layer to add to the ashwood, but hitting differently. It seemed to fizz against her nerves and send currents of shock against her skin.

And then the footsteps came closer and closer still.

Then they stopped.

Corvina couldn't lift her head from the floor, but her eyes strayed up to two different pairs of legs on the other side of her prison. There was a muffled curse and then...

Fire.

It crawled in licks up the iron bars. It was slow and small, and yet it only enveloped the bars for a few seconds when it started to melt. Corvina's lips shook as she watched a gaping hole form where bars should be. The iron pooled on the floor like molten lava, crawling slowly in Corvina's direction.

Her fingers should have been singed, but the advancing lava stopped as it itself was enveloped by cold. By a sheen of...

Of ice.

Fat snow drops fell from her cell, coating her skin in an ashy layer. She blinked the cold from her lashes and a breath exited her lips in a cloud. Her body rolled slightly, angled a bit to the side, head tilting so she could look up at the two figures that stepped inside.

Boot-clad thighs appeared in her vision first. With a traveling gaze, her eyes flicked up to a tall woman. She flashed white teeth at Corvina, and though the expression seemed to be more of a grimace, Corvina could not doubt this woman's beauty. As weak as she was, she saw it clearly. Smooth ebony skin expanded against a muscular body. White tufts of curls were shorn close to her scalp and her ears...

The second woman stepped forward. This one didn't flash a smile, but sucked in a breath at what a pathetic figure Corvina probably made on the floor. Lying in her own filth, starved, and poisoned. And because she was beautiful with her dark waves of hair that trailed down to her waist, her golden-brown skin and piercing, amber eyes, Corvina's own face found the ability to flush.

She knew she probably looked more corpse than human. And the pain kept her immobile on the ground. She could scarcely move as the two figures stepped forward.

Finally, Corvina found her voice. It rasped out of her, lower than a whisper. "Are you here to kill me?"

Be ready, Gale had told her.

If this was death, then perhaps it would not be so bad. Perhaps they would let her go quietly. Even if she didn't want to. Even if a part of her still clung tightly to life.

The women shared a glance. It was the ebony-skinned woman who answered, "No. We are here to save you."

Her gaze flicked between the two. The longer she stared, the more strength she felt surge inside her... Strength she hadn't felt in days.

"W-w-who are you?"

"We're the Re—"

"Don't say it," the long-haired one interjected. "Just don't fucking say it."

The ebony-skinned woman smiled wryly and lifted her fingers to her ears. Ears that were as pointed and curved as Corvina's own. She'd thought it an illusion. A figment of her own poisoned imagination. But the woman's fingers swiped over the tips. Corvina itched to do the same to her own.

She felt... something here. Like this moment was integral and would stay with her for the rest of her life.

"We are... friends."

Iona Wylde

Magic shot from Iona Wylde's fingers. Ice sliced across the ground, coating it in a thick layer meant to knock the approaching Fae off his tracks. But he saw the move coming. He whirled, the turn graceful for someone of his gargantuan size. His feet pounded against the grass, making the ground beneath their feet tremble. He barreled towards Iona, his body lowered, his shoulder out like he meant to tackle her down.

She let him come.

She was not afraid.

Because when he was little more than a few feet away, a wall of fire burst between them, sending him jerking back with a startled cry. A giggle mingled with the rising flames of fire as Iona shifted her sword of ice into her hand and jumped through the heat.

They met with a clash of blades; her opponent startled at her sudden appearance. The pommel of his sword slid from his grasp. She took advantage of the moment, hitting it hard with her blade and sending it clattering to the ground.

He jumped back as she advanced, but was met with magic once more. It encircled him along the ground and emerging from them, as if born from their depths, rising like a phoenix of legend, came Shula Azzarh.

Her blade was encased in flames, glowing brighter than her own golden-brown skin. Together, the two Fae Elementals attacked with magic, strength, and sword. They swept his feet out from under him and he toppled to the ground, hitting it with a grunt. His hands lay sprawled next to his face and it was almost too easy to send their swords flying to his neck, stopping just inches from his throat.

He winced as Iona's blade nicked him just beneath the scruffy orange beard. The magic of fire and ice illuminated the color rising in his ruddy cheeks. She knew him well enough to know what it signified.

He was *turned on.*

Flames extinguished and ice melted. Shula lowered her sword, her breaths heavier by the minute. Iona opened her palm and the sword burst into a shower of snowflakes that shattered against the Fae's face.

He smirked up at her then Shula.

"Finally managed to knock me on my ass."

The sword twirled in Shula's grip before she shoved it into her sheath. Her smile was an easy thing to touch her lips. Easier now than it would have been weeks ago. Iona hardly recognized the Fae. Every day that passed, Shula seemed to break out of her shell more and more, taking the power that had always lived deep but unclaimed in her soul.

"And I could've done more than that, too."

Julius snorted. "Don't let one victory make you too cocky, Fire Dancer."

"Ha! The only reason I didn't burn that beard off your smirking face is because Iona likes thigh burn."

Iona cackled and winked down at her mate. "It's true. I do." Then she held her hand out to him. He took it and she grunted as she pulled his massive body to a stand.

Then, the three of them turned to face their audience.

Fae of all shapes and sizes sat around watching them with lifted brows. There was a tinge of awe in their expressions as their gazes drifted back and forth between Iona and Shula.

Julius noted where they stared and chuckled. "That was the power of the Elementals," he addressed them. "It's effortless and deadly, and it's the reason the Emperor of Illyk wants them." A jolt slid around the group. "This is war. The final war. We will take back our homeland and get the respect we deserve. But to do that, you need to be trained."

Iona stepped forward. "The emperor stole from me as much as he did you. My family..." She broke off, took a breath. Speaking of them hurt, knowing that her blood were all dead, all gone, ruptured something inside her that she felt would never fully heal. "They died beneath his tyranny. Our lives will never be the same. He broke your bodies, your hope, your spirits. But we will take what's left and make you a weapon. A fucking *force.* And we will make him regret the day he decided to cross us."

A chorus of cheers rang out that pulled a smile from Iona's lips, despite the heartache. Despite the dire circumstances. For weeks, she'd felt lost within herself, desperate for revenge.

Years ago, her family had faced the humans on the sandy battlefields of the Jade Court. They'd died there and Iona had been reborn in grief, sand, and blood. She'd lived a life of numb fighting until hope had been given to her. The hope that maybe her sister was alive. Even that had been taken from her, printed in a cold hand on parchment in iron camps, forcing her to accept the truth.

Her sister was dead.

Hope was dead.

Her faith in Mana had been shaken. She still felt like she was balanced on the edge of wanting to believe in something greater than herself and the loss of all that was good.

But when she stood here before these Fae, she was reminded that there was good in the world. There *was* hope. And it existed in this.

In a group with a singular goal in mind.

Revenge.

And justice.

"If you are willing to fight and take back what is ours, stand, Fae brothers and sisters, and take your weapons." They did. Slowly but surely, firmly. Once they all had swords in their grasps, Iona's smile widened.

Shula clapped her hands together. "Then let us begin."

Training new recruits was not easy. But they had one thing, if not talent. Determination. And that was all that mattered.

Ever since King Regent, Valerio Ashera of the Seelie Courts, declared war upon the humans, their group of what had been composed of eight Fae and two familiars had grown exponentially. With every city in every kingdom they traveled, they breached the walls of iron camps.

They unleashed their magic and their rage and brought them to the ground until they were nothing more than scraps of metal and ash and memories rising with the smoke. Their numbers grew.

Before, King Valerio would have taken the refugees behind the walls of Castle Aileach to keep them safe. That dream had decimated along with their stronghold. Months ago, humans had invaded their home in the mountains of Tuath. How they'd found it was a mystery, but find it they did. Boulders had been launched at the rickety castle, bringing it crumbling to the ground.

They weren't sure anyone made it out alive. Not even the King of Seelie. And so Iona, Julius, and the others had pledged themselves to Valerio as their new king. He refused the title until he knew with absolute certainty that his father was alive, and so they called him King Regent instead.

And so their journey had begun. Once they destroyed one camp, they couldn't help but destroy them all one by one. They saved the Fae from any more suffering. They brought them to their fold, healed them, tried to give them what they needed.

And they offered them this.

A chance of retribution.

It was difficult. Some had missing limbs and fingers, so holding their weapons pained them. Some had such fragile minds that even the sounds of steel made them curl onto the ground and sob. It was the unresponsive ones that hurt the most to see. The ones that could scarcely move or talk. Those who stared at an empty void that no amount of coaxing could pull them out of.

She wondered if death would have been a mercy for them, but that wasn't her decision to make. And when asked, they couldn't even respond. So they were stuck in limbo. In between that place where life and death met. Their minds long gone, even while their bodies still breathed.

The days since the fall of Castle Aileach were filled with traveling, eating, and training. There was little room for rest, and what free moments they had were spent plotting as they journeyed to find the next Elemental.

Neither Shula nor Iona were sure which Elemental awaited them in Port Bay, Dana. All they'd known in that moment months ago when they tossed the stones was where they landed and the feelings that lanced through their bodies when one of them hit the sea-side kingdom.

Fear.

It was a visceral sensation that coated their tongues and souls. It felt almost as oppressive as the iron that was rooted through Illyk. The Fae needed them because he or she was in trouble.

The feeling hadn't been overbearing. At least, not at first. It gave them time enough to plot how they would make it through the crowded city of Port Bay and find the Fae. But each day they crawled closer to Dana, the unease grew.

The stone had landed in the capitol city, right on the edge where the Danarish King's castle was located.

"We have to think the worst case scenario," King Valerio had said as he stared at the map, his eyes tracing invisible lines that he couldn't see. But Iona and Shula could. "And right now, that worst case scenario is telling me the Elemental is enslaved."

Either that or the Fae was very good at hiding. Right in plain sight, like Shula had when she'd traveled with Piriguini's Circus, back before she'd met the Resistance.

But of all the possibilities, that was the worst one.

"That means we will need an army to protect our camp while a handful of us go find the Fae," Valerio continued. He pointed at the map of Illyk, where Dana met the Arcana river, further up near Port Lays, keeping his finger in between that city and Vallart. "Their borders are likely patrolled, but we do not know if it is by the king's soldiers or the emperor's..." He broke off, contemplating the map with a stoic expression.

"You want to fight your way through," Clay guessed, a tinge of surprise in his lilting voice as he seemed to read whatever was on the king's face.

Valerio had already said as much. That war had been declared. That the moment the Fae Resistance had attacked the military camp in Tuath, it was a call to fight. But so far, all they'd done was travel across Illyk from one camp to the next, freeing Fae who needed them.

"We are already at war. We just have to turn the tides in our favor and regain the numbers we lost."

And so they did.

They gave the Fae a choice. To fight or to flee. And almost all of them wanted to fight.

When the day bled away into night, they stopped the training and gathered the new recruits in a circle. Julius stood at the center. Of everyone in their original group—Valerio, Clay, Uric, Weylyn, Ryker, Julius, Shula, and Iona—it was Julius who had the most experience in battle.

Yes, Valerio was no stranger to it, but more often than not, he was morose, so busy with planning and plotting that his ability to shine light and hope on anyone else was all but gone. Uric, while from the Obsidian Court, the court of spies and shadows, knew the battle of silent assassins. Not war. Clay had experience fighting, but he was a High Lord, made for peace negotiations and flirting with anything in a skirt. Ryker was a healer, not a fighter. So the task fell to Julius and Iona. Shula was determined to help as well. She was by far no expert in battle, but she was getting better every day. She'd learned to masterfully combine the skill of a sword with her newfound control over magic. It inspired the recruits.

"You've all done well," Julius complimented, holding gazes as he swept his eyes across the group. "However, you still have a long way to go. I know this is no easy task, what we ask of you, but you have proven yourselves loyal and determined and there is no greater gift than that. Go rest, and may Mana watch over your dreams."

The sentiment was echoed in a choppy, broken chorus before the Fae dispersed. Either to the bonfires being lit by women where they roasted game over the flames, or to their tents to fall into a deep sleep. Shula waved her fingers and disappeared into the throng along with the others.

Iona turned to Julius. Sensing her gaze, her mate prowled towards her, gripping her by the hips and yanking her body against his own. Their hips aligned and she could feel the heat of his erection through the tight material of his leather pants.

Iona quirked a silver brow at him. "Fighting excites you, eh?"

He bent down a fraction so the tips of their noses touched. At this proximity, his beard scraped against her chin; the growling timbre of his voice was enough to send a sliver of desire down her own spine. "Fighting *you* excites me." His hand cupped her cheek, thumbing against her skin. "I love it when you kick my ass."

Iona stood on the tips of her toes, her own hands clasping either side of Julius' neck. Her thumb met the silver mark on his skin. *Her* mark where her canines had sunk into his flesh to pull desire and a bond into a tight knot between them. She grazed it with the edge of her finger and a desperate sound keeled from Julius' throat.

"Stick around," she whispered. "There's more where that came from." The words were a promise.

His bright grass-green eyes flared as he ground her against his erection. "Keep touching me like that, my love, and I'll take you right here for everyone to fucking see."

"Please don't. I just ate dinner."

Julius snarled, the sound half-hearted and jesting, and they both turned mock-glares on Clay as he approached.

"What do you want, little lord?" Iona teased.

"To not witness you two maul at each other out in the open like wild animals. That would be nice." The High Lord of the Sapphire Court, and King Valerio's cousin, smirked. His pretty boy good-looks were almost too ethereal to be true. Vibrant green eyes regarded them humorously, and the dimples that concaved his perfect skin were teasing in their appearance.

"You know you like it," Julius retorted.

Clay's smile kicked up. "You're right. I'd watch and give you pointers on how to please the lady."

Iona's eyes narrowed. "He pleases me just fine."

"Don't be nice for his sake, Iona."

"Is there something you needed, runt?" Julius asked playfully.

Clay's expression suddenly sobered, and Iona's body tensed at the rare expression. "Valerio wants to speak with us," he said. "Now."

An Entirely Different Beast

"Our numbers are growing." Valerio's hair was loose of its usual bun, the sharp strands sweeping over his face, curtaining his view of the others. "We have too many."

"Isn't that a good thing?" Shula asked.

Her scent of confection and embers was heady in the tent. Valerio tried to hold his breath and free himself of it, yet he found his nostrils flaring, pulling it deeply into his lungs. Like he could bottle the Fae there somehow.

What foolish thoughts.

"No." He pushed himself away from the table and the map sprawled there to look up at his companions. The only people he had left.

He trusted the Fae currently in his presence. Except Weylyn, but the golden Fae's mind-reading magic was useful enough that he did not bother kicking him out of his most trusted circle of friends. Besides, even if he did, the Fae would know their every secret.

He already did.

"I'm not following." Shula's brows pulled together, and Valerio had to avoid looking at her. She was a changed Fae from what she used to be when they'd first found her at the Temple of the Brotherhood. She'd been shy before. Uncertain in her own skin, uncertain of her own magic and power. And they'd fed on the weaker parts of her, adding to her self-doubt. Until Iona.

Now it felt like the two Elementals were conspiring against Valerio at every turn. And because of that, he noted a burst of confidence in the fire Fae. Though perhaps it had something to do with Ryker as well. They'd never been open with affection before. They still weren't, but they shared glances between them that spoke thousands of words in different languages of love than Valerio could ever understand.

"The more Fae we rescue, the more our supplies dwindle down to nothing. We have no food, no clothes, no armor..." He trailed off with a shake of his head.

"I can take them hunting," Julius offered.

"There is only so much game we can catch and still too many mouths to feed. It will not be enough. We can no longer survive at this camp. We need something far more sustainable." His eyes raked over the map of Illyk once more. "We need a city of our own."

"A city?" Clay parroted. "You want us to conquer a city?"

There was an incredulous note to his voice as he guessed what it was Valerio wanted. He understood. So far, they'd taken the discreet route. The same route they always did. Freeing Fae, running, hiding, forced to portal from one place to the next to avoid detection. But those days fell alongside Castle Aileach months ago.

Things were different now.

Valerio would not be like his father, secretive and hiding behind the walls of a stone castle. He could no longer rely on hidden places to keep them safe. They needed to take action. To be aggressive.

To go to war.

His finger landed against Port Bay on the map. Where the Elemental was. Where they were headed.

"You want to conquer Port Bay?" Iona's brows rose and he could feel her admiration. The loyalty of the Fae made him want to smile, but he kept his lips pressed firmly together.

"It is a small city, rich in food, weapons, and supplies. It is close to the sea, reclusive so as to not worry about being attacked from many sides. And we are headed there anyway."

"The capital city is bound to be protected by soldiers." Julius stroked his beard. He could see the wheels of the ginger's mind whirling as he tried to think of a plan of attack.

"Do you think the Fae are prepared for battle?" Valerio asked.

"Against seasoned soldiers? No. But if we play this smart, there's a possibility we can win."

"We cannot portal to Dana," Uric cut in. His dark, judging gaze cut across Valerio's figure. The scowl was a permanent fixture on his friend's face and no amount of coaxing would pull the expression into a new one.

They had not been able to portal for weeks now. Uric's magic was only so strong and could withstand only so much. He could not create a portal big enough for every single Fae at the camp and their supplies without suffering dire consequences. It was why they had remained right where they were for weeks. Training... *plotting*. Always plotting, but not finding a solution to their problems.

He was getting sick of feeling like they were at a standstill.

Valerio knew there was a question beneath his words.

"How are we going to get there?"

"We travel through small towns," Valerio answered. "We are close to Covenglen. We can go through the town and take boats to cross the Arcana." Shula opened her mouth, presumably to argue. He cut her off before she could. "We have lost too many numbers with the fall of Castle Aileach. I do not want to risk anyone's life unnecessarily, so when we arrive in Dana, we will lay low. Our priority will be to save the Elemental. It will have to be a stealth mission. Afterwards, we will figure out what to do about our own people and how. *After* we cross the Arcana. Julius, you and I can—"

He grew distracted, cutting himself off as he watched Weylyn's body suddenly go slack. His head jerked back and his eyes rolled until nothing but the whites of them were visible. Everyone in the tent froze. Valerio's own breath caught in his chest as he waited.

For months, he'd waited. And every time Weylyn's eyes rolled, he felt like he was balancing on the edge of a particularly high cliff, waiting to be pushed to the jagged rocks below. It had been nearly a month or more since the fall of Castle Aileach. More than a month since his father had ordered Uric to take Valerio and flee. More than a month since he held on to the hope that his father was still alive.

He had never gotten along with his father. In fact, he had gone through most of his life despising the king. More than one vicious thought, especially after the mysterious death of his mother, was that he wished for the king's death.

But when faced with that possibility, when hearing the pain in his father's voice right before Uric dragged him through that portal, all Valerio had known was guilt. As if he'd committed patricide himself by wishing for it. Like he was somehow to blame.

He still didn't know how the humans had discovered the location of Castle Aileach. It was a coveted Fae secret. One only they were supposed to know about. So how—

Weylyn's chest rose with a sharp inhalation. His eyes rolled back and he blinked his dark depths before turning slowly in Valerio's direction. Composed, as if he had not just been completely useless. A smirk tilted his thin lips that spoke of mischief.

"Your scouts are approaching," he said in his musical voice. "And they come bearing gifts."

The commotion in the camp had them all filing out of the tent. Uric went first, blade already in hand. Shadows seemed to swirl around him. His rage always became a tangible thing whenever he felt Valerio's safety was threatened.

He was the first outside, everyone following alert. Two of their scouts who had been posted on the outskirts of their camp led a struggling human between them.

The smell of blood and sweat became prominent in the air as they led him closer. Valerio settled a hand on Uric's shoulder and his friend moved away to the side, but he did not lower his blade.

"King Valerio." He cringed at the name. He had asked them to stop, but it did not seem to matter how many times he insisted they not call him that. At least not until they found proof of his father's demise. How he expected them to get that proof, well, he was waiting on Weylyn. "We found this human scout prowling the grounds of our camp." They shoved the man forward on his knees.

His armor clanked as he fell. Gone was his helm, and he bore the colors of the Emperor of Illyk. Blacks and reds. Dark eyes rimmed with hatred looked up at Valerio. While there was a sliver of fear, there was still defiance.

And then the fool did something utterly stupid.

He spat at Valerio's feet.

For a moment, everyone held their breath. A shift in energy cackled and he knew they were waiting to see what he would do. If he would react like his father, with unbridled violence and disdain. But Valerio was not his father. The king's shadow cast a far and wide reach, and it touched Valerio wherever he stepped.

"Cute," Valerio commented on the action. "What is your name, human?"

"I'm not telling you anything, Fae scum!" he cried out.

The tediousness of interrogations grated on Valerio's nerves. He had no energy, and far less patience, to deal with this fool of a human at the moment. He turned to Weylyn with a quirked brow.

With a smirk, the Fae stepped forward while Valerio moved aside. Weylyn crouched before the human. There was something prowling about his movements. Every single Fae present was a predator, but Weylyn was another beast entirely.

And the human felt it as Weylyn leaned forward where he was crouched, his long black braid swaying over his shoulder like a snake. His ringed fingers reached out to touch the human's face, and the man whimpered. Valerio fought not to roll his eyes. He knew that Weylyn did not need touch to tap into another's thoughts. He was doing it to unnerve the man and make him piss himself.

Which he did. But Weylyn did not shy away from the stench or the growing pool at his feet. He just smiled wider, more manic. And then he stiffened.

The human scrambled away from Weylyn's stiff form, falling on his back with a cry. When Weylyn came to, he stood up and turned to face Valerio. With little emotion in his voice besides mischief, he said, "We are about to be ambushed by a group of human soldiers. Apparently they've been following us for days."

"H-how did you know that, you devil?!" the human cried.

Valerio turned first to Julius. "Ready your Fae," he ordered. "We will put their skills to the test." Julius nodded and both he and Iona broke from the group and rushed around camp to get everyone ready. Then, Valerio turned to his cousin. His hand waved in the direction of the human. "Will you do the honors, Clay?"

His cousin sauntered forward with a smile on his face. Clay didn't usually relish in violence, but things were different after the fall of Castle Aileach.

They were all different.

"Gladly," he answered, holding out his palm.

And then blood exploded from the human and he fell to the ground. Still.

Dead.

Clay's own nose dripped a drop of blood, which he wiped away with the back of his hand.

"You, Shula, and Ryker will protect those who cannot fight. Uric, Weylyn?" Both Fae looked at him. One with bright golden eyes that all but glittered with the prospect of violence. The other, his eyes dark and somber. "We have a camp to protect."

Sipping Fire

"Five minutes," Clay whispered. "We have five minutes."

Shula swallowed the nerves that rose up in her throat. Soldiers were fast approaching and this was the first time confronting them. Their first time being ambushed. Sure, over the course of the past couple of months, they'd been going through camps and burning them to the ground. They'd fought soldiers and had come out victorious.

This was different.

It was an actual battle.

While Shula wouldn't be in the thick of it, she worried for her Elemental sister. Iona may not have been her sister by blood, but something bigger than that connected their fates and sealed their friendship. It hadn't been easy to accept the other Fae at first. Not when Shula felt like she was cast in her much larger shadow of greatness. Knowing how brave Iona was compared to her had been a blow to her already fragile self-esteem.

That was before Shula realized there were different types of strength in the world. That was before she realized that she and Iona were as different as the Elements they wielded. Fire and ice. Both powerful in their own right.

And once Shula learned to accept her own power, her world shifted.

The fear was not something that could go away over night. She knew that much with absolute certainty. She was afraid for the Fae. Afraid of the humans. But no longer of her magic. Not with what she could now do.

Beside her, Ryker vibrated with energy. His body was hot and she leaned into the warmth he offered like it was the most natural thing in the world. As she did, his hand tunneled through her long hair, pulling her towards him.

Their gazes met and held, words unspoken passing through the spaces between them.

Eyes on me.

They stared, sharing silent words of caring and support, and she smiled, feeling her anxiety melt. He'd known what was bothering her, what tightened in her chest, and he'd eased her nerves with a single glance.

They hadn't always been so close. But this was new, this mating bond and closeness, and they were still learning to navigate certain aspects of it. But it was growing stronger by the day. That line they'd balanced on where hatred and lust met was disappearing. It was nearly gone, the hatred completely eradicated.

There was still something tentative between them. Neither one used to love. To *this.* And so every moment together was tender and shy. So different from when they'd first came together. An explosion of fire between them where they both wanted to go up in flames.

Those flames still fanned, steady and warm. And sometimes it burned too hotly, but they were still unsure how to come together like they had so long ago. When they'd sipped from one another's mouths and bodies and sunk canines into flesh, intertwining their fates together forever.

She wasn't sure why she was thinking about that in that particular moment.

Perhaps she didn't want to think of the possibility of dying before she got the chance to taste him again. To feel him inside her. To be enveloped by the soft, comforting scent of herbs.

She started to drift on the tips of her toes towards him. Hoping to meet him somewhere in the middle where emotion met passion.

"It's time," Clay interrupted before she could, causing them to pull away from one another.

"Get everyone huddled together," Shula ordered. Her determination steeled and she turned to meet the faces of the Fae they were meant to protect. The ones that couldn't fight. The ones that were lost souls and drowning in their traumatic memories. She felt a strange kinship with them and prayed that, like her, they could rise from the ashes of what had been done.

And come out stronger.

More powerful.

Clay and Ryker ushered everyone into a tight huddle, and once they were ready, Shula called forth her magic. Flames sliced across the ground, surrounding them all within a protective circle of fire. Protecting those who couldn't fight for themselves. That way, anyone who dared try to come towards them would find their skin melting from their bones.

And a pissed off Elemental protecting those who couldn't protect themselves.

They'd had but a few minutes to plan an ambush against the ambush. The Fae had spread out through the camp, some hiding in the trees while others pretended to walk about the camp as if there was nothing amiss. Once they caught sight of the humans, they'd give the signal and the battle would begin.

Iona watched from her perch up in a high branch. She heard the crackling of leaves and twigs as footsteps approached. They were followed by a whistle. It cut through the air, shrill and loud. *The signal.*

Behind them, Shula's fire blazed and Fae burst from their hiding places as the humans approached. Steel swords clanged together. From below, Julius exploded through shrubbery with a fierce cry that reverberated through Iona's spine. She smiled to herself as his body rammed into humans, shattering their bones on impact.

His Mana-given gift was strength; the price he paid was that rage. He tore through them all like a beast, shattering bodies, breaking bones, taking lives with his fists and his sword. Iron arrows zipped through the air, heading straight towards her mate.

With a cry, she sent out a wall of ice as a shield to protect him from the impact. The iron hit ice, and she let her magic shatter into snow. Then, she pushed herself off the bark and she was falling.

Her feet hit the ground just as humans came towards her. She jumped up, a sword of ice forming in her hand. She met them with a grunt of ferocity, pushing them back. There was a dance of violence between them. She whirled, swung, attacked. Blood coated her face, plastering her short white curls against her scalp. She saw red as she tore through sinew and bone. The force of her rage propelled her on. Her fellow Fae fought alongside her and she didn't spend time fearing for their safety, even if the sensation was there in her chest.

Humans broke past them and darted towards the camp. They barreled past Fae, lancing their iron swords, and some of the Fae cowered back from the poison it emanated. Like it was instinct to fear and recoil.

"Hold the line!" she screamed.

But it was too late. The humans burst through into the camp, only to be met with the burning flames of Shula's magic. Fire licked across the ground, as if the fire Fae had sensed their arrival and fortified her wall of protection against them. The suffocating press of her magic forced them back. They screamed, crying out as their skin melted beneath their iron armor.

Iona's legs pumped beneath her as she ran towards them, spearing them through the necks with her ice sword.

She wasn't sure how long the battle lasted. But it lasted. And when it finished, Julius let out a roar akin to a victory cry. Shula's fire died to nothing but mere embers as she rushed out of the fray, her chest rising and falling.

For a moment she froze, and Iona and Shula's gazes met. They smiled at one another. And though Iona knew that she hadn't been directly in the battle, she still felt simmering relief beneath her skin. In the few months they'd known each other, Shula had grown to mean a lot to her. As much as Iona's own sister had meant, before she'd been sent to her death.

Everything after happened too slowly.

Shula stepped forward. One step was all she managed before the arrow tore from the sky and slammed into her chest. The impact jerked her back. Blood sprayed and bodies moved in a blur. Clay caught her in his chest, turning with her in his arms like he meant to be her shield.

Iona's mind struggled to process the scene. The spray of blood, Shula's cry of pain, Clay's shout of worry. Her heart thundered within her chest, and she felt the sword in her hand begin to disintegrate into flakes of snow. Her fingers traced a pattern against her leg. For a second, she was yanked back to blood against sand. To fingers clawing against the beach as her sister was pulled away by soldiers, calling Iona's name.

A beastly wail pulled her back to the present. More animal than human. More animal than Fae. It roared straight from Ryker's throat. A cry Iona felt shatter down to her soul. A sound born of pain and rage. And then he was moving, running, his eyes trained on a single spot.

Iona followed with her eyes, turning as Ryker charged past her faster than even Julius and slammed into a hidden human. He ripped him from his hiding place in the shadows, pulling him out by the neck. He snapped his canines, his every movement feral as he tightened his grip and *tore,* pulling the man's throat out with his fingers. Blood sprayed against his scarred face. He looked demonic, monstrous, with blood dripping down his cheeks, beard, and arm.

Then he turned and rushed back to where Shula had been standing a moment ago. She lay half on the ground, her legs splayed out, her upper body pulled close to Clay's chest. She inhaled harsh, gasping breaths. The kind Iona recognized as the breaths of the dying.

Iona moved then, shaken out of her stupor. Determination swelled through her veins. She'd watched her family die years ago. She'd spent her life alone. She'd found hope only to lose it again. She'd had her faith shaken, but in this moment, it rose up and she called out a prayer to Mana. One she hoped would be answered like her other prayers hadn't been.

Please, save Shula.

Her feet ate up the space between her and her Elemental sister. Her knees jarred as she fell to them, watching with shallow breaths as Ryker gently pulled his mate into his arms, careful not to jostle her as he took her from Clay. His blood-smeared hands shoved away thick locks of her hair. Their gazes clashed, like a silent conversation passed between the two and held them captive, but when he dropped his eyes to her wound, Ryker threw his head back and he roared.

Ryker's eyes were flashing, wild and desperate as he took her in. Her name pressed to his lips, but he couldn't seem to make a sound beyond harsh breaths and strangled noises. His heart beat against his chest, the same chest where the soul that was intertwined with Shula's essence lay. And her chest, it was soaked through with blood.

His hand shook as he reached for the arrow. Her hand intercepted his, shoving it away. "No," she argued on a whisper. "Don't. You promised."

He snarled at her. "Fuck your promise."

The promise he'd made to her when he said he would no longer use his magic to heal others. Because she was afraid. Afraid of what would happen to him, that he wouldn't wake up from an injury that could prove too great.

It went against everything he ever stood for. Every vow he'd ever taken. But when she'd made him swear it, when she'd looked at him with that desperate, fearful expression in her eyes, he'd realized he wanted time.

More time to get to know her as what they were now. As mates. As friends. As more.

And with everything going on, there had been scarcely time to know one another. To touch, to taste. To sip from her fire. She was bleeding out before his eyes and still wanted to hold him to that fucking vow?

"You promised," she argued again, her voice weak.

"What if it were me?" he snapped. "What if it were me on the other end?"

Her mouth opened, then closed, no argument leaving her lips.

He let out a strangled sound and cupped her cheek, softening his voice a fraction. "Will you really let me watch my mate die?"

Her eyes widened at the cold bite in his words. At the growl. Mostly, at the heartbreak he let bleed freely through. He hadn't shown emotion before, but now it leaked out of him like the life force was leaking out of her.

"I am going to save you," he said. "And when I do, then I will continue to keep your promise. But you will not lie here and tell me to watch you bleed out."

For a moment, she stared, and he knew there was a war behind her eyes. Then she leaned up and he knew what she wanted, what she searched for. He met her in the middle, careful with her wound, and their lips touched.

It had been so long since he'd last tasted her. The first time they'd give in, she'd tasted of hatred and chocolate. Now she tasted like confections and freedom. Like desire. Like a future he desperately wanted and meant to have.

With a quick move of his wrist, he yanked the arrow from her chest. She cried against his lips, but didn't sever their connection, even as his hand pressed against her breast and magic flowed against her wound. Her flesh knitted together and in exchange for the life of his mate, he took her pain.

It didn't matter.

He would take that and more if it meant having one more day, one more hour, one more *minute* with the woman he was growing to love.

A Crow Cawed

"I'm fine." Shula waved off Ryker's stare of concern. His eyes hadn't left her chest since she felt the arrow pierce through it and blood bloomed across her body. It'd been more shocking than painful at first. But then the agony came when Clay jostled her, turning her away as if he meant to be her shield against the impact of more weapons.

Then there was Ryker. She'd never seen him look so distraught. Never quite heard a sound burst from his lips like when he'd roared her name. For a long time, she'd felt like she was tip-toeing on the outskirts of their mating bond. Like neither one could fully submerge themselves into the commitment towards one another.

It was easier to hate and push away than to give someone else your whole heart and soul. Even when they'd already cemented their mating bond by sinking their teeth into each other's flesh, there'd still been reluctance. And then there hadn't been. Their touches were still tentative, unsure what parts of their broken selves aligned, where they fit.

Getting shot had also taken away her doubts. Obviously, he cared about her. Not just because they shared pain and emotions through that magical bond. But he cared about *her.*

Shula's chest warmed at the realization, right where the arrow had pierced her skin. Her hand reached up to rub the spot, which she regretted doing as Ryker's eyes honed in on the movement.

He let out a low growl and stepped towards her, shoving away her hand and yanking at the front of her shirt to look down at her skin.

"Ryker," she warned. "I'm *fine.*"

He made a noncommittal sound that had her rolling her eyes.

"Insufferable Fae bastard."

His gaze shot up, that single black eye of his flaring to life, his nostrils inhaling deep. The feral movements should have annoyed her, but all they did was warm her body over every single inch. Her thighs pressed tightly together, staving off the zing of pleasure that accumulated there.

But, bastard that her mate was, he could smell her.

A growl rumbled through his chest. His body tilted towards her, pressing close enough that their lower halves aligned, and she could feel him hardening through his pants.

Their affection was always subtle, beating on the unsteady wings of a small bird just learning to fly. It was either awkward or ferocious.

Right then, it felt like it would consume them.

His hand reached out to cup the back of her neck, fingers threading through her long strands of hair. He pulled her closer, yanking her up so she pressed onto the tips of her toes. His lips hovered over hers, beard scraping against her chin.

"Never again," he whispered darkly.

She didn't need to ask him to clarify. She knew what he meant, but with the lives they led, it was impossible to know if their next moments would be their last. The thought of death still petrified her as much as the humans did. She was still afraid of them and their weapons and of what they could do to the Fae. But she learned to face that fear and confront it head-on. She'd learned how to fight back.

And that made all the difference when it came to survival.

She tried to look away, but Ryker's growl trailed straight to her core.

Eyes on me.

She blew out a breath. "Ryker..."

"If I made a promise, then you will too." A command, growled angrily. But beneath the primal demands, she could see something else.

The brokenness of him. The *fear.*

He'd already lost Mairin, his sister, to the humans. That had been decades ago. She knew he feared losing her too.

Her body softened and she leaned closer, letting their foreheads touch. What kind of a mate would she be if she could not gift him a promise in return for the one he gave her?

Though promises were fickle things and could change or be broken. But Shula wouldn't break this if she could help it.

"I promise," she whispered.

He breathed a sigh of relief and their lips met tentatively. His mouth was soft, a perfect contrast of the rest of his body. The raised ridges of his scars scraped along her skin, as coarse as his beard almost. It was nothing but a brief touch at first, but then she daringly slid the tip of her tongue against the seam of his lips. He opened for her and within moments, they were devouring one another.

A groan rumbled through her, a desperate sound that she didn't recognize. Her hands reached for him, gripping at the front of his shirt. Beneath the material, she felt his scars like a brand against her palms.

"Are you two done yet?"

Shula pulled away with a gasp, her face flushing brightly. For a moment, she'd forgotten where she was, what they were doing, where they were going...

The Fae stood around, shuffling uncomfortable as they waited for Shula and Ryker to extricate themselves from one another's bodies.

"Can you two break it up?" Clay teased again. He was perched atop a white stallion, one of the many they'd stolen from the humans at those camps. The beast snickered, almost as if it were laughing alongside its new master. "We have a town to get to, in case you've forgotten."

Slowly, Shula pried her fingers from Ryker's shirtfront.

Clay's brows kicked up to his hairline when Ryker didn't release Shula. "Perhaps I can ask Valerio to give you five minutes? You'll have to bear with an audience, though."

At that, Ryker growled and released her. "Fuck you," he snapped at Clay.

"Aw, sorry to disappoint you, but you are not quite my flavor of Fae. Shula, however..."

With a snarl, Ryker made a lunge for Clay only to be stopped by Valerio pulling his horse in front of him.

"If you children are done... We have to leave now."

Shula cleared her throat, resting her hand against Ryker's arm. Despite how things had changed between them and the trust they had, his jealousy still hadn't abated. And Clay didn't help matters with his open flirtations. She didn't think Ryker would ever breathe easier in regards to her friendship with Clay. At least, not unless he found himself a mate.

That didn't seem likely, and it didn't seem like Clay was eager to settle down into the mated life, either. Not with the way he spun through camp, lifting skirts. More times than she could count, Shula had caught him walking out of a lonely female's tent in the middle of the night.

He didn't do it sneakily and had made it clear to the women he bedded that he wouldn't stay the night with them. Ever.

There was a reason behind that, she was sure, but she didn't ask.

Ignoring the others, Ryker turned to her. Horses were on low supply, so the two shared one. A chestnut female with a sleek coat and kind, wide eyes idled nearby and they walked towards her. Shula's fingers grazed along the animal's side before Ryker gripped her by the waist and hoisted her atop it. The horse teetered a bit before settling and Ryker followed after.

Before he ordered the horse into a cant, Shula's eyes searched the camp for Ryker's familiar. She found the little black cat perched on Weylyn's shoulder. The feline had taken a liking to the eerie, golden Fae ever since the fall of Castle Aileach. It didn't make sense, but she'd spent a long amount of time on his shoulder.

When Shula had asked Ryker about it, he'd shrugged. "She is my companion, not my property. She knows her own mind. If she sees something in Weylyn, he should count himself lucky that she finds him worthy enough to be around."

While the Fae still made Shula uncomfortable, she took comfort in the knowledge that Ryker's familiar didn't find him totally despicable. And in the fact that she was still Ryker's companion, regardless of who she spent her time with.

"Move out!" Valerio called from the front of the procession. He was shadowed by Uric, both atop pitch black steeds with hair that gleamed like the night sky. Iona and Julius followed behind them, both of them sitting atop Iona's familiar, a massive polar bear who held Julius' heavy weight as if it were nothing.

Ryker's arms wrapped around Shula as he took the reins and snapped them lightly, spurring the chestnut horse forward. Once they settled into a steady rhythm, Ryker's mouth pressed against her temple and he whispered, "I am glad you are okay, Fire Dancer."

They arrived at Covenglen by nightfall. The town was situated beneath a small hill near the Arcana. It was unimpressive, the homes all but dilapidated shacks made of slanting wood and metal. From the distance, it looked a miniscule and unimportant place, but Shula knew that they had large boats.

Most towns close to the Arcana had sturdy wooden boats they rented out to travelers or used themselves to cross the miles-wide river. Usually, it helped bring income into their pockets.

The Fae waited on the cleft of the hills, staring down at the place they were meant to pass through. They were waiting for Valerio's signal, and Shula found herself holding her breath in front of Ryker until Valerio spoke.

"Swords out," he ordered.

The slide of steel against sheathe had her releasing a breath in a rush.

"Look alive," he ordered. "We will take this town by force if we must." And then he nudged his horse into a gallop and the others followed. Tension rang through the air and Shula felt the compress of unease baring down against her chest.

By force?

Her fingers dug into the chestnut's mane. "Ryker," she gaped. "Does he mean to *conquer* that town?"

She knew he'd meant to conquer a city for their own. While she hadn't been in complete agreement, there was something different about fighting a city drenched in iron versus taking over a small town of humans who could barely defend themselves.

"Shula..."

But she didn't wait to her what else Ryker had to say. She dug her heels into the side of the horse and they were off in a sprint. The wind was knocked from her lungs, and she welcomed the reeling sensation, urging her to gallop faster until they cut through the line of Fae and intercepted Valerio.

His horse reeled back with a whinny, and when he settled back to all fours, Valerio's expression was irate. "What do you think you are doing?"

"You can't conquer the town." Her chest heaved as the breathless words left her lips.

Valerio's brows rose. The slashing lines of his beautiful, dangerous features were as cutting as any blade. When he glared, she always felt the full force of it. Even now. "You are mistaken if you think you are in charge, Fire Dancer."

She rolled her eyes. "Cut the shit."

Uric growled from his side.

"These humans have done nothing wrong," Shula argued, ignoring him. Behind her, Ryker's arms tightened, but he didn't interrupt her. He let her speak. She did not think he would agree with her, but she appreciated his silent show of solidarity anyway. "And you mean to slaughter them all for their boats?"

"I will not take a chance with the lives of my people."

"You don't know those people!"

"I know enough!" he shouted.

Somewhere in the distance, a crow cawed, startled from wherever it was perched. Then there was silence.

"Humans have degraded us for decades," Valerio continued tightly. "Look around you, Shula. Every Fae here has suffered at the hands of humans. Even you. What else would you have us do? This is the only solution we have in order to protect ourselves."

Her chest ached at his words and how true they were. Yes, humans had degraded the Fae, but no Fae was wholly good and no human was wholly evil. There were good humans out there. Humans like Des, Orna's mate—friends who had died too soon. Just like there were Fae whose own morality was questionable. Like Valerio's father.

Like Valerio himself sometimes.

But if Shula knew one thing, it was that she could not stand idly by and watch Valerio lead the Fae to slaughter innocents. It was one thing to storm the camps and kill the soldiers manning the walls. They had chosen their fates. They stood there while Fae were tortured and pushed into fires that burned them alive. They watched the ashes of Fae drift over the sky and laughed. These, though? These were innocents.

"It's not the only solution," she gritted out with determination. Steeling her spine, her fingers tightened within the chestnut's mane. And down the bond she shared with Ryker, she felt his admiration for her resolve. "These humans aren't soldiers and you can't trump every human with those who have harmed you. There is good in them. I *know* it. And there's good in us, but they don't know that." Her eyes swept over everyone listening. "They discriminate because they are afraid of us. Because of what we can do. If we go in there now like this, we will only be proving right all they've heard about us." She looked Valerio in the eye. "That we're monsters."

His expression hardened. "What would you have us do, Shula?"

"Prove them wrong." The answer came immediately. "Instead of fighting, let's go in peacefully. Let's request the use of their boats, instead of taking what we want by force."

The animosity ran deep. She feared their hatred of humans was too great. But this couldn't be all that they were. Hatred was an infection. It spread through bodies and minds and time and generations. It was a disease that poisoned even the purest of minds. Hatred was a wound, and Shula meant to be the balm. At least for a moment. If they'd just listen.

Valerio's steed whinnied, clomping his hooves. Valerio's hand stroked down the beast's neck and with a heavy sigh, his eyes closed then reopened. "Alright, Shula Azzarh," he whispered with caution and resignation. "We will enter peacefully. And I pray to Mana your plan works."

"It will."

In the distance, a crow cawed.

Their presence was met with shouts of fear and running bodies. Humans tripped over each other in their attempt to escape. Women carried crying babies, corralling their children away. The men rushed forward with farmer's tools in the form of weapons.

Fear was palpable in the air. It had an acrid taste to it, one that coated the tongue and felt heavy in the throat. The scent was worse. The winds were rank with piss and sweat, of hay and shit, and something deeper, darker.

Valerio yanked his stallion to a stop, though the horse canted nervously from side to side at the sight of the weapons pointed in their direction. Uric cut in front of Valerio, angling his body sideways, his weapon already in hand and up in a defensive position. They trembled in fear at the sight of the pale Fae; at his almost translucent skin, pale hair, and darker eyes that were like that of a devil.

He probably looked ethereal to them, with his hair pulled away to show his ears and that feral glare.

"You have nothing to fear, humans," Valerio said. His voice caused stillness to settle over the gathered crowd. Their apprehension was obvious as they shuffled from foot to foot, eyeing every movement the Fae around them made. "We come peacefully."

"Lies!" someone shouted, causing the crowd to stir.

"Devils!"

"Leave!"

Shouts rang out, thickening the tension. Things were quickly spiraling and would get out of hand without them having accomplished anything. Shula nudged the chestnut forward. Ryker growled from behind her, his arms tightening around her.

"What are you doing?" he whispered darkly near her ear.

She ignored him and approached the empty space next to Valerio. He glared at her from her peripheral, but he went ignored as well.

"Who's in charge of your town?" she asked, loudly enough for everyone to hear.

It made them stop. Pause. Several gazes swiveled in her direction, breathing her in with scrutiny. But she was used to the attention, though not the blatant hatred. Not the blatant disgust as they took in her ears. She had the sudden urge to pull her long locks over them but refrained herself. That scared little Fae was long gone. She swore to herself she would not be that weak again. But beyond the disgust, she knew they were enthralled with her. She made sure of it. Not by using glamor to pull them into a false sense of security, but by using her body.

Every movement she made was calculated. From the way she pushed her hair away from her shoulders, the way she positioned her fingers, to the way she angled her body and slid from the horse, and touched to her feet with a single, lithe pounce.

Ryker growled a curse and followed her, looming behind her like a very scary tree. Eyes bounced back and forth between the two of them. Her much smaller frame, and the controlled, alluring movement of her body as opposed to Ryker's protective, angry stance.

The humans parted down the middle, separating to let a man through. He stepped to the front of the other humans. Unimpressive, short in stature, and with a rounded belly, he swiped a hand over his sweaty, bald head. "I am Lord Clifford Addington. I am in charge of Covenglen."

Shula smiled warmly at him. It disarmed him. His blinks were slow as he took her in, the kindness she tried so hard to radiate. She knew they were mistrustful, and Uric wasn't helping their situation with his glares, nor was Ryker with his growling stance behind her.

"We are the..." *The Resistance.* The words were poised on the tip of her tongue, but she choked them back. Those words always made her eyes roll, no matter how badly Clay wanted to claim that title. It sounded... she wasn't sure what it sounded like. But she knew she didn't like it. Nor did Valerio. And if she were to confess that that's what they were, the townsfolk would surely turn on them. "We are merely travelers passing by, looking to rent your boats in order to cross the Arcana."

At her words, Valerio slid down from his own horse, standing beside Shula in a show of solidarity. He bowed low to the lord, careful and stiff.

"Lord Addington," he drawled. "I am Valerio Ashera." He left out his title. "What my companion says is correct. We seek safe passage through your town and across the Arcana. We mean no ill will."

Turning away from Shula, the lord looked Valerio up and down. There was a coldness in his eyes. Despite the nervousness, this human seemed intelligent.

"Harboring Fae is illegal," he stated. "You know the laws."

"I am aware what laws your emperor has passed, but my people are not human and we do not follow the same rules of men," Valerio countered. "We are a peaceful group—"

"Hence the weapons..." Lord Addington eyed the swords suspiciously.

"These roads are dangerous, and we need some form of protection. I am sure you understand."

"Sure. And I am sure you understand that as Lord of Covenglen, I cannot just allow Fae to pass through and use our boats without facing consequences from the emperor himself." His fingers flicked across his forehead.

Beside Shula, Valerio tensed even further. She wondered if he was fighting back the urge to use his magic, of casting an illusion over the man in order to get his way.

Shula stepped forward, drawing his attention to her. "We understand you have a duty to your people and your emperor. We understand that our very presence here puts you all in grave peril. It is not easy, to be the leader of this place where every decision rests on your shoulders. I know what you're thinking. If you let us past, will we betray you? We won't. Look at us." She gestured behind her at the Fae in wagons, the ones who couldn't ride, the ones who were so obviously broken, bruised. Who couldn't lift a finger to fight. "We just want peace. Please, Lord Addington. *Please* let us pass."

It wasn't a grand speech. It wasn't cemented in the kind of strength that Clay once said he believed Shula possessed. She didn't know if she could move mountains and cities. She didn't know if she was capable of something so grand. But her words were sincere. They came from the heart.

And that was all she had to give.

She hoped it would be enough.

And if it wasn't, she feared what Valerio would do. But she hoped, even despite all odds, even knowing what humans felt about them, that it would be such a slim chance they would want peace. She had to believe. Because when hope died, so did their chances of survival.

"Okay," Lord Addington said stoically, his gaze flicking between the Fae and their weapons. Then, he turned to his crowd of shocked humans. "Covenglen is yours, Fae. I'll not turn away when you want peace. However, the hour is late and the boats are not available to rent until morning." He turned back to them. "Stay. Enjoy our food and our lodgings."

Shula startled at the offering. Beside her, Valerio's eyes narrowed. "Why?" he asked, rather demanded. "Why would you offer us a place?" The suspicion was laced heavily in his voice.

Lord Addington shrugged. "What is our other option?" His eyes were drawn back to the weapons. "To say no and die when you take our town by force?" His lips kicked up into a mirthless smirk. "Call me cowardly if you wish, but like the female said, these are my people and I'd rather have peace than war. If it will please your people to stay and rest, then you will stay and rest."

Shula's body leaned back into Ryker and she took a breath. Perhaps it wasn't the reason she wanted them to allow passage. Perhaps it wasn't from the goodness of their hearts or because they weren't prejudice. Maybe the lord's reason was only to protect his people and not because he cared about the Fae. It was because he feared for their lives.

At least there would be peace, though.

At least there would not be death.

The tavern was subdued, the energy as morose as a funeral. Their people had filled up the space of the inn above stairs, as well as almost every table below. Those who hadn't the energy, the Fae whose minds were too far gone, had stayed in the barn, guarded by Iona's familiar. They could scarcely walk, let alone climb a flight of stairs to lay in bed. So after they'd gotten them situated and claimed their own rooms, they came down to the tavern.

A few locals crowded together near the bar, watching with suspicious gazes. Even the tavern whores were slow to wander, hanging near, unsure on whether or not they should approach. Clay flashed them a welcoming smile. The charming twist of his lips had them relaxing, a few of them sauntering towards him with exaggerated twist of their hips. He held out his arms as they approached, both plopping themselves on one leg each.

"Ladies," he greeted. "Fine night, isn't it?"

They tittered and draped their upper bodies all over him. Heavy breasts smooshed against his chest. His fingers itched to reach out and grip them in his hands, but he was respectful above all else, no matter their professions.

"Stars above, Clay." Julius snorted, even while he had Iona perched on his own lap and was halfway buried into the skin at her neck.

At the sound of his voice, the two ladies on his lap tensed, stopping their ministrations and staring at him warily. Clay's hands drifted towards their hips, stroking up and down until he felt goosebumps break across their exposed flesh and they relaxed into him.

"Don't mind this bastard, ladies. He's despairing because he now only has one woman to give his love and attention to instead of two." He pulled them closer so their breasts all but pressed against his cheeks.

"One woman is all he needs," Iona retorted, her eyes narrowing on Clay and the hands roaming over his body. "And far more fulfilling than meaningless trysts."

Already, they'd tossed back drink after drink. It wasn't Fae wine, but it was decent ale. Not strong enough to get them drunk, but it did the trick. Julius' cheeks were flushed as red as his hair, and Clay was feeling more relaxed than he had been when they'd arrived.

"I am not one for settling down when I have so much love to give," Clay teased, though the words soured his stomach. It wasn't precisely a lie. He loved women, and burying himself between their thighs and in the recesses of their minds was his favorite past time. There was enough love in his heart for women to go around.

But Clay wasn't a hopeless romantic like his cousin. He knew the odds of finding his mate were slim. That wasn't to say he didn't ache for what they had, but he was content as he was. There wasn't an emptiness in his chest where a mate should be. He wasn't lonely.

Others would argue that he slept around and sought attention from women to fill a void. There was no void. It was just that women were fascinating creatures. How opposite they were to men. All soft, supple flesh instead of hard, angry lines.

One of the women was already grinding against his leg. He watched, letting her take her pleasure and wet his thigh with her desire. And he hadn't even done anything yet. He wouldn't even necessarily have to touch her to make her want.

"One day you'll find your mate, little lord," Julius jested as he trailed kisses along the back of Iona's neck. His mate leaned forward, her lids fluttering as he snaked his way down. "And I can assure you now that she will not want anything to do with you. And when that happens, I am going to laugh in your fucking face."

With a roll of his eyes, Clay hoisted one of the women higher, settling her over the hard ridge of his erection. She squealed, grinding herself down tighter on him. The other woman gripped his wrist and pulled his palm, placing it over her breast.

And if she wanted to fuck in front of an audience?

Well, who was he to deny her?

"I hope everything is to your liking." The innkeeper was a fearful woman. Her eyes danced around the room, looking everywhere but into Valerio's eyes. Like he was some Unseelie creature who could kill with a single glance.

"Everything is perfect. Thank you."

She bowed low and scurried backwards out of the room. As soon as she was gone, Valerio made his way to the tray of food she'd left on the table. He picked up a tankard of ale but as he brought it to his lips, Uric was already knocking the drink away.

"Are you daft, my King?" he hissed.

Valerio blinked with surprise, first at the mess on the floor and then up at his friend. There was an urgency to Uric's tone and the insult that was not usually there.

"What, Uric?"

"It could be poisoned with ashwood."

Valerio rolled his eyes. "If it were, I would have smelled it." Despite his words, Uric was already digging through his food, poking at it with the tip of his knife and bending down to inhale deeply. "I do think you are exaggerating."

Uric's body snapped up and he pierced Valerio with a glare. "And I do not think you are taking this seriously, my King."

He had already asked him to stop calling him that, but of course his friend would not listen.

“I was as suspicious as you at first, but Lord Addington’s claims have merit, my friend. Perhaps it is not the peace Shula wanted, but it is peace nonetheless. Even if it is an uneasy one.”

Uric snarled. “I do not like it.” His feet began swallowing up the length of the room. Back and forth, back and forth. He paced like an agitated, caged animal. “Something is... off.”

“Perhaps that feeling has more to do with the fact that the Fire Dancer was correct in her assessment. Besides, Lord Addington is right to fear us. We would have taken his town by force anyway. He knows it. This solution helps everyone involved.” Uric did not stop pacing so Valerio intercepted him, placing his hands against his friend’s shoulders. “Uric,” he snapped. “Stop, my friend. Please, relax. It will be fine.”

It took a moment. But as if Valerio’s hands were a balm that soothed him, Uric’s shoulders drew down. The skepticism still took residence in his gaze, but it was not as prominent as before.

“Fine,” he conceded. Then, as if Valerio’s touch hurt too much, he pulled away and settled himself into a chair next to the door. He gripped his blade tightly and focused his gaze on the entrance.

As if someone, or something, would burst through at any moment.

Valerio did not fear.

At least not for himself.

Not with a guard as dedicated as Uric Adriel Nova.

Shadows cloaked the town of Covenglen. Black clouds curtained the moon, preventing the dull, silver light from touching the floor. Weylyn Xanth’s feet danced along the ground, his long, lithe legs as silent as the flutters of a butterfly wing. The earth held its breath and somewhere in the distance, a crow cawed.

Where he was from, that was considered an omen of death bleeding along the horizon.

Scary things happened in the dark. Creatures prowled and feasted upon flesh and souls. They stole children from their cribs and harvested them in jars. They were nightmares incarnate that would kill you with a single glance. He was familiar with an array of dangerous beings. Some that could suck out love and happiness like the marrow out of bone. Or even rip a soul to shreds with talons dipped in shadows.

A smile threatened to curve up his lips.

Violence. He relished in it. He breathed it. Craved it like a Fae addict might crave Unseelie drugs in their system.

He knew the force a craving could have on the body. He was no stranger to drugs or the hallucinations they brought. One might even have called him an addict before the world changed. He would have done anything back then, absolutely *anything*, to drown out the *bullshit* and the agony and the memories.

Those fucking memories.

Funny, how he relished to know everyone else's secrets, but he buried his own so deeply, it was like they had never really lived within him at all.

"Melancholy thoughts." The cat perched on his shoulder purred.

With a silent chuckle, he reached a finger up and scratched beneath her neck.

He was unsure why Ryker's familiar had taken a liking to him. Beasts had a tendency to gravitate towards those who saved them from certain demise. Perhaps this cat was no different. It was odd, however, that the little black feline had decided to speak to him.

As far as he knew it, familiars only spoke to their chosen Fae and few select others.

Lucky him.

"Lucky you," the cat echoed in his thoughts.

His chuckle was as inaudible as his strides. He continued through the piss-poor town in search of... something. At this point, sleep alluded him, and he would not seek it out.

Valerio Ashera might have been fool enough to trust the word of the fat lord, but Weylyn was not. It was not because he searched his mind. No, Weylyn did not go shoving his consciousness into every slimy bastard he saw. And sometimes, he did not even need to use his magic to know how chaotic certain minds could be, or to perceive deception where it so obviously was.

Nor was it his job to warn Valerio of the mistakes he was making.

Weylyn had been King Ashera's bitch for far too long, the loathsome creature, and now the pretty prince expected that same loyalty. But Weylyn had never been loyal to the Seelie King, like he would never be completely loyal to the Seelie Prince either.

The only being he served was himself. His reasons for following the Resistance were his own.

So Weylyn prowled the night in his restlessness, waiting for what he knew would unfold. Whispered voices pierced past the quiet night, and he followed with a curve of his lips. There, in an unassuming home, a window peeked open. Weylyn did not need to see inside to recognize the voice of the fat lord who had greeted them earlier. He was with his townsfolk.

He soaked up the press of their anger in the air, shivering as it caressed his skin. It was like an aphrodisiac, these human emotions. None more potent than rage or fear.

"What were you thinking, letting them stay here?" a voice hissed.

"They will steal our children in the night!"

At that, Weylyn smiled. Only Unseelie stole children from their cribs, switching them out with the sickly Fae babes. The little people of the wood were tricksters like that.

"Do you take me for a fool?" The fat lord's voice was cunning. No trace of that nervousness he displayed outside. He did not sound the sweaty, incompetent, fearful lord then. No. Now he sounded vengeful. What an unlikely and yet entirely too predictable turn of events. "They would have slaughtered us all."

"They will do it anyway!"

"*Not* if we slaughter them first."

Oh, how *interesting.*

"However do you mean?"

"I offered them hospitality, which they so readily accepted. When they are at their weakest, we will end them all in their sleep before they get a chance to murder us. Ready the iron weapons. No Fae will be left alive tonight."

Weylyn pushed away from the window, slinking deeper into the shadows as the humans filed from the little house, a skip in their step.

His own body felt elated at the prospect of violence and death. So many of his problems could be solved if he stayed back and watched these events unfold.

"Cruel Fae." The cat dug her claws into his shoulder. *"Cruel, beautiful Fae."*

He knew the words were not a compliment. He resisted the urge to shrug. It was in his nature to want to see everything fall. In chaos, he prevailed. And there would be no greater moment than this.

To watch the great Valerio Ashera fall victim to his own stupidity.

The asshole.

He deserved that and more. For being too trusting. Why should Weylyn warn them that danger was coming when Valerio should have predicted this? *No one* was innocent. That was a lesson Weylyn had learned the hard way.

And everyone deserved to die.

"You must warn them."

"No," he hissed softly.

"You must."

He suddenly wanted to shove the cat from his shoulder with annoyance. Maybe cook it over a spit for being entirely too irritating.

As if reading his thoughts, the cat swiped a paw against his face, splitting his skin.

"It is a shame Ryker has not yet named you. Maybe I shall call you dinner."

That slit gaze blinked at him, unamused.

"It is no business of mine that Valerio was not cautious enough."

The cat said nothing.

So easily had he fallen out of its favor?

Whatever.

He did not want it.

He went to shove the thing from his shoulder but earned another swipe to the cheek.

"Manipulative creature," he growled.

"Hateful Fae," she replied.

He was hateful, that he would not deny. Nor would he apologize for his own bloody nature. But for a moment, he felt at a crossroads. Witnessing death would be satisfying, but only for a moment. Yet it did not agree with his own plans for the future. If the Resistance died here, now, then he could never go back home.

Could never claim that which he so desperately wanted above all others.

With a sigh, he moved, his feet carrying him fast through the town, hidden from the folk who were preparing for bloodshed. He knew where Valerio was lodging and when he made it to the side of the inn, he began to climb, jostling the clinging cat.

At the window, he pushed it open and leapt inside the room. He was so silent, it startled both Valerio and Uric, who was keeping watch by the front door.

"Weylyn, what—" the fool of a prince began.

Fucking asshole.

Weylyn smirked and though he did not like speaking, he was forced to tell them the truth. "The humans mean to murder us all."

Black Feathers and Blood

The second the words left Weylyn's lips, Uric hopped up from his seat and ran in Valerio's direction. His hand clamped around his friend's arm, and a portal opened and they fell through the crystalline surface. Weylyn followed, hopping nimbly behind them until they disappeared.

Everything happened so fast that Valerio barely had time to take in a breath before his feet were hitting the ground on the other side of the portal. His arm shot out as he tried to find his balance, but one was shackled in Uric's iron grip. His friend didn't let him fall, but he did trip when a second body rammed into him from behind, nearly knocking him off balance. He shot a glare to Weylyn, though the Fae feigned as though he could not see it. The movement had been almost purposeful. Valerio did not have time to worry about that, though. Not when he glanced around and breathed in their surroundings.

"Uric, where did you bring us?" He whirled on his friend, yanking his arm away in the process.

Uric, unfazed, smoothed down the front of his dark shirt. "Away from that town."

A growl snapped out of Valerio's chest. "Take me back!"

"Those treacherous humans were prepared to murder us all in our sleep and you want to go *back*?" he scoffed.

"Oh, do not blame the humans, Adriel," Weylyn purred. They turned to him, watching him luxuriate against the ground, leaning back against the thick trunk of a tree. As if their world had not just imploded moments ago. He reached to pet the cat, but Ryker's familiar hissed and dug her claws into his shoulders. Weylyn did not even flinch. "The prince really should have predicted this."

"How could I have predicted this?" The words were right there, poised on the tip of his tongue, gleaming like a dagger. He did not say them aloud, but Weylyn's eyes fluttered, and he pulled the words from Valerio's mind regardless.

He smirked, the action mirthless and cruel. "A prince, or in your case a king, as you have so proudly paraded yourself, must exhaust every option. You were too complacent. Entirely too quick to trust that lord. And that, *Seelie Prince*, will cost you dearly."

Valerio's jaw snapped shut angrily. Denying the words seemed fruitless at this point, and he hated Weylyn for saying them. But there was that small part of him that could not deny that the golden Fae was right. The truth was, he *should* have predicted this. He should have thought of every possible outcome. He should have known that most humans were vicious, hateful creatures.

He had been so desperate to believe in goodness, to believe that what Shula had said was true. He had taken advice, instead of deciding for himself.

And it would cost them dearly.

He turned from Weylyn's smug expression to look at Uric. "Take me back," he snapped. "Now."

Uric's level stare met his own. "No."

Valerio fought not to rock back on his heels from surprise. "Our people are still in that town. We need to get them out. We need to fight back."

Indecision warred on Uric's face. The desire to protect his prince, his *friend* from harm. And the struggles of obeying him. Of putting him in danger.

But what type of royal would Valerio be if he left his people behind?

"The Elementals are there," Valerio said tightly. "As your prince, I command you to fucking *take me back*, so I can save our people."

Uric's jaw tightened, but he opened his palms and the air near them shimmered. "As you command, prince."

Julius' hips snapped against Iona's, blunt nails digging into her skin as he thrust into her from behind. They cried out in unison as their flesh slapped together, their harsh breaths echoing through the walls of the inn. His hand slid up her bare spine, grasping at the back of her neck to hold her in place.

Iona pushed back against him and a satisfied grumble vibrated through his chest. He couldn't get enough of his mate. While he'd heard what the mating bond entailed, experiencing it was another matter entirely.

He was completely consumed by her. Every thought, every desire, every fucking nerve ending was suffused with the memory of her kiss, her touch, her taste. He wanted to pull her into him, connect their souls into one single being.

Fuck, maybe that was the very definition of love. To be consumed entirely by another person, to want them in a capacity that transcended Mana itself.

His hips slowed, rolling against her in loving movements. He couldn't see into her eyes, but he could convey his love this way. And he would convey it for the rest of their lives, or for however long they had left. His touches became tender, reverent, and the change of pace had her trembling against him as release overcame her. It overcame them both. He shuddered his own release and, after a moment to catch his breath, rolled away from his mate. With a sigh, Iona landed on her back next to him.

"Fuuuuck," she whispered, the content in her voice obvious. She turned towards him, propping her head up on her palm.

The smile she gave him was his weakness.

"I should let you be on top more often," she teased.

Julius snorted and pulled her against his side. Already, he was growing hard again just by having her near. He could spend an entire lifetime with her and never grow bored. He could spend an eternity with her and always want her. He would spend his whole life loving and caring for her.

He didn't realize he was staring at her intently until she grabbed his nipple between her fingers and twisted. "What are you staring at?" she demanded.

He chuckled, rubbing a hand across the injured peak. "Just about what comes after all of this..."

Her fingers tapped against his chest in thought. "After seems so long away," she said finally. "We still have a long way to go."

"I know." He was used to conflict by now. To wars. No matter how small, it was always never-ending. Peace was all but a fantasy. That didn't mean he wouldn't fight for it just the same. To change the subject, he rolled over her, pressing his hips down on her. "Another round?" he asked.

She smirked up at him, but before she could open her mouth to reply, the door to their room burst open. Caught off-guard, Julius started to move, but Iona was faster. Her hands shot out, caging around his berth. There were shouts, footsteps, and the unmistakable scent of ice.

When Iona's hands dropped, Julius rolled and hopped to his feet. The wood shook with the force, his anger a tremor along the ground. His nostrils flared. He prepared to charge against their adversaries...

But they were already frozen in place.

All but ice statues, they were still in the middle of the room, their weapons raised and poised to strike. From behind the ice, their eyes moved and it didn't take much to catch a whiff of their fear.

"They were going to kill us."

Julius turned and found Iona already slipping into her clothes, tugging on her tight gray pants and tunic. He followed suit, dressing quickly. He had no idea what the fuck was going on, but it was obvious these humans had betrayed them. He had to wonder if it was just this handful, or if there were others.

Fuck, was it the whole town?

"Ah!" He whipped around to watch Iona stumble as she pulled on her boots. Breathing hard, his mate clutched tightly at her chest, gasping for breath. A pained expression marred her features and she gritted out the words, "Something is wrong... My familiar..." The sentence trailed off and then she was running from the inn, leaving Julius behind. He cursed and ran after her, every instinct in his body demanding that he protect.

Sometimes Julius forgot that Iona was an Elemental and could protect herself.

Ice bodies wobbled down the halls. Where his mate touched, she wreaked this in her wake. Cold. Death. He shoved past the statues and they shattered against the ground as they fell. He heard shouts as he passed rooms, and while he wanted to check on his companions, while the soldier in him urged to find his leader and make sure he was okay, then come up with a plan, he couldn't. Not when his mate's silhouette was disappearing through the inn and out into the night.

He burst out and was greeted with smoke, fire, and blood.

It wasn't Shula's magic. It wasn't her fire tearing through the barn that sat near the inn. There was no trace of confections or embers in the air. Just acrid smoke and burning flesh. He gagged.

"No!" Iona was running towards the barn. Julius felt his own heartbeat catch in his throat as he watched the wood going up in flames. He followed, faster than he'd ever run before. The outside doors were barred with an iron rod.

He reached it before Iona did. His palms closing around the rod. The burn came instantaneously but he ignored it, channeling his magic as much as the iron would allow. But it was enough. It had to be. The rod snapped in half as he tugged and the doors burst open.

Smoke poured from the barn, flames licking out to kiss his skin. He startled backwards, dropping the twin rods to the ground. Iona's magic met the flames with a force. It pushed them back, the cold diminishing the heat.

"Come on!" she cried out, a desperation to her voice.

Julius' own throat felt clogged with emotion. The fucking barn... Their people were in there. Without enough room at the inn, the majority of them had stayed together at the barn with Iona's familiar as protection.

Growls rose from within the smoke, and a moment later, the polar bear came bursting from the barn, his fur steaming. On his back, he carried Fae. They hung tightly, sobbing against him. The minute he burst free, they slipped their hold and fell to the ground. Then the familiar was turning, running back in with Iona following close behind.

Julius' legs wanted to carry him into the building after her, but he knew she had things under control. Instead, he went to the injured Fae on the ground. Their skin was charred, their flesh bubbling up grotesquely. He wanted to touch them, help them up, but he knew it would only hurt them more. The healing process needed to set in and even then it would be painful, and there was no guarantee they'd fully heal. Not when they were already so weak.

They needed Ryker.

They needed—

A shout had his attention jerking up. Humans, so many humans, ran towards him wielding their weapons. Iron swords, rakes, and shovels. It was a mutiny, and Julius wasn't sure whether he should be impressed or pissed off. It was poorly executed, and yet they'd also done it so well. Allowed them in, allowed them to let their guards down.

They charged and Julius reacted on instinct, running in front of the injured Fae to protect them. Too late, he realized he had no weapons. He didn't want to hurt the humans, because a single glance at their fearful expressions made his stomach coil into knots. These weren't warriors. They were fucking farmers.

But all those thoughts flew from his mind the moment they approached. He didn't dodge, and the weapons pierced and scratched his skin. He howled his pain, eyes honing in on the weapons. His fists struck out, snapping the wood of their rakes, but the iron that struck bruised his skin. Despite his superior strength, he wasn't immune to their brutality. Iron spikes embedded into his skin, and he cried out as blood raked down his arm.

He swiped his arms out at them, connecting to flesh and bone. Humans exploded against his fists, bathing Julius in gore. It rained over his face, staining his vision crimson. Copper burst against his teeth and tongue and his rage was ever-rising, even as the iron weakened him, his fury was at the forefront, being unleashed. His movements grew sluggish as a spike entered his side and stayed. The iron within his flesh had him dropping to his knees.

It was all the humans needed. An iron rake swiped towards him. He flinched back, exposing the arch of his neck. He felt the blood drip down his neckline before the agony hit. A gargled howl escaped his lips. Fire encased his insides, the iron debilitating his magic, him. His hands reached up to staunch the flow of blood, but it slipped through the cracks of his fingers.

The Fae around him, though burned and in pain, cried out for him. He felt them crawl on the ground in his direction. And Iona? He couldn't see her, couldn't feel her.

The humans were surrounding him and never before had a hatred burned brighter.

And somewhere in the distance, a growl of rage sounded.

And somewhere in the distance, a crow cawed.

Shula lay at the very edge of the bed, trying to make herself as small as possible. Not from fear. That eluded her. But because Ryker's massive body took up a great amount of space. While they shared a single sheet or cot on the ground when they traveled, they'd never really shared an *actual* bed before.

She could hear her heart pounding wildly in her ears, and she knew he could probably hear it, too. Feel the rhythm of it beating along the mattress. He lay on his back, his eyes closed. In this position, he looked peaceful, less tortured. When he was awake, he was always shrouded in despair, the scars stark and silver against the olive tone of his skin. In sleep, they were imperfect, raised flesh pulling smoother skin together. Less severe, somehow.

Her fingers twitched as she ached to reach out and smooth over the scars. More specifically, the ones behind his elongated ears. Scars that should have belonged to her.

Ryker took a deep breath, his chest expanding. He slept fully clothed, though that might have been done more out of habit regardless of where they were. Shula was the same. She went to bed in her tunic and pants and boots, though the garments felt too confining. Too hot. Her skin itched, but it wasn't her magic forcing discomfort against her flesh.

It was Ryker.

It was his proximity, his peacefulness. It was her own desire to feel his body against hers.

The last time they'd been together had been months ago. Back at Castle Aileach. Back when their bond had sealed and she felt his canines sink into her skin and her own did the same in return. When they'd joined in spirit, in soul, in bodies. They'd moved together in tandem. It had probably been the only time since they'd known one another that they'd been in perfect synchronization.

Mana knew that afterwards there was nothing but heartache.

But that too had faded. They'd found their own sort of camaraderie. A friendship, if nothing else. But the desire was still there. It was invisible between them, and neither one acknowledged it. Not because they didn't want to, but because there just hadn't been an opportunity.

They couldn't be like Julius and Iona, who fell easily into each other's arms and slipped off into the woods for a quick fuck that could be heard all over the camp. Doing it like that only reminded Shula of Orna and Des, and she had no desire to sneak off like that, because it didn't seem like it would bring anything except horrors.

They'd done nothing more than sleep beside one another. Sometimes pressed close. Sometimes with Ryker's arm wrapped around her middle. Sometimes with Shula's face buried into the crook of her mate's neck.

Now they had privacy and Shula wondered if there was something broken about them, preventing them from gravitating towards one another. Preventing her from slipping her hand within the front of his pants and gripping his length like she hadn't before. She wanted to explore every part of his body like he had to hers.

Her face flamed and her breaths came in shallow pants as she recalled it. Desire between them had been consuming but easily smothered. Shouldn't they be different now that they were mated? Why were relationships so confusing? Should she just reach out and touch him? Wake him up with a kiss? Ask him?

Ryker's nostrils flared and his breathing stopped. It was quick, the way he moved, turning on his side and pressing his palm against her hip. His eyes opened, pupils inflamed as he stared at her.

He can smell me, she thought. She'd almost forgotten about the Fae senses, and the realization made her face burn with embarrassment. How many times had he known by her scent alone what it was she wanted from him?

How many times had he pushed it away as much as she had?

His big hand slid over the curve of her hip. He didn't speak. Half the time he didn't need to when their eyes conveyed precisely what they wanted to say.

Eyes on me.

So that's where she kept them. On his bicolored eyes. They drank each other in and his hand moved slowly, languorously, over her hip and to her waist, kissing its way to the front of the waist of her pants. His fingers tugged confidently at the drawstring, and her breath caught at the action as if this was their first time touching.

She arched her hips forward the slightest fraction as her pants loosened and his hand dipped inside. Every movement was slow and torturous, but it was everything she wanted. Everything she craved. His fingers found her wet and aching. And when they slid against her slick folds, she bit down on her lip. Hard enough to draw blood and taste the coppery tang of it in her mouth.

His other hand reached out reverently, cradling her cheek, thumb swiping across her lip until she released it from between her teeth. He smoothed it out, catching a drop of blood with the pad of his thumb. He looked like he wanted to heal her, but remembered his promise and leaned forward instead to lap up the injury with his mouth and tongue.

She melted into his embrace, drinking him in as much as he did to her. His scent swirled through her nostrils. Calming, a balm to her erratic breathing. Her own cloyed through as well, clashing against him until their scents intermingled.

Herbs and embers and confections. Together, they were warm tea and chocolate cake. A soothing, addicting combination innately their own.

Ryker's fingers dipped inside her folds, stretching her tight channel. She cried out against his mouth and he swallowed the sound, drowning it out with a feral growl of his own. His thumb circled her clit lightly in circles, making her head spin with headiness only he could sate.

Her hips pressed into him, riding against his fingers to create a delicious friction. She wanted to reach out and grab him, to study his body the way he already seemed to know hers, but her hands were trapped between them. He held her smooshed close, like he meant to pull her into him.

Become one being, one entity.

"Ryker," she moaned his name against his lips. She wanted to touch him. Needed it like she needed her next breath. She tugged at her hands, pressing her palms against his chest and shoved him. They rolled until he was on his back with Shula straddling his waist. His hand was still trapped between them. The position was awkward, but so delicious. She undulated, riding his hand and breathing harshly into the room. Fire danced beneath her skin, begging for release. Begging to be pushed over that edge.

Shula braced her hands against Ryker's hips, her thumbs teasing the scarred skin visible beneath his tunic. She toyed with the waist of his pants, silently asking permission. She stared at that space before her gaze flicked up to him.

Brazenly, she whispered, "I want—"

Ryker grunted. She was familiar enough with his sounds now to know what that one conveyed. Desire. Permission.

It made her bolder. "I want to feel you..."

Her hands started pushing down the waist of his pants. He arched, easing the way...

"I am afraid you will have to feel your mate later, Fire Dancer."

Shula yelped at the sudden voice that came into the room. Her first instinct was to hide, bury herself in Ryker's arms. But the more violent part of her reacted before she could even move. Her hands lifted and fire darted out, shooting into the direction of that voice.

It was only once the smoke cleared that she realized who the voice belonged to and reminded her why she didn't recognize it.

"What the fuck, Weylyn?" She tried to scramble off Ryker before she realized his fingers were still deep inside her. Her face heated to epic proportions, but it didn't take long for Ryker to remove himself from her and sit up, angling his body in a way that blocked her from Weylyn's view.

While she tugged the drawstrings of her pants together, she glared at Weylyn. The golden Fae's eyes were glittering with malice and his nostrils flaring beneath the dark smoke staining his skin. Behind him, the silver mirror of an open portal hovered. Which meant Uric was just on the other side.

What was going on?

"I do hate to interrupt," Weylyn crooned, but he said the words with such joy that they seemed like a blatant lie. "You seem as though you were having fun. However, it is time to go now."

"Why?" Ryker was already standing up, gathering his bag and pulling the straps over his shoulders. Shula scrambled to follow suite.

"Because the humans plotted a mutiny and are picking us Fae off one by one..."

Shula froze as she bent to pick up her cloak. Her heart stuttered until she felt like it would stop beating entirely in her chest. Her arms moved, the cloak settling against her shoulders like a thin barrier of protection against the truth of his words.

The humans... They wouldn't. Would they?

"They certainly did," Weylyn said, answering her silent thoughts. His ringed fingers now held a thin dagger. It bounced and twirled on his palm and between the spaces of his fingers. The hilt was gripped tightly between his fingertips. His arm arced back and he sent the dagger flying...

Just as the door to the room opened. The blade landing thick into the skull of the axe-wielding human. He fell dead to the floor.

"Mana..." Shula breathed, her chest rising and falling.

Weylyn shot her a grin full of mirth. "Time to go." And he stepped backwards into the portal.

Ryker gripped Shula's hand in his and yanked her into the mirrored surface. When they landed on the other side, it closed behind them, but they were greeted by Valerio's scowl and behind him...

Fire and chaos.

Valerio aimed his glare in Shula's direction. In that single look, she felt the entire force of his hatred like a tsunami wreaking destruction. Even worse were the screams and cries suddenly piercing through the air around them. The air was sharp with the scent of blood, fire, and iron. Of death and havoc.

The results of a decision she'd helped to make.

"This is what happens," Valerio whispered darkly. "This is what happens when humans are blindly trusted."

He turned, a swish of dark cloak and hair.

And Shula nearly fell to her knees, a scream working its way up her throat to join the symphony of the dying. And through all the noise, somewhere in the distance, she could hear a crow caw.

⁂

Livia and Tyra sucked down air in an attempt to calm their erratic breathing. Their eyes were peeled open, surprise evident in the twist of their lovely features.

Clay sat between them, the single sheet pulled up at his waist. He smiled to himself. Another successful night of pleasure. Another night well-spent with his face buried between thighs and his dick being hugged by slick heat. Another night with their cries filling something inside of him. Women were happiness. Beautifully complicated creatures.

He enjoyed deciphering them.

"Wow," Livia breathed. Her body shifted, the sheet sliding down against her smooth curves to display her breasts. She pressed them against his body. She trembled and even beneath the scent of her release, he knew she wanted more. "That was..."

Tyra leaned against him, raking her fingers through his already disheveled hair. "Clay," she hummed. "I had no idea a Fae could be so..."

He shot both women a smirk as he pulled them closer to his body. He would not spend the night with them, but he would relish in their presence a moment longer before they had to leave to the boats in the morning. "Not every Fae, love. Just me."

"No one ever worries about our pleasure."

Clay made a noncommittal noise. That truth had been evident when they'd stumbled into the room and they'd pounced. The noises they'd made had been falsetto music, too practiced and inauthentic. A damn shame that women like themselves were used merely for a man's pleasure while not feeling any of it on their own.

He'd changed that. Had focused on their pleasure throughout the night, only taking his own after he'd made them come no less than five times each.

It had been such a fun night.

"Men are always taking," he said softly to them, letting his fingers trail against their curves. "Some can go a lifetime without really giving. And you women? You deserve the world..."

There was silence, and he wondered if his honest words had been far too poetic for them when Livia burst into sudden tears.

Clay's eyes widened at the display and he tugged her close, ready to push her head into his neck and let her weep against him. Had he done something wrong? No, he knew he hadn't. Had he moved her so much that he'd reduced her to this?

"Clay," Livia hiccupped. "W-w-we're s-so s-s-sorry..."

His brows pulled together. “For what?”

Tyra’s nails raked across his skin as she pushed herself off of him. She hopped off the bed and began collecting his clothes from the floor, tossing them against his chest. Her movements were rushed, desperate. “You need to hurry,” she said, an urgency to her voice that was *not* pleasurable. Rather, fearful.

Livia extricated herself from him as well, swiping at the tears sliding down her cheeks. “We didn’t think... we didn’t know you’d be so...” She made a noise and hopped up as well. “Get dressed Clay, please.”

Noting the franticness of the both of them, he obeyed, quickly slipping into his clothes and shoes. An uneasy feeling settled in his gut. “What’s going on?”

Livia sniffled. “They made us do it...”

Tyra sighed as she threw his bag in his direction. “Lord Addington. He... he told us to distract you.”

Realization and surprisingly *hurt* speared through him. “He what?”

Livia took a cautious step towards him, placing her hands against his chest. “We were supposed to distract you. Keep you busy so they could come in and... and...”

“And kill me,” he guessed.

She bit her lip and nodded, a tear tracking down her cheek. On instinct, he lifted a hand and wiped it away. The move seemed to surprise her.

“We’re sorry,” Tyra stepped close. “We didn’t know that Fae could be so...” Her gaze raked over his body. “We were afraid of you, but you’re... you’re *sweet.*” She sounded disgusted with herself. “This would have been easier if you’d been a dick instead of having a magical dick.” She waved a hand in the direction of his crotch.

Clay snorted a laugh. “Magical dick?” That seemed an apt enough description. But it wasn’t even about his dick. Dicks didn’t matter when it came to pleasure. You could have any girth or size and it wouldn’t matter. What was important was how you *used* it.

“Don’t gloat. Just get out of here. They’re coming for you. We’ll lie and say you snuck out or something,” Tyra grumbled. “We won’t be responsible for your death.”

Livia nodded her agreement. “We like you.”

He flashed them a wide smile. “I like you, too. Both of you. And I thank you.” He pressed a hand to his chest. “I will remember your kindness, your faces, *always.*” He pulled Livia forward and speared her mouth with a scorching kiss. One he knew she’d remember for the rest of her life. Then he did the same to Tyra before pulling away and shouldering his bag. “May Mana watch over the both of you,” he said.

They swooned where they stood.

Then he was leaving, sneaking out of the inn's window and climbing down below. It wasn't until he touched the bottom that he heard the door above burst open and frantic, angry voices. He disappeared into the night before they could look out and catch sight of him.

And even as chaos rained down around him, Clay wore a smile on his face.

Smoke stung her eyes. Fire suffocated her lungs. She countered it with her magic, feeling the press of iron trying to weaken her. But she was strong. She was an Elemental and her ice and snow cooled the heavy licks of angry flames, settling over the burning skin of the Fae inside.

Their screams were spears to her heart. Their pain her own. She breathed it in, as heavy and clogging as the smoke. Her familiar rushing for everyone they could possibly help.

The humans. These fucking humans had barred the Fae within the barn. Helpless Fae. Fae already broken, the Fae who could scarcely fight. And they'd tried to burn them alive.

Many of them caught fire and the sight was a nightmare, a horror she never imagined she'd see in her lifetime, and she'd seen so many things. So many terrible things. Her snow coated their skin, but their screams didn't cease. It was a struggle to get them out of the barn without hurting them further. It was complete chaos, and when the flames finally died, it left the charred remains of Fae behind. Some dead, some alive yet agonizing.

She wanted to ease their pain, but for the first time in forever she felt afraid. That the world was composed of such cruelty to do this to the weak, to children and elders... Her heart ached for them and vengeance seared through her anew.

She tore her gaze away from their suffering as her familiar gathered them up. He was as gentle as he could possibly be and still they cried out. Iona gritted her teeth against their pain, her breathing growing hard and labored. She allowed herself a single second to absorb this pain before she marched forward with determination. Ice and cold pooled against her palms as she helped gently place the Fae across the back of her familiar.

She went along the barn, finding most of them huddled in a corner together. One by one, she put those that could fit across her familiar. Their skin bubbled on the surface and she loathed to even touch them. She bent to the body of a small Fae boy.

"This is going to hurt, okay?"

He didn't respond. She reached out but as her hands hovered over his body, she realized he wasn't breathing. Wasn't moving or groaning in pain like the others. Tears stung her eyes and trailed down her cheeks. Anger, visceral and deadly, rose up in her chest and begged to rip out in a scream. The boy... He was dead.

White noise drowned out the sounds of the agony, and Iona tilted her head up to the charred ceiling of the barn. A crow flew across and a feather drifted down. She watched its slow descent, following its path until it landed softly against the chest of the dead Fae boy. Right over his still heart.

And in the back of her mind, she heard the crow caw.

His ear drums rang with the deadly sound of a battle that wasn't meant to happen. Not like this. They were not supposed to be bested, they were supposed to go through victorious. But he had taken the wrong advice, listened to the wrong Fae, and now his people were suffering. Dying.

In the distance, he could see Julius felled. The giant of a Fae dropped to his knees, and it caused the ground beneath their feet to shake. Humans surrounded him with their weapons. They were slashed and cut through his skin. Julius roared, swinging his hands out blindly. But even he was not immune to the effects of iron. He was too weak and the humans too vicious. A streak of blood cut across his neck, causing a river of crimson to pool down his chest.

And Iona, she was nowhere to be seen, but a quick scent of the air and he smelt her magic at work. Ice and peppermint and apples.

Valerio could not stand by and watch as his friend was harmed. He narrowed his eyes and the magic he hadn't used in so long exploded into fragments of illusion. A monster of his own creation roared from Julius' chest and swiped out at the humans attacking. They screamed their fear, dropping away from the Fae and scrambling back as shadows broke apart into things of nightmares, clawing after them, wrapping around them.

In all actuality, there was nothing there. It was a fabrication, one Valerio twisted and weaved for his own pleasure. Their screams were a thing of beauty and he smiled cruelly, though the expression was borne of the madness that came at the price of using his magic.

He pushed his illusions further. There was no controlling the cruelty that built inside of him. He unleashed it, letting his anger and his rage take over. In the distance, he saw Iona and her familiar rush from the charred barn. On the back of the polar bear, there were Fae and Valerio could just make out their burnt skin. He could hear their cries of pain.

At the sight of her injured mate, Iona gave a cry and rushed to him, dropping to her knees at his side.

It was too much. The emotions that were heavy in the air clogged through his senses. They blinded him, and the madness was too close to keep at bay. All he knew was that he wanted the humans to pay. And because he already hated himself for his own mistakes, he shifted those emotions onto someone else he could take it out on. On the enemies he could kill.

A laugh escaped him. Crazy. He sounded it, he knew. And Uric hovered near him, his worry palpable. But Valerio could focus on nothing but the destruction the humans had wreaked. Illusions exploded all around the town. He pushed his magic. Past iron, even though it weakened the effects, the fabrications still flickered like ghosts or phantoms. Humans screamed and exited their homes. They gathered outside. A group of them. A whole town of them.

Them against Fae.

The Fae had never stood a chance, and now their numbers had dwindled even further.

He sensed Clay before he heard his cousin. He approached behind him, looking on with horror, but it didn't register in Valerio's brain. All he knew was his own feelings, his own anger and his own hatred.

He didn't turn to his cousin. "Kill them," he ordered.

He felt Clay startle behind him. "What?"

"Kill them all."

"Valerio—"

"I order you to kill them all."

Something tugged on his arm but he didn't budge. Confections and embers tickled his nostrils, and Shula appeared in his line of vision. "Valerio," she pleaded. "Please don't do this. There are innocents..."

"We were innocent," Valerio growled. "The Fae in that barn were innocent and look at them!"

Shula rocked back. "*Valerio...*"

"I am your king," he whispered, and it was the first time he acknowledged what they'd all crowned him to be. The first time he acknowledged his father's death as a sure thing. He did not regret it. He would not. "My word is the law. And this? This is your doing Shula Azzarh. Our people are dead because of you."

She stepped back and gasped, but he did not focus on her pain when everyone else's was so much stronger.

"Clay," he growled. "Do it."

His cousin stepped forward reluctantly, holding his hand forward. A sharp burst of pain came behind Valerio's eyes. He was weakening. His magic already taking its toll. He pulled back the illusions just as Clay gave a cry.

Red exploded throughout the town and one by one, the humans dropped to the ground. As quickly as they drew breath, it was stolen from them. As quickly as the blood in their veins pumped to their hearts, it was redirected out of their orifices until they collapsed.

Dead.

"It is done." Valerio laughed, and his companions turned to look at him sharply. With hatred, quite possibly, or something else. He did not care. "Let's go," he ordered. "Gather anyone of our own who are still alive. We cross the Arcana tonight."

He walked down the slope. Blood blanketed the ground, seeping into his boots. Black feathers dusted the pools of crimson, and in the stillness of death, a crow flew overhead, leaving behind a trail of feathers...

...and the creature cawed.

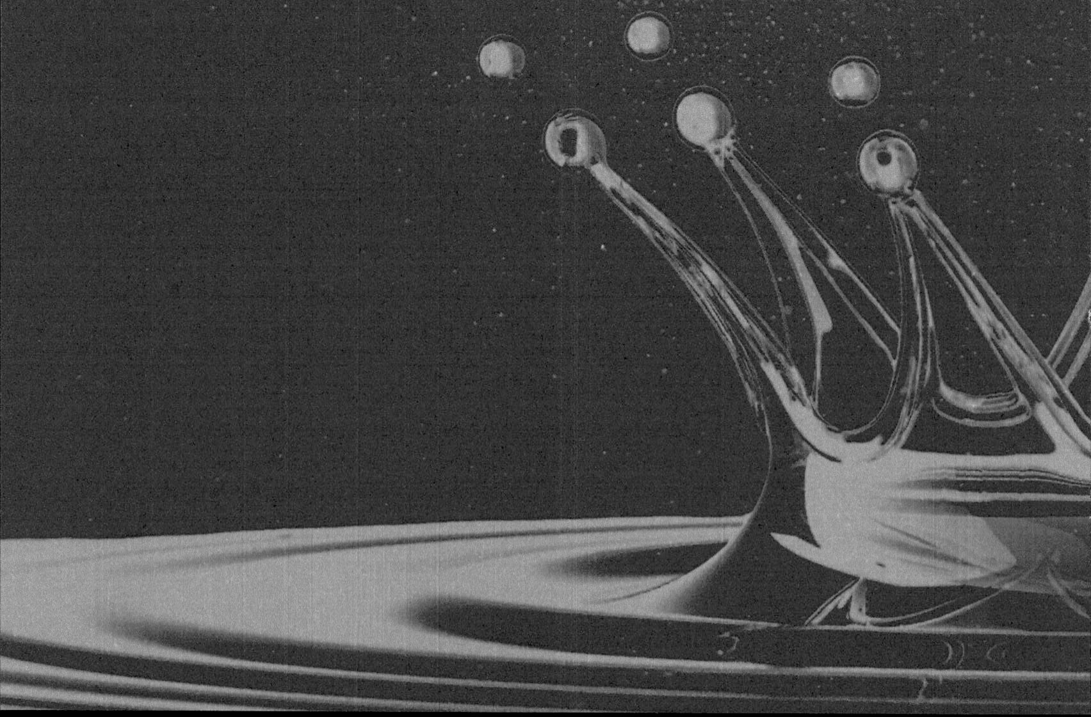

Heavy Head, Heavy Crown

The Arcana was steady, pushing the boat through the water with the lapping of its waves. It rocked slowly from side to side, lulling Shula into her thoughts. Her nails dug tightly into her palms and beneath her skin, her magic stirred. It was wakeful, caressing lines down her insides as if it was seeking both comfort and destruction. Just a reflection of her own tumultuous thoughts.

Guilt threatened to consume her whole. It was difficult not to take what Valerio said to heart. To let his words wash over her like the waves of the sea. But was he right? Had her actions led their people to death? People had died. Fae and human *both.* When would the killing end? All she'd wanted was for both sides to come out unscathed.

Why was it so hard to try and keep the peace? Why was it so hard to believe in *good*?

"Shula..."

She breathed out a sigh as Clay took the seat next to her. She leaned into him, the movement natural. She felt closest to Clay and he was always there when her emotions were a storm. He was always there to listen and offer an ear. It was easy to lean against him for comfort, even when it wasn't easy to forget the ease with which he'd killed the humans.

"You can't blame yourself," he whispered, voice tight. "We are all to blame. We all did things..."

"You killed all those people... innocent people..." She pulled away from him. Not from disgust. She wasn't sure it was possible she could ever be truly disgusted or horrified by the things he'd done. He'd been following orders, after all. It wasn't right. He'd fucked up, but he was right. They *all* had. It didn't make what he did the right thing, but she could see the haunting truth of it in his eyes.

He was disgusted with himself.

"I didn't kill them all," he whispered. A confession. "I swear, I didn't. I took enough blood to knock some of them unconscious. I did kill, but I did not kill them all."

She breathed a sigh of relief. Even still, those lives taken... She could tell they weighed on him. There'd been so much blood, her boots were still coated in it. Bile rose to the back of her throat at the thought. That someone's life force was still stuck to her. That the people she'd gotten killed were following her to remind her of her sins.

A shadow loomed over them, boots stepping into her vision. She followed the strong legs up to the harsh panes of Ryker's scarred face. Her mate jerked his chin, causing Clay to sigh. He pushed to a standing position, resting his hand on Shula's shoulder before he walked away, leaving her and Ryker alone.

Their gazes held.

Eyes on me.

She sighed as he bent in front of her. Kneeling like a knight, like a worshipper. His palms encircled her knees, holding her steady. It was comforting, which she had to admit was surprising. Usually when her emotions were this high, it was to Clay she turned to. It was Clay who could make her feel better.

"Shula," Ryker whispered. "I'm here."

I'm here. I'm listening.

Tears burned the backs of her eyes. If she needed any proof to how far her and Ryker's relationship had progressed here it was. He wasn't walking away from her. He wasn't chasing away her source of comfort only to leave her in the dark. He was here and he was trying. He wanted to listen, and she found that she wanted to tell him.

"I killed them," she whispered. A single tear slid down. "My advice killed them."

Ryker made a noise of disagreement. He didn't reach out to wipe away her tears but let her emotion show. "The humans would have died regardless."

"And the Fae—"

"They would have, too." That black eye flicked over her face. "We were outnumbered."

A sob wrecked its way free. "But they didn't deserve to die. None of them. Not the humans and not the Fae."

He met her with a level stare. "No," he agreed. "They didn't."

It was like a dam broke within her. The tears came in a stream of pain and regret. Her body crumpled forward, and Ryker caught her in his arms and held her close. Something clicked into place between them. Their jagged edges pressing together like they had a tendency to do. Every imperfect inch of him pressing against every imperfect inch of her.

He held her close, her lips moving against the crook of his neck. "Do you really mean that?" It somehow seemed very important in this moment that she knew the truth. If he was saying the words to be complacent to her emotions or if he honestly, truly believed them. She knew what he thought of humans. Knew his hatred for a lot of them ran deep. She didn't want him lying just to make her feel better. The truth was hard, but it was better than a lie. That was one thing her relationship with Ryker had taught her.

"Of course," he whispered. "I... I do not hate humans, and those betrayed us after we were lenient with them. I do not like them, but I do believe the conflict couldn't have been avoided. You should not blame yourself."

She pulled away to look into his face. She saw past the scars to the man underneath. Though, she admitted, she wasn't sure what Ryker would be without the scars. He wasn't the monster he thought he was. He could be kind when he wanted to be. When he tried.

"I told Valerio to trust them."

"And he chose to listen. That does not make it your fault." His thumb rubbed circles against her cheek. "Shula, for so long I have said that your ability to find empathy with the humans was a weakness, but I know now you just want peace. I am sorry it took me so long to realize this. I am sorry I could not see past my own prejudice. I won't lie; it might be difficult to get rid of, but I understand you. I understand your motives."

He always had, even if he couldn't accept them before. He could now. He was here, pulling her into his arms for comfort. And while his words eased something in her chest, she didn't think the guilt would ever leave. It would eat at her. It would consume her. It would make her question every decision she ever made.

"Maybe humans really are as terrible as you all make them out to be." Even as she said the words she couldn't believe them. There'd been humans in their group. There'd been Des, who had looked at Orna as if the sun rose and set upon her bright blue skin. Like she was a star in the sky and he meant to drown himself in wishes and light. There'd been the blacksmith who had freed her from her iron shackles without truly knowing her.

But for a moment, the negative, darker part of her believed that she'd been wrong. That there could not be peace between the two races. That they were destined, for now and forever, to despise one another.

"Eyes on me." Ryker grabbed her chin and pulled her in his direction. She hadn't even realized she'd looked away. "Don't," he growled. "Don't you dare let their hatred take anything else from you. Their hatred stole Mairin from me. It stole your parents from you. It nearly tore us apart. Don't let it shake this." His hand pressed to her chest. Right over the pounding of her heart. "Don't let their hatred take away your faith, your love, or your innate belief in goodness. Because when you believe, Shula, you make *me* want to believe too."

In a few short hours, they would arrive on the other side of the Arcana. Valerio stood at the edge of the ship, staring ahead at light of the rising sun. Mottled colors of purples and pinks and blues stained the sky like a bruise.

His breathing came out in silent, quick bursts of anger and guilt. The madness had already slipped from his mind, but the aftermath of it left him feeling too much yet hollow at the same time. Emotions were a conundrum and they weighed all too heavily. He felt that pressure on his head, like an invisible crown was perched over his brow, the heaviness of it threatening to snap his neck.

Then there was the rage. Boiling beneath his skin. It pressed against him like his magic was demanding a release. And he wanted to give into it. To scream at the sky for all the lives lost, dwindling his armies when they could have gone through unscathed. But Shula's idea...

"You fucking asshole." Clay's voice snapped him out of his thoughts. He turned sharply to glare at his cousin only to find the bastard glaring right back.

"Careful how you speak to me," he warned.

Clay's eyes rolled hard. "Or what? You'll use your magic on me? Go right fucking ahead if you think that's a battle you can win." The threat in his words was evident, and then there was the stirring of magic in the air. Valerio's blood ran beneath his skin, expanding through his veins. He gripped his chest as he felt his heart squeeze. "In a battle of magic, cousin, we know that mine is far greater than yours."

Valerio's eyes flicked up, catching sight of a rivulet of blood sliding down Clay's nose. The pain expanded through his body, making him gasp for breath. But as quickly as it rippled through him, it eased. Clay took a step back, not bothering to wipe at the blood spilling over his lips.

Valerio straightened, his eyes narrowing into thin slits. His canines elongated in threat and he gnashed them in his cousin's direction. "How dare you—"

"You're one to fucking talk, Val," he snapped. "What the fuck was that back there?" His voice rose and Valerio wondered if they'd garnered an audience. He felt the press of stares but avoided snarling at his people. He had already made a mistake of colossal proportions, he would not give them more reason to fear.

"Shula's plan—"

"Stop fucking blaming her, you dick!" Clay's palms met Valerio's chest and shoved. Valerio planted his feet on the ground, jerking back only a fraction.

"Put your hands on me again, Clay, and I will forget that we are cousins and take great joy in watching you writhe on the ground."

"Maybe if you got your head out of your ass..."

"*My* ass?"

Clay's mouth twitched. "Yes, you stupid bastard. You keep blaming Shula for that shit show back there, but you can never place the blame where it truly belongs. On yourself."

"You think I do not blame myself?" He threw his head back and barked out harsh laughter. "You know nothing. You have no idea what it means to rule. You've spent your entire life drinking and whoring. You don't know what it means to wear a crown."

"Oh, cousin..." Clay stepped forward, placing a palm against Valerio's shoulder. His expression fell into one of sympathy. "See these tears I cry for you, the poor baby Fae prince."

Valerio shoved him away. "Stop joking!"

"No, you stop joking! Mana, you're such a bastard. Why are you even blaming Shula?"

"It was her idea, her advice, that led to this."

Clay laughed, though the sound was entirely without humor. "Fucking idiot. Yes, she gave you the advice, but in the end it was yours to take or discard. You took it, and the fact of the matter is that Shula is not the ruler of the Fae. *You are.* So suck it up and take responsibility for what you did." He got quiet a moment then tore his gaze away as if looking at Valerio hurt too much. "My father told me that to rule, you had to look at the world like an enormous game of chess. You have to strategize, plan. If one piece falls, know how to fortify a strong front. The truth is, you didn't do that. You didn't strategize, you didn't plan."

Weylyn's words came back to him.

"A prince, or in your case a king, as you have so proudly paraded yourself, must exhaust every option. You were too complacent. Entirely too quick to trust that lord. And that, Seelie Prince, *will cost you dearly."*

Valerio bowed his head. "I know," he whispered. "I *know.* They are dead because of me."

"Because of *us,*" Clay corrected. "We all got lax. We all trusted too fucking easily because they seemed welcoming. But, cousin, you cannot keep shifting the blame onto others because it is the easier solution. That is not what it means to rule."

"And you know what it means to rule?"

His cousin shrugged. "I'm just a drunk whore. I don't know shit. But you fucked up and you need to own up to it. What you made me do..." He shook his head. "I do not relish in killing, and you forced my fucking hand."

Their gazes met and something in Valerio's chest fractured. He saw the torment in his cousin's bloodshot eyes. He'd put that expression there, all because he'd ordered him to kill. To murder. They'd killed his people, they were the enemy, and yet it disturbed something in Clay's soul.

All their lives, Valerio had known that Clay was one of the best of his family. He had his flaws like anyone else, but he was too kind to wield the destructive power that lived within him. And Valerio had made him use it for evil.

"They were trying to kill us," Valerio tried to reason, though the words sounded hollow in his own ears. "They hated us from the beginning, so it does not matter."

"Perhaps they hated us, but if you'd gone about it differently that could have changed. Your actions have only ensured that they hate us more."

He sighed and turned back to the horizon. The sky had lightened already. It was a new day, but Valerio still carried with him mistakes and guilt of days passed.

"Maybe you should be the one wearing the crown," Valerio mused.

Clay burst into laughter and slapped a hand against Valerio's shoulder. "I don't want that shit," he said. "It's too heavy even for my pretty head."

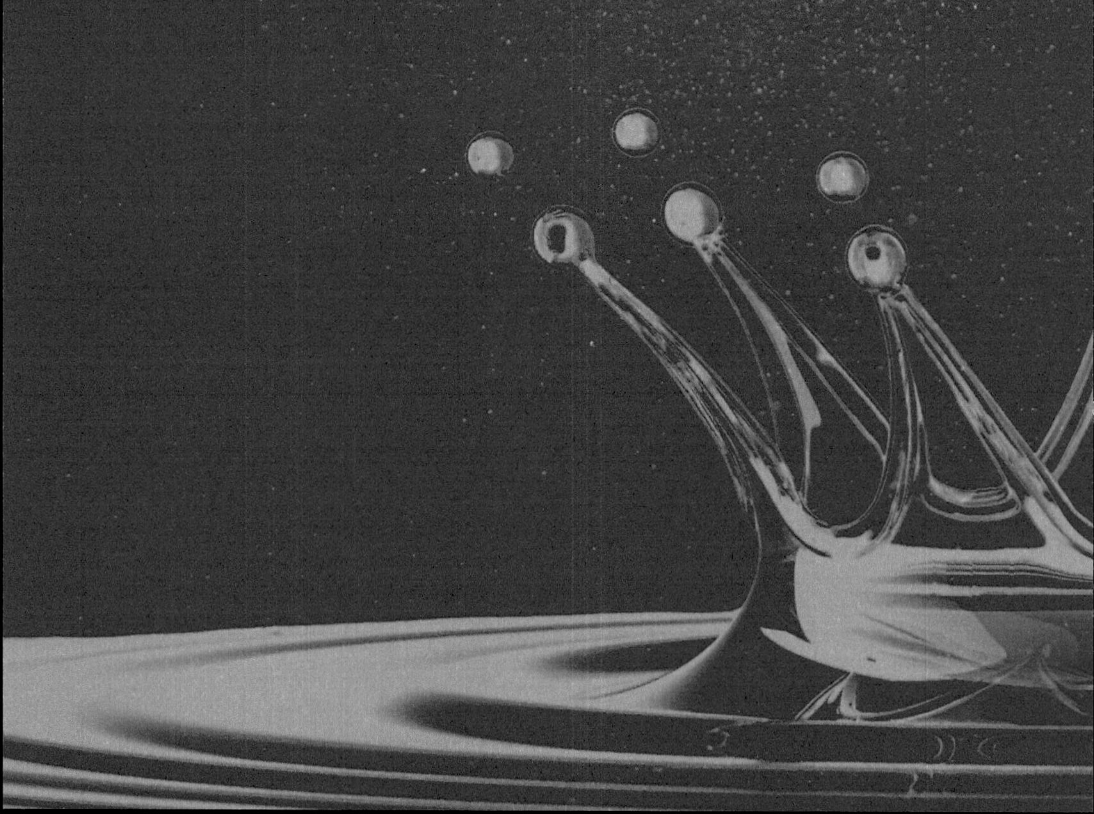

A Taste of Consciousness

They were down about three dozen Fae. In certain terms, it wasn't such a great loss considering a lot of the dead had been on the line between the living and afterlife anyway. And yet, every loss was just that. It hurt Iona's heart that so many had gone, dwindling their numbers even further.

Even so, they were still sizeable enough to be a small army. They nowhere near compared to the emperor's soldiers in quantity, but she had every faith that they would find more Fae in need of salvation and revenge.

They traveled slowly because their Fae were still injured. Julius had taken the brunt of the humans' hatred. He was still weak, the iron wounds slow-healing. But it didn't stop him from being his regular smiling self, at least. Iona's heart had almost stopped when she saw him surrounded by the humans and their weapons.

She'd seen him fight before, on the West Isles, surrounded by humans and their iron. He'd torn through them in his rage, busting through bone and skin like he was snapping twigs in half. But he'd had help then. This time he'd been alone and had gone down much quicker. Because of the iron in his side. Because of the wound at his neck that was slowly healing and making his voice hoarse. Because he'd dared to feel compassion even as they'd meant to kill him.

But he was okay, and that was all that mattered.

As an army, they laid low, traveling by night and resting during the day because Valerio said it would be safer. The Fae king spent his time in his tent, plotting their next moves in silence. He didn't consult anyone, and Iona wondered if it had to do with the advice Shula had given him. If he didn't trust himself to make the right decision when others whispered in his ear.

She'd gone near Shula herself, placing a hand on her shoulder in support. She knew it hadn't been Shula's fault, what had happened, and she knew that deep down Valerio knew that too. She didn't envy him his position, but she knew he couldn't do it alone. This war came with risks. No side would come out unscathed. They all had things to lose, but so much more to gain in the end. She understood that Valerio would take every loss personally, because these lives?

They were dependent on him. They rested on his shoulders. It was up to him to keep them safe.

Realistically, he couldn't keep everyone safe. If only the king would realize that and stop beating himself up over it.

When they finally reached Dana, they stopped along the outskirts of the kingdom near a city called Port Lays and set up camp.

Dana was hot, the wind drifting sand through the air. It was lush and bright, swathed in colors of golds, brown, blues, and porcelain. They were near smaller towns and surely there would be soldiers patrolling the kingdom.

"We will stay here indefinitely," Valerio declared. "All the Unseelie who are strong enough will take turns patrolling the camp and glamoring it in case any humans happen by." His eyes slashed across each of his closest friends. "All of you, come with me." He turned sharply, making his way towards his tent. He shoved the flaps aside and disappeared within.

The rest of them followed.

When they were inside the confining space, they all looked expectantly at their leader. His arms were crossed against his chest and his gaze swept down the line of them. They stopped on Shula and stayed long enough for a low growl to rumble through the tent on Ryker's behalf.

Valerio sighed. "I owe you an apology," he said.

Iona blinked at the words and fought back her own satisfied smirk. He looked as though admitting as much cost him, and Iona took great joy in that, almost as much as hearing the apology that Shula rightly deserved.

"I am your leader, and I need to take responsibility for what happens here on out. I will need to strategize better to avoid more incidents such as that one. I will take into account your ideas and advice in the future, but in the end the decisions will be my own, as the fate of the Fae is in my hands."

There was a beat of silence. Shula didn't speak. Not to accept or recognize his apology. Her stare on him was hard and unyielding. Iona was proud of her. It took a brave person to be that level of petty against a king.

He deserved every bit of it, too. She let him know that with her glare.

With a sigh, Valerio turned back to the rest of them. "That being said, we are in Dana and we need a plan to find the third Elemental."

Iona cracked her fingers with a smile. "I am so ready for it."

"Good," he said. "Because we leave to find them at first light."

•⋙—•♦•—⋘•

Weylyn loathed to suffer foolish people. None more than the Seelie Prince. The most foolish of all the Fae. He snapped his fingers at Weylyn and expected him to obey.

Have you located my father yet, Weylyn?

Come with us, Weylyn.

Are you reading my mind, Weylyn?

Are you giving up my secrets, Weylyn?

Pfft, as if the prince's brain were in any way interesting. He had read the thoughts of insects and found them far more invigorating and interesting than Valerio could ever be. He was a sad fool, with an even worse mind that Weylyn hated shifting through.

It felt like wading through shit.

Some minds were like that.

More chaotic than others. Each one savored differently; he touched the surface of them and felt a thousand different textures and flavors and emotions. For example, Shula's mind? It burned as hotly as her magic. It was strange to think about minds this way, but they were as unique as scents and the dips and curves of bodies. When Weylyn invaded minds, it was like his consciousness was reaching out for the other person's. He could glide his fingertips for surface thoughts or dig deeper, plunge his hands inside to rip thoughts from days ago. Years ago. Shula's was all warmth at the surface. Like standing before a campfire. When he plunged deep, he ached.

Iona's were wild like the snowstorms on Castle Aileach. They swirled and swirled, cold and biting and desperate for revenge. Sometimes there was a touch of softness inside, but more often than not, she was chaotic in her musings.

Weylyn rather liked Uric's mind. The hopeless, desperate thoughts of the sad sap made him smile every time. Uric's woes were like a sweet nectar that Weylyn drank up. The constant questions, the constant doubt, the constant pining after the prince who would never be his... His mind was sharp and violent, and Weylyn had always relished in the violence.

But Weylyn's favorite of them all was undoubtedly Clay's. The pretty little lord tasted like bubbling cider, the kind that burst magic on the tip of the tongue like back home. It made Weylyn ache for more. For home. For something he knew he could not have.

He was familiar with the different versions of consciousness of their minds. The Elementals savored of the powers they wielded with a touch of something more. It was similar to their scents, in a way. Warmth and confections and chocolate. Cold and mint and apples.

"Find the Elemental, Weylyn," Valerio ordered.

Because every time Shula and Iona tossed the stones on the map, it landed in a single area. Port Bay. And Port Bay was a bustling city. Perhaps he could have let the Elementals be guided by their own buzzing, by their own humming magic beneath their skin.

But Weylyn had stupidly smirked as they strategized how they were going to find the third Elemental and caught the irritation of the Seelie prince.

"That is, if you can."

Never one to wither back from a challenge, Weylyn let his magic loose. Distantly, before his eyes rolled to the back of the head, he heard someone whisper.

"He can do that?"

"I do not have to be touching someone or be in close proximity with someone to read their thoughts. Just like I do not have to have met them beforehand."

There was silence and he found satisfaction in that before he plunged into the deep depths of unconsciousness. It was a scary thought for them. That he could read any thought, from anyone, anywhere. He did not usually stretch his mind so far. The risks were always far greater than the reward. But in this case, he did not want to give the Seelie Prince the satisfaction.

Besides, he liked causing unrest.

He could feel their questions burning through their minds.

"Why didn't he do that before?"

Simply because he did not want to.

Simply because he liked to watch them suffer.

Fuck their wishes. He was not their lap dog, and some secrets he liked keeping close. Well, this one was out now. Cold calculation on his part, he supposed.

His mind drifted, traveling at lightning speed through the various cities of Dana. He was not sure how it was possible, how he could send his mind across places he'd never been or seen. But it had nothing to do with location and everything to do with souls and minds and the conscious thoughts. It was like blindly casting out a net into the water, and reaching for the one that felt right.

Hundreds, thousands of minds slipped past him. All in different tastes and textures that didn't feel quite right. He was looking for the Elemental. The third. He was not sure what this one would smell like, so he kept his senses open for something similar to earth, air, or water. What spirit felt and smelled like, he could not be sure, but failure was not an option for him.

Not when throwing the response back at the Seelie's face would be gratifying.

His net cast out, reaching further and further until it latched onto something. Like a fish ensnared, the conscious wriggled against him. It was a slight invasion; one they would scarcely feel if he was careful. He ran his fingertips across it, tasting sea salt on his tongue and something else. Water in all its forms. Ponds, oceans, depths unknown. There was something completely tranquil about it, and he smiled as he reached out into the mind.

He caught flashes moving quickly. Flashes of a roaring ocean beneath a balcony. Of pale, golden hair like wheat drifting in the breeze. Of pillars and an opulent ballroom. Of the flash of a body in a mirror and atop a head...

A crown.

Weylyn sucked in a breath and was hauled back into his body. He opened his eyes and the first words he spoke were, "She tasted like sea salt."

The others stared at him with varying expressions of severity. He ignored them, choosing to smooth out the wrinkles in his shirt instead.

"So you found her?" This came from Iona.

He took in a slow breath, his ringed fingers pulling the length of his long braid.

"If you could find Elementals all this time with that magic of yours, why the fuck didn't you do it sooner?" Clay complained.

"Because finding them is your mission, not my own. Besides, it is never a sure thing when I try it. There are too many minds, and while a lot of them are similar, Elementals have a particular... brand on them that make them easier to make out. Yet it is dangerous." He did not elaborate. Let them not know his weaknesses. Let them not know why doing so was perilous. So they could never use it against him.

And let them not know how he only did so now just to spite the prince.

Although he suspected Valerio knew, with the way he glared. "So?" the prince demanded.

This brought on Weylyn's smirk. "So," he drawled. "You will never believe who, or what, the third Elemental is."

Dana

Port Bay was alive in the most spectacular way. Life was bustling, bodies choking up every crevice of the streets. Vendors were lined up in rows. Humans hawking their wares. Scents of oranges and fish filled the air, a very heady combination.

"Ugh." Iona wrinkled her nose. "Fucking fish."

They had slipped in between buildings to scope out the city. Their hoods were drawn over their heads, casting shadows over their faces and the expressions they wore; Iona's of disgust as her nose tilted up in the air, and Shula's of something that seemed quite like a mixture of awe and horror.

The others hovered behind them.

Ryker, Julius, Clay, and Weylyn. Valerio had stayed behind to watch over the camp with Uric. If they found themselves in trouble, all Weylyn had to do was send a mental message to Uric, who would open a portal to safety.

"There are Fae here," Julius whispered, leaning over Iona to get a look at the bustling on the streets.

It was true. It was part of the reason Shula felt rising horror in her chest. Fae were just... openly walking around. A majority of the people milling around them were *Fae*.

"So it's safe to walk around Dana with our hoods off?" Clay started to pull his off, but Shula caught his arm before he could.

"Don't," she warned. "Look at what all the Fae are wearing around their necks."

Iron collars choked at their skin. Beneath the gleaming metal, she caught sight of raised flesh spiderwebbing their skin in scars wrinkled with age.

"They're slaves," Shula whispered.

"Fuck," Julius cursed, his voice low and hoarse. "We'll have to keep our hoods up, keep a low profile. We don't know what could happen." His bright gaze darted wildly in thought. "Okay, we need to split up in smaller groups to find an easier way to make it to the castles. Iona and Shula, Clay and Weylyn, and Ryker and I." He waited for everyone to nod their agreement before he continued, "Weylyn will check in every ten minutes to make sure everyone is okay." Then he flashed a feral smile in his mate's direction. "We can make a game of it if you're up for the challenge."

Iona snorted, a beatific light in her eyes. "You're on. And don't think we'll take it easy on you just because you're *injured*, either."

"Wouldn't dream of it."

After a few more words back and forth, they dispersed, separating into groups to setting out into the city. Shula pulled her cloak tightly around herself as she walked forward, careful with any jostling movements so it wouldn't fall from her head and expose her ears. They moved carefully and with purpose.

They knew a few things from Weylyn. One, the next Elemental wielded water. He gave no explanation other than it was in her scent. Two, she was female. Three, she resided in the castle of Port Bay. He wasn't sure which one, which was why Shula and Iona would guide them there with their own connection.

Port Bay had three castles, each one set on a high cliff overlooking the Lagnh Sea. They sat side by side, pillared, opulent structures that could be seen from down in the city. It looked like it would take a long climb to reach them, but Shula knew they couldn't just walk up to the castle and knock on the doors.

They needed to find another way in.

She couldn't believe that the Fae they were looking for was at the palace. She'd wondered aloud if she wasn't trapped or a servant or slave, but Weylyn had shaken his head adamantly at her inquiries.

"I saw a crown," he'd said, and there was delight in his voice. As if seeing a flash of a crown had been all it took to convince him that the Fae was somehow royalty. But she wouldn't pretend to know his mind and his magic better than him.

But after spending a few minutes in the shadows of Port Bay, they'd heard the whispers of a Fae princess up at the castle.

So maybe he wasn't a total liar.

Bodies rammed into Shula from all angles. She felt a tug on the hem of her cloak. Probably street urchins looking to pilfer from her pockets. Her hands went to grasp at the cloth, and as they left the neck of her hood and traveled lower, she felt a hard yank and the hood slipped from her head.

Exposing her ears.

Fuck.

She quickly tried to pull it up, though her fingers trembled with the move. The crowd was too bustling, perhaps no one would see her...

Shula stopped in her tracks as the people parted in front of her and a single person was made known. She felt the world slow for a second at their approach. So familiar, it felt like she was lost in time, in another time that no longer belonged to her. One before the Resistance, before Iona and Orna taught her the true meaning of friendship. Before when she'd taken scraps of affection without realizing it for the true abuse that it was. Before she'd known her own worth.

She never imagined what it would be like to come face to face with her again. Now that she did, she could see the burning hatred of her eyes, hear the clinking of the bag of coins as it was tossed into her hand, and feel the effects of ashwood in her blood.

"Fanny..." The word came out strangled. It gave Iona pause some distance away, as if realizing that Shula wasn't following anymore.

Shula wasn't sure who met who in the middle. She just knew that between one moment and the next, Fanny was in front of her, sneering, though a hint of surprise lived in her pixie-like features.

"Shula?" It sounded more like a demand. Like Shula was a plague and not a person.

Suffocated with memories, Shula tried to hold her head high as she met her gaze. As her fingers finished pulling the hood over her head. Betrayal swarmed her all over again. Just the memory of it was a wound that was suddenly ripped open with a knife.

"Fanny."

"How—?" She broke off, shaking her head. "Soldiers are looking for you. I see you got away."

How was this happening? How was Fanny standing before her conversing as if nothing had happened between them? As if something even existed between them after her betrayal? She still looked at Shula with hatred, with disgust. It was no different from the last time they'd seen one another.

Fanny wore simple traveler's clothes, rolled up at the sleeves. She'd probably come to the market to purchase more ribbon or accompany the food vendors to purchase meats for the circus. It didn't matter, though. What mattered was that Shula's tongue felt glued to the roof of her mouth.

Shula wanted to speak, but all her words died. Words about how she'd never been a true friend. Even before she'd known Shula was Fae, Fanny had degraded her, had laughed, had victimized herself in certain situations to make Shula appear the villain. She wasn't selfless or kind. She was petty and mean. So unlike Orna. So unlike Iona.

Over Fanny's shoulder, Iona leaned close, her dark eyes flashing. The sudden proximity had Fanny startling. "*This* is Fanny?" Iona asked. The joviality had gone from her voice; it now dripped with anger. "Fucking Fanny."

"Who the fuck are you?" Fanny's voice rose almost to a shriek. The simple sound had Iona's hand slapping down against her mouth, her other arm yanking her backwards through the throng of people. There were so many that nobody seemed to pay them any mind as they pulled Fanny into a side-alley. She barely struggled and Iona didn't release her until they were in the shadows. She shoved her against the wall with a snarl.

"I can either be your best friend or your worst nightmare," Iona whispered.

But Fanny was too stupid for her own good. Her hands reached up to shove Iona's shoulders, though Iona didn't budge. And Shula could only watch like a silent spectator.

She hated how she had lost her voice. How she was filled with such uncertainty.

"Crazy Fae bitch," Fanny said.

Iona laughed and took a step back, giving Fanny the illusion of space. Her head tilted in Shula's direction. "So, what do we do?"

She knew what Iona was really asking. Her friend knew the whole story. She knew how Fanny had betrayed her by turning her into the emperor's soldiers, who then took her to the Brotherhood. Shula answered honestly. "I don't know."

A flash of sympathy in Iona's expression. "She will betray us."

"I know."

She would. If they let her go, Fanny would run to the nearest authorities and let them know there were wanted Fae to be found in the market. It would be chaos. It was a wonder she wasn't screaming now, though Fanny had always thought herself more powerful than others. She was too cocky. Too confident. Looking into her eyes now, Shula knew what truth lay behind Fanny's eyes. She thought Shula weak and disgusting just like she always had.

"Do you want to...?" Iona trailed off.

Do you want to kill her?

Yes. Shula did want to kill Fanny. She wanted to hurt her the way that she'd been hurt. Betray her the way she'd been betrayed. She'd been able to put what Fanny had done behind her. Yes, the ache was there, but it wasn't as if she was sad because she missed Fanny. Not when she knew she'd never been a real friend to her.

The injustice of what had happened made her chest rise and fall with emotion she couldn't conceal. And how pathetic was that, she thought? "She ruined me." She hadn't meant to speak aloud.

Fanny was a big reason Shula found it so hard to trust. The pain was a reminder. It was sharp and vicious. She wondered if it would always be there. If it would always be the reason she couldn't go near others. If it would make it hard for her to open up to people because she feared that betrayal.

She'd trusted the Fae, but she wasn't sure if it was full trust or if she gave it out in snippets. Was that why she couldn't touch Ryker without recoiling in fear and nerves? Was she still living in that past?

"I'm angry," she said again.

"You have a reason to be," Iona agreed.

"No, she doesn't!" Fanny cried out in a harsh whisper. "She's Fae! She's illegal and disgusting, and so are you!"

Once, those words would have hurt her heart. Now, she stared at Fanny. Really stared at her and realized something. If it hadn't been for Fanny, she never would have met the Resistance. She never would have met Ryker and her friends. She never would have found herself. She'd still be living in uncertainty, in the shadows of her terrible past.

She couldn't help but think of Ryker then and his own anger. He had held onto that for years, letting it mar the skin on his body, twisting and distorting him until his insides had been just as twisted as the evidence of his hatred for the emperor. He'd let it fester for years. He had let it alter his treatment of Shula just like she'd let her fear rule her.

And it was then she realized she didn't want to be that way. She didn't want any more of those negative emotions getting in the way of her future. Of her relationships. He was changing and so was she, and Shula knew she didn't want to regress back to what she'd been before.

"I don't want to be angry anymore."

And she felt like she could finally let it go.

Shula took a breath. "I don't want to kill her." It would only stain her hands.

Iona gave her a nod, and Fanny seemed to breathe her own sigh of relief. "Good," she trilled. "Now let me go."

Iona laughed. "Who said we were letting you go?"

Fanny blinked. "But she—"

"She isn't going to kill you." Her hand lifted and caressed the side of Fanny's cheek. "But Shula has always been a much better person than me. And I? I like revenge served cold."

Magic prickled in the air and before Fanny could scream, it enveloped her from the neck upwards, ice encasing her entire head. And Iona was a blur, a sword appearing in her hand that she swung with all her might. It hit the side of Fanny's head causing her to shatter like fragile glass.

Her body slumped to the ground, pieces of her head scattered against her prone form. They were little more than shards, the magic holding them together. How strange, Shula mused, that someone could be reduced to pieces within a single moment.

"I hope you won't be upset with me for that," Iona said as the sword in her palm sprinkled into wisps of snow. "I just really hated that bitch."

"It's fine."

"She would have turned us in the minute our backs were turned for a sack of coins. I'm not sorry and won't be sorry."

"You did what you had to do. Just because I didn't want to kill her myself doesn't mean I'm upset that you did it."

It surprised her how true that felt. She would not mourn Fanny. She hadn't cried when she'd been betrayed, and she wouldn't cry now that she was dead.

"We should go," Shula urged. "We have to find a way to the castle."

Iona didn't argue as they stepped out of the alley with caution in their steps. They didn't speak to one another as they pushed through bodies, trying to get out of the city. Their trek was slow and demanding, and after a while, the crowd started thickening with soldiers.

Sweat prickled against Shula's skin beneath the cloak she wore. She felt eyes on her, exposed in a way she hadn't felt before.

"We look out of place," Iona hissed, seeming to read Shula's thoughts. "We're wearing fucking cloaks and everyone else is practically naked. Plus, I'm sweating."

"We should climb the cliffs," Weylyn's voice slammed into their mind, quietly laced with amusement as if he'd somehow been listening in on their conversation. He appeared like an apparition in their minds, making goosebumps climb over Shula's covered arms.

"That is the worst idea I've ever heard," Iona snapped.

"Is it? We could trek through the city of you wish, risk more soldiers discovering us. Or climb the cliffs, where I am sure there are no soldiers stationed at all."

"And how do you know that?"

The image of him flicking his fingers and smiling appeared in their heads. The Fae was a mystery and not easily read no matter how hard Shula tried.

"The cliffs are dangerous," Julius weighed in, his voice sounding misty and far away. *"We could fall to our deaths."*

Weylyn's chuckle echoed like a sinister voice in shadows. *"Then I suggest you hold on tight."*

The rock was wet and slippery against Weylyn's grasp. The Lagnh Sea roared, splashing waves against the side of the cliff, and the sunlight beat down from the sky, unrelenting and cruel. But he had suffered fates far crueler than this, so it did not bother him quite like it bothered the others.

He found a firm hold and began to climb up higher. He was not sure if the smallest castle was where the Elemental Fae was, but it was closest, and they would start there. Besides, just beyond the edge of the cliffs there were trees and bushes, greenery they could hide behind instead of being out in the open and under the blind eye of human soldiers like at the market.

This plan was better than walking through the city. All they'd had to do was veer down to the beach and follow the coast up to the rocky cliff side. The rest was smooth climbing from there.

"Fuck, fuck, fuck," Clay cursed from his side.

Weylyn chanced a look in that direction and smirked as Clay nearly slipped. "Having trouble, Lord Valentino?" he mocked. He couldn't help himself. Clay was so fun to tease.

"Mana save me, you're like a fucking spider," Clay retorted breathlessly.

"I'm just very good at climbing." To prove a point, he went up, up... Then looked down with a smirk at the other Fae. They were all breathing heavily and carefully maneuvering their way up. Clay though looked green.

"Show off!" he called out.

"Do not worry yourself unnecessarily, Clay. If you fall, I will catch you."

The others blinked up at him as though surprised by his easy banter with the other Fae. Weylyn just smirked. Let them wonder what his true mask was. They would never guess it, never know. Besides, it was so easy to speak with the other Fae rather than the others. Ever since they'd nearly died together at Castle Aileach. The both of them had been trapped on a ledge, looking at a chasm of chaos below. Something about the prospect of your own imminent demise seemed to bring people together. In this case, it made them more susceptible to teasing than ever before.

"If I fall, I'm taking you with me, asshole," he grumbled.

Weylyn's laugh was drowned out by the crashing waves. The rest of the way was made in silence. Weylyn reached the top first, jumping over the edge of the cliff with nimble feet and landing in a crouch. He rolled, scooting and hiding behind the shrubbery and waited for the others so they could do the same.

Up close, the veritable castle gleamed against the sunlight. The pillars shone as if made from polished porcelain and chips of alabaster. Servants milled about on the grounds, cutting through grass and sand, walking beneath wisteria plants carrying baskets of foods and laundry.

"Well?" Iona demanded in his ear, her voice harsh.

He turned to meet her icy gaze with a stony one of his own. Iona despised him. She'd proven so by breaking his nose, though that had been more to keep his mouth shut regarding her treachery rather than actual hatred. He admired that strength in her. Though she would regret doing what she'd done and her treatment of him.

Eventually.

She was also obviously annoyed that he had this hidden power within him, casting out and sensing thoughts, and had not mentioned it before. His secrets were his own, though, and no one would steal them from him. Their secrets, however, were like plump fruit hanging from branches, begging to be picked. Like the fact that he could pick up the truth. She already had the answer she wanted. It was that Elemental connection they shared. She just wanted to take him for a fool.

He turned away from her and back to the grounds, peering between bushes at the human and Fae slaves milling about. He cast the net of his magic out, reaching for the minds of those in front of them. He shifted through their thoughts like piles of wriggling fish, batting the more festering ones away.

Flashes were caught in his mind.

Princess Corvina.

Prince Reginald.

Sick.

Locked away.

Thoughts swirled. Some cruel in their glee for what was happening to the Fae princess of this castle. Others, the kinder ones, filled with worry over her fate. There was one among them... One that would serve their purpose.

He went back to his own mind and sucked in a breath. "That servant." He pointed to the young woman walking slowly across the grounds with a basket of laundry. "She will lead us to the Elemental."

"You're sure?" Iona sounded skeptical. An unnecessary sentiment, he was sure.

"I am positive. Shall I retrieve her?" But he was already standing. Already moving despite their hissing protests. He was a blur to human eyes as he darted forward and grasped the servant around the waist. The basket in her arms dropped. She let out a cry that he muffled behind his palm before he was running back to their hiding place. She fell to the grass, Weylyn looming over her with his hand against her mouth.

He could read the fear on her expression. He didn't need to read her thoughts to know.

"Do not fear," he said, but her heart was pounding against his chest like a caged animal wanting to break free from its confines. Her eyes dilated with fear, a wild look overcoming them as they darted between the Fae looming over her.

"What the fuck, Weylyn?" Iona hissed. "You're frightening her."

He ignored the ice Elemental and stared down at the servant. "You are safe," he assured her, his tone soothing. "We will not harm you. We require your help. If I remove my hand, will you scream?"

She gave a tremulous shake of her head.

"Very good," Weylyn praised and slowly removed his hand from her mouth.

True to her word, she didn't scream, but she took in their ears, the ethereal beauty, and the obvious lack of collars.

"W-what do you want?" There was only a slight tremor in her voice. How brave, she was.

Weylyn did not move from her body, but kept her weighted down on the ground with his thighs. "We want to know where they are keeping the Fae princess."

Her eyes widened and she tried to scramble away from him, her nails digging into the dirt. "Whatever you want with her, I won't give it to you!" she hissed.

Iona made a snickering sound of approval.

"I commend you for your loyalty," Weylyn drawled. "But we do not want to harm her." He leveled her with a stare. "We want to save her."

This gave her pause. Her eyes darted between them again, taking them in all over again. Minutes went by as she assessed them, measuring them up in her mind.

"Let me up." He obeyed, pushing away from her body as she sat up, leaning against a trunk of a tree. After a couple of deep breaths, she shook her head back and forth. "This is crazy. Positively crazy."

"That's us," Clay flashed her a smile. "A crazy group of friends trying to do good by the world."

Her laugh was strangled, but he didn't miss the shine in her eyes as she took in Clay. Weylyn supposed that pretty face came in handy in moments like these. Who needed to torture answers from a person when a pretty face sufficed?

"Is it even crazier that I believe you?" the servant asked, leaning her head back against the tree. "I don't know how you evaded the guards, but if you are looking to save Princess Corvina, then you will have a difficult time of it."

"We have had difficult lives. We are used to trials and tribulations," Iona answered.

"She is locked up."

"But... but she's a princess!" Shula gasped.

"A princess who lied to her husband and is suffering the consequences in the dungeons." The servant pushed aside errant strands of hair. "The rest of the staff thinks me daft and frivolous, but I care for the princess. She is kind and does not deserve ill treatment. So if you promise not to harm her, then I will help you. I hear Fae are magically bound when they make oaths."

Only Unseelie Fae. No one said that, though.

"We would never hurt her," Clay declared adamantly. "We promise we would never do that."

She measured his words carefully and seemed to believe him. "Then I will help you."

"Just like that?" Shula cut in skeptically. "How do you know we aren't evil with nefarious plans?"

"Shula, babe, you aren't helping," Clay muttered.

The servant waved his words away with a soft chuckle. "You're Fae and you aren't collared. Plus I get this feeling..."

"It's Mana." Iona's eyes widened. "Mana is with us."

Weylyn fought back an eye roll. Iona was too overzealous with her beliefs. She would find a sign from Mana if an animal whizzed by and let out a flatulence near her. It was irritating.

"You're the Fae Resistance, aren't you?" she whispered.

Clay gifted her with a smile as the answer.

"What do you need from me?" Her eyes went bright with steely determination.

"We need access to the castle. A pathway to free her from the dungeon. And we need her to be ready to come with us."

The servant nodded. "I will make sure she is ready." She stood and smoothed down her skirts. "I will meet you here tomorrow. Please, do not get caught."

And then she was gone.

"Can we trust her?" Julius asked skeptically.

"Yes."

They could. Her thoughts, while shallow on the surface, held an edge of something deeper just beneath. Of something caring. Different from others he'd invaded. It would not be in her nature to betray them. He had noted that immediately.

She cared for Princess Corvina Rhian, High Lady of the Gold Court.

And strangely, after looking through her thoughts, so did Weylyn.

The next day, they met the maid in the bushes once again. Only this time, there was a fearful air about her. Almost desperate.

"What has happened?" Iona demanded the moment they caught sight of her trembling body.

The servant sniffed and pushed aside strands of hair. "My lady is getting worse. He's feeding her food laced with ashwood. She's skin and bones and can barely open her eyes. If you are going to save her, you must do it now. I fear..." She let out a sob. "I fear if you do not, she won't last the night."

Clay let out a curse, and Iona felt cold rise up inside her chest. For years, she'd witnessed injustice being done throughout the world. For years, she had seen Fae fall to the tyranny of humans and die. It was why she had not hesitated in ending Fanny on Shula's behalf. It was why she charged into war with a smile on her face. They would not lose the Elemental. She refused to let her life go by knowing that there was something they could have done to stop it.

So they would protect her.

They would break her out.

And they would bring the emperor to his fucking knees.

"Can you clear a pathway for us?" Iona asked, a plan already forming in her mind.

The servant sniffled. "I can. But we must hurry. The prince is up to something. I know it."

Iona looked to her friends, giving them all firm nods. "We go in. We go in now and we go in together."

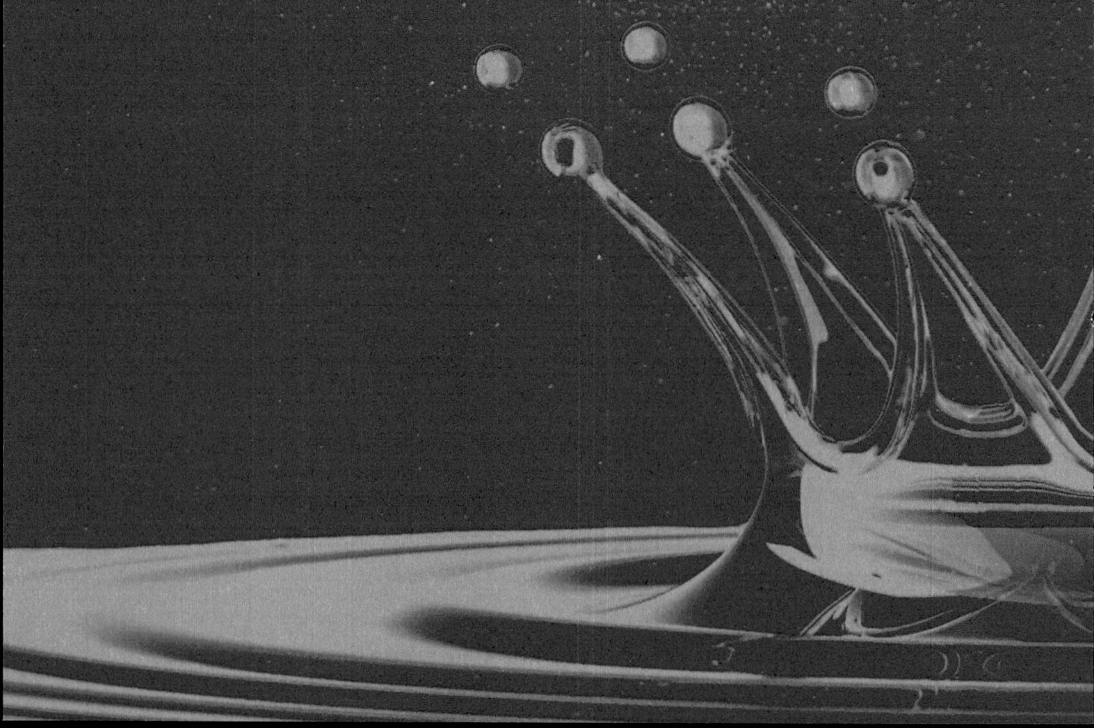

Liberation

Clay rubbed a hand across his chest and winced.

"You okay?" Shula eyed the action with pulled brows.

He dropped his hand but the moment he did, that strange ache built up in his chest again, nearly making him reach for his chest to rub at it once more. "I'm fine," he said. But he didn't feel fine, and he doubted she believed the words.

He just felt... strange. Like something was stirring beneath his blood. A calling of some sort. Like an invisible string was tugging, yanking, demanding his attention. And he wanted to give in, but he wasn't sure what that sensation wanted exactly.

The castle was quiet beyond, quieter than it had been before. He wasn't sure what it meant. Perhaps the servant had cleared the way for them, but they wouldn't know until she gave them a signal of sorts.

He felt bad referring to her as 'the servant'. She had a name, though none of them had bothered to ask her what it was. That didn't sit well with him, but they had more important things to worry about. Like this Elemental. How she was trapped. Locked away by an angry husband.

Just the thought of what she was going through made rage splinter through his chest and rise. His blood boiled, magic stirring as if begging to be unleashed. And he would. When he came face to face with the bastard that mistreated the woman, he would end them.

Women were too fierce to be kept within a box. They were too wild to be kept in a cage. Intelligent, beautiful. His mother had been confined in her own little prison back before the courts fell. Though her prison was never as confining as Valerio's mother's, it was still suffocating. He watched her wither until his father died, and even then it had seemed like she could never break free.

His father had never been physically cruel to his mother. Yet there was no love between them, as it usually was in those types of marriages. He did have a way of using cutting words, though. From a young age, Clay had watched it unfold and knew he didn't want to see that dimness in a woman's eyes. Ever. He vowed to always make them smile. To make them happy.

They dealt with so much, endured such hardships as opposed to men, and the least he could do was give them that.

So he would give this Fae her revenge if that's what she desired. And he would make her smile. This he vowed.

A sharp whistle rang from across the yard. From a great distance away, they caught a ruffle of skirts and a pale face peek at them from behind a pillar.

"It's time." Iona stood to her full height. "Do you feel the connection, Shula?"

Shula stood. "I do."

"Then let's go find her."

They led the charge with their mates flanking behind them and at their sides, weapons already drawn. Weylyn and Clay brought up the rear. While Clay wanted to forge ahead, his determination heightening with every footstep forward—that ache in his chest growing stranger and more prominent as well—he let them take the lead. This was a sort of camaraderie for the Elementals. It was their mission, their purpose, and so he would stay back.

He understood the importance of bonding. It was in all sorts of things. In fucking, drinking, fighting. For them, it was finding one another.

They made it inside the castle, meeting the servant in the middle. Her breathing was hard; she looked fearful but determined. "I told the guards the prince had need of them. They don't know he's not at the castle presently. The servants are also otherwise occupied. We must hurry!" She turned, lifted her skirts, and ran.

She went down twists and turns of hallways and they didn't pass a single soul. Each step led them closer, and each step made Clay's breath come out harder.

"You okay over there or are you about to faint?" Weylyn teased.

Clay was jerked from his thoughts. He would not get used to Weylyn teasing him, but before he could come up with a proper retort, they were intercepted by guards.

And the real fun began.

"Keep going," Julius growled at his mate, Shula, and the servant moments before he charged at one of the soldiers. Ryker went for the other. They were a clash of steel and iron. While they took care of the guards, Weylyn and Clay went forward after Iona and Shula. They were charging down a part of the castle that veered off from porcelain to stone.

"Down here," the servant said, pointing at a door. "But there are guards."

"We'll take care of them." Clay stepped forward and his booted foot shot against the door. It burst inwards and he charged down the stairs where he met with more guards. He cleaved through them with a ferocity he didn't know he possessed, the magic inside him demanding. He answered the call of his blood. To save and protect.

The iron weakened him, but he pushed forward anyway, dodging the whizzing blade by a hairsbreadth. It sliced off the delicate ends of his hair, and he was slammed against a wall. His sword swung out, piercing through the exposed part of the soldier's neck. He slumped to the ground. Weylyn was finishing off the other one and they went ahead, clanging and fighting their way through men while Iona and Shula zipped past them. As if they weren't there at all.

And when all the guards were discarded, Clay and Weylyn made their way down the end of the dungeons. People were silent behind the bars, pressing themselves up against them and watching with leering, dead eyes. They looked half starved, skin clinging to bone and dirty, tattered rags clinging to their frames. He wondered what crimes they committed or why the prince of the castle deemed them criminals and threw them in here.

He tore his gaze away from them and followed the scent of magic. Confections and embers, peppermint and ice. And there were others scents too. The scents of the prisoners, but the Fae always had sharper smells, more prominent ones, and he scented one just beneath Iona's and Shula's.

There was the crackling of Iona's ice magic, and then their voices rang through the iron. Their words—Iona's and Shula's—confident. And there was that third voice. Tremulous. Weak. His chest ached and he rubbed it despite the blood coating his hands and staining his clothes as he approached.

"We are friends."

There was a gaping hole where iron bars should have been, having been melted into a pool on the ground, which was covered in ice and snow. Iona and Shula stood in the center of the dungeon, peering down at the Fae on the ground.

Clay stepped into the room, trying for levity in a situation that was tense and tragic. "It still surprises me to see your magic against iron."

They ignored him, rightfully so, hovering over the female. His heart beat faster in his chest when Shula's body angled away and he finally got sight of the woman. Her body was broken, for lack of a better word. Her face was swollen and battered, her skin raised on her ankles where iron manacles were clamped down on her.

Blonde hair strung against her cheeks. Her lips were swollen and cracked. She looked dead, like she'd suffered such a great deal, and that familiar rage at the sight of a harmed woman came surging up. His chest tightened with that same discomfort, and the moment Iona used her magic to break the manacles from her ankles, Clay was dropping to his knees beside her, pulling her gently into his arms, holding her with reverence.

She smelt like sea salt and water. Like oceans and ponds and coconut and something citrusy. The scent of her tingled through his nose, and he found himself inhaling deeply before he caught himself.

The woman—Princess Corvina's—eyes fluttered open, and that flare in his chest intensified as she looked at him. Their eyes met and his breath caught.

She opened her peeling lips and rasped, "My son..."

Before she fainted in his hold.

Drowning Magic and Mating Bonds

Corvina felt herself drifting in and out of lucidity. Words rasped from her sore throat, begging for the one person she wanted above all others. The one she worried for. The one that was being taken from her.

"My son..."

Blackness danced behind her vision and she gave into it for a moment. A single moment, because there was a voice in her head. Her own, or someone else's she couldn't be sure, telling her to be strong. To wake up. To find Basil and protect him from Tobias.

It was hard, but she managed to pry her eyes open a fraction. As she did, only light registered for a moment and a weightlessness that made her wonder if she were dead. But no. Her eyes adjusted and the first thing she saw was the face of the most beautiful man she'd ever seen. A golden-brown halo of hair surrounded his head in twisted wisps. Eyes, green like chips of ice, like the sea, stared down at her. Though he wasn't smiling, dimples concaved his cheeks and chin.

"My son," she repeated, pushing aside the stupor his looks threatened to pull her under. "I need to find my son." She no longer felt the manacles around her ankles. The two Fae women had taken them off of her body.

Friends, they'd claimed to be. A quick glance at this man's ears let her know that he too was Fae. They twisted upwards like arrows pointing at the sky. Her hands fumbled against his chest, lightly pushing him away. She willed her legs to cooperate but she found herself wrapped in the Fae man's embrace.

Panic clawed at her throat. She felt trapped in his hold and hated how weak her voice sounded when she pleaded, "Please let me go."

But he didn't pull her closer or tighter. Tobias would have. This man slowly let her slide to her feet. When she wobbled and the room spun, he caught her, steadying her until she found her footing and was able to stand on her own. She pulled away from him and looked around the small dungeon room. At the gaping hole they'd created with magic, even though it was iron and should have been impervious to it. She looked at the Fae man again, but his face was so beautiful it hurt. So she looked to the women instead. They were safer than the man, that much she knew with certainty.

She had so many questions. Like who they were and why they would risk the wrath of her husband to break her from her prison. But even as her mind took in many facts about them, like the lack of collars choking their throats, like the strange attire that did not fit in with Danarish customs, like how they were staring at her as if she would fall apart at any moment, there was still only one thing on her mind.

"I have to find my son." She took a step, then two, then three. They didn't try to stop her so she pushed forward. But even if they would have tried, she would have fought them. Her legs trembled like a newborn calf as she wobbled out of that cell. When she tripped, her hands flung out to grasp the iron bars. A hiss of pain pushed through her clenched teeth, but she ignored it, only focused on finding Basil.

"You can't walk," a voice said. "You're too weak." Corvina didn't turn to look at the Fae who had spoken. Her voice had been soft, pleading. It was the Fae who smelled of confections and fire.

"I have enough strength for this." She started forward again. Her palms pulsed from the burn of iron, but it was a single flash of pain against a whole, dreadful ache. Her feet dragged. Out in the hall, there were more Fae. Men. One of them, a gargantuan ginger with a thick beard, wielded a sword and was bathed in blood. Another man had his cloak up, but it did nothing to shadow the vicious scars that bisected across his face. The third male had brown skin and a long braid that hung over his shoulder. His eyes were golden and he seemed so familiar. Like she knew him from somewhere. A dream, or the dream of a dream...

"My lady..."

Her attention turned to a cell she recognized and the Fae pressed up against the bars.

"Dawn!" She tripped and nearly fell in her rush to get to her friend, but strong arms wrapped around her middle. A rich scent tickled her nostrils. One that smelt bubbly, one that could make her drunk with a few mere whiffs.

"Careful," the Fae's voice glided along her ear, down her spine and made her shiver. Her fingers dug into his arms, but he didn't let her go.

"Dawn," she gasped. "We need to get her out..."

"We will," the man promised. "I swear, we will."

Her eyes met Dawn's, and there was no trace of malice in her old friend's gaze. Just an infinite well of sorrow that cut Corvina deep. "Go, my lady," Dawn urged. "Go get him."

She bit her lips, the sting of pain nearly making her gasp. She was still being held, almost reverently by the male behind her. She didn't like how close he was, so she pulled from his grasp, and this time he let her go. Down the hall, there was the evidence of violence. Blood and bodies covered the crevices of the place and Corvina couldn't bring herself to look. She stared ahead, holding her head high. Footsteps followed behind her. None tried to stop her. No one tried to speak to her.

She had questions of her own. *Who are you? Why did you set me free? What do you want?* But those questions could come later. After she found her son.

At the top of the stairs, she met with Gale. She skidded to a stop, taking in her human maid with surprise. She vaguely remembered how she came in and bathed her, fed her, and then whispered words of warning.

"Princess!" Gale rushed forward, throwing her arms around Corvina in such a way that made her flinch. When she pulled away, there was relief. "We must hurry. The prince planned on taking Reginald away *today.*"

It clicked in her mind then. The words hadn't been a promise of death. They'd been a promise of freedom. Gale had done this. Her frivolous maid, her maid who hadn't understood what it meant to be Fae. What it meant to suffer like they suffered. Who was blissful in her own ignorance. It had been she who had brought these Fae to break her out.

Who they were, she didn't know, but she had a feeling...

"We must hurry," Gale urged, turning and rushing. Corvina followed. Every step ached, but when the two Fae women stepped on either side of her, hands supportive against her shoulders, she felt something surge through her. Something that felt a lot like magic. It reinvigorated her. Her aches were still present, but renewed energy and fierce determination darted to the forefront of her mind, her soul.

"Where are we going?" the Fae that smelt like ice asked.

"To save my son."

Up the stairs and down the halls they ran until Gale stopped before Basil's room door.

She pushed the doors open, but it was Corvina who stepped inside first. To be greeted by her son and something else far more horrifying. He stood in the middle of the room, his dark eyes wide and fearful. Tears tracked down his face, and behind him a soldier stood, pressing the edge of a knife to her son's neck.

"Don't take another fucking step, Fae bitch," the soldier snapped.

Corvina felt her entire world slip from under her, and she was falling down a hole, down a place she feared she couldn't climb back up again. Her son, her Basil. No violence was supposed to touch him. She was supposed to protect him from it. From his father, from the difference in his blood, from this. Yet the violence was touching him. It was pressing a blade to the delicate curve of his tiny neck. There was fear in his eyes, and the tears wouldn't stop flowing.

"What are you doing?" Corvina found her voice steady while her emotions were anything but. "That is your prince—"

"I don't give a fuck!" he spat. "You were imprisoned, but I heard them breaking you out." His chin jerked in the direction behind her where she felt the presence of the other Fae. "I am no fool. You'd kill me without blinking, and this fucking brat will ensure my safe passage out of this castle." He jerked against Basil and her son gave a cry, throwing his arms out.

"Mommy!"

"It's okay, Basil," she reassured. "Everything will be okay." It was a promise. She'd been weak her whole life. She had let Tobias alter and mold her into something new, into something she wasn't. She had let him break her. From the wounds inflicted upon her body to the wounds upon her mind. She became weak, so far from the person she'd been before that she feared she could never go back to being brave or headstrong. She would always be a shard, a fragment. He'd torn her to bits, razed her soul and hollowed her out.

But for Basil, she would not be cowed.

She'd taken the brunt of abuse so he wouldn't have to. She'd suffered for his happiness. And if she had to kill this son of a bitch to save her child's life, then she fucking would.

Violence, foreign and hot, swirled at the pit of her stomach. "Let him go," she ordered the soldier. She could feel the Fae behind her closing in. Feel ice and fire at her back, and it gave her a surge of strength that she didn't question. She'd been tortured for weeks. Starved, forced to choke on ashwood and suffer iron. It still ran through her system. She was still weak.

But *this* made her strong.

"Stay the fuck away!" the human roared. His hand trembled, and she could smell the acrid scent of his fear. She wasn't sure what he saw in her gaze, but hoped it was the reflection of her murderous intent.

"Basil, baby, close your eyes."

Her son, despite his tears, did as she bade.

And for the first time since arriving at this dreadful human kingdom, Corvina unleashed her magic in a torrent. The human didn't see it coming. Though why would he? No one knew what she was. No one knew what lived beneath her skin. That water was an element she'd wielded since her youth. That her father had trained her in secret to use her magic. And while she'd avoided it since, she could do so no longer.

It felt as if she were snapping free of chains. Water dripped from her hands, swirling between her fingers. She didn't need water around her. She didn't need matter for her magic to work. She could create it of her own volition. So she lifted her hand and she did just that.

And she drowned the soldier where he stood.

The knife clattered from his grip as he convulsed, accidentally pushing Basil forward. Her son fell to his knees with a cry, but kept his eyes firmly shut. And Corvina didn't ease her grip on the magic. She waited, watching the man twitch along the ground like a fish out of water until he stilled. Only then did she pull back. Water burst from his mouth and nose, but the soldier did not get up again.

"Basil..." Her voice broke and her head spun. She fell to her knees in front of her son and pulled him into her arms.

"Mommy!" He wrapped himself around her, all legs and arms and tears. "Mommy, Papa was going to take me away without you! He said you were sick!"

A sob lodged in her throat. At what could have been. At what Tobias would have done.

"I'm here, Basil," she whispered. "I'm *here*."

Weakening from the exertion of magic she used, but here for her son just the same. The weight of everything came crashing down on her. Exhaustion, pain. Her eyelids drooped to half-mast, and through her thick lashes, she watched as that same beautiful Fae male walked in their direction and bent so their eyes were level. Her heart pounded at his proximity and an ache, one different from ashwood and iron and beatings, built in her chest. It was like an ache in her soul, an itch that needed scratching even when she didn't know where to begin.

"We have to go," he said. "It's not safe here."

She was too weak to ask, but Basil surprisingly spoke up. "Who are you?"

He smiled. "We are the Resistance."

The Fae Resistance. The one that had been whispered about through the castle by her maids. The one that was marching into Dana that she'd overheard many times in the last few weeks. They were here and had freed her from her prison.

Her eyes lifted and met the bright green of the man. She wanted to recoil from his beauty, frightened at the cruelty that could be lurking underneath of it. Though they'd saved her, she wasn't sure what to make of it. No one ever did anything for free, and if they'd gone through all this trouble, she didn't doubt that they wanted something from her.

"I don't—" Her head spun as something seemed to flash over his eyes. That tightness in her chest seemed to snap, like an enormous knife slicing between them and cutting whatever invisible line had been there. She gasped as something zapped through her body. A jolt of electricity that she knew, *knew*, that the Fae man felt as well. He fell back against the ground, his eyes widening as he took her in. His hand clutched his chest, his breathing growing rapid and harsh in the silence.

"You..." The magic was a maelstrom around them. Violent and invasive and foreign. But something... Just fell into place. Something she tried to reject, even as the sensation nestled itself into her soul. "It's..." He shook his head to clear it. "The mating bond."

Mating bond.

The words echoed through her hollow mind right before darkness crept through the edges of her vision. She fell backwards, cracking her head against the ground.

And this time, she didn't wake up again.

Broken Mate

Her head cracked against the floor before Clay could catch her. The violent, painful sound had the child, the one still wrapped around her body, bursting into tears.

"Mommy!" he wailed, wrapping himself tighter around her, throwing his body over hers like he meant to protect her from them.

Clay was still reeling from the realization of what this woman was. Of the bond that had snapped into place and was still pulsing between them. He could feel the enormity of it, a frisson of electricity and magic. He could practically see it. Threads tying the two of them together.

His chest heaved with every breath he took. His mind ran in miles at lightning speed, his thoughts trying to catch up to the events that had happened within the last few moments. The ache that had been near-bursting in his chest since he'd arrived had imploded. And this was why.

Because of her.

Princess Corvina.

His mate.

Fuck, he had a *mate.* One who smelt like sea salt and ocean and The Pool of the Sapphire Court—crystal waters that reflected off the night sky, like the waters themselves were made of starlight. Like lily pads and fresh rain. She smelt soothing and bright. He'd been surrounded by pleasant scents before. Shula's and Iona's... But never one he wanted to wrap himself in. Drown himself in with as much ferocity as she used her magic.

His mate. His mate. His mate. His mate. His mate—

"Shall I kill the wailing brat?" a voice echoed in his head, causing him to turn his attention sharply to Weylyn. The Fae had spoken within his mind and was staring at Clay with a rather cynical expression twisting his lips, though only the whites of his eyes were visible.

"What the fuck?" Clay shook his head. "What's wrong with you, you psycho?"

"Then get your shit together and do something about your mate."

The entire conversation had taken place within Clay's mind and lasted a few seconds before he realized the bastard was right. He was sitting there like a dumbass while his mate was lying unconscious on the floor. He wanted to get to her. Needed to.

He scrambled forward on his knees, reaching for her body almost blindly. His breaths sawed in and out of his chest and his hands trembled as they neared her, only to be intercepted by the boy.

"No! Leave her alone!"

He jerked back. Fuck. He'd forgotten about the child. Her son. His mate's son. Fuck. His mate had a *son.* A *husband.* Panic clawed up his chest, making him damn near fucking useless until Shula stepped forward and bent to the little boy's level.

Clay's head cleared as she lifted her hands and began to speak. The panic started to abate a fraction and he observed the boy more closely. His unruly curls covered the points of his ears. They weren't tipped as sharply as a full blooded Fae's. They were a cross somewhere between Fae and human.

The boy stopped wailing when he caught sight of Shula and heard her sweet voice.

"We aren't going to hurt you or your mother," she whispered. "We're friends."

Big wet tears flicked from his eyelashes. He sniffled. "You smell like chocolate," he whispered, his tone almost accusatory.

"Do you like chocolate, Basil?"

Basil. That was the boy's name, and Shula was handling him better than Clay could. At least not right then. Not when his instincts were trying to override his common sense and thoughts. He wanted to be impulsive, to damn everyone else and reach his mate. But he couldn't do that. He could do nothing except be lost in the swirl of his tumultuous thoughts.

"I do."

"Me too," Shula whispered. "Chocolate cake is my favorite. Can you come with me? Your mother is hurt and we have to get her to a healer. Is that okay with you?"

Basil looked torn between Shula and his mother, but in the end he climbed off her body and stepped towards Shula. The fire Fae picked him up with ease of practice and set him on her hip. "You smell like oranges," she told him with a smile.

"I like those."

And they were stepping away, giving Clay free reign to reach over and pull his mate into his arms. He cradled her with care. She felt too fragile in his arms. Her bones poking against his body like a pile of sticks. Smoothing away her wheat-colored hair, he caught sight of the wounds around her neck. A band of red circling her delicate throat like an iron collar had been closed around her neck. Her lips were chapped, hollows sunken beneath her eyes and marring her face with shadows. She was covered in scars over the flesh he could see, and he had no doubt that more dipped beneath the rich dress that hung from her frame. But despite all the wounds that covered her, there was no doubting she was beautiful. Her nose was a bit long and pointed, the tip curving up ever so slightly. Her breaths came from her nostrils in quick spurts.

He stood with her in his arms. She was too light, his mate. Broken. Hurt. She was fragile and he felt like he would crush her if he pulled her to close. Her heart fluttered against my chest, as weak as the flapping wings of a baby bird. So weak. So fucking *frail.*

"We have to leave," someone said from behind him. He turned with his mate in his arms. The servant who'd helped them storm the castle was there, twisting nervously at the folds of her thin skirts. "The prince could come back at any moment and the guards..."

Everyone was crowded around the doorway, staring at him and the woman in his arms. There were three new additions to the group as well. One of the females that had been locked away in the dungeon, haggard and in little more than rags, and two other females with iron collars around their throats. They were staring at his mate, limp and hurt in his arms. Their mouths dropped open and they clutched at their chests.

"My lady..." one of them whispered.

Clay ignored her. "Weylyn."

But the Fae's eyes were already flickering, and in a few moments a portal opened. Shula stepped forward first, holding the boy tightly in her arms. "I'm just going to walk through that mirror, okay, Basil?" He nodded in response and they disappeared through it, inciting gasps from the servants.

"It has been a long, long time," the haggard Fae whispered. She stumbled forward on weak legs. "Since I have last seen magic." Her gaze was held enraptured on that portal. "Since I have last been with my people..." Another shaky step and then she was moving, pushing towards the portal and slipping through it.

"We have to go," Julius urged, speaking directly to the maids. "Come with us or stay here, it is your choice."

One of the servants straightened. "Where our lady goes, we go." And as regal as queens, the three stepped forward together.

And the rest of them followed.

⋆⋆⋆

“Is this her?” Valerio asked as they clamored out of the portal onto the other side. He gazed down at Corvina, wrapped tightly in Clay’s arms, his eyes flicking over her with a cold calculation that made a snarl rumble from Clay’s chest, the sound unbidden, feral, born of some instinct that suddenly pounced from his soul.

Valerio rocked back on his heels, eyes widening. Clay pulled Corvina closer to his chest, unable to quell the instinct that rose in him to protect her.

“This ought to be good,” Julius grumbled, amusement in his voice.

Clay growled, low and dangerously. “Fuck off. She needs to be tended to.” He pivoted on his heel and marched away, ignoring Julius’ laughter behind him. They’d landed smack in the middle of their camp, and the three Fae maids and the haggard woman were staring around like they’d landed in another dimension.

When they saw Clay marching on with their mistress, however, they followed hurriedly after him, yanking up their skirts and all but running after his fierce, quick strides.

He wasn’t thinking clearly. Or maybe he’d been living his entire life in a fog until the moment he set his eyes on her and the bond snapped into place. Maybe his existence had been sad and pathetic until this very moment. Everything inside him burned to blistering proportions and all he could think about was protecting her. Getting her to safety.

With single-minded focus, he walked right up to where his tent was erected, pushing aside the flaps and walking into the vast space. He’d set it up himself, content to see his space lavish as well as comfortable. Or as comfortable as he could make it in their travels across Illyk.

Luckily, not all of their things had been pilfered by the humans when they’d been ambushed back in Covenglen. A few small tables were set around the tent, atop which sat oil lanterns; and there was a decent sized cot with blankets and a mountain of pillows. He aimed that way, setting her down with slow care.

The female servants fluttered in after him. They were a flurry of skirts and movement as they bent low to examine her, tittering and whispering over her prone body.

“He went too far,” one of them whispered. The one who’d helped them get to his mate. She pushed aside a lock of Corvina’s hair and Clay caught a glimpse of her ears.

A roar rose in his chest at the sight.

The tips were mangled and scarred. Like the flesh had been twisted with a knife and hadn't healed properly. Like Ryker's scars.

"Did you expect anything different?" another maid hissed as she pulled the brown cloak from Corvina's body and set it gently aside. Their movements were quick and efficient as they began undressing her. As if they'd forgotten Clay was present at all. But he did not blame them. They seemed to worry about her and it was the only reason he didn't interfere. Though he felt helpless standing there, he could not peel his eyes away as piece by piece, they removed her clothes until she was in nothing but a thin shift. But even that scrap of material wasn't enough to hide the figure beneath.

Too thin. Like she'd been *starved.* Her bones poked through the dress.

"I expect a prince to care for his princess," the woman retorted. "Not... *this.*"

"You live in a fantasy, Gale," one of the Fae servants snapped at the human. Gale. Her name was Gale. "You did ever since you arrived at the palace. You thought this would be some romantic tale, but it wasn't. Prince Tobias is a cruel master who beats, rapes, and tortures his wife."

Gale sucked in a breath, the harsh sound of surprise that Clay's own mind echoed.

The words pierced through him like weapons. *Beats. Rapes. Tortures.* His body began to tremble with rage. A fucking human prince did that to his own wife. It was a despicable crime, to hurt a woman. Even more despicable to hurt your own wife. The evidence of it all lay on her body in old scars. Her arms, her neck, her calves and ankles and feet.

Fuck.

His gaze stopped on her bare feet. She even had scars on her toes.

No woman should have to suffer what she suffered. *No one...*

He seethed and suddenly felt like he needed to know details. To catalogue every single injury she had suffered if only to avenge her and let the one who'd done this to her suffer tenfold.

"What did he do to her?" *My mate. My mate.* The words echoed in his head. He wanted to pull her into his arms. He wished he had Ryker's magic just then so he could heal any ailments. Instead it was blood magic that coursed through his veins. Useless blood magic.

"Prince Tobias—" Gale started.

"Gale!" one of the others hissed. "It is not our place to say."

Gale clamped her lips shut and turned back to Corvina in silence.

He assessed the small group of them. The two Fae were outright hostile towards Gale, but Gale had been the one to help them find Corvina. Though human, in the end, it was her who had brought them together. And for that, she would always have his gratitude.

"You should leave," one of the maids suggested. "It's not appropriate for you to be here." Her gaze pierced him, and he did not want to argue because she was right. He wanted to stay, but she was in a vulnerable position, being bared in his tent. If she woke up and found him there, after everything she suffered, he knew she would fear like anyone would fear the unknown.

She was his mate. He wanted to stay. Needed to.

"Is there anything you need?" The words sounded too far away. Like they were spoken by someone else and were little more than a distant echo.

"Water, towels, salve if you have it."

"I'll send our healer."

The servant gave him a strained smile. "That would be perfect."

Clay gave one last lingering look in his mate's direction before he exited the tent.

Though the air outside was fresh and warm, he felt like he couldn't breathe. The blood through his veins roused, his magic jumping forward, demanding exit. He slowed the rush, the fast pumping of his heart, as he stormed across the camp. It was easy enough to spot Ryker. The scarred Fae was hovering over the sick and injured, as usual. But for a moment, Clay didn't care about them or their ailments. He didn't care that Ryker's attention was elsewhere. He grabbed hold of the man by the arm, yanking him off to the side.

"She needs you," Clay all but growled. "Help her."

Maybe Ryker would have snarled at him for the audacity of bossing him around, but he'd seen her body. He'd known what had happened to her. At least, a small extent of it.

He nodded slowly. "I was just coming to get my supplies and going to see her next."

Relief eased something in Clay's chest. He gave a single, grim nod, and then Ryker was sweeping past him, disappearing into his tent to tend to his mate. To help her in a way that Clay couldn't.

He raked his hand through his hair out of frustration and turned to walk aimlessly through camp. He caught sight of Julius and Iona speaking with Uric and Valerio, likely filling them in on what had happened. Clay's attention snagged on them for a moment. On the confident way Julius spoke and looked in the direction of his mate. On the not-so-subtle way her hand slid up his back and rubbed circles of encouragement. Of the way her own fingers began tapping against her thighs and Julius' hand closed around them and squeezed in reassurance.

He couldn't help but to compare the mated pairs.

Julius and Iona.

Shula and Ryker.

Julius and Iona had always been proud of their bond and confident in their feelings towards one another. Iona swept Julius off his feet and had bonded with him right away. They were a perfect unit. Strong and fierce. He was a fucking soldier who had led troops into battle. She'd been a soldier as well. Together? They were the very definition of a force to be reckoned with. Of a loud, boisterous love with little inhibitions of showing what they meant to one another. Clay often caught them lost in their passion as they kissed or undressed. He cracked jokes at his friends' expense, but he loved seeing Julius so happy. No one deserved it more.

Then there were Shula and Ryker. Their feelings had been a battle. Walls were wound so tightly around the both of them, but they were slowly learning to peel away those pesky layers brick by brick. Clay admitted, he'd confronted Ryker purposefully, trying to get him to pull his head out of his ass and be the man that Shula needed him to be. She was beautiful and kind and deserved happiness. She deserved to be treated with respect, to be treated like she fucking mattered because she did. And if Ryker hadn't fought to be that man, then Clay would have dueled him to protect Shula from the asshole. But they were beyond that now. Ryker was still a miserable bastard, but he wasn't the same miserable bastard that had been before. Back when he had nightmares over Mairin and hated everyone because of what had befallen his sister. Now, their bond was a tentative thing. It wasn't as loud as Julius' and Iona's, but it was surer than it had been before. They were a more quiet couple, content with sharing glances and tender touches rather than passionate kisses in the shadows.

And all of that made Clay wonder exactly what kind of couple him and Corvina would be, if she would even accept him as a mate. Because... she was fucking *married.* Granted, the human prince was an asshole and if she wanted to go back to him... Clay didn't think he'd have it in him to respect those wishes. Valerio wouldn't. He would keep her here like he kept Shula and claim it was for her own protection. But would Clay stay idly by and watch it happen? He believed in freedom of choice, and if she didn't choose him, could he live with that?

He would have to. You could no more force a mating bond than you could force a human to be Fae. It wasn't something that was possible. A mating bond was a gift freely given. If she wanted him, she would let him know. They would mark each other, and that mark would be a binding. It would solidify the bond that was already pulsing between them. Officially tying them together.

But would she accept him?

Would she *want* him?

He stared longingly at the tent where she lay. Bruised, broken. And Clay longed for something only she could give. And a part of him feared that her answer would be no.

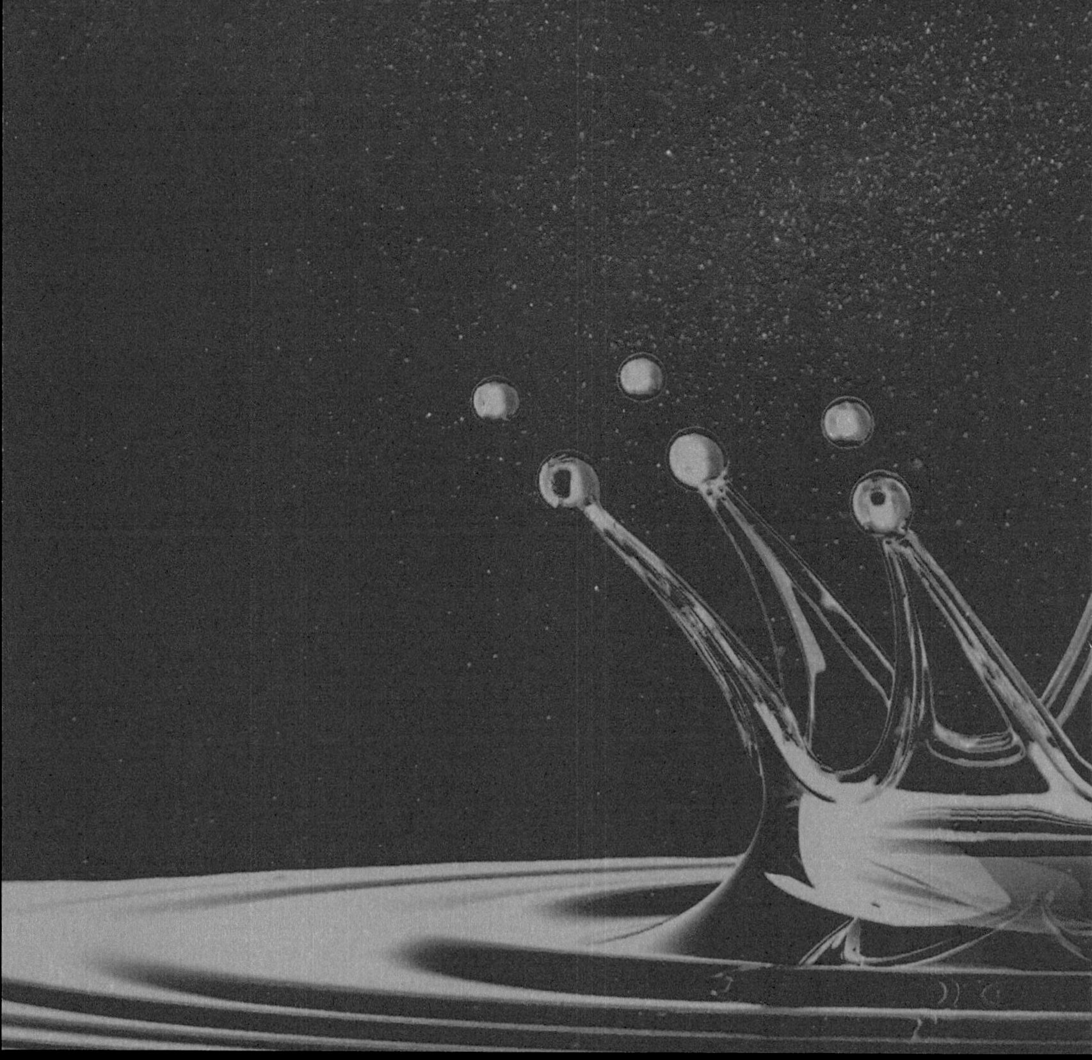

Kings, Elementals, and a Choice

Consciousness came slowly, and with it Corvina was aware of every ache and pain in her body. This was the normal of her life. Just another day woken up in her husband's bed, released from her iron bonds, and suffering the aftereffect of his hatred and rage.

It took a moment for her to take inventory of her wounds. Her throat ached something fierce like she'd swallowed broken glass. The coppery taste of blood was coated heavily against her tongue, and it took great effort to peel her eyes open. She didn't register her surroundings. Not at first. Usually, Juniper and Wren would be the first to arrive to clean and press healing salve over her wounds. But they weren't there.

The sounds came a second later. Unfamiliar and strange. She pushed herself up, fighting back the nausea and her spinning head. When her vision cleared, she realized she wasn't in her husband's bed at all.

She was in a tent.

That's when the memories came rushing back. Of the torture, the dungeon, the smell of magic, the Fae, the soldier with the knife to Basil's neck...

Basil!

She stumbled to her feet. Her thin shift made her quicker than her dress would have, and she barely gave a moment's thought to the fact that her clothes were gone as she forced her way out of the tent. Light blinded her and the soft sea breeze told her she was still in Dana, but she recognized little else. She was in a camp of some sort. Tents were erected all over, several spits of fire were going with a dead carcass of an animal roasting over it.

People walked around in clusters or alone, all of them busy with some task. Meanwhile, Corvina felt as if she'd been dropped in the middle of a different world. All around her there were Fae. Fae without collars, and no one she recognized.

Panic started clawing up her chest. She whirled around, her feet scraping against stones on the ground. "Basil!" she screamed through the pain, stumbling across the camp. She couldn't see her son, couldn't find him. Was he okay? Was he hurt? She wouldn't forgive herself if he was. "Basil!"

Fae stopped to stare at her as she stumbled past. She knew she likely looked crazy. A half-naked Fae woman covered in bruises shrieking for her son. She didn't care.

"Basil! Basil, where are you?" The tears came, tasting like salt against her lips. "Basil!" She almost tripped against a rock, felt the skin on her toes split. She cried out. "Basil!"

"Corvina, please calm down."

Her attention snapped up to the man who spoke. He'd approached on silent feet. Both of them. Two Fae men that seemed to contrast one another. The one who had spoken was tall, with a slight tan staining his skin. Long black hair was tied away from the planes of his sharp face and pointed ears. Dark eyes regarded her with caution and something dangerous that she couldn't make out. His tall, lithe body seemed to loom over her even from a distance.

The second Fae was pale with silver-white hair that cut just past his shoulders. He wore a sneer of displeasure and disdain as he watched Corvina. In his hands he held a black dagger that he flitted through his fingertips with expert precision.

She ignored it. Just like she ignored the feeling of cowering her body demanded she do. She was afraid, but her protectiveness was stronger. "Where is my son?" Her fingers twitched at her sides, magic buzzing against her fingers.

The black haired Fae noticed the movement and held up a hand. "Look, just calm—"

He didn't get the rest out. Magic imploded against her fingers. Water rushing out in his direction, intercepted by the silver-haired Fae. He rushed at her, his dagger raised above his head. That threat made her scream, made her cower away from him. Her hand closed into a fist and water invaded his lungs, choking him.

He fell to his knees, dropping his weapon and clawing at his throat. Now that her attacker was immobilized, she stomped in his direction.

"Where is my son?" Her fist closed tighter, filling him with so much water, it spit from his pale mouth.

"Stop it!" Someone cut into her line of vision. Corvina recognized her from before. She was one of the Fae who had helped free her from her prison. The one with long dark hair and golden-brown skin. The one who smelled like fire and confections.

The sight of her made Corvina's magic ease back. The man's choking stopped and he gasped for air as he sputtered the rest of the water out of his body.

"My son..." Her hands, which she had thought incapable of violence before, trembled.

The woman's eyes softened. "He is safe."

"Mommy?"

Corvina whipped around and saw Basil. Before she could wonder if he had witnessed what she'd done, she was running towards him, dropping to her knees and pulling him into her arms. Her body shook with relief, and she could do little about the tears staining his clothes. She gasped and pulled away, running her hand over his body in search of injuries. He looked unharmed, but there were a lot of ways someone could be hurt that didn't involve fists.

"Are you alright, my love?" she asked frantically.

His mouth widened into a toothy smile, and that was all she needed for her body to sag. For her to know he was fine. Basil wore his emotions on his face and her son would never lie to her. "Shula gave me chocolate, mommy, and fish."

Corvina blinked her surprise. "Oh?"

"And she showed me her magic and showed me around the camp! I wanted to wake you, but she said no because you were tired. But you're awake now, mommy. Do you want to see the camp with me?"

She breathed a sigh of relief. He was fine. He was completely fine. Better than that he was... happy. Happier than she'd seen him in a long time.

"Thank Mana," she whispered.

"Corvina..."

With reluctance, she dragged her gaze away from Basil and stood to turn and meet the small group of Fae that had gathered silently near her. The silver Fae had already gotten up. The whole front of his tunic was soaked, the white material clinging to his pale body. He started towards her, and she felt the murderous intent in his posturing. She stumbled backwards, blindly reaching for Basil to protect him from the Fae's wrath.

"Uric," the dark-haired Fae snapped at him, stopping him in his tracks. His voice had been full of command, hard like a royal's but not cruel like her husband's. Just firm and steady. Then he turned to Corvina. "Perhaps we should speak in a more private—"

"Corvina!"

Her attention was pulled in yet another direction. This time towards another Fae male. This one with blond-brown hair, ruffling against the wind. He ran towards her, shoving aside the others. She flinched back as he charged forward, the action causing him to freeze and pause his trajectory. Close. Not close enough to touch but close enough that she felt a frisson of electricity stab between the two of their bodies.

Bright green eyes regarded her with concern and a jolt made her gasp. The intensity of his stare, the way he flexed his hands at his sides as if he were holding himself back from reaching out to her...

Everything about him was familiar and foreign. This newcomer smelt like richness. Like cider and bubbles, the kind that made her drunk. As it was, being so near him made her feel it. Her head spun with the headiness of his scent. It wafted up her nose. Magic was somewhere in the spaces between them. She felt it as surely as she felt her own. It was like... like there was an invisible string wrapped around her shoulders, tugging her towards him.

A strange instinct demanded she lean in his direction, but the fear clamped that sensation down almost immediately. She cringed at her own thoughts, at her body and what it demanded. She was still bruised, frightened, broken. And yet that beautiful Fae male in front of her was staring at her as if she held up all the stars in the sky.

"Do... do I know you?" she whispered, not knowing what else to say.

He blinked, whether it be of surprise or something else, she wasn't sure. "You... you don't remember?"

Her head tilted to the side a fraction. "No?"

He looked disappointed. She ignored that, too. Just like she ignored the strength of the mating bond pulsing between them. It sang, a song of beckoning. Likely lamenting her lies. She did know who he was. Of course she knew.

And the truth frightened her. The truth of what he was and what he represented.

A mate.

When she was a little girl, full of happiness and illusions, she dreamt of her mate. Of who he would be, what he would look like, how he would treat her. Her parents had not been mates, and she had not known her mother, but her father had loved her fiercely. And then the war swept all that away. And in her own foolery, she had tied herself to a man who shattered the dreams that had lived in her mind. All childish fantasies had been pushed away. The reality was she was destined for marriage with Tobias. Her punishment for her weakness. For not keeping her strength to somehow save her people or be anything but a meek wife.

A mate was in her future no longer. Regardless if he was standing before her now. He was beautiful, and she was broken.

She did not deserve a mate.

Not with her cowardice.

"Come," the dark-haired one ordered softly, mindful of her state. "Shall we speak in private? We can explain everything to you and answer any questions you might have..."

She hesitated, unsure if she should go with complete strangers. They'd saved her, but she didn't really know who they were. But she supposed that didn't matter, did it? If they wanted to overpower her, they could. It didn't matter if she wanted to or not. They would get what they wanted...

"It's okay," the Fae woman whispered. "You'll be safe."

Safe. That word was as foreign to her as the home she had left behind.

"Okay," she conceded reluctantly. "We can speak in private."

They led her to a large tent erected in the middle of camp. She followed slowly after them, where the dark-haired Fae gestured at a seat. She gladly took it, as her ankles were screaming, and set Basil in her lap. She'd not let her son leave her sight. He was safest with her, where she could protect him.

After she sat down, more Fae filed into the room. There were six Fae total. Four of them men and two women, the ones who had freed her from the dungeons. She memorized the features of the men. The dark-haired man and the silver-haired one named Uric. There was the blond, her *mate*, and a large ginger. The ebony-skinned woman stood next to the ginger, her dark eyes intent on Corvina. The penetrative stare made Corvina shiver.

Magic thrummed within the tent. It was all Corvina needed to know she was among a group of powerful Fae. And since she was so used to suffocating her magic, to seeing Fae collared, they were an attraction in and of themselves.

Her eyes dragged over to the blond and when she found him staring at her, she looked away.

"Introductions are in order," the dark-haired Fae said. "I am Valerio Ashera." He paused. "King of the Seelie Court."

She blinked, her breath catching in her throat. Her father had spoken highly of the King of Seelie. Though at the time, the reigning king of Seelie had been Amos Ashera. This... this was his son. Which meant the king was dead. Had her father been alive, he likely would have mourned the king's death. She herself didn't know what to say. She stared dumbly at him, realizing, perhaps a beat too late, that she'd nearly drowned the king of her people.

Shame heated her cheeks. "Your Majesty..."

"No need for formalities here, Corvina. You are royalty too, after all."

Her throat grew tight. Royalty. Being a human princess who suffered the cruelty of her husband seemed so miniscule in comparison to what her title could be. High Lady of the Gold Court. Until Basil took the title himself...

"This is Uric Adriel Nova." He gestured at the silver-haired Fae. She nodded at him. He didn't sneer at her this time, at least. "This is Julius Darah." It was the big ginger. He flashed her a smile full of canines and mischief.

"Hey, beautiful," he greeted.

She tried not to jolt back at that. It was a lie, though he said it with such sincerity she almost believed it. She surely looked a horrid sight.

"That's Iona, his mate." King Valerio gestured at the pretty, ebony-skinned woman.

Iona shot the king a glare. "Why didn't you introduce *him* like that?"

She spoke to the king like she was speaking to a commoner. Corvina's eyes widened.

"Iona..."

"I'm serious. Next time either introduce the both of us like that or don't belittle me." She turned back to Corvina and gifted her with a radiant smile. "I'm Iona Wylde, ice Fae Elemental."

Elemental...

"And that's Shula Azzarh."

Shula was the Fae her son had seemed enamored with. If she had won over Basil, then Corvina felt no ill will towards her. Despite the fact that she was sought after by Captain Brannon. Despite the fact that her face was plastered on posters all over the city. She gave the woman a nod, and Shula smiled back warmly.

"I'm a fire Fae Elemental." She said the words almost timidly. She reached up and tucked a long lock behind a sharp tipped ear.

"And this is Clay..." The king's voice trailed off as Corvina's and Clay's eyes collided. If he spoke again, she didn't hear what he said, because her mate—no, *Clay*, she had to think of him as *Clay*, not her mate, because he would never be hers—was staring at her intensely, like he could see down to her withered soul.

She shrunk away from his attention and turned back to the king. He was safer to look at.

"I am Corvina Rhian and this is Thorne Basil Rhian..."

"Rhian..." The king's eyes widened a fraction. "The High Lord of the Gold Court..."

"Was my father." She gave him an almost rueful smile.

"I don't remember him having a daughter."

That ache in her chest built as she thought of her father. "He kept me well protected within our court."

"So that would make you High Lady of the Gold Court. Welcome to our camp." King Ashera bowed as if they *were* in court. She had the urge to curtsey in return but feared her weak ankles would not allow it.

"What is this place?" She'd guessed, but she wanted to hear the answer straight from his mouth.

"It is a Fae camp. We have been traveling across Illyk and rescuing the Fae from the emperor's camps, helping them and building our numbers for the inevitable war. And... we've been looking for you."

"Me?"

"You're the water Elemental, Lady Corvina."

Her fingers flexed against her son's stomach at the reminder. She knew very well what she was. The aches and pains on her body were evidence of what she'd hidden. Her throat still felt raw from the ashwood Tobias had made her swallow. Her insides still burned from what the priest had forced down her throat.

"And the emperor is looking for the Elementals," she whispered.

"Yes. How did you know?"

"The emperor's soldiers marched into Port Bay with a Priest of the Brotherhood."

At the mention of the priest, Shula jolted where she stood. "A priest?"

Corvina slowly angled her head in Shula's direction. "Yes," she whispered, her hand going to her throat as if she could feel the pain of the fire clawing down her throat still.

Shula eyed the movement and sympathy flashed in her eyes. "The ceremony..."

The ceremony that had outed what she was. Understanding rang between them and Corvina knew she had found someone who had lived through what she had. Here was someone else who had understood what she'd gone through, what the water tasted like as it burned holes down her throat. The look in Shula's eyes let Corvina know that she'd suffered the same fate.

But of course she had. Hadn't she heard of her? The infamous Fire Dancer of Piriguini's Circus. The one who had escaped the emperor. The one who had posters of her face plastered on every surface of Port Bay. This woman was a survivor. A fighter. The haunting in her eyes told Corvina she'd suffered through horrible things. And here she stood. With her head held high, showing no weakness or hardly any evidence of her ordeal.

Admiration was easy to feel and accept. She wanted to reach out and hold the woman's hand but refrained.

"Water that burns like fire," Shula whispered absently.

"It felt like I was dying," Corvina confessed.

"Me, too."

They stared long and hard at each other until someone cleared their throat, breaking the spell and drawing Corvina's attention away from Shula and back to the king.

"So you know that the emperor will stop at nothing to find you," he said.

He would have if Tobias had gotten the chance to tell everyone she was dead, though he never would have brought to light that she was an Elemental. He had killed the priest who had confirmed it, but Captain Brannon suspected what she was. If Tobias told the captain she was dead, he would be forced to leave Port Bay. But something told her Captain Brannon was no fool. He would not believe such a thing. Besides, who knew what Tobias would do now that she was missing.

Fear choked up her throat.

What would he do to her if he caught her? And Basil? She felt her hands begin trembling, but she said nothing as the king continued, "Elementals are the very foundation of Fae magic, Seelie and Unseelie alike. If he destroys the pillars, in this case, the Elementals, then he will have the power to destroy the Fae in one fell swoop, eradicating us all."

Her heart pounded against Basil's back. Her son thankfully wasn't paying attention to the conversation. He'd dozed, his head lolling forward. She was glad he couldn't hear these tales of violence.

"We are trying to find the remaining Elementals before the emperor does. To protect you and to seek your help. You can either make or break the Fae. We need you, Lady Corvina. Will you help us?"

They looked at her expectantly, the pressure of their gazes felt like too much for her to handle. Help them save the Fae race? How were they even supposed to do that? If the entirety of the camp was what they had in ways of an army, then she didn't think they would be a match for the emperor's forces. They'd not even be a match for her husband's forces.

And when he found out who had taken her, he would march here and get her back, and this resistance they'd created would die before it even got the chance to live. The Elementals would be captured, she would be captured, and who knows what would happen then.

Just the thought of Tobias finding them here...

Her hands tightened around Basil and she took a breath.

She couldn't help them. Not because she didn't want to. She did, but she was afraid. Afraid she wasn't strong enough. Afraid for Basil and his future in the inevitable battle and war. That was the reason she had stayed after all. Because the world outside of Dana was unknown and at least Tobias had provided her son with protection.

A war would change that.

Traveling around and living in a camp with these Fae would change that.

"I am sorry," she whispered, feeling the burning sting of tears in her eyes. "But I cannot help you."

Their disappointment was almost palpable.

"Thank you for pulling me out of the dungeon," she continued. "I do not want to seem as though I'm ungrateful, because I'm not, but I would appreciate it if you took me back to the castle."

Iona looked at her with a dumbfounded expression. "Why would you want to go back there?" she asked incredulously. "You were locked up! And they'll give you to the emperor—"

"They won't," Corvina interrupted with certainty. "My husband is a proud man; he would rather die than give me over to the emperor." He'd said as much as he shoved ashwood down her throat.

A snarl ripped from Clay's throat at her words. When her eyes snapped to him, his lips slammed into a thin line, but the look in his eyes was murderous. Frightening. She leaned away from it, clutching her son tightly to her chest.

"He hurt you," Clay whispered, a trace of anger and that feral side in his voice. As she stared at him, something rose, magic zapped and made her breathless. "If we take you back, he will hurt you again."

She knew that. Just like she knew what she looked like. How haggard her appearance must have been, how pathetic she surely looked with bruises covering her skin. Shame rose to color a blush along her cheeks. These strangers had seen her at her lowest. They'd seen her locked away in that dungeon. How could they ask her to jump from one terrible situation and into another? How could they even imagine she would ever be brave enough to do what they do? To be a part of a resistance like they were? It was impossible. This whole thing was impossible...

For as little he knew her, Clay must have read the reluctance on her face. He stepped forward, cautiously like he would approach a frightened animal. She supposed that's what she was, after all, but the thought still hurt. She tried not to flinch back as he knelt before her. She remained stiff as his eyes lifted to hers. Bright green on blue for a moment.

"I know the thought of us must be frightening. The thought of the danger we might face will not convince you. I know you might think that your husband is the better option. You don't know us and therefore have no reason to trust us, but please..." He started to reach for her and she flinched back, causing him to stop in his tracks. "Please, let us keep you safe."

Tears threatened to fall, but she held them back. "He will come," she warned. "He will come for me if I stay." It hurt to look at Clay, but she kept her gaze there, because she was used to the pain. Physical and emotional. Above all, she was used to wanting things she could never have. "He will come and kill you all."

And she did not want them to die because of her.

"Have faith in us, Lady Corvina," Clay said with a smile. "We are the Resistance. We are not so easily felled."

In the background, Valerio groaned. "*Stop* calling us that."

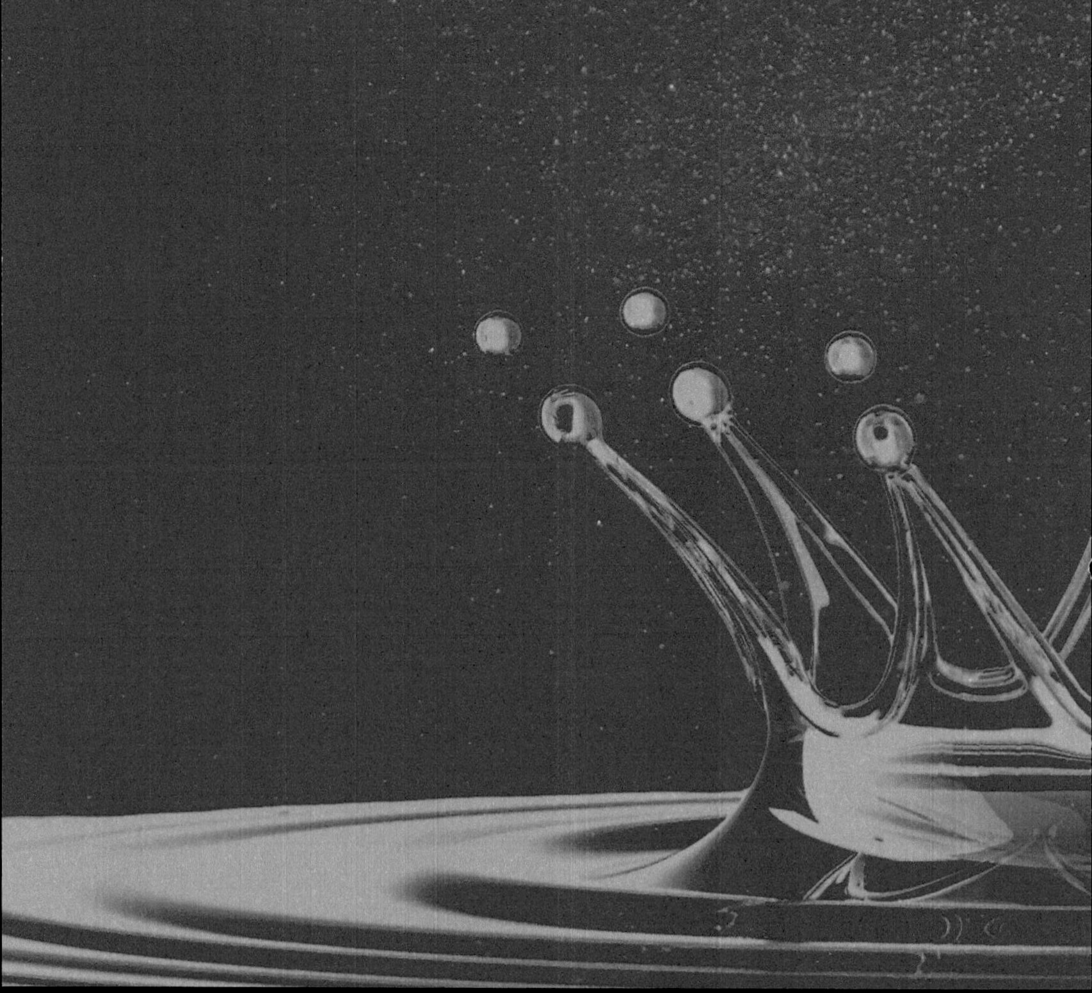

Bring Them Back

Prince Tobias knew something was wrong the moment he entered his castle and was met with stillness. Even so, his steps remained unhurried through the halls. When he met pools of blood staining the floors, he did not balk. When he saw the bodies of his soldiers, he did not wither. When he saw the cage open down in the dungeons where that Fae servant bitch had been held, he did not care. It wasn't until he saw melted bars of his wife's empty cell did he roar.

That fucking treacherous bitch.

She'd gone, disappeared, and had taken his son with her.

He would make her pay. Tobias vowed he would make her pay. But he knew she hadn't done this on her own. She wouldn't have been able to. After taking inventory of the servants still left alive at the castle, he found her three maids missing.

Whoever had helped those bitches escape would pay dearly.

In his rage, he drew his sword. It met the flesh and bone of servants and guards alike. He did not care who he killed at the end of the sword. He did not care that their blood splattered against his face and teeth. That he looked fucking manic in his rage. He left them all dead and rushed to his father's castle and stormed into the throne room.

He threw the doors open wide and marched inside, not giving a single fuck that Captain Brannon was present before the king or that there were soldiers and servants both.

His father's eyes widened as he beheld Tobias. Blood staining his face, sword dripping in his hand.

"She is gone," he growled up at the king. "My wife is *missing*."

There was silence at first as they took in his frazzled state. The evidence of violence against his person. And then, a huffed laugh came from a far wall. He glared at his impetuous brother.

"Oh, dear," Arthur murmured with amusement. "That is problematic, isn't it? Have you checked behind the draperies, dear brother?"

"This is no joke," he spat then dismissed him to turn back to his father. "She was taken along with my son."

The king stood to his full height, looming above Tobias on his throne. He stepped down until they were at eye level. Despite everything his father was, the king cared deeply for Reginald. It was in the narrowing of his eyes and the tight line of his mouth.

"We will get them back, son," he promised.

"But who took them?"

This time, it was Captain Brannon who answered, his tone droll, bored. "It was the Resistance." His gaze was knowing. Like all along he'd never believed their lies regarding Corvina's whereabouts and what had befallen her.

Tobias hated the captain, yet for a moment he felt as though the soldier could prove himself useful somehow.

"I told you they were searching for the Elementals, Your Majesty. They found and took her because you did not heed my words." He leaned forward just as Tobias opened his mouth to speak. "Let us do away with formalities, prince. We both know that the emperor's priest did not just go missing on his own accord. Let me be clear, I do not care for the fate of that fat fuck. My only concern here is for the princess. She is valuable to the emperor, and therefore to me."

Tobias wanted to snarl at him, but his father's hand squeezing his shoulder held him back.

"You can understand our reluctance to trust anyone outside of our own family, Captain Brannon," the king said diplomatically. "We were unsure if your intentions were impure or not." He released Tobias. "Now, I think we can come up with an agreement that benefits everyone..."

Captain Brannon glared suspiciously at the king. "What sort of agreement?"

"The emperor wants Corvina. If you agree to help us get her back from this pesky Resistance, as you call them, perhaps Emperor Laurel can... *borrow* her for a certain amount of time, and you return her to my son, unharmed of course, after he has no need of her."

"And would the prince..." Captain Brannon's gaze slid towards him. "...approve of such an arrangement?"

He wanted to scream out that no, he did not approve. Corvina was his to do with as he pleased. Not the emperor's, not anyone else's. But a glance from his father told him to be smart. That there was more to this than he could even begin to imagine. And he was right. For the first time in his life, Tobias would not let the anger rule him. Because his fucking wife was missing and he needed her back. And Captain Brannon had knowledge of the Resistance that they did not. He could help them get her back.

And when Tobias had her in his grasp again, he would show her the consequences of leaving him. She would rue the day she left and took their son with her. He would make her pay for her insolence. And he would relish in it.

"I want her back," Tobias conceded. "I do not care what it costs. I want them *both* back."

And Captain Brannon smiled. "We will," he assured. "We will get them all."

The King's Message

"Dawn?" Corvina's knees almost gave out as she exited the king's tent and came face to face with her friend. The last time she'd seen her, she'd peeked at her from between the bars of iron, her eyes begging for rescue.

Her friend still looked pale and tired, though no longer that haggard version of herself. She stood tall, wearing new clothes, old and frayed, but they were not tattered rags like she'd had before. It was a simple brown dress, a dull color that made her skin look brighter.

Gale, Juniper, and Wren were behind Dawn, as if standing in wait for Corvina as well. But her sole focus was on her oldest friend. The friend she had failed. The friend she had gotten locked up and tried to protect despite it.

Once upon a time, Dawn would have dropped into a curtsey to greet Corvina. She did not. There was a hard edge about her. She was no longer soft and caring, but something else. Anger and resentment wrapped around her like a shield she dared not drop. She didn't smile or appear to be happy to see Corvina like Corvina was to see her. Then again, they'd led very different lives. She'd suffered in a cold dungeon and Corvina had lived in a lush palace. Dawn likely hated her, and that thought brought a fresh pang of regret and hurt in her chest.

"So that's the boy, then." Dawn nodded at Basil, who was asleep in her arms. The talk of adults had bored him drastically.

Dawn had never seen Basil before. She'd seen Corvina large and pregnant the times when she went to visit her in her cell. She'd never actually met her son.

"This is Basil," Corvina whispered.

"Hmm," Dawn hummed, "He looks like your father, my lady." That was her acceptance. That even though Basil was half human, born of cruelty and malice, he was accepted by her oldest friend. Before a smile could tug at her lips, Dawn said, "We will stay here, my lady." It was a command, not a request. And just another way in which Dawn had changed.

"Dawn..."

"I am *not* going back to be locked in a prison cell and tortured, and neither are you."

"We are not safe here—"

"We are not safe *there* either, my lady. And this time, I will not stand by and watch you ruin all of us again."

Corvina felt their presence at her back as they exited the tent and stopped to watch. Her face heated. She did not want the Fae to hear this conversation. To think her more weak than they probably already did. After Clay professed to keep her safe, she told them she would think on it, for she didn't know what else to say. Then she stood and left.

"For so long you hoped our people were still alive and they are. We will be protected here. We will be free." Dawn stepped forward and gave Corvina's shoulder a squeeze. "Think on it." She pulled away, leaving before Corvina could say anything to her.

As soon as she was gone, her three maids surrounded her. Wren took Basil from her arms, hefting him up and pressing his head into the crook of her neck.

"She is very rude," Gale commented. She was staring at Dawn's retreating form. She turned to Corvina. "Would it be imprudent of me to say that I agree with her that we should stay here?"

"Gale, it is not your place," Juniper admonished.

Corvina blinked at her maids, ignoring their banter. "Your collars!" she gasped. They were gone, with nothing but the puckered scars as evidence that had been left behind.

Juniper's hand encircled her neck. Her smile was shy, tentative. "Yes... They found a blacksmith to take them off."

"That's..." Tears threatened to choke her once more. "That's *wonderful*, Juniper."

Corvina was well aware of the Fae at her back, taking in this interaction with unabashed curiosity. She didn't want to focus her attention on them, but they made it too difficult. Especially when Clay stepped around to stand next to her, setting his body at an angle so he could glance between Corvina, Juniper, Wren, and Gale.

"Ladies." He gave a proper bow in the direction of her maids. When he turned to Corvina, she nearly jolted at the heat she found there. She tried not to flinch from the intensity of it. "If you'll allow me, I will show you around camp?"

Out of her peripheral, she saw Gale swoon and Juniper and Wren share conspiratorial glances. None of them spoke, leaving the decision up to Corvina.

"I—" She didn't want to spend any more time around the Fae male. Just being near him was a sharp reminder of *everything.* She was determined to put him as far in the back of her mind as possible. But... She searched her maids' gazes, finding them all but bouncing on the tips of their toes. Surely a single tour around the camp... Corvina sighed in defeat. "Okay," she conceded.

She ignored the bright, near-blinding smile he tossed at her and started forward. She had no clue where she was going, but walking ahead helped her steel her nerves against Clay and this strange place she suddenly found herself in. She felt like she'd been shoved out the life she knew and everything around her was spiraling.

"The camp stretches out for a few miles." Clay caught up to her, swaggering in his gait, his voice calm as he explained. "Thanks to the Unseelie, there's a glamor set around the camp so humans can't see it. We all have a job here and try to work in harmony. Over there is the tent where Ryker tends to the sick." He pointed to a fairly large tent at the edge of camp where several Fae hobbled in and out through the flaps. "If you feel unwell, don't be afraid to seek him out. He's a scary bastard, but he is happy to help."

The sight of the tent made Corvina shudder, and immediately her hackles rose while her weak, broken body filled with shame. Why had he shown her that particular tent first? Her haggard appearance seemed suddenly much more conspicuous.

"I am not sick," she whispered, the vehemence strangling out of her on a whisper. She was aching, hurting, covered in scars, but she wasn't *sick*. Not like the others were. She didn't have a disease, and her heart ached to think they thought it as such.

Clay's steps faltered. "I didn't say that," he said softly.

She didn't realize they'd stopped walking and were staring at each other, measuring the other up. She had to force her gaze away and march forward as best as her weak knees would allow.

"Lady Corvina..." She could feel his hand hovering near her body, and she gritted her teeth to avoid flinching away.

"The tour?" she reminded him.

He was silent a moment before continuing, "If you are hungry, food is usually prepared around the evening. Everyone is welcome to help themselves, however the children and elders are always the first to take their meals before the women hand food out to the men."

"Is that what's expected of us, then?" Gale asked cheerily from somewhere behind them. "To make ourselves useful around the camp, I mean. Will we serve meals?"

Instead of ignoring the maid like men usually did, like Corvina expected Clay to do, he turned fully to place his whole attention on Gale. Corvina turned to look and found Gale blushing with obvious surprise, especially when he flashed her a dazzling smile.

"If you decide to stay..." His gaze veered towards Corvina for a single moment. "There is plenty of work to be done. Choose what makes you feel most comfortable. Whether that be caring for our orphans, sewing, cooking, or serving meals."

"What about that?" Gale pointed.

A blacksmith was hammering away at a blade, his thick, strong arm rising over his head only to come swinging down to create a clang that resonated throughout the camp, becoming a sort of drum beat to the rest of the noise.

"If you want to pursue your time as the blacksmith's helper, I am sure there will be no objections, my lady."

Gale giggled.

"I've sent a few Fae to procure materials to build a tent for you." He continued walking, passing around the camp. As he did, more than one Fae waved and called out to him. Corvina noted it was mostly women, tittering flirtatiously. "You can stay here if you wish." He stopped before a tent. Corvina recognized it. It was the one she'd awoken in. "The tents for your maids will be set around you if it will make you feel more comfortable, Lady Corvina."

She avoided his stare by looking at her provisional home. It did not matter that she was used to a lavish life. Finery didn't matter in the face of unhappiness. She'd been filled with riches galore and had been miserable. And Clay's voice held hope that this tent would be adequate enough for her, but it didn't matter.

She wouldn't stay here long enough for it to be of consequence.

"Thank you," she said to Clay without looking at him. "I think I would like to rest now."

"Of course, my lady." He bowed low in her direction. She didn't see his bright green eyes shining, as she avoided his gaze, but she could feel them trained on her. His stare was demanding, penetrative. Like he was searching for something within her. Expectant of something she could never find strength enough to give. Something she didn't deserve to give, nor did she want to. It didn't matter.

Nothing did.

She belonged to another.

"Good day." She pushed through the tent flaps, breathing a little easier inside with him away from her. But she could still feel him on the other side, standing a moment, and she pictured him staring longingly after her before he turned and bowed to her maids.

"Ladies," he whispered.

Then he was gone, and her maids pushed into the tent. Wren walked over to the cot to set a sleeping Basil against the pillows. He barely stirred.

"Will you sleep as well, my lady, or would you prefer to dress?" Juniper asked.

Corvina looked down at her shift. The hem rose above her calves scandalously. The material hugged her thin body, against every poking bone. They'd all witnessed how haggard she was. That thought had her saying, "Dress, please."

Juniper nodded and went to the corner of the room. "It is not of fine make, but Lord Valentino found it for you..." She turned with a simple, blue and white dress in hand. It looked easy enough to move around in. There was no corset or all the accoutrements a princess was obligated to wear, a fact she was grateful for once Juniper brought the dress over her shoulders and it fit snug against her body.

"Who is Lord Valentino?" Corvina asked. Her stomach twisted at the thought of finding the man, but she was not so far gone that she couldn't thank him for his hospitality.

"My lady, Lord Valentino is Clay." Juniper pulled the ties at Corvina's back, securing it in place. "Now, are you hungry? I am sure they would not mind parting with a bowl of soup for you." Juniper's eyes roved down Corvina's form. Words she didn't dare say were on the tip of her tongue, but Corvina read them anyway.

Did everything think her so pathetic?

"A meal would be nice, Juniper."

Juniper curtsied.

"I shall go help her, my lady." Wren scrambled after Juniper, leaving Corvina alone with Gale.

The quiet pressed around them uncomfortably. Gale stood off to the side, stealing glances at Corvina's still form. She opened her mouth, closed it again.

Corvina let out a deep sigh. "You have something to say, Gale."

"My lady, the others have made it quite clear that it is not my place—"

"I am not so formal as to prohibit you your freedom to speak, Gale," she said gingerly. "You have been very kind to me. It was only because of you that I was freed from that prison in the first place. Please, if you have something to say, I will hear it."

Gale twisted the hem of her apron. "Well, my lady, you see, I know you think me very daft, but I *am* a maid. I do know the ways of the world, and I have witnessed suffering firsthand. Despite that, I like to think on the bright side and imagine a different hand than the one I was dealt..."

Her fanciful thoughts suddenly made much more sense then. Corvina supposed not everyone who suffered wallowed in that sadness. Everyone perceived and moved forward differently as they wished. She didn't know Gale's story, but her maid looked on the bright side of things. Perhaps Corvina and the others had judged her too harshly without knowing what it was she'd gone through...

"Forgive me for saying this, my lady, but frankly your life before was sad and drenched in violence. The way I see it, you've been saved. Given a second chance. It would be such a shame to waste this opportunity without experiencing it first. Perhaps..." Her face flushed. "Perhaps you might even find your happiness here." There was an undertone to her words, the same look she got when she mentioned handsome men. It was in that dreamy eyed look of hers.

Corvina knew she was thinking of Clay.

"I am married," Corvina reminded her, keeping the bite from her tone. "As you well know. I cannot leave Tobias..." Even saying the words hurt. She had no love for him, and he would have killed her besides. Everyone knew it, so why was Corvina fighting this?

It was because she feared the villains unknown more than she did the known. Because she feared a war. She feared bringing her husband's wrath down upon these people.

She tried to imagine Clay skewered with her husband's sword. He would do it, if he knew. It was another reason she would reject the bond between them.

She would not be the reason for their demise.

"I know, my lady," Gale said sadly. "But if we all go back, the prince will not take kindly to us leaving in the first place. And, well, there is quite a possibility that he will kill Juniper, Wren, Dawn, and myself. And imagine all he would do to you if he had you back. You are free from his clutches now. I know you might be afraid to explore this freedom, but don't let fear hold you back from something that could be an amazing future."

"Thank you for your words, Gale. I shall think on them."

But Corvina didn't know what to do. The future was dripped in uncertainty as much as it was dripped in violence and blood and death. Either hers or others. And Corvina would always much rather die than be responsible for the pain of others. Not to mention her son...

How could she protect him outside of the castle, where she knew nothing of the world, where she had no money, no connections?

Her head began to pound at her temples, and she felt exhaustion start to pull her under. She didn't want to contradict Gale and tell her that she was living in a fantasy, because she was no one to decide that for anyone else. Gale's thoughts were her own.

But for the moment, Gale was right. Corvina was too weak to go back, and she feared the Fae wouldn't let her leave. Not if she was as important as they all claimed her to be. For now, she could do nothing. Nothing except eat a meal and rest.

And try to gain her strength for what she knew was to come.

Two days passed and Corvina couldn't find solid footing within her camp. It was evident that none of her maids could, save for Dawn and oftentimes Gale. Dawn was studiously ignoring Corvina. Sometimes it felt like a punishment, but more often it felt like she didn't know how to approach her former lady. Not now, not after what had become of them both. Corvina felt the same sensation, whereas Gale had fallen into place due to her friendliness.

Already she had learned the names of everyone at camp, and they all passed by and greeted the human. At least, most of them anyway. A lot of them looked at her with fear.

"How odd," she commented around the fire they all sat near. Her fingers fluttered nervously against her skirts, like they were searching for something to do.

They hadn't volunteered to help around camp just yet. They were still getting their bearings. Or they were waiting for Corvina's permission. She didn't feel comfortable with her maids out of her sight for long periods of time. They were the only thing she knew in this strange new world, and she found herself tethering herself to them as if they were a crutch she needed to walk, to survive.

Her maids didn't comment upon her weakness, but she knew they saw it. Knew they looked at her with pity when they thought she didn't notice.

Gale leaned forward. "They stare at me like I'm some circus animal."

Juniper snorted. "It is because you are human," she clarified.

Gale sat back again with a soft huff. "Is that how you all felt, then? Like your every move was being watched? Like they were looking at you like some monster waiting for you to snap?"

It was Wren who answered, pressing her fingers to the scars against her neck where the collar had been. "Yes."

"Hmm, interesting."

"Mommy, I would like to see Shula again." Basil tugged on Corvina's skirts, pulling her away from the conversation. The fire crackled, shining brightly against her son's skin, painting him bronze. An enormous pot rested over it, a fish stew bubbling from within.

Corvina sighed at the question. It wasn't the first time her son had asked to see the fire Elemental, and he was growing increasingly irritated every time Corvina said no.

It wasn't that she didn't trust the former Fire Dancer. In fact, of everyone in camp besides her maids, Shula Azzarh was the one she admired the most. She was just wary to let Basil out of her sight and didn't want to impose on the other Elemental.

"No, Basil," Corvina said softly.

He let out a whine and crossed his arms against his chest. She blinked at his reaction in surprise. He'd never been one to throw tantrums or pout. She supposed it had been bound to happen sooner or later, especially now that he'd found a friend.

"I miss her," he said.

Corvina felt her heart crack, but she didn't have long to contemplate the feeling when a ruckus at the far end of camp drew her attention away. There were shouts of surprise, the clang of swords. Her heart felt as though it would burst from the sounds alone.

Was it Tobias? Had he come to take her back?

She pushed to her feet, waving at her maids and Basil. "Watch him," she ordered before her feet carried her towards the noise. She still wasn't at her strongest, as her injuries hadn't completely healed, but she did feel better. Her strength was returning, and though she wobbled as she hurried towards the commotion, not every step pained her.

A crowd had formed and she was at the very back, catching snags of the conversation.

"How did you get in here?" a voice demanded.

She caught sight of a soldier atop a gray steed. He wore the colors of Dana. She felt her heart plummet to her stomach.

"Your glamor is not so effective on half-Fae," the man on the mount sneered down. "I would have a word with your leader, for I bring a message from King Archibald and Prince Tobias of Dana."

The High Lord's Message

Their wards weren't as sound as they had let themselves believe. Not if this soldier had managed to get through simply because he was half-Fae. He had slid from his mount, confident in his success, and pulled the helm from his head to reveal hair shorn short and the tips of his ears. They weren't sharp like Valerio's, though they did have a slight curve. He faced off Julius with a smug smirk, staring at the tip of the sword as though he did not fear death.

As if he were so confident in his survival.

Valerio nodded. He would meet with the half-Fae and hear what it was the king and prince had to say. He had expected something like this. Perhaps not a messenger, but rather outright war. This was preferable, he supposed, to finding his men dead surrounding the perimeter. Though that was still an option.

He sent a mental message to Weylyn to fortify their borders in case of attack. He would not let himself be distracted by this messenger.

He led the soldier into their war tent. He was not alone. Uric, Julius, Clay, and Iona were with him. As far as protection went, he felt the utmost confidence in his companions.

Julius led the half-Fae by the tip of his sword into the tent then circled so they were all facing the smirking man.

"Nice little camp," the messenger began, too cocky, too confident.

Valerio did not listen to the obvious bait. "I have heard of your kind before," he said, pressing his palms to the desk and leaning forward. "Half-Fae who whored themselves out to the Emperor of Illyk..." And because they were still part human, they had been allowed to live and thrive in a way that full-blooded Fae had not.

The soldier's smile faltered, lip twisting into a sneer. "If I follow the emperor, it is because Fae like you have done me no fucking favors in my lifetime."

Julius snorted. "Traitor."

The soldier met him with a cool gaze. "Call me all the names you wish. I do not care for your opinion. I come bearing a message from the royal family of Dana, and you will hear it."

Valerio slowly lowered himself into his chair behind his table where the map and pieces were spread out. "What is his message?"

"They want the bitch back and his heir."

"Over my dead fucking body!"

Valerio closed his eyes against his cousin's tirade. Of course Clay had to go and open his big, fat mouth.

The soldier leveled an amused glance at Clay. "Those are his wife and son. According to Danarish law, leaving your spouse is an offense punishable by death. Harboring the prince's bride and son will cost you dearly. However, he is willing to offer a truce if you merely give him back what rightfully belongs to him."

Clay felt the blood within his body begin to stir to life, heating to a boiling point as he stared at this soldier. This half-Fae who had betrayed his own kind to hunt them down like fucking dogs. Perhaps Clay would have felt sympathy for him, but he only knew rage as he stared in the face of the man who was threatening his mate and her son.

He was no abuser, but he knew their minds. Knew how obsessive they could become. How angry. The truce this soldier was offering was nothing more than smoke and mirrors, an illusion of peace in the hopes that they would bend the knee and lower their gazes, only to find a sword cleaving through the backs of their necks.

Clay met the man's gaze with fury of his own. He stood to his full height. "You can tell King Archibald and Prince Tobias that the Fae accept no truce. We will not yield to him or his whims. High Lady Corvina and Basil are under our protection."

The half-Fae gritted his teeth. "You are making a mistake. Fail to hand them over, and you will be met in battle and drown in blood."

At this, Clay smirked. It was a funny turn of words, surely, for the only ones that would drown in blood would be them if they dared try and take his mate from him.

"I will repeat, Lady Corvina and Lord Basil are under the protection of the Fae Resistance. They are under *my* protection as the High Lord of the Sapphire Court, and they are under the protection of my cousin, the King of all Seelie. A slight against them is a slight against us."

The soldier snorted. "Your 'Resistance' is going through an awful lot of trouble over one stupid Fae cunt. Tell me, my lord, does she have a magical pussy? Is that why you and my prince are so willing to fuck everyone over for the bitch?" He barked out laughter, harsh and mirthless.

Clay barely blinked. It was instinct to wrap his fingers around the pommel of his sword and unsheathe his blade.

The man stared at it with a scoff. "My king and prince will not take kindly to that, so I would think twice about it if I were you, High Lord."

"Oh, I have." He swung the blade, rendering his opponent immobile at the same time with the force of his magic. Steel connected against the flesh of his neck and sliced through. Blood splattered, staining Clay's grinning face. As the head tumbled to the floor and the body followed, Clay sneered down at the dead man. "And I do not take kindly to anyone threatening my mate."

The man was already dead, yet Clay still spoke as if he were alive. He bent, picking the head up in a single hand. "Let this be a message from the High Lord of the Sapphire Court to the Danarish King and Prince, shall it? Uric? The Danarish throne room."

Uric snickered and a moment later, a portal opened in front of them, the mirrored surface portraying Clay's feral expression. It was one that was startling and unfamiliar. One that arose when he found his mate threatened, and one he would wear time and time again if it meant her protection.

"Let this be our message of war," Clay whispered to himself a second before he threw his arm back and tossed the head into the portal.

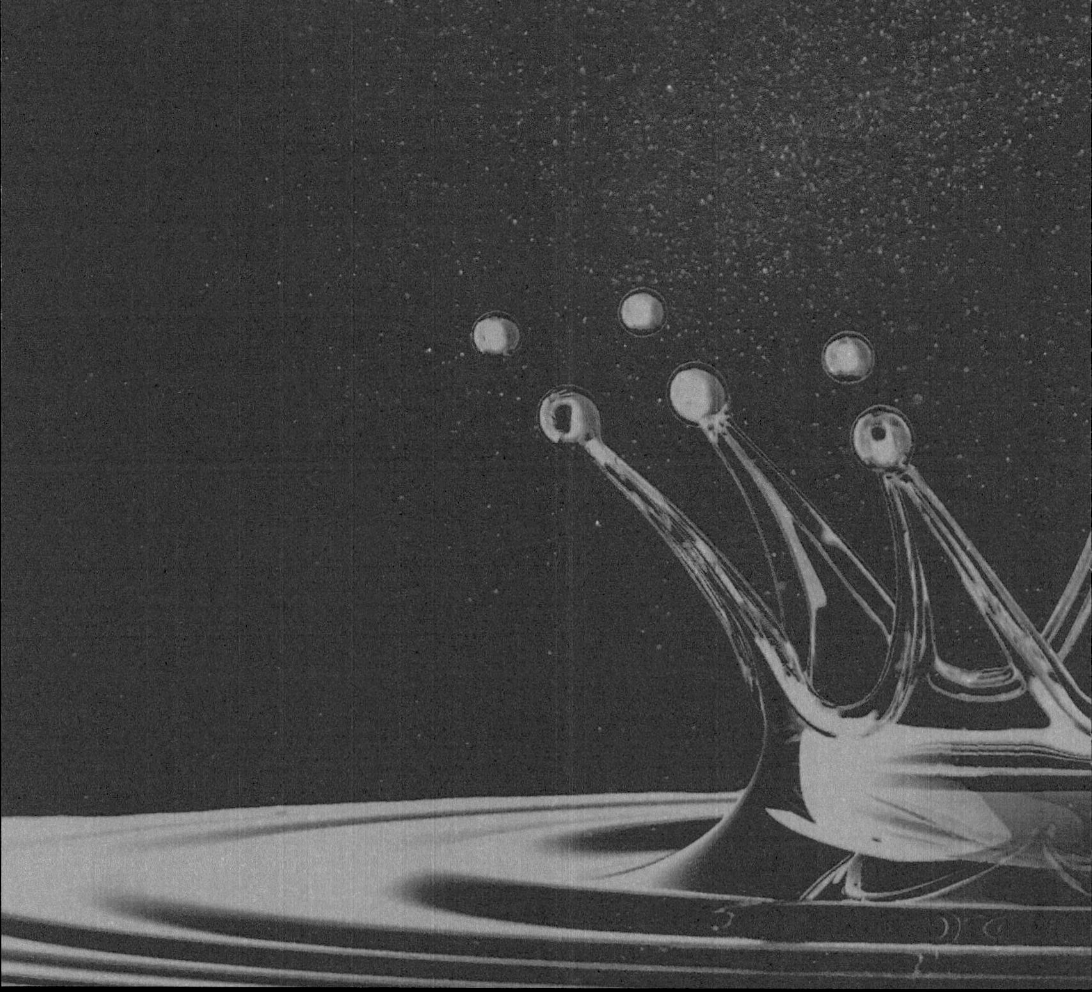

Dawn's Truth

Corvina bit down hard against her hand to avoid crying out at the violence she'd just witnessed. At the ease with which Clay sent a sword slicing through another's head and tossed the appendage through a portal with little remorse. In fact, he smirked as blood spattered his face while he defended her honor in violence and brutality.

She shivered and slammed her eyes closed. She didn't want to see anymore. Didn't want to hear anymore. She was used to Tobias' violence. She was used to him inflicting pain on her behalf as well. This... this wasn't what she wanted. Not from Tobias, not from Clay, not from anyone.

Maybe that made her weak, like so many other things made her weak. She didn't care. She never *asked* for this. For death to stain her hands, her soul. All she'd wanted was to give a chance for her people to survive.

Slowly she backed away from the tent, letting the flap fall back into place. The smell of blood was still sharp, and she tried to muffle it and her heavy breaths behind her hand. She walked backwards blindly until she was far enough away from the tent that she was sure she wouldn't be heard. Only then did she drop her hand and give out a choked sob before she turned and ran.

Tobias' threat rang in her head. The death of his messenger was an act of war, and the Danarish would bring it upon this camp tenfold. Over her and over Basil. He would stop at nothing until they were back in his clutches again. He would bring the might of his armies to these people. These people who had been nothing but nice and accommodating. The people that Gale spoke about every moment of every day. The ones that stopped by to smile tentatively at her before rushing away.

None of them were safe. No one was. Not when Tobias was raging. Not when he set his mind to violence. He wouldn't stop. And when he came and decimated this camp, Corvina would have no one but herself to blame. She should have never left that dungeon. She should have never went with the Resistance...

She came to an abrupt halt when her body smacked into another. She gasped, blinking away tears she hadn't known had fallen against her cheeks, and met Dawn's stern expression.

Once upon a time, Dawn would have comforted her. She would have held her close like friends did and soothed her with a few words. But that time had long been forgotten and this Dawn was someone else. That much was evident by the sneer she wore.

"Crying again?" She sniffed in Corvina's direction with derisive sort of disdain. "You never used to cry so often."

Corvina had to take a few moments to catch her breath, to blink away the tears. Her patience with Dawn suddenly felt like it was fraying. She had dealt with her comments and sneers for far too long already and had borne the brunt of her hatred because she'd felt responsible. She had cowed, because she felt she had deserved it. Now, she felt as though Dawn was merely being hateful for the sake of it. "You would be weeping too, Dawn, if you knew what I have had to live with for years. What I still have to live with." Her voice shook. She wanted to be strong, to make decisions, to be a force like Shula, like Iona, but she was weak and afraid.

"I know what you have had to live with. Do you think just because I was locked up, I did not hear the whispers of what that bastard prince did to you for years?"

Corvina's head tilted a fraction. "Knowing and experiencing are different things."

She snorted. "Oh, I am very intimate with what it means to have a human man force himself between your thighs. You are lucky, my lady, that it was only your husband. I suffered a rotation of guards for years."

"Dawn..." Corvina started to reach for her, but her maid stepped back. She masked her hurt with compassion. "You never told me."

"I was not going to further add to your self-piteous thoughts. You are too self-sacrificing, my lady. It's why we are in this fucking mess in the first place."

Corvina jolted back as if she'd been slapped. She'd never heard done speak so crassly. "I was trying to protect our people..."

"And I commend you for it. Back then, I wanted to jump. I wanted to end this precise suffering I knew we would go through for your benefit and not my own. I knew you would break. I knew he would take that goodness in you and twist it until my lady was unrecognizable. I watched you, day after day become something you never were. At first, I was sad. Now, I think you are pathetic."

"Dawn, how dare—"

"It's true. Do not try to deny it. Look at yourself... You come running with tears on your cheeks because you witnessed, what was it?" Dawn tilted her head to the side, waiting for the response.

"T-they killed the messenger."

"Pft. The messenger that would have dragged you and Basil back to that bastard and you weep for him."

The tears flowed freely even as Corvina tried to stop them. She didn't dare swipe them away, but she glared at Dawn. "I do not weep for him. I weep for this camp, for the people. Tobias will come and slaughter them all for me. How can I live with myself if I allow it to happen?"

Dawn stepped forward and gripped Corvina's arms in her hands. Her strength was surprising as she shook Corvina, as if willing sense into her.

"It is no fault of yours what others choose to do. Your responsibility lies only in how you deal with it, how you confront it. If you run back to him, then what these Fae went through to save us all will be for nothing. Once upon a time, you were willing to sacrifice yourself to save your people. Well, take a look around, my lady. These *are* your people, and they need you. Not me, not Juniper or Wren, but you. An Elemental. To save us all. And if you aren't willing to fight to save them, then you aren't the High Lady I thought you could be."

Dawn pushed away, still wearing her glare.

"I am not the same as I once was, Dawn," she whispered, feeling the fight seep out of her.

"No," Dawn agreed. "You are far more deplorable."

Her words hurt and cleaved something in Corvina's chest. While they were true, they were spoken harshly, with little remorse. They beat her down, made her feel smaller...

"My lady, you come from a long line of Rhian royalty. You were brave, but you have become the weak, frightened mouse that *he* turned you into. You are out of his clutches. Find your voice again, rediscover who you are because you, my lady, are the daughter of a High Lord. You are a High Lady in your own right, and it's time you started *acting like it.*"

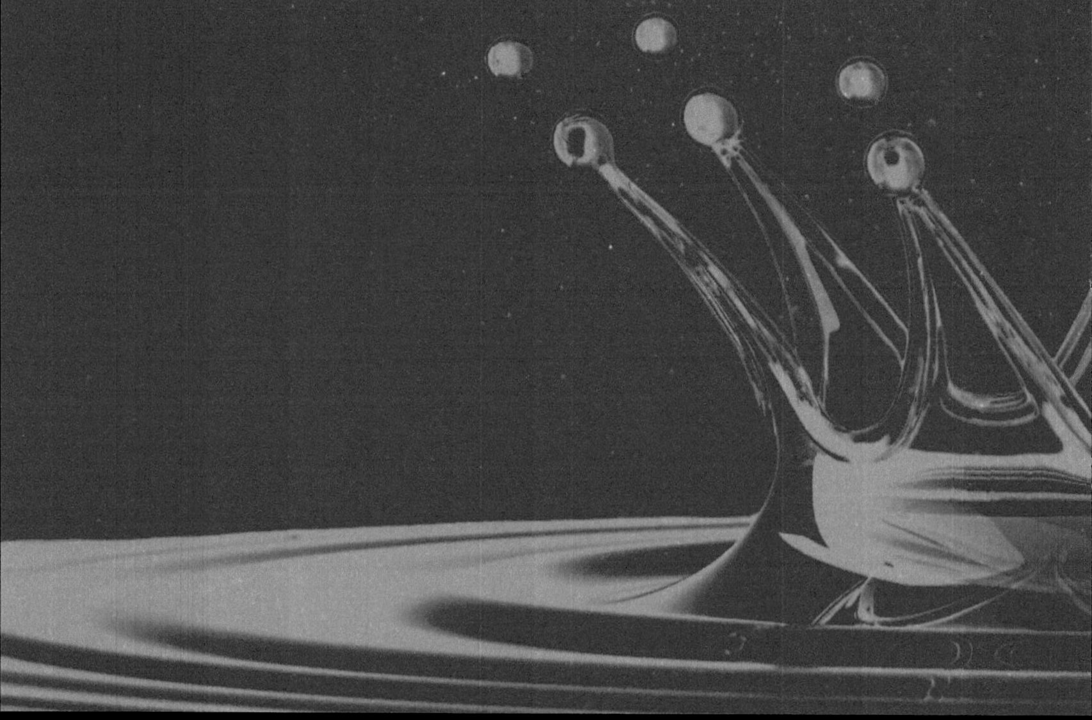

This Means War

They were in the throne room when a mirror shimmered into existence. The guards cried out and circled around the Danarish King on his throne to protect him from the strange Fae magic.

Tobias leaned forward, curious and anxious to see what would arrive. Magic meant Fae, and that likely meant his wife. Was the messenger bringing her and his son back with this strange magic?

A mirror appeared. As tall as a doorway, the surface shining with their own reflections staring back in a waving, distorted way. Something flew from the surface, a blur, before the mirror disappeared and the object bounded with a wet squish against the floor. It rolled like a ball, sliding and leaving a trail of red behind it before it settled to a stop.

A guard moved forward cautiously, turning the thing with the tip of his sword.

It was the severed head of their messenger.

Tobias sneered in disgust at the sight.

"Someone clean this mess up," the king ordered with impatience.

Guards scrambled to obey, searching for maids. Meanwhile, Arthur and Tobias both turned to their father. But the king's eyes were not on them. It was on the head, the blood. He stood to a slow stand and stepped down from his throne. His robes trailed against the floor and he came to a stop before the head, setting his foot atop it as he stared down at the dead man.

"You know what this means, my sons," he said slowly. They didn't need to answer. The king kicked the head away and finally turned to face them both. "This means war."

A Monstrous Healer

No one mentioned what happened to the messenger, though the whole camp knew he'd been killed, and no one confronted Corvina about her eavesdropping. They probably hadn't noticed. Her stomach still felt unsettled, but Dawn's words resonated louder than her own discomfort.

She should have heeded the words, but she couldn't. Physically, mentally, what Dawn said didn't register. Yes, it hurt, but it was hard to contend who she was now with who she had once been. How could she find herself when the future was so uncertain, when she was destined for death at every turn?

Tobias' voice, and the fear he'd implemented into her, were louder than Dawn's. It was a cocoon around her, and nothing else was able to get past it. Not bravery or Dawn's truth. It was just easier to become what she'd been made into rather than find her courage again only to be torn back down. And it was an inevitability, because Tobias would bring his armies. He would come. And he would destroy them all.

It was a thought that plagued her for days.

Even now as she sat amongst the others, watching the two Elementals, the last of their kind, train together, she felt a sort of sadness. That they would have to fight the Danarish when they came for Corvina and Basil. That Tobias would be at fault for the eradication of the fire and ice Elementals.

But as they started to move, those thoughts were blown away to the back of her mind. She felt herself being hypnotized as Iona and Shula faced one another and began to battle. At first they were little more than a parry of swords and a blur of hair and fabric as they twirled and jumped away from one another. They clashed, raising shield arms to block and push back. Their grunts were like a song of battle, their movements lithe and fast.

Iona was a brutal fighter and when she struck, she struck true and with a jarring force of strength that rocked Shula back. She huffed out breaths that clouded in front of her as if she were cold, but there was a sheen of sweat shining against her ebony skin.

Meanwhile Shula was a quick, elegant fighter. She wasn't brutal or vicious like the former, but she was determined. Strength washed over her features and her feet moved like a dancer flying across stage. That quickness seemed to give her an advantage as she darted away from blows, tiring out her opponent.

Corvina found herself enthralled by them both, but her gaze strayed to Shula more. And when magic burst around them, she could barely suppress her gasp. Fireworks and snow exploded between them, perfectly controlled within the space of their battle. Yet Corvina felt the heat of Shula's sparks touch the bare skin at her arms. Their every movement looked effortless, perfectly trained. Corvina knew her water magic could likely never compare to this power, to this grit and determination.

A kaleidoscope of colors burned her eyes. Fire and ice warring, pushing the two Elementals away from each other. They fell back, landing on the ground with great huffs. They breathed in deep then sat up slowly. Iona smirked at Shula from across the space that separated them, flashing the elongated points of her canines.

"You're doing amazing," Iona called out as she pushed herself to her feet. Her smile was sincere, and her dark eyes were glowing with pride.

Shula hopped up on nimble feet, dusting off the backs of her pants. "So are you," she replied, her tone softer than Iona's but no less firm.

They walked, meeting in the middle, where they slapped palms together. Then Iona was turning and making her way towards Corvina while Shula followed. Corvina jolted as their attention turned on her. She thought herself all but invisible, a strange thing to feel because when she was near the other Elementals, it felt like a frisson of magic had been emptied across her every nerve. Her skin came alive and her magic responded. Like it wanted to be unleashed.

"Hey." Iona was hardly out of breath as she greeted Corvina.

"Am I bothering you?" Corvina asked, her voice lowering to a weak whisper. "I—I can leave if my presence is a distraction."

They hadn't approached her before now in almost the entire week she'd been at camp so she could only think that that's why. Because her staring upset them. She would hate to pull them from something as important as training, especially if it meant their life or death.

They shared a glance. "Of course not," Iona said slowly. "We were actually wondering if you'd like to join us."

"Me?" Her palm met her chest. "Train with you?"

Iona shrugged, flashing her dazzling smile. "Why not? It'd be interesting to see what our magic can do together."

Sure, Corvina thought, except for the fact that her body was too weak to even hold up a sword, not to mention a shield. That she would only get in their way and embarrass them and herself. She would rather not. Her head shook back and forth before the thought fully formed.

"No, thank you."

Her eyes strayed away before she could catch sight of their disappointment and they landed on Basil in the middle of the field, bending to lift a sword.

Corvina shot to her feet, shoving Iona and Shula away as she called out, "Basil, don't touch that!"

Her voice startled him. He jumped, his hand slicing across the edge of the blade. Blood came later, followed by his howling cry of pain. He dropped the sword as she made it to his side, dropping to her knees and lifting his palm up for examination.

"Basil what were you thinking?" she admonished. Her heart pounded with worry as she looked over his cut. Was it deep? Would she need to stitch the skin together? Mana, he was too young to be hurt, too young to receive an injury like this, and certainly too young to hold a sword.

Blood seeped from between his fingers down onto her own. Tears stained her eyes and she lifted her apron to try and clean the blood away.

"You know better than to touch weapons, Basil," she snapped. He wouldn't stop crying and his pain only put her in more distress.

"Ryker's coming, it'll be okay." She barely registered Shula's words before she was surrounded by the scent of confections and embers. It was a comforting smell and Corvina breathed it in before another scent permeated her nostrils. Of herbs like chamomile, lavender, and sage.

A body bent next to her and a man's massive, scarred hands slowly pried Basil's hands from Corvina's. She turned, catching sight of the scarred Fae male she always saw by Shula's side. The one who tended to the wounded of the camp. The one her maids said helped *her.*

It was only because of that she yielded.

Basil, however, took one look at the Fae and screamed.

It was due to the scars slashing over his face, distorting features that would otherwise be beautiful into something entirely different.

"It's okay." Shula bent to reassure him. "This is Ryker. He is the healer and will take away your pain."

At the sound of Shula's voice, Basil stopped his wailing. All it took were a few words from her for him to feel reassured. Something in Corvina's chest eased and a swell of admiration for Shula grew.

Basil's big, wet eyes regarded Ryker as the healer began swiping a wet cloth against his hand. "Are you a monster?" Basil asked unabashedly.

"Basil!"

But Ryker didn't seem offended. He let out a low, rumbling chuckle. Something that seemed foreign coming from him. He swiped the rag across Basil's skin again, clearing away the blood before he answered.

"No," he responded.

"Are you a soldier?"

Ryker smirked at her son. "I am a healer first and a soldier second."

"So you're a man?"

Ryker's head tilted slightly. "Yes."

"Do you fight and fuck?"

"Basil!" Corvina cried out, aghast at what just had come out of her son's mouth. "Where in Mana's name did you hear such a thing?!"

The admonishment, combined with his current pain, had tears filling his eyes again. "P-papa said it to me. He said that's what men do..."

Her eyes prickled and shame coated her cheeks as the Fae around her listened to this. It was nonsense, and she was surprised Tobias had influenced Basil at all. She supposed it had only been a matter of time for it to happen. He was his father, after all.

"Do not speak like that again, Basil, do you hear me?"

His lip jutted out. "Yes, mommy."

"Basil." Ryker drew her son's attention once more. "You will feel a sting of pain, is that okay?"

He sniffled. "Okay."

And then Ryker covered his palm over Basil's wound and he glowed. A white-yellow light emanated from his skin to envelop her son's injury. It lasted a second before he pulled away to reveal the smoothness of Basil's skin.

"All gone," Ryker rumbled. "How do you feel?"

Basil's eyes went wide. "Wow! Was that magic?"

"It was."

"Will you do it again?"

While Ryker and Basil chatted, Corvina slowly pushed to her feet. With the injury gone, the ache in her chest eased. Ryker and Shula would always have her gratitude. That much was evident.

"Corvina..." She turned her attention to Iona and Shula. They were looking at her with twin expressions of severity. "Can we have a word with you? In private?"

Want For No One

Corvina was a frightful creature whose shoulders pushed up to her ears and whose eyes darted around anxiously. She would jump at the sight of her own shadow or the slightest sound or raised voice. Iona watched the water Elemental closely and felt a surge of sorrow and sympathy for her. For what had been done to her and how it had twisted her.

There was strength in there. There had to be. Iona refused to accept anything less. She was an Elemental. She had that magic coursing through her veins. She was one of the most important Fae walking Illyk, and Iona wanted Corvina to believe that as fiercely as she herself did. As Shula did.

They left camp and pushed towards a spot that would give them a modicum of privacy. Both Iona and Shula turned to face Corvina. She seemed to wither under their gazes, and Iona wondered if the Fae was even aware that she was doing it.

"What did you want to talk about?" Her voice was soft, quiet. Her eyes darted between them, and Iona could catch a glimpse of a hint of mistrust and wariness. Iona wanted to reassure her, but because she didn't think the Fae would appreciate to, she bit her lip instead.

"We know we sprung all that information on you the other day, and for that we apologize," Iona said.

Corvina shuffled on her feet looking awkward as though she wasn't used to anyone apologizing. "I... It was quite a surprise to learn that the Emperor of Illyk was searching for me." Her gaze was shy as it bounced between them, stopping on Shula.

"We were surprised, too," Iona assured, drawing Corvina's gaze back. "We thought we were safe, or at least as safe as we could be in this world. Then we find out the emperor wants to find us and use us to eradicate the Fae?" She shrugged. "Puts a damper on our existence."

Corvina didn't laugh as Iona had hoped she would. Instead, she took her bottom lip between her teeth and chewed ferociously on it. "My husband wasn't going to turn me over to the emperor," she said softly. A flush rose on her cheeks as if she were embarrassed to utter the words. "He locked me up when he found out what I was and killed Brother Bastien so no one else would know..." She took a shuddering breath and shifted on her feet. "He wanted to keep me for himself."

"The emperor would have known you were alive anyway." Iona tried to match Corvina's softness, but her voice came out too firm. "He would have found out and come after you regardless of where you were hiding. Here or there, it's the same. The emperor knows we are alive and he wants us."

Corvina made a strangled sound that resembled a sob. Tears glistened in her bright eyes, but they didn't fall. "I have to hide... I have to take Basil and—"

"You *can't*," Iona interrupted, taking a step towards her. She didn't miss the way Corvina flinched back as if she'd been struck. "Don't you see? It doesn't matter where you hide. The Emperor of Illyk will find you. The only way we can beat him is like this. Together."

Iona's words were frightening Corvina with their intensity. Shula knew this because she had once been in Corvina's position. She had been on the other side of the Fae who wanted her to fight, vehemently denying anything to do with them and their war. Iona didn't understand, and Shula didn't think the ice Fae ever could.

She'd taken up the mantel of a warrior all on her own. She'd fought because she'd wanted to. She'd known fear, but not like Shula had known fear. Not like Corvina had obviously known fear. And it would take a lot more than simple words to get the water Elemental on their side.

It might take days, weeks, months even. Like it had taken Shula so long to accept her part to play in this war. But she wasn't focused on convincing Corvina. Not like Iona was. Not like the others were. Shula wanted to understand her. Reassure her. Become her friend. Because that's what she would have liked. That's how she'd wanted to be treated instead of thrown into their camp.

And after all, weren't Shula's and Corvina's situation similar? Both reluctant parties too afraid to reach for the power that lived inside them?

Shula shot Iona a look of exasperation then focused her whole attention on Corvina. "The concept of war is intimidating," she whispered. "When I first arrived, I wanted to be here about as much as you probably do right now. I get it. We shouldn't have to fight, and it's okay to feel that way." She told Corvina everything she wished the others would have said to her. She didn't admonish her; she *understood.*

That's all anyone in the world ever wanted, Shula supposed. To be understood.

"You don't have to fight if you don't want to. And I know the prospect of this camp seems daunting. How could it not? We are a massive group of Fae sure to draw attention to ourselves with our numbers alone. You're afraid of who will come after you, after Basil, and it's ok to feel fear. I felt it, too. But I'll be honest, these Fae will protect you and Basil with their lives. We will protect each other with our lives." She dared a slow step forward, careful to lift her hands at a snail's pace to not frighten her. She didn't flinch away, so Shula grabbed her hands, smoothing her fingers over Corvina's knuckles. Her skin was scarred, her bones disjointed. Evidence of her hardships lived on her skin. Shula had the urge to kiss each one of her knuckles like a mother would, like a sister would. And touching her? It caused magic to zap between them. The Elemental part of themselves recognizing each other. "We are stronger together, and together we will rise."

"I am afraid..." Corvina whispered as tears streamed down her cheeks.

Shula lifted a hand and brushed them away. "So am I," she confessed. "I am afraid every day of my life because I don't know what's coming. But I know what world I want to live in, and I know that I am going to fight for it to come true."

"I don't know how to fight."

"I didn't either, but I learned. And there's nothing wrong with not wanting violence. The world is cruel enough without seeking out war and retribution."

Behind them, Iona was quiet. Shula wondered if she disagreed with what she was telling Corvina. If she felt like she was discouraging her from helping them. Shula didn't care. She was being what no one could be for her at the time. She was being the friend she'd wanted and needed when she'd fallen into their clutches, forced into a war she wanted nothing to do with but had eventually accepted. She'd always thought that if someone would had treated her better, she would have been quicker to join. Maybe that was the case with Corvina.

The water Elemental needed gentleness. Understanding.

Shula had that in abundance.

And she hoped Corvina understood that.

Corvina felt power surge through her the longer Shula kept a firm grip on her hands. A part of her wondered if the fire Elemental had done it purposefully, touched her so their magic could intermingle and so Corvina could feel the truth behind her words. That they *were* stronger together.

She knew it to be true already from the moment they'd stepped into the dungeon to save her. She'd felt their magic, had felt strength surge through her. How else would she have been able to use her magic against that guard if not for them?

And Shula's words? They touched every fear Corvina harbored inside her heart with care. Here was another woman, touched by tragedy, who understood what it meant to fear. She did not think Iona fully understood. And if she did, her approach to her problems was different than Shula's and Corvina's. She seemed headstrong and resilient.

But Shula was telling her not to shove away her fears. She was telling her that she and Basil would be protected. That there was strength between them. That it was okay if she didn't want to fight.

That it was okay to be weak.

But was it, though? Was it okay to not be like them, these strong and proud women who fought with swords and used their magic so openly and viciously?

It was hard to fathom that Corvina could be like that. That she could ever be as strong as them. When all she'd ever been for the past four years was pathetic. She didn't know if she could even find her old strength and forge ahead like Dawn wanted her to do. If that was even possible for someone like her.

Slowly, she pulled her hands from Shula's and broke the connection. She took a breath, trying to sort her thoughts. Would she be safer with them? Or was it all pretty words disguised as lies? Tobias would stop at nothing to find her. When he came, did she want them there to witness his cruelty? To suffer because of her?

"I will think about it." She gave them the same answer she gave the Seelie Prince. The truth was, she didn't know what to do, what voice to listen to. Tobias' was the loudest. His threats of harm and war pushing aside the hope the others had in her. It was a misplaced hope, she thought. They were foolish to believe Corvina could ever be great.

She shook her head and took a step back. "I should go see to Basil now."

"Wait." Iona spoke, stepping forward. Her smile was almost arrogant. "Do you have the scars?"

Corvina froze. "Scars?"

"Yeah. The scars that mark us as the last of our kind. Down your back?"

That's what the scars had meant? She hadn't known. She'd known it was magic and it represented something important, but...

She closed her eyes against the sudden onslaught of memories. Of the pain searing down her back, of Tobias plowing into her body with little remorse as the first waves of pain hit. At the feel of his rough hands against her hips as blood flowed down her spine. At his hands shoving her away before his cock pulled out of her.

She felt like she couldn't breathe.

"I—I have to see Basil." She turned from them and ran away. Her legs tangled against her skirts so she hiked them up with trembling hands until she was far away from the Elementals and their harsh truths. Yet the memories still trailed after her. Shadows and phantom of previous pain. It made her skin itch. It made her want to reach for her scar. It made her want to sew her legs closed so Tobias could never enter her again.

Everyone was demanding pieces of her life, her heart, her soul, pieces she could not give. She was too broken already, and if she gave anymore she would disappear into dust and smoke.

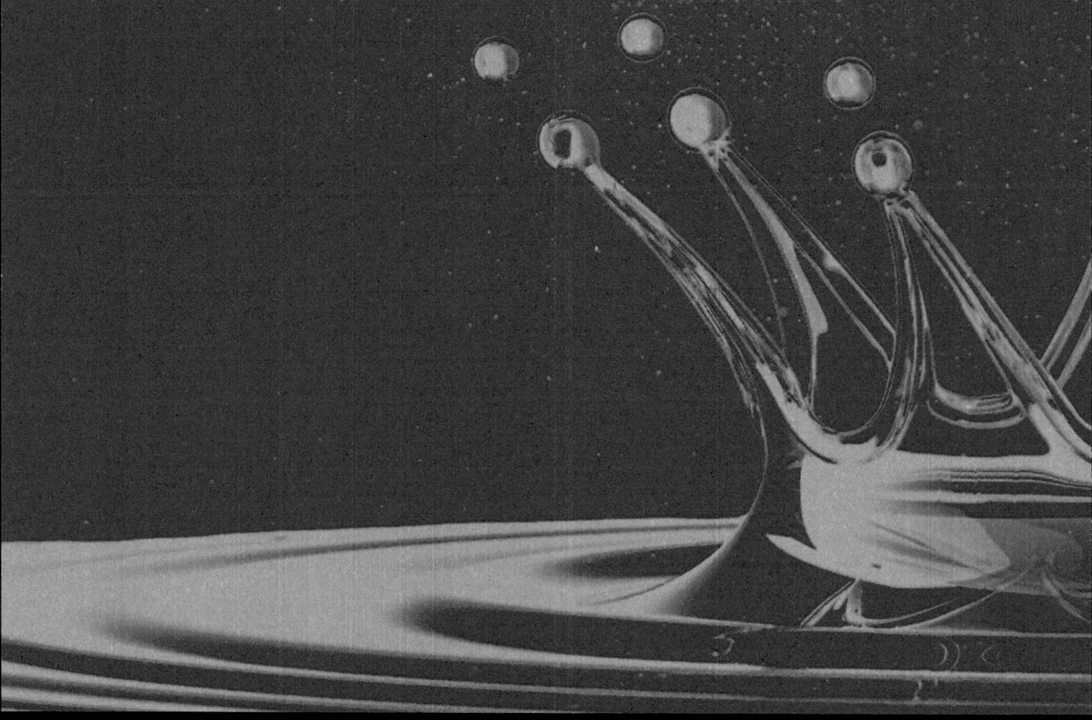

A Shield of Water

Corvina wondered what it would be like to be so free. So strong. To not cringe from everything. To be like Iona and Shula. To partake in the sweaty, violent mess of battle with determination on her face.

They hadn't asked her to fight again. Though she'd expected that, it still hurt and she couldn't fathom why. They saw her as something she wasn't, as something she feared she'd never be. At least they didn't mind that she still sat and watched them.

Every time their swords met in the middle, clanging together, she felt something zap down her soul. An itch. To use magic, to be as incredible as they thought she could be. But as quickly as the sensation arose, Iona and Shula would turn to her in unison, and it would dissipate.

But every night after they finished training and dispersed, Corvina would linger late when most of the others had gone to sleep and the fires still cackled and the patrol lingered on the outskirts of their camp.

That night was no different. She breathed harshly, staring at the space Shula and Iona had occupied hours before. She could imagine herself in her wildest of day dreams, in armor of gold, wielding a sword and shield, facing down all those who had ever wronged her.

On tentative footsteps, she walked into the space, reaching a shaking hand towards one of the swords. She picked up the one Shula had been using. Her arm trembled at the surprisingly heavy weight of it. The weapon was foreign in her hand, like something that didn't quite belong. Still, she lifted it and her shoulder ached. But for a second, she wanted to imagine what glory would be like. She wondered what it'd be like to fight beside the other Elementals.

Iona, wielding her sword of ice; Shula, making fire dance around them; and Corvina... The sword in her hand lifted as she mimicked a fighting stance Shula had done. She felt awkward and disjointed, holding it one-handed, but she ignored that and focused on her own magic. In her left hand, she let water come to life. It swirled and swirled around her arm until she carried a shield of water.

Her skirts threatened to tangle against her ankles as she took a step, thrusting the sword. She kept her balance, whirling, sparring, lifting her makeshift, magical shield against an imaginary opponent. None of the movements she made felt natural, and yet she felt fierce.

Was this what heroes in stories felt like? Powerful, yet strange? Like the weight of the sword was too heavy and yet somehow it fit within the palm of her hand perfectly? Even her magic felt like a strange combination of both, the shield whirling in small waves. She wasn't sure how protective such a thing would be in an actual battle and knew she'd never find out.

But for now, she could pretend. Pretend she was a hero. Someone worth fighting for. Someone unafraid.

With a grunt, she whirled, the heaviness of the sword causing her entire arm to tremble. She tried to hold strong, but weakness gave out and she dropped both with a cry, the pointed end of the blade sticking into the ground. Her chest heaved with every breath and tears pricked at her eyes.

Then a voice cut through the moment. "You are holding the weapon wrong."

Corvina's body jolted as she whirled. Her magic fractured, raining down to wet the earth as the shield vanished. She thought she'd been alone. That no one was watching her delusions of greatness. Anxiety prickled up her body, making the back of her neck itch.

Clay sauntered forward, a swagger in every step he took. She watched him warily, though she had to admit that she felt strangely like prey. Like he was hunting her. Maybe it was the way his bright eyes roamed over every inch of her figure. Not in a lewd way, but in a way that was far more intimidating.

She'd been very careful about avoiding him. For the most part, it worked, considering he was usually busy around the camp anyway. But sometimes he found ways to wedge himself into her personal space, charming her maids into senseless giggles and making a joke that would bring a smile to her son's face. No matter how hard she tried to ignore the connection between them, it seemed to pulse especially heavy when he was near.

It was maddening, to want something so badly and have it so close, only to pull back because you knew you didn't deserve it or trust it. That whatever lay there could never be because it was too good to be true. It was best for them both if the bond went ignored, so she pretended as though she didn't know it was there at all.

But it was hard to ignore as he stopped in front of her. Up close, she could make out the perfection of his every feature. From the dimple in his cheeks to the one in his chin that made him even more endearing. His hair was unruffled, and yet there was a method to the madness of it. There wasn't a single speck of sand on him, his posture perfect, his clothes even more so.

Once she would have fallen for his easy charm. She would have embraced what readily lay between them. But Corvina wasn't who she once was. She'd always been naïve, still was, but if there was one thing she'd learned since being in Dana, it was that sometimes the prettiest things were the most poisonous. He was no exception. She already knew of the violence he harbored inside. How long until he realized his charm failed and he turned that savagery on her?

"I suppose there is really no proper way to grip the sword, but in your case, you should hold it like this."

And then Clay was touching her. Her breaths froze in her throat as his fingers glided over her own. She was aware of him positioning her hand, but every touch was almost sensually deliberate, and she lost her focus on the task at hand. All she knew was his fingers trailing a delicate path against her skin. Never before had she been so lost in a touch or so hypnotized by it. It felt like magic, the kind that transcended the bonds of Mana. This was something else entirely. It made her breathing quicken and her chest constrict.

Corvina had never felt desire before. Only cruelty. But with Clay's hands on hers, she knew what it was that rushed through her veins and slid to tease between her legs. Foreign, it made her itch to bring her thighs closer together beneath her skirts, but she feared if she moved he would know what she was doing.

The thought shamed her. Was she so broken that she craved whatever gentle touch was given to her, even knowing blood stained his soul?

His fingers encircled her wrist. His body moved like it was a dance. Even though she was still, he loomed behind her, his chest crowding against her back. She felt the thundering of his heart against her body, heard his breath hitch as he leaned closer over her shoulder so their cheeks touched.

"Like this," he whispered. Closing her hand against the pommel of the sword, he kept his touch over hers, branding her skin with something that felt like a promise to never let go.

And Corvina couldn't move. She was frozen, in fear and desire, however strange that new feeling may have been.

This was a dangerous game. He was pushing past her walls. He was seducing her with his gentle touch. And she was falling for it. Because she was naïve. Because she was easily fooled. But despite all that, this just felt different.

She tried to imagine Clay's gentle touch wrapped around the blade without her interference. Of him in battle, facing against Tobias. They'd be a clash of swords and anger, and Tobias would *rage*. His sword would thrust forwards, bursting through Clay's chest—

Just like that, Corvina came to her senses. She jerked away from him with a gasp, dropping the sword. It was difficult to meet his gaze, but she forced herself to face his confusion. She didn't think he'd ever been rejected before. That much was evident. But she had to. For his own safety. For hers.

"Thank you for your guidance," she forced the words out. "That was very kind of you."

He looked like he wanted to scoff. "Kind. Yeah..."

"I think I will take my leave now." She picked up her skirts and prepared to flee his suffocating presence.

His gentle voice stopped her. "Lady Corvina, I—"

She half-turned and caught his unsure expression. "Yes?"

The smile he gave her was sad. "Never mind. Good night, Lady Corvina."

She nodded and turned, her feet carrying her away from him. With every step she took, she left behind the strange sensations he'd provoked. It would do no good to relish in them when they'd not be everlasting. Instead, she built a shield of protection around her heart, her soul.

Only that was enough to give her the strength to leave him behind.

"Would you like to train?"

Corvina startled from where she sat, glancing warily up at Clay as if surprised he'd asked her the question in the first place. He hid his concern behind a smirk, trying to make it look like he actually felt casual and carefree when, in reality, he didn't.

It had been days. Corvina was healing, a slow process when Ryker refused to use his magic, and even slower because her wounds had been inflicted with iron. Even with the dresses he'd provided to her maids hugging her thin body, he could make out the raised silver scars beneath the material and on her skin.

The night before he'd seen something in her that he hadn't before. A bright spark of life as she wielded sword and magic, like it was something she was meant to do. He wanted to see that expression again, hated the thought of her broken down.

He didn't want to imagine what it felt like to suffer what she had, what kind of effects it could have on her very soul, but Clay wanted to believe that hope was still prevalent within her. He'd seen a glimpse of it in her awkward form, with the pommel of the sword in her hand and the shield of her own making against her arm.

He remembered the touch of her, however small and gentle it may have been; it still seared him down to his bones. Maybe he wanted that again. Selfishly, he wanted to feel her, but more than that, he wanted her to feel safe and happy.

Slowly, Corvina blinked at him. He could feel her maids' gazes on them both, questioning and perhaps even a little smug.

"Excuse me?" she questioned.

He hefted one of the extra swords he carried in his hands. "Would you like to train with me? I thought we could work on your form, get you used to the weight of the sword and work on your stance if you're up for it."

Please be up for it.

She stared at the sword then back up at his face. He witnessed the flash of her eyes, of the same energy he felt her exude last night while she tried to train on her own under the cover of darkness. Perhaps secrecy was what she needed. Not all eyes on her, judging. She likely lived with daily scrutiny at the castle. Too late he realized that he'd fucked up by asking her publicly and stepped away.

"Sorry." He felt his face flushing, felt himself floundering. He stepped backwards, one step at a time. "I must have misunderstood..." He tripped over his own feet and was nearly sent careening to the ground. He wobbled then shot up, his face enflamed. Corvina's maids tittered behind their hands at his expense, but that was the least of his worries. He'd embarrassed Corvina. Her face was flushed with the evidence.

"Lord Valentino..."

He almost closed his eyes at the sound of his name leaving her mouth. He wondered what it'd sound like if she called him Clay. If she moaned it, whispered it, *revered* it.

"I apologize, my lady."

He turned and all but rushed away. He couldn't bring himself to meet Iona or Shula's eyes, knowing they'd witnessed that whole fiasco. And when he stormed past a cackling Julius, he rammed his shoulder into the other Fae.

"Fuck off."

"Yes, little lord," he laughed. "I told you this would happen."

That he had.

He'd never imagined trying to woo his own mate would be so difficult and yet he'd never been one to give up so easily. So he wouldn't. He would put happiness back into Corvina's eyes. He would see the fight again.

If it was the last thing he did.

She should have left with the others. It's what she'd wanted to do. But the call of the fire and the blade was too strong to ignore. So Corvina waited until they'd all gotten up and left. Then she sat, staring at the flames and the row of swords nestled side by side across from her.

She itched to pick one up again. Something held her back. She didn't know what, not until she heard the footsteps approach.

Even though she heard him, even though his scent wrapped around her like a dense fog, she still jumped when he called out to her.

"Lady Corvina, I thought I'd find you here."

Her hands broke out into a cold sweat. Last night, she'd been so overwhelmed by his presence that she hadn't realized the position she was in. Alone at night with another male. She eyed him like a prowling predator, fearful because even though her strength was growing every day, he was still infinitely stronger than she could ever be. He could harm her in any way.

She wondered if he'd let her scream.

"W-what—"

He was still dressed in the same clothes from earlier. He moved like a ray of sunshine, soft at first, getting bolder by the second as he walked over and hefted up two swords. Clay turned back to her with a smile. "I apologize if I was too callous earlier. Perhaps you like your privacy. Anyway, the offer to train still stands..."

Take the sword, something in her whispered. She forced the voice away. She couldn't take the sword. She wouldn't. It had been a passing fancy before. Imagination, delusions of her thinking she could be as great as the rest of them. But the reality was different. The reality was that her limbs were shaking, her heart was pounding. If she picked up that sword in front of him, he would see what a weak imposter she really was.

She feared the look in his eyes when he realized.

Corvina no longer felt as though he would harm her. He gave no indication that he would lunge or move closer. Yesterday he had. Yesterday he had put his hands all over her in a caressing, gentle manner. Was it shameful to say her body wanted more of that?

"Lord Valentino." She stood slowly, cautiously. "I'm not sure what gave you the impression that I would like to train with you at all."

The words hit him like a blow. She watched him wince and the guilt gnawed at her insides, but she shoved that aside too. It would do no good if he thought anything could happen between them.

"Surely you want to learn—"

"No," she snapped. "I do not. Good night, my lord." She whirled quickly, not letting herself see the disappointment in his gaze. It would be nothing new. Everyone was disappointed in her. What was one more?

Corvina was discovering something about Clay Valentino. He was an addicting force, and it was better not to give in to that.

She slowed into a fast walk. Her chest heaved with every breath and her ankles pulsed. She tried not to limp. She wasn't strong enough yet and being away from the other Elementals, while it gave her room to breathe, also sapped the strength from her body. Holding the sword the night before hadn't done her any favors either.

She felt weaker than ever, and she wondered if it had more to do with the aches and pains in her body or Clay. His expression, his tender touch and how she craved more of it. But it was too good to be true, she thought.

And everyone always let her down.

Corvina slept in late the next day after tossing and turning all night. She'd had vivid dreams of violence and carnage, of the wheat fields of her court and of the stalks withering and crumbling onto an earth splattered in blood.

Mostly, she dreamt of Clay's touch. It didn't matter how hard she tried to shove it from her mind; it was there, and she swore she could still feel his fingertips on her skin. It made her body itch with discomfort. It made her legs tangle against the sheet on her cot. She woke up with a sheen of sweat against her body and her mind buzzing with a million thoughts. None she could sort through.

She felt frazzled and couldn't explain why. She awoke alone, her maids already tending to Basil most likely, so she hurried and dressed. But swiping a damp rag across her clammy skin did nothing to ease the aches that seemed to embed down to her bones. Slipping into a dress and her shoes, she hurried out. But not even the fresh air or Danarish heat could ease her mind.

She couldn't put a name to the sensation that slipped over her. She wondered if a name even existed for the type of anxiety she was feeling. Perhaps breakfast with Basil could ease her fears.

Her eyes scanned the camp until she locked her sights on Basil. Her son wasn't with her maids. He was with Clay.

Her heart beat up to her throat, gripping her in a choking hold of panic. She found herself running to intercept them as they played. By all accounts, it should have been innocent. It looked harmless enough. Clay had Basil on his shoulders and was twirling him in circles. They both laughed as if they were friends. Or, Mana forbid, father and son.

What right did Clay have to pick up that mantel? What right did he have to demand anything of Corvina or her son? It didn't matter what twisted claim he thought he had on her. It was unacceptable. It was infuriating. Those emotions swelled and exploded in her chest within seconds.

The remnants of that dream still clung to her. Of Clay's hands sliding gently down her body, caressing the skin at her neck only to close around her and choke the very life from her body. Perhaps that was explanation enough for her rising anger.

"Put my son down this instant!" she shouted, uncaring if others turned to look. If others found her manic.

Basil was the most precious thing to her, and she didn't want him being used for Clay's amusement or anyone else's. Since he was born, she had worked hard to protect him from the evils of men and would continue to do so. Even from Clay. Because in the end, she didn't know him beyond what she'd seen. And what she'd seen so far had been nothing but violence as he took a sword to a messenger's head and tossed the remains into a portal. It was the promise of war and death.

She wanted none of that.

Clay stopped twirling, his brows pulling together.

"Mommy!" Basil called out from on his shoulders.

Corvina tried to keep her temper in check, but it was bubbling just along the surface. "Put my son down right now!"

Slowly, Clay obeyed, sliding Basil down the length of his back and setting her son to his feet. As soon as he did, she reached for him, pulling on his shirt and angling him behind her.

"How dare you?" she accused. "How dare you come near my son?"

His earlier demeanor changed into something far more cautious. "We were just playing..."

"Do not try and use my son in your games! Do not try to use him to get to me because you think I am yours. I will not be manipulated into accepting a mating bond, and you'll not use my son to do it!"

Behind her, Basil clung to her skirts as she shouted.

Clay's expression darkened. "I thought," he began slowly, "you said you did not remember..."

Corvina cursed in her head, her panic rising higher. She had not meant to give it away. She had wanted to move on as if they were nothing to each other, but now that she'd acknowledged it...

"Fine," she conceded through her teeth. "I do remember what you are. But so what? It does not matter that you are my—" She broke off, unable and not daring to say the word.

Mate.

It would make it more real. It would give power over the bond that she didn't even want. She didn't want a mate, and she didn't want him.

She wanted for no man ever again.

"I apologize," Clay began. "If I crossed a line with Basil, but I can promise you that I wasn't using him to get to you. I would never do that, least of all to a child."

He sounded sincere enough, but plenty of men did, didn't they? Right before they stabbed you in the back.

Corvina tilted her chin up a fraction. He apologized, but she wouldn't extend him the same courtesy when she had nothing to apologize for. Her fears were sound, and she still didn't trust the man. With her or her son. Despite the fact that he smelled rich and decadent and could make her dizzy with scent alone. Or that he was the most beautiful man, human or Fae, she'd ever seen in her life.

They were nothing.

Clay cleared his throat. "I... I was wondering if you would like to walk with me? Perhaps we can talk..."

"No," she answered angrily.

He staggered back with the force of the word. Like it'd been a blow to his chest.

"It does not matter what you think we are, Lord Valentino. I am *married,* and I will not have you demanding things from me that are not yours to have!"

She registered the shock on his expression. But before he could open his mouth to say anything back, she whirled and marched herself and her son forward.

Away from him, and the temptation he offered.

He wanted her, but he didn't know her. Didn't know how weak she was. He only wanted her because of what she represented, not because he knew anything about her. If he did, he'd surely be disgusted. And anyway, he could want and demand all he wanted.

Corvina had nothing left to give.

Clay watched Corvina march away, his chest heavy with wariness and anger. She knew. All this time she'd been at camp, she'd known that they were mates and had denied it. For days he'd been suffering, tormented over whether or not he should tell her again. For days he'd spent his nights sleepless and in agony, wishing she'd look his way. For whenever she did, she always turned away too fast. As if she couldn't stand the sight of him.

Her words echoed through his skull. Her rejection stung, and it sent the magic of their tethered bond into a frenzy of pain. He gasped, clutching his chest. A growl emanated from his lips that he couldn't quell at what he assumed this pain meant. It was the start of a rejected mate bond.

He'd heard of them. After all, even if Mana chose mates, that never meant they were truly destined. Humans and Fae had free will and could accept or reject it if they so wished. And she started the rejection process. The bond inside him would become a painful thing as it slowly severed.

She might as well have stabbed him in the heart.

"Fuck," he cursed aloud, rubbing at the ache that didn't ease.

He knew when he saw her, broken and bruised, that his mate would not trust him easily. That she would have her reservations because of all the abuse she'd endured. He thought he could at least make her smile. That he would have time to get to know her, for her to get to know him. Maybe he'd been to arrogant to think that they were destined. To forget for even just a moment that their bond could be broken.

"Ah, but men are such fools. Especially rich, royal men."

Clay turned to the voice and found one of Corvina's lady's regarding him with amusement and contempt. Her name was Dawn. She was the one who'd been locked up in the dungeon near Corvina. She'd been covered in dirt and rags then. A malnourished version of what he knew she once was. Now, she was regaining her figure even after a few days. Her pallor was no longer pale and sickly, but becoming a steady yellow-orange.

Half-Unseelie, if he had to take a guess.

"Excuse me?" He dropped his hand from his chest, but her eyes zoned in on the spot where he'd been rubbing before flicking back up to his face.

"You are a foolish High Lord," Dawn said again. "An entitled whore of a man who chases anything with a skirt."

He blinked at her audacity, though amusement made his lips twist. "You know me so well."

"You are all any female at this camp talks about, Lord Clay."

He flashed her a wicked smile. "I take that as a compliment."

"You shouldn't. Tell me, why are you pursuing Lady Corvina?" She drew closer.

His answer was swift. "Because she is my mate."

Dawn snorted. "Foolish. Like I said."

"I am confused..."

Dawn looked away from him, staring at the horizon and the bright risen sun. "I told her to jump, you know," she whispered.

Clay wanted to ask what she meant, but he didn't dare speak. Not when her eyes became distant, her voice haunted.

"When we first arrived in Dana with our courtiers, we were pariahs, outcasts. Yet my lady kept her head held high, because she believed she was doing right by her people in the Gold Court. Her father thought that by offering her up to the royals, he was saving his court and sparing her life." She took a breath and her eyes found his again. "They slaughtered them all. One by one, we could smell the blood and hear the dying cries of our people. I rushed her within her rooms and barred the doors. I begged her to jump into the sea, because drowning was a better fate than what soldiers had planned for two virgin Fae."

Clay gulped, his hands tightening into fists. He imagined it. Two lone females, suffering at the hands of Danarish soldiers; his mate suffering at the hands of Danarish soldiers. No one deserved such a treatment.

"Then Prince Tobias came into the room and offered her marriage in exchange for our lives. Her father was dead, our court had fallen, and we were stuck. So she did what she thought she had to do to survive." She sighed, shaking her head. "She spread her legs for the Prince of Dana."

Clay gulped, choking down the snarl that wanted to emerge. His reaction was visceral and feral. He didn't like that part of his instincts. He was no fool. He knew she was married, had a child, but he didn't want to imagine her beneath that human scum. Not after he'd witnessed the aftermath of that man's cruelty.

"And you would have her do the same for you."

Clay reeled back as if he'd been struck. Dumbfounded, slack jawed he could only mutter, "What?"

"You think you have some claim over her simply because she is your mate. Prince Tobias is not so different. He thinks he has some claim over her because he is her husband. The truth is, you do not love her like the prince does not love her. You want to possess her without really knowing her. You think you are entitled to her because of the magic that binds you. And that, Lord Clay, makes you no different from the man who tortured her for years."

The realization of what she was saying speared through him like a weapon. He gasped, wanting to close his eyes against the onslaught of her words. It wasn't true. Was it? He remembered all the times since he'd met her. He hadn't pressured her, but what Dawn was saying had merit. Did he really feel like she was his possession just because the bond told him she was his?

Mana, Dawn was right.

He was acting like a feral, possessive jackass, thinking he deserved her simply because Mana said so. He hadn't gotten the time to know her. Granted, he'd tried, and she wanted nothing to do with him. It only made him that much more persistent.

But to be compared to her stain of a husband?

"I would never hurt her," he gritted out.

"Oh, of that I have no doubt. I have seen true evil, my lord, and that means I know a good man when I see one." She reached out and patted his cheek. "You are a good man. Entitled, rich, and a foolish whore, but a good man."

"Thanks?"

She smiled at him, sad but genuine. "You're welcome. Now, as for my advice. If you want to get to know Lady Corvina, you will have to do so slowly and cautiously. Do not presume to think she is yours when you don't even know her. Respect her wishes and stay away. Do not push." She stepped away. "She has had her will and spirit broken. She has been taken from enough already."

Clay watched Dawn retreat, blinking away the emotion from his eyes. He took a breath, realizing that she was right. He was acting like a fucking fool. Corvina wasn't his just because magic claimed them to be a good match. He didn't know her and she didn't know him. He'd be lying if he said he didn't want the chance to know her better. But Dawn was right. Corvina wasn't ready to hear him, and that was fine.

He was going to respect her wishes. He was going to give her space and pray that eventually she would give him a chance to get to know one another. And if she didn't want him as a mate, that was fine. It would be her decision. He would suffer the pain of a severed bond, and he would get over it. They could be friends, or they could be nothing if she so wished.

There was nothing else Clay could do except stay away from her.

Brands of Strength

The next few days were filled with the cacophonous symphony of Fae preparing for battle. Corvina watched with dread curling in her belly as Fae bustled around, training and forging weapons by the dozens. With everyone busy doing something, Corvina felt useless. She hadn't lifted a finger to help anyone since she arrived. She wondered if it had been an unconscious form of protest on her part.

She felt petulant and foolish. These Fae were risking themselves on the impending war with Dana because of her, after all. What would her people think of her if she just sat around and watched?

She didn't like the idea of it, so she approached the Seelie King cautiously. He was a frightening presence, though not more frightening than the sentinel at his back. Uric glared at her as she approached, twisting the folds of her skirt in her fingers.

"Lady Corvina." The king gave her a low bow. "Is there something I can do for you?" He appeared to be busy with his own planning, but he stopped and gave her his whole focus.

It was unnerving to have that dark gaze on her. She swallowed past the nerves in her throat.

"Your Majesty, I was wondering if there was a way my maids and I could help prepare?"

He offered her a small smile. "That isn't necessary."

"I want to."

If they were going out to battle for her, the least she could do was something for them. She wondered if he read that in her expression. He conceded after merely a moment.

"Our soldiers need uniforms."

"My maids are proficient with sewing and mending." Corvina was passable at best, but she didn't say so when she wanted to be of use.

That was how she found herself with her maids and gaggle of other women in a circle, sewing up the uniforms for the Fae. They were nothing like the Danarish uniforms, which were bright and colorful to represent their kingdom. The Fae had to make do with what they had, pulling apart fabric they no longer used and putting it together again into poorly patched uniforms.

For days, that's how Corvina kept herself occupied. When she wasn't sleeping or spending time with Basil, she was sewing with the other women, listening to them prattle on about things of little consequence. She ate, she slept, and above all, she avoided Clay.

He hadn't sought her out after she yelled at him for all to hear. He hadn't sought Basil out either. Corvina wasn't sure what to make of that. She had told him to leave her alone. Had she even dared to raise her voice to Tobias, she wouldn't have been able to sit for a week, and he would have visited her every hour just to spite her. Clay had... He'd respected her wishes.

She'd caught him in passing. The camp was so small, it was impossible to miss him. Especially when he was so beautiful, he practically glowed. Like he carried rays of the sun in his pockets. But he didn't seek her out, his gaze barely strayed to her.

It made the bond in her chest ache, though she shoved that feeling aside.

She didn't know how she should feel about the fact that he'd actually listened to her wants. She was unfamiliar with such a thing and didn't know how to navigate the emotions in her mind. How to perceive a man who actually listened and put what she wanted above what he did.

Corvina couldn't help but wonder if it was a trick. If he was just waiting for the right moment to pounce. She didn't know what to trust, so she tried to put him far in the back of her mind. By sewing and washing and avoiding her conflicting emotions all together.

"Someone needs to take this to Julius. He asked for his shirt to be mended the other day."

Corvina turned to one of the women who held out a folded tunic.

"I'll do it," Corvina offered, setting aside her needle and thread.

"My lady, I can—"

"It's fine, Juniper." She stood and took the folded fabric from the Fae. She hoped her nerves weren't alive on her face. The gargantuan ginger made her nervous because of his girth alone, but he was easy to smile and easier to crack a joke.

To be honest, all men made Corvina nervous. She was afraid their plans were always nefarious, that they would be as cruel as the Danarish guards and her husband, but she was coming to find that the men at this camp weren't at all like the human men she'd come to know. Even still, she needed to face those fears.

She wasn't sure what her future held, where she would go, if she would even go back to Tobias, but she knew that she didn't want to be a frightened creature any longer.

"He is likely in his tent," the woman said.

Corvina gave a firm nod and went to find him. At a camp as small as this, everyone knew where everyone's tent was. Julius and Iona shared one, and Corvina weaved her way towards it quickly enough. She paused outside of the closed flaps, listening for anyone within.

"Julius?" she asked tentatively. "Iona?" There was no response. For a moment she debated just going in and leaving his shirt inside, but she decided against it. It seemed like a violation of privacy to do such a thing, so she backed away slowly.

"You looking for Julius, my lady?"

She turned at the craggy voice, facing an old, bent half-Fae.

"I am."

"Saw him head out to check the perimeter with his lady love. That way, I think." He pointed in the direction of a small copse of trees.

There weren't a lot of forests in Dana, when sand and beaches overpowered the kingdom. What few trees they did have provided a good amount of shade and plump fruit. She followed where the old Fae had pointed.

A small cluster of orange trees pressed together around the perimeter of the camp. Soldiers were stationed all along the lines of the camp where the Unseelie had glamored them. It wasn't a very strong glamor, and it only lasted a while. They had to reinforce it every few hours. Usually, Unseelie could only glamor appearances, mainly of themselves to hide their animalistic features. They altered the appearance of their camp, but because it required a great use of magic and energy, it always flickered and failed, which meant they needed extra protection around the camp.

She walked slowly, careful of where she stepped. Up ahead she heard voices, recognizing Julius' and Iona's. She hadn't really spoken to either of the Elementals since the day they'd asked about her scars. It was probably unfair of her to push them away. And maybe they hadn't suffered the same fate as her own life, but they were tethered together by something more than what Clay wanted from her. And they weren't asking for as much as he was.

She would smile at Iona, say hello, and maybe they could become friends. The Elemental was intimidating and intense, but she did seem like a good person. Corvina was afraid she'd judged her too harshly, and she wanted to make up for it.

She hadn't ever really had friends before. All she'd ever had were ladies maids and courtiers. She was used to people bowing to her in passing or averting their gazes. She was used to cruelty, too. She had to find a way to navigate through the different personalities of the camp, no matter how hard a task.

A smile tilted her lips as she got closer to the voices. She pushed aside a hanging branch, and her feet stuttered at what she witnessed on the other side of the foliage.

The feral growl tore down her back, causing goosebumps to rise against her skin. Her eyes widened as she watched Julius' big frame push against Iona. His hand gripped the back of her neck, shoving her against the trunk of a tree.

Their pants were down to their knees, and Corvina feared she couldn't look away from below Julius' waist. She wanted to, but her gaze was riveted on his... his cock. It was a monster of a thing, and Corvina was sure she'd never seen one that big. Engorged, long and thick. It jutted upwards, the tip beaded with drops of liquid.

Julius kicked Iona's legs opened wider, and then his hips were pistoning in her direction, impaling into her from behind.

Iona cried out and Julius dug his nails deeper into her neck, keeping her pinned against the tree as he *brutalized* her.

Corvina's mouth opened, but no sound came out. She was frozen in fear, and no matter how much she wanted to run forward and help Iona, her limbs felt frozen where they were. She couldn't believe Julius would do this to his mate, but then again, men were vile creatures, presenting a certain air in public and changing in private.

She'd lived through this herself.

Through the guttural grunts as hips slapped against hips. Corvina wanted to whimper as his body kissed Iona's tighter. Iona's nails ravaged the bark. Her mouth opened and cries came out of her mouth. Cries of pain?

But Julius was so lost in Iona that he didn't see Corvina. He kept moving inside her...

"Julius," Iona groaned. It sounded like a plea.

His elongated canines grazed her shoulder. "Yes, mate?"

Iona smirked, the expression jarring and foreign to Corvina. It confused her due to the situation. Iona's palms pressed against the tree and pushed away from it, all but stumbling backwards. Julius stumbled with her, pulling out of her center. Iona turned, grabbing him by the shirtfront and whirling, shoving him against the tree.

The sudden change in dynamic had Corvina's eyes widening even further. What was going on? Why would Julius let Iona handle him that way?

"It's my turn now," Iona purred, the sound laced with seduction, not fear.

It made Corvina's earlier thoughts freeze. This... this was...

Julius chuckled. "Always fighting to be on top," he growled in a teasing tone.

"Damn straight." Iona kicked out of her shoes and pants and gave a powerful leap, wrapping her arms around his neck and legs around Julius' thighs. With a slowness, she positioned herself against his tip, but didn't slide down on his considerable length.

"Iona," Julius growled, the sound a warning.

"Beg me for it," she replied breathlessly, rubbing herself against his tip.

Corvina should leave. She knew that watching this was wrong, and yet she was entranced. Entranced because of the way Iona pushed Julius around. Because this was a dynamic she hadn't known existed. Iona seemed to be experiencing... pleasure. Something that didn't quite measure up in Corvina's mind, when all she'd known was pain. She knew this act as a chore, as something her husband demanded. She'd never enjoyed it before, had never felt even a fraction of what Iona seemed to be feeling as she rubbed herself against her mate.

And what Corvina thought had been brutality earlier... it hadn't been. It had been, what? A change of roles? They'd been dominating each other like it was a game they liked to play.

Julius leaned forward and nipped Iona's lips. Corvina almost thought he wouldn't beg. That he was too proud, like most men were proud. But the big ginger surprised her. "Please, love," he groaned. "Stop teasing, please."

With a triumphant smile, Iona slowly lowered herself against him. Using her thighs for momentum, she started bouncing up and down on his cock, swiveling her hips occasionally and crying out sounds of ecstasy.

And Julius just stood there and let her set her own pace. He didn't control or take over, because now it was her turn.

And watching this change made Corvina's face warm. She'd never known anything like it. A rush of heat sweltered over her body, and she couldn't stop it from teasing her own folds. An embarrassing flood of wetness pooled between her legs. She rubbed her thighs together, but doing so only made them ache. Only made her crave when she'd never craved before.

Was something wrong with her? She'd only known brutality and pain, and now she was craving something inside her. She only felt hollow, desperate the more she watched Iona dominate her mate and issue out commands. Her nipples puckered against her shirt front. She felt too hot, too itchy. She wanted something...

With a start she realized she wanted what they were doing. She wanted that control. The control to say no and be obeyed. To know what it felt like to ask someone to stop and they listen. To know what it felt like to have that pleasure instead of pain. To have someone else beg for once. For there to be a mutual agreement.

She stepped back, the couple still oblivious to her presence.

When she was far enough away, she darted into a run.

As if she could escape what she just witnessed. As if she could run away from the desire that was suddenly coursing beneath her skin, pressing up against her body, slipping through every crevice in a demanding, eager pull. She gasped, feeling her heart pound...

"Corvina!"

Her feet skidded to a halt. Her eyes darted frantically until they settled on Shula's approaching form. She waved at Corvina, a smile on her face, but her forehead creased in a worried line. She came to a stop in front of Corvina, eyeing her up and down like she was searching for injuries.

"Are you okay?" She looked around. "Is someone chasing you?"

That was worry in her tone, and Corvina would be a liar if she said it didn't warm her heart. The fact that Shula was worried about her.

She let out a breath, easing her grip on Julius' tunic. She'd wrinkled it in her run, and had forgotten that she was even carrying it.

"I'm fine." But her smile was wobbly, and she wasn't sure Shula believed her.

"You're sure?"

Her heart calmed down, warming up to the steady sound of her voice. "I'm fine." The words felt true. She was fine. For the first time, she didn't ache. She wasn't choking on ashwood or chained in iron. Basil was happy here, surrounded by young Fae that looked like him. She was still nervous and skittish about a lot of things, but a part of her felt... well, like she could nearly be happy.

"I'm glad. I realize we haven't had a chance to talk much and I was hoping, if you weren't busy, we could..." Shula's voice trailed off with uncertainty.

Corvina's grip on the tunic eased. She would give it to Julius later. That is, if she could even look him in the eye without seeing the image of his giant cock float through her mind.

Her face flushed and she cleared her throat. "Of course."

"Would you like to go to my tent?"

"Sure..."

Shula led the way to her tent. The inside smelled strongly of herbs, but being enclosed in such a small space made Shula's scent of embers and confections that much more prominent.

"There's not much, but take a seat..." She gestured at a single chair within the space. While Corvina sat, Shula took a space on the cot. It left their gazes unleveled, but she didn't seem to mind. "I wanted to apologize if Iona and I crossed a line when she asked about your scars..."

Corvina gulped. "It's fine."

"It's not. That's private, intimate. She had no right to ask you."

Iona, she was finding, did what she wanted. Corvina wouldn't fault the woman's curiosity. She had to learn to not take everything as if it were an attack. But there would be times when she wouldn't be able to control her own reactions, or the visceral pain, or the memories that jolted through her mind. And she didn't want to be treated like she was weak, either. Didn't want people tip-toeing around her, watching everything they said just because they were afraid to hurt her feelings.

"It's fine," she reassured, her voice firm. "You're all curious. I understand. I would be, too."

Shula let loose the breath she'd been holding. "Okay, good. How are you faring here?"

"I'm doing as well as can be expected. Basil loves it, though."

At the mention of her son, Shula's smile broadened and Corvina's breath caught. She was beautiful when she smiled.

"I'm glad," she said. "Basil is such a sweet boy. So full of energy and life."

She liked the way Shula spoke about Basil. It was obvious the fire Fae had grown a soft spot for Corvina's son, like he had for her and Ryker. It meant a lot to her. Basil didn't trust often and when he did, he loved with his whole heart and soul. And Corvina didn't know Shula that well, but she had a feeling the woman would do anything for Basil.

"He is. He's always been shy before, always hid his spark. But here..." A lump formed in Corvina's throat. Tears stung behind her eyelids. "He's happy here."

Shula didn't say anything for a long moment, staring instead at Corvina. When she finally did speak, her voice was low, almost hypnotic. "I know it can be daunting." She gestured with her hands. "All of this. When they found me, they wouldn't let me go. I tried to run at every turn."

"What changed?"

"Everything."

Then Shula began to tell Corvina her story. Of a little girl raised in Fae camps, of two loving parents ripped from her arms. She told the story of the old woman who took her to have her ears altered so that no one would know what she was, about how she hid in plain sight at the circus. About a Fae named Davina and her prophecy, about twin flames in flesh and the agony searing down her back and her best friend's betrayal. When she got to the part about the Brotherhood, Corvina felt true fear slice through her. For herself. For Shula. Though logically she knew Shula had escaped, she felt that anxiety and adrenaline as she tried to escape their clutches.

Then she met the Resistance, and they took her against her will despite her protests. That part made Corvina's chest ache. She couldn't believe that they would do that. Then again, Valerio looked like the type of Fae who would stop at nothing until he got what he wanted. But the others?

Shula went on about a Fae named Orna and her human mate, Des. Tears shone in her dark eyes as she recounted their deaths. She spoke about Castle Aileach, a Fae stronghold. About her journey to Tir na Faie and through the Iron Mountains and the metallic beasts that reside there. She spoke of her connection to Ryker that they both fought, of getting captured and escaping and accepting a bond that had been there since the beginning. And when she spoke of Iona, her voice stuttered and her cheeks heated as if she was embarrassed.

Softly, she confessed, "She intimidated me because she's so... strong."

"So are you," Corvina blurted. When their gazes locked, Corvina flushed. "I thought it since the moment I saw you. You've suffered so much, and I never would have guessed all that pain you hide." Her fingers twisted into the fabric of Julius' tunic. "You just seem so strong."

And I'm so weak.

Shula gifted her with a smile, as if she'd plucked the thoughts from Corvina's brain. "I've come to find out that everyone wears their own different brands of strength. That it's not linear or subjective. That there's strength in surviving and fighting wars. There's strength in watching your loved ones die." Their eyes held. "There's strength in a mother's love and in surviving what you have."

Her breath caught in her throat and tears threatened to spill. Never before had she been called strong by anyone. Least of all by someone she liked and admired. By someone she saw as strong, an unmovable force. "That's good advice," she whispered past the lump in her throat, sure Shula could hear her tears.

"Isn't it?" She smiled. "Clay gave it to me."

She expected to feel like she'd been splashed with cold water at the sound of his name, at the shine in Shula's eyes that was the slightest hint of mischievous. Instead, Corvina's insides warmed and something in her hummed.

"Did he?"

"He's a really good listener."

Interesting. Corvina didn't reply. Instead she observed Shula again. Was there a reason she was bringing up Clay? Was there some ulterior motive? Or what was she to him?

"Good friends are hard to come by these days," Shula continued, oblivious to what was going on in Corvina's head. It was obvious she was thinking about the friend from the circus who betrayed her to the emperor's soldiers. "I was hoping we could be friends."

Corvina smiled genuinely. "I'd like that."

"After Fanny, it's been hard for me to trust friends..."

Corvina jolted. "Wait, did you say Fanny?"

"Yeah."

"From Piriguini's Circus?" She'd known of course that Shula had lived her years out there. She'd heard the rumors, seen the posters, but she hadn't imagined it would be Fanny. Fanny who had sneered at Corvina's ears. Who crawled on her knees to kiss her shoes.

"Yes..."

Corvina leaned back in the chair. "Small world. Piriguini's Circus is in Dana. We went and I met Fanny." She winced at the memory. "I am sorry she was such a terrible friend."

Shula smiled a little sadly at her. "It's okay," she whispered as she leaned forward and reached for Corvina's hand. Corvina let her, relishing in the brief moment of connection before Shula pulled away once more. "I have new friends. Better friends than I did before."

So do I, Corvina wanted to say. Instead, she smiled and swallowed past the lump in her throat. For the first time in a long time, she felt content.

Smiles and War

"Look at him."

"I *know*."

"The eyes—"

"The dimples..."

"That smile!"

"I've never seen a man so beautiful."

Wistful sighs echoed around Corvina, distracting her steady fingers from sewing. The tittering females had been going about it for a few minutes now, and Corvina had been steadfast and focused on her task, not wanting to give into her curiosity. But those last words had her snapping her attention up.

"Who are you talking about?" The words were out of her mouth before she could stop them.

She'd learned the names of the Fae women sewing in a circle. There were her own maids of course, Gale and Wren, and a few newer faces. Of Fae from camps as well as those who'd come out of hiding and had joined the Resistance along the way. Karlotta, Liv, Mabel, and Perri.

Perri was a pretty young woman with violet eyes and skin, and a considerable number of scars on one side of her face that twisted up towards her pointed ear, giving her half of a grotesque expression. She leaned closer, her voice lowering to a whisper. "Him." Her chin jutted out in the direction of said male. Corvina turned, gaze following the path to where he stood. "The High Lord of the Sapphire Court. *Clay*."

Corvina's breath caught as surely as the bright beams of Danarish sunshine shone down against his skin, giving him a golden-tan hue. The material of his clean, crisp white tunic clung to his frame, highlighting the contours of his body. He was all lithe, lean muscles, with strong arms and thick legs that his pants and boots hugged tightly.

Blond-brown hair plastered to his reddening cheeks, and he heaved a laughing breath as he lifted his sword and made a series of jabs.

The women around her sighed and it tore Corvina away from him. Her own cheeks felt hot, and she wouldn't admit it was because she'd been admiring his form. The elegant way he held a sword. He was careful with the weapon, as careful as he had been when swiping her hair away from her face and cradling her body to his chest.

The woman's voice tore her from that memory, though. "The way he holds his weapon..." Because the words echoed her thoughts, Corvina bit the inside of mouth. "He's always so gentle, so... passionate."

The other women echoed their agreement. "He has the gentlest touch," Karlotta, a Seelie with dark hair and bright eyes, said.

"But he can also be rough if you ask," Mabel added.

"I've never met a man so intent on a woman's pleasure instead of his own."

"And that prowess?" Perri sighed, her violet eyes glassing over with a dreamy expression. "He's so..."

"Wait," Gale interrupted. "Have you *all* been with him?"

They looked at her, as if she said something utterly ridiculous. "Of course we have."

Gale and Wren shared a look before turning it to Corvina. She was surprised at the sudden spark of jealousy that burned in her chest. She tamped it down as Gale sat forward, not concealing her curiosity. "Why?" her maid asked.

"What do you mean?" Karlotta tilted her head.

"I can see the appeal he has. But why would you all... knowing he's been around the camp..."

"Do you have some strange delusions that he will fall all over you if you keep going back for seconds?" Wren asked with a sniff.

Corvina resisted the urge to blink at her maid. It seemed like since they'd arrived at the camp, her companions were determined to make Corvina see all of Clay's good qualities. That meant they looked down and sneered at any woman who made mention of him or went near him.

"It's not that," Perri said. "We know we can never be with him. He makes it clear that he will not offer us a relationship besides friendship. That honesty is more than what we've ever gotten before. There's something enticing about it, but more than that, he..." Her hand rose, hovering over the scar that twisted her expression. "Clay listens. He makes us feel seen. Makes us feel beautiful in an honest way that is real. And we crave that, not sex, not a bond. It's..."

"It's friendship," Liv supplied.

"Yeah." Perri smiled. "Precisely that."

They huddled together, whispering again and sighing wistfully.

Corvina turned back to where Clay was standing. He wasn't alone anymore. Shula was in front of him, circling him like they were ready to train. Intensity vibrated off the two of them. Clay's eyes were twinkling mischievously as he stabbed his sword into the ground. The action caused Shula to stumble backwards.

Clay laughed as he prowled closer towards her. He caught her around the waist and lifted her, twirling her in circles. She let out a peal of laughter that sounded almost odd coming from her throat.

The close press of their bodies made Corvina shift uncomfortably in her seat. Emotions she couldn't recognize churned in her gut as she watched everything they'd said unfold. Everything they'd said about Clay, she could see. The friendship, the way he listened. And hadn't Shula mentioned something about his advice? About what he thought of strength?

He was close to Shula, that much was evident. And although Corvina knew that Shula and Ryker were mates, she couldn't help but wonder if Shula was somehow... wandering from her mate's bed for Clay.

She didn't know why the thought speared through her chest with discomfort. She didn't like the idea of her friend with Clay. Which was ridiculous. He wasn't hers. She wasn't his. They didn't belong together and he could do what he wanted with whoever he wanted. That was typical male behavior, after all. To stray. To be cruel.

But even as she thought it, she couldn't believe it. There were a lot of men here that seemed kind. And despite her reservations about him, he seemed kind enough...

As if he could feel her gaze on him, Clay turned and looked at Corvina. Their eyes held. Usually, Corvina would look away from the intensity of his green-eyed stare. Except this time, she couldn't look away. And when he smiled, it was tentative.

And Corvina couldn't help herself.

She smiled back.

Her smile nearly knocked Clay on his ass. She gave it without restraint, though it was shy. He could see that the pain was slowly easing from her body. Her mind. She was incorporating into camp and hadn't run away. Not when her son and her maids were so happy here.

Maybe she was realizing she was better off with them rather than with her husband.

The thought of her husband was just enough to sour his mood and make his stomach churn. He didn't drop his expression though. They stared and stared until a flush crawled up her neck and stained her cheeks with color.

"You should talk to her," Shula suggested.

Clay didn't take his gaze off of her. "No. I promised I would leave her be."

"She looks like she wants to talk to you."

He hoped. Wished. It wasn't that simple, though. Nothing ever was.

"Valerio wants to speak with you."

Clay groaned aloud and turned to face the speaker. "Weylyn," he greeted.

The Fae smirked at him, as if he and Clay had some long-standing joke that they shared together. Just because they'd almost fallen off the side of a castle and nearly hurtled towards their deaths didn't make them friends. Or because they'd scaled the side of a cliff together.

Or because...

"Your thoughts flash across your face," Weylyn purred. "I don't even need to read your mind to know what you're thinking."

Clay bared his teeth. "Stop reading me."

"But you make it so easy." Weylyn leaned forward, his long braid swaying over his shoulder. "Now, let me repeat myself. Your prince is asking for you. Says it's urgent. Better hurry, cousin dearest, before he gets impatient."

"Yeah, well, thanks for the message, lapdog."

Weylyn's golden eyes flashed with murderous intent, but he just smiled. It was chilling. Eerie. And Clay regretted the words as soon as they left his mouth because of that look alone. Feral and ready to rip his heart straight from his chest.

A second later, the expression was gone and Weylyn was smiling again. "You are lucky I do not hate you, my lord." He gave him a soft pat on the shoulder. "I would have torn your guts out and hung you with them."

"Thanks?"

Weylyn chuckled and walked away. Clay just watched him go. If that's how he treated those he liked, Clay didn't want to be on the receiving end of Weylyn's wrath.

"He is so creepy," Shula mumbled.

Tell me about it. He was afraid to say those thoughts aloud, but then remembered that Weylyn could read minds from a distance, so he quickly tried to shut his thoughts off. "Quick, let's go see what Valerio wants."

•⟫—•◆•—⟪•

"You want to *what*?" Clay's knuckles dug into the table, nearly tearing the soft parchment of the map they rested on. His head shook adamantly back and forth. "We can't, Valerio. It's too soon!"

"We have no other choice," his cousin and king argued. "Scouts have informed me that Dana is making their move. They're marching nearer as we speak."

The tent held only Valerio's closest comrades, and they were all staring down at the map like it was magic waiting to explode.

"They'll be near in a few days," Valero went on. "We have to fight."

There was silence preceding his words, and Clay felt a stirring of discomfort in his gut. War. He knew it was coming, but it seemed like it was approaching too fast. Regardless, he was prepared to face the Prince of Dana on the battlefield and end him. If nothing than to free Corvina from his evil.

"We will have to meet them out on the battlefield," Julius said, stepping forward to observe the map. "The first battle is always a test of force between two opposing sides. The Danarish are going to want to play with us first by measuring the size of their dicks."

"They are proud," Valerio agreed. "They will want to toy with us. They will expect us to be easily felled, but we will have a plan in place to show him that Fae are not so easily cowed."

"They'll come in with iron. We have to put the strongest on the front lines to try and get rid of it so the rest of our soldiers don't weaken immediately."

"We will have a plot in place by nightfall." His dark eyes rose. "Prepare yourselves for war, my friends. For the time has finally come."

A Promise of Tomorrow

That night, they sat around the fire. The energy was subdued and quiet, though Corvina couldn't be sure why. Something was happening. Her instincts were frazzled and she had the urge to ask, but was too afraid to approach anyone to do so.

They sat around the fire, a hearty bowl of fish stew in her lap. Flames crackled in front of her, illuminating the camp. Wren was sitting with Basil, who couldn't keep his eyes open and was lolling to the side. Corvina smiled a little bit at that. Her maids huddled together, leaving the spaces on either side of Corvina opened.

When someone came to sit next to her, her body tensed and she turned, meeting the golden eyes of a Fae male. She sucked in a shocking breath. He seemed... familiar somehow, though she couldn't remember why.

His skin was brown and glowed a bright orange next to the fire light. A long black braid hung over his shoulder, atop on which a black cat perched. The man was staring at her silently, eerily, his eyes flickering over her form. Like he was assessing her.

He should have made her feel uncomfortable. Maybe in a sense he did. But not like other men made her uncomfortable. His gaze wasn't leering or probing or calculating. He was merely... looking at her.

"Hello." His voice was nearly ethereal, deep and soft.

"Hello..."

The cat on his shoulder purred.

"My name is Weylyn."

"Corvina."

He flashed her a toothless smile. "I know."

What a strange interaction. She eased her body to the side, angling away from him. He only seemed to follow. Either that or his presence was so big that she felt he swallowed her whole. It was nothing compared to Clay's presence of course. This man wasn't comforting, but he didn't make sensation ooze down her spine.

She didn't know what he made her feel, but she knew she wasn't too happy with it.

"Are you well?" he asked.

"I am." She was surprised by how true those words were when they had never been before.

"Good." He nodded once. "Should you ever need anything at all do not hesitate to seek me out. I will do all in my power to help you."

Why would he do that? In her experience, no one offered their help for free. Freedom always came with price, sometimes people thought they were willing to pay it but when the time came, it was always vicious and bloody.

"You are my High Lady, after all," he went on.

Her eyes widened. "Are—are you from the Gold Court?"

His smile was an answer, and yet at the same time it wasn't. She wanted to ask him more, to see where he'd been when the Fae fell. To hear where he'd been that terrible day. Had he seen the court fall? Had he lost anyone? What of their people?

But she didn't get a chance to ask any of that because Shula came and sat on her other side. Just as she did, Weylyn stood and slipped away into the darkness cast by the flames.

"Are you okay?" Shula asked. Her gaze was riveted on the space where Weylyn had disappeared to. "Interactions with him always leave a Fae unnerved. I thought I'd save you from that."

Corvina eased a tightness in her shoulders she hadn't realized was there. She would have time to ask later, she supposed. She'd seen Weylyn around camp, but not often enough. He was like a spectral figure, appearing and disappearing at will.

"I'm fine." Corvina dipped her spoon into her bowl. "Why is everyone so subdued?" she found herself asking. She didn't have the bravery to bring it up with anyone but Shula. Because she felt close to her.

"Ladies, may I sit here?"

Corvina startled, the stew sloshing over the sides of the bowl. Hot liquid burned her fingers and stained her dress. Heat that had nothing to do with the camp fire slid up her cheeks. She hadn't noticed Clay arrive. Thankfully, he wasn't focusing on her embarrassing lack of grace, but looking at the vacant spot next to Shula.

Corvina's stomach did an uncomfortable twist as Shula gestured for him to sit. He did, and even though there was a whole another person in between them, it felt like he was right next to her. His heat, his scent. It clouded through her senses. She knew a part of it was the bond, while the other part was the sighing words of all the females that professed and praised.

"What are we talking about?" Clay bumped his shoulder against Shula, jostling her slightly. She threw him a look that Corvina couldn't quite decipher—not that she knew the Fae well enough to decipher her looks—before she answered.

"Corvina was just asking why everyone seems subdued."

Clay sighed, his shoulders sagging. His attention found itself riveted on the bowl in his hands and the stew inside. Surprisingly, it was him who answered instead of Shula. "We ride out to meet Dana on the battlefield tomorrow."

Her heart fell to the floor. For a second, her tongue felt leaden against the roof of her mouth, and she had to pry it off and work her jaw before she could even speak. "Battle?"

"They're marching here. To keep the camp and the children safe, we are going to go out and meet them far away."

Her head spun with this information. She wanted to scream suddenly. This all felt like her fault. Because she was here, the Danarish were on their way to destroy the Fae. Because she'd dared to escape her husband and bring Basil with her.

All those lives... People she'd come to know in the past few weeks... What they would face on that battlefield. Her husband was a cruel adversary, and he would find joy in cutting the Resistance down.

If she'd only just—no! She shut those thoughts down as soon as they'd formed. The voice of uncertainty was clashing against other voices, other words. Of Dawn's. Of Shula's. Voices of people stronger than her tried to penetrate through that guilt.

If she gave herself over, did she truly believe that he would cease his cruelty? He would take her and kill the Fae anyway. Or enslave them, as was the Danarish way. Then he would kill her slowly and torture Basil by taking him to the Brotherhood to choke on that unholy water.

And that was why she hadn't tried escaping. Because somewhere deep down, she knew that these were her people. That she and Basil belonged here more than they ever belonged in Dana. She didn't deserve it, their kindness or protection, but she was High Lady, and she had it anyway.

She recalled the look in the golden Fae's eyes. Weylyn. *"You are my High Lady after all,"* he'd said. That meant something to her. It meant that her people still thought of her. Still looked to her.

And for a glimmering moment, the woman she'd used to be flared to life in her chest. The stubbornness beneath the sweetness. The determination. The ferocity. It broke though the broken bits of what she was now and rose to the surface. Naked. Afraid. Bleeding. But there just the same.

She took a breath. "Is there anything I can do?" She didn't know how to fight. She didn't know how to wield shield and sword like Iona and Shula. She wasn't the strongest, but she couldn't let the people march out and die without trying to help.

Shula blinked, as if pleasantly surprised. But Clay, his smile was radiant. As if he never doubted her like everyone else doubted her. And she took that silent praise and held it close to her chest.

"I think Ryker could use help with the injured... Let me go ask him." Shula stood and disappeared, making her way towards her mate. And Corvina suddenly felt suffocated by Clay's presence. Not as stifling as before, not as terrifying as the thought of war. She didn't fear afraid of him in that moment.

She felt... worried about what was to come.

"The Danarish armies are mighty," she said to him.

Clay seemed surprised that she'd even spoken to him. Had she been so terrible that that's what he seemed surprised at? She felt ashamed of herself for a moment.

He gave her a rueful sort of smile. "So are we."

She shook her head. "You don't understand... They are vicious. They have iron and ashwood—"

"We know they do, my lady."

The words 'my lady' curled around her skin, as soft as a caress. It felt like he was tracing his fingers down her arm with nothing other than his voice.

A shiver made its way down her spine.

"Let us speak of something else. Like... this soup."

She blinked at the sudden change of subject, her body too slow to get rid of the remnants of hypnotism his voice left her under. "The soup?" she repeated.

He held up the bowl to accentuate his point. "Yeah. The soup. Positively delicious." He smirked, flashing bright white teeth.

"I suppose."

"There's no supposition about it. This soup is one of the most delicious I have ever had. Perfect consistency." He lifted his spoon and let the liquid fall from it, splattering. A drop tainted his crisp shirt, and he looked down at it before looking back at Corvina sheepishly. She swore she caught a flush of embarrassment on his cheeks.

Her eyes narrowed. "You don't like the soup, do you?" She couldn't help but feel like it'd been either a joke or a sad way to keep their conversation going.

"Mana, no." He cringed. "No offense to the Danarish, of course. Perfectly fine fish, but we've been eating it for weeks now. I feel like I'm sweating fish stink."

"Try living here for four years. You eventually become one with the fish."

Clay threw his head back and laughed. It was a pleasant sound and when he finished, his face was flushed. She felt like her own cheeks mirrored his. Had she just made a joke? It had been so long since she'd felt free enough to do so.

"If I hadn't seen the Danarish for myself, I would think they all had beady eyes and fishtails."

"Oh, they're a far cry from the merfolk of the Unseelie." Her body tilted closer to him, hair slipping over her shoulder. He leaned close enough that she could breathe in his scent. "They smell worse," she confessed on a whisper.

He chuckled, the warmth of his breath pressing against her lips. It jolted her back, as if realizing just how close they were. It surprised her, how easily they fell into conversation. How easily the fear suddenly dissipated. Like he'd joked because he knew it was what she needed. He'd looked at her and he'd known. He wasn't being flirtatious like he had been before. He was just being kind. Acting like a friend.

And it had been so long since she'd last had friends.

She understood what the women meant then. How he wasn't just someone they thought about falling into bed with, but someone who made them feel seen. And after being invisible for so long, empty in her chest, it was nice to be spoken to like she was a person.

It was something she'd forgotten about.

"How did you find yourself here?" She gestured at the camp with her spoon.

"Here as in here in the camp? Or here as in alive?"

"I mean here with the Resistance."

"Ah." His face fell. "That is a rather sad story."

"You don't have to tell me." She started scooting away, ashamed she'd even asked for something so personal.

"It's fine," he reassured quickly. "I don't think anyone here has a pretty story. And I'll tell mine, if you don't mind listening."

There was such sadness in his tone, it drew her to him in an inexplicable way. "I'll hear it."

"I was born in the Sapphire Court," he began. "My father was High Lord. I would say that I'm sure you know what it was like to have a High Lord father, but mine was a cruel bastard. Yours sounds decent."

A smile twisted her lips. He was a decent man, though he'd made mistakes in the end. At least he'd done so thinking he could make a difference.

"He died in battle and I became High Lord. When humans began invading Tir na Faie, the Seelie King asked for the High Lords to get together so we could plan our counterattack. We fought for years until the day we couldn't fight anymore. By then, we were being overrun with humans and iron. We grew weaker in our own lands and the Fae king didn't know what we could do to save ourselves. Weylyn suggested we hide at Castle Aileach. It was our stronghold for years until..."

Until it was decimated.

Her hand reached out to grip his. No one was more surprised by the action than she was. Still, she didn't pull away. "I had already been in Dana for years when the courts fell. I only knew we'd been overrun when the soldiers started murdering my courtiers." She didn't dare tell him the rest, lest he think she was weak. But he'd probably guessed it all anyway.

She started to pull away, to slip her hand away from his, but he held on. She gasped as the contact sizzled up her body. "We all had to do things to survive, my lady." His grip eased, fingers smoothing across the tops of her knuckles and down her fingers. She knew he could feel the crooked joints, the scars. Embarrassment made her want to pull away, but she felt frozen. "Some of us suffered more than others, but we did it. We survived when others did not. We are here, and we are honoring them every day we draw breath. You're a survivor, my lady. Do not let anyone tell you different."

He pulled away, and Corvina almost followed him. *Tell me more,* she wanted to beg. She wanted to hear the words of her worth because when he said them, she almost believed that they were true. But he was right. She had survived when others had not. Maybe it had not been out of bravery, but she was still alive, and she had the opportunity to be brave now.

"You're very kind, my lord."

"I'm honest, my lady. There is a difference between being kind for the sake of being kind and telling the truth." His eyes burned on hers like green fire. "I would never lie to you. That I can promise."

"Then I will promise the same."

His smile was radiant. "Then tell me, Lady Corvina, what is your favorite food?"

Clay donned his armor in the early hours of the morning before the sun had even risen across the sky. Despite the upcoming danger, he wore a smile on his face, though he knew he had one person to thank for that.

He'd stayed up well into the night talking to Corvina. They'd shared stories and tales of their childhoods before the war, before the fall of the Fae. It had been nice not worrying about wooing her, about trying to get her to accept him as her mate. Dawn had been right. He'd only thought about claiming her and not getting to know her.

That had changed last night as the last embers of the fire died down with their laughter and the night grew quiet around them. Something had shifted. They weren't lovers, they weren't even really mates. But they were friends. And Clay found that he liked that even more. He liked getting to know her. He like hearing her laughter because it was so tentative. Like she'd forgotten how and was just now remembering to find her voice again.

Once more, he felt his hatred rise for her bastard of a husband. Every time his eyes caught sight of her scars as she reached up to brush aside a curly lock of hair or she gestured with her hands. He pretended not to notice, because he knew how humiliated she was regarding what she'd been through. He fought the urge to reassure her every few minutes that there was nothing to worry about. He would not judge her.

But he could avenge her.

He stepped out of his tent among the hurried chaos of the start of a battle. He was familiar with this, though not as familiar as Julius. During the wars, he'd been relatively safe. He didn't fight in every battle, but he'd planned and plotted and tried to keep his court safe. They'd all failed, but this was another chance to restore Mana's balance.

He walked over to the weaponry, grabbing a shield and sword. First, he sheathed the sword at his side, but he didn't strap on the shield. He would tie that to his steed, and once they made it closer to the battlefield, he would prepare.

Amongst the chaos of the morning, he heard his name being called. He turned as Corvina pushed her way through the crowd. She was out of breath, her chest rising and falling. The sight of her made his heart beat faster. He'd just seen her last night, having escorted her back to the tent she shared with Basil. He'd wanted to kiss her then but instead had leaned backwards on the balls of his feet.

"Goodnight," she'd whispered, a flush on her face. It made him wonder if maybe she'd wanted him to kiss her, too.

"Goodnight," he echoed before turning and walking away.

She stared up at him now with that same flush rising high on her face.

"My lady, is everything alright? Is Basil okay?" Basil was important to her. He admired that because her fierce, protective ferocity when it came to her son reminded Clay of his own mother and how much she'd loved him.

Her eyes warmed at those words. "Basil is fine. You'll be fighting today?"

He hadn't mentioned that last night. They'd avoided topics of battle and heartache. Mainly because he was afraid she wouldn't care that he was going to ride out and face certain death. He realized later what a silly notion that was. Corvina cared, and she cared deeply.

"I have to."

"No, you don't."

He frowned. "I cannot let my people ride out and not help. My magic could make a difference in battle."

She swallowed. Her fingers twisted on the folds of her dress. "You'll be careful?"

He flashed her a smile. "You worried about me, my lady?"

She stepped forward, so close that their bodies touched. He felt the heat of her zap through him even through the metal of his armor. "Yes," she whispered, her voice husky. And she stood to the tips of her toes and pressed a kiss to his cheek. She pulled back, her bright eyes shining. "Be careful, Clay. Please."

A moment later she was gone.

And Clay stood there stupidly. Blinking at the spot she'd been standing. Feeling the press of her lips against his skin like a brand. Like a promise of tomorrow.

It felt a lot like hope.

And he felt new determination grit through him. He would ride out into battle, and he would help his people win. Because he had a lot left to live for. Because he wanted more of what he saw in Corvina's eyes. More trust. And more kisses.

"What the fuck do you mean we're staying here?" Iona demanded. She was way too close to shoving the Seelie King at his shoulders until he started to make even an inkling of fucking sense.

"You are staying here," Valerio repeated, his eyes daring her to test him with her anger.

She gritted her teeth, closing her hands into fists. If Julius was here, she would have punched him in the dick. Likely her mate knew this had been Valerio's plan all along and was avoiding her, which would explain why she hadn't really seen him all morning. Or maybe he hadn't known. It didn't matter; none of this was on him.

It was on Valerio.

"Shula and I could make a difference in battle," Iona argued, gesturing between herself and the fire Fae. "We can help against the iron."

"I know that, Iona. But we do not know what Dana has up their sleeve. We cannot risk either on of you getting captured. And we cannot risk showing our hand too soon since this is merely the first battle."

It made sense. Of course it made sense. But it didn't sit well with Iona. "Do you expect me to knit by the fire while you all go out and risk your lives? I won't do it, Valerio."

"Of course not. You must stay here and protect the camp. This battle might be a ploy of Dana's to come sneak in here and take Lady Corvina back and decimate us while our warriors are distracted. You and Shula will be the best defense for our camp."

The tightness eased in her chest. The anger was still there. But he was giving her a purpose, even if it wasn't in the midst of the action like she wanted it to be. Justice was calling to her to fight and it's what she wanted to do. To honor Mana and protect the Fae.

"We'll protect them," Shula conceded. There was a note of fear in her voice, but more than that there was determination. She really had come a long way from what she'd been before. The fear still lived brightly inside her, but she had a fiercer edge now. It had arisen because it had already burned within her. It just took her a while to follow that light.

"Fine," Iona huffed. There was no other choice and besides, he was right. They had people to protect. And so she would protect them.

With her life.

Sometime later, Iona found Julius before they marched off. She greeted him with a fist to the gut, though through armor and his giant bulk, he barely even flinched. He pursed his lips down at her, amusement glittering in his grass-green eyes before it was replaced by something else.

Just like that all her anger dissipated. She sighed and they stepped towards each other, arms reached out. For a moment she wished his body wasn't clad in metal armor so she could feel the warmth of him underneath. So she could garner his scent just for a moment longer.

"Stay safe," he whispered against the top of her head.

She sucked in a sharp breath and released it. "You too, dick face."

He chuckled, the words breaking the tension as he pulled away. His big hand cradled the side of her face. "Fight, Iona. If someone who doesn't belong comes into the camp, you fucking fight and you fucking kill them. Do you understand?"

"The same goes for you. Make them pay. Make the Danarish pay for what they did to my sister."

He knew what she meant. Knew she didn't mean the sister who had died in the camps, the one who she'd shaved her head for in mourning. The other sister. The Elemental. Sure, they hadn't had much of a connection since she arrived, but that didn't matter. What mattered was that they *were* connected. What mattered was that she was a woman who had suffered and her abusers deserved to rot.

Julius' smile curled at the ends in a malicious way that sent shivers down her spine. Not out of fear, for she could never fear her own mate. But he wore the cloak of the Unseelie, of the Wild Hunt he told her he'd witnessed as they tore across the sky in a shadow of darkness and star dust. Of warriors of old who killed and reaped souls. Older even than Mana.

He'd confessed to her one night in between whispers and sighs that he'd wished he could have been a part of the Hunt when he was young. How those were foolish dreams now that he'd found her.

She didn't think them so foolish now. The calls of the wild had been captured in his heart, like a song within a music box, and he was ready to open his mouth and let that violence sing on the battlefield. He would wreak havoc, and he would make the humans bleed.

Words were unnecessary now. Their lips met in a desperate clash of tongue and teeth as they devoured. Like it could be the last time. But it wouldn't be. Iona sent a loud prayer up to Mana, asking for the protection of their troops. The Danarish soldiers were greater in numbers. They had iron and ashwood. But the Fae had something the humans didn't.

Nothing left to lose.

And that could make anyone desperate enough to win any battle.

And they would win. She felt it deep in her bones like hope and determination.

Like a promise from Mana.

"Remember your promise to me," Shula whispered up at Ryker.

Ryker cradled her smooth cheeks in his scarred hands. The contrast between the both of them made his heart beat faster, as did the words and the reminder of the vow he'd made. For a greater part of his life, he'd suffered so others wouldn't have to. He bore the scars so others could live.

That had been his single mission in life.

Now he felt like he was destined for something more.

"I remember."

Her sigh of relief tore through his veins. He dropped his forehead to hers and breathed in her scent. He should have stayed behind at the camp. It's what he'd wanted to do. It had actually been a part of the original plan. But Valerio needed all the soldiers he could spare on the battlefield and he wanted Ryker in case... But Ryker had made a promise to Shula and he wouldn't break it.

Not even for his prince.

So he would go out there and he would fight. And when needed, he would bring injured soldiers back to the camp to treat them. But he would not use his magic.

"Be careful," Shula said.

"I will." But Ryker didn't want to spend the last minutes they had left talking. He pulled her face closer to his and their mouths touched. Like every kiss they shared, it started off just the slightest bit tentative before it blazed. He kissed her like he was pulling her scent into his body. He inhaled her like he was tasting the chocolate off her lips wrapped in something else.

Not hatred or contempt, but something more.

Their tongues moved, drawing out a few moments of pleasure and sighs before he was forced to pull away from her. Their eyes held and he said nothing when he finally stepped back from his mate and turned. He heard a strangled noise, but he didn't turn. He already had every aspect of her memorized. From the first moment he'd seen her, he'd committed her figure to memory. From the first moment he touched her, he memorized how she felt beneath his scarred hands. And the first time he'd kissed her, he knew he'd never forget the taste of her lips and tongue.

It was only with that in mind could he go forward.

To battle.

Corvina didn't know what had possessed her to press her lips to Clay's cheek. All she knew was that something had shifted between them. It wasn't the mating bond; no, she could differentiate that magic and her real feelings. And what her heart told her was that Clay was a good man. A friend. And she didn't want anything to happen to him during this battle.

A battle that everyone was marching off towards. She committed the moment to her memory, feeling despair at the fact that this would be the last time she saw several of the people currently walking away to fight Dana.

Her heart ached for them, and she felt worthless as she watched them with their swords and their shields ready to protect what they believed in. It did, however, give her a moment of strength. A moment of clarity. Strength existed. Her people were alive and vibrant and ready to defend themselves from the tyranny.

Right then Corvina realized that she would be, too.

If they could wield the weapons with their gnarled fingers and scars after suffering in a camp, then she could do the same.

Squaring her shoulders, she whirled, ready to put herself to good use, and nearly rammed into Dawn.

She blinked at her maid, focusing on the metal armor she wore, and the sword she held in her hand.

"Dawn?"

"I am going to fight, my lady."

"Dawn..."

"No! Do not try and convince me otherwise. I am going with the soldiers, and I am going to fight. Dana took *everything* from me, from *us.* The soldiers on that field tortured me day and night. I had no reprieve from their cruelty and you suffered as much as I did. So I am going, my lady, and even if I die out there on that field today, at least it will be taking vengeance into my own hands." Tears were streaming down Dawn's face. She'd kept her emotions tightly locked behind a wall of anger, and now it finally began crumbling and making way for something new.

And that was this.

"I was not going to stop you," Corvina reassured. She stepped forward and reached for her friend's empty hand, giving it a squeeze. That was all the touch she gave, for she wasn't sure if Dawn would allow for more, before she pulled back. "Make them pay, Dawn. Take your vengeance."

Dawn blinked, surprised by the ferocity in Corvina's voice or the answer itself, she wasn't sure. She gave her a firm nod and started away, but Corvina couldn't let her go off without saying something first.

"Dawn!" Dawn whirled around. Corvina blinked away her tears. "I am sorry."

Because it was Dawn, she didn't need to say anything else. Her maid already understood. "I never blamed you, my lady, despite what I said in anger. I never blamed you. For any of it."

Corvina almost crumbled at the impacting force of those words. They'd been everything she'd wanted to hear. Forgiveness. For what Corvina had done. For how she felt like she'd failed. What Dawn had given her was a gift, one Corvina didn't think she'd ever be able to return. And she couldn't even reply, because Dawn had already been swallowed up by the crowd.

And now all Corvina could do was wait. Wait and make herself useful around camp before the fate of the battle made itself known.

Battle and Blood

The thing about healing magic was that it was more extensive than just healing. It was never as simple as curing ailments and absorbing the pain. It was more than that. It was every aspect of agony, one that others could never quite comprehend.

They'd marched their way into battle with Valerio leading the charge. Ryker had stayed a little ways behind, but still close enough that he'd seen how it started. How the first arrow flew into the neck of a Fae, felling him instantly.

That's when the agony began. As shields and swords clashed, as the grounds were swallowed up with carnage of battle and blood, Ryker nearly keeled over as his magic pulsed, sensing pain and injuries from those around him.

He didn't absorb their pain, but he felt it there and his skin itched, demanding he put his powers to use and heal like he was meant to. He had to shove the urge away with every swipe of his blade. Every time he fought, he winced for his opponent. Every time his blade tore through the flesh of a human's neck, he resisted the urge to reach for his own.

They were the enemy, he kept reminding himself. But the readiness of his magic, wanting to burst beneath his skin, made it hard to tell the difference. How could he when pain belonged to everyone? No pain was greater than others.

That was something Shula had taught him.

His mind whirled and he huffed in heavy breaths. The armor weighed him down, making it hard to move. Iron burned through the air, weakening him. He was glad Shula wasn't here for this, but despaired too because she and Iona would have been able to melt and destroy the iron the soldiers wielded, giving the Fae an advantage.

Beside him, a Fae fell. His convulsions had Ryker dropping to his knees. His chest was pounding so hard it felt like it would burst straight from his chest. It was suffocating, demanding, and he tamped it down, desperate to keep his promise.

"Fuck!" he screamed, slamming his fists into the ground. "Fuck!"

Agony seared through him, making his chest heave and saliva pool from his lips.

"Ryker!" He looked up as a body came into his line of vision. Clay dropped to his knees at his sides and helped him up, groaning as he threw Ryker's heavy arm around his shoulders. "Fuck me, you're heavier than you look. Get up, big boy, we have a battle to win and Shula would kick my ass if I let you die."

Soldiers rushed for them, but before Ryker could cry out a warning, Clay's palm lifted in their direction. He closed his fist and blood burst from them. They dropped to the ground in a heap of dead limbs.

Clay reached up and swiped at the blood dripping from his nose. "Come on," he said. "I'm getting you back to the camp. There are a lot of injured who need you."

Ryker gritted his teeth, pulling himself up. He gently pushed Clay away. "I can walk on my own," Ryker assured. "You keep fighting."

Clay breathed a laugh and clapped Ryker on the back. "Now that's what I like to hear."

When the injured began pouring into the camp, Corvina found her legs moving at a fast pace. She tried to help as best as she could, but she wasn't a healer. Experience with her own injuries helped her manage cuts and bruises, but these Fae came in with wounds far greater than what she knew how to heal.

Shula helped guide the injured onto cots. Because they wouldn't all fit into a single tent, their cots had been set outside at side-by-side intervals. It wasn't an ideal setting, but it was what they had. Shula worked through the masses as if she were used to this type of chaos. She began binding wounds, treating the more severe injuries first.

Corvina followed her lead, doing what Shula did and mimicking her movements. She felt her expression twist with pain the more she worked and was surprised with Shula's equanimity. It only made Corvina's admiration for the woman grow in increments.

Then Ryker arrived. He limped into the camp, oblivious to his own injuries. Shula took a single flicking look at her mate, as if doing a quick assessment if he was truly alright before they fell into perfect synchronization together. They moved around each other as if they'd been doing this together for years, though Corvina new it had only been months since they'd met. Yet they were a unit.

She forced her eyes away from them and helped, looking at the faces of the injured. She knew these faces, though none of them were Dawn's or Clay's. She looked in the direction from which Ryker had come, but Clay didn't appear. Knots made her stomach sick, but she swallowed the bile and uncertainty back.

She wouldn't think about all the horrible things that could have happened to them both. Instead, she turned back to the injured and she worked.

And she worked.

And worked.

Magic was unleashed. It ripped through the human's ranks, altering their memories until they didn't know what was real and what wasn't. Blood exploded from orifices, and even the small pulse of iron in their arsenal couldn't push the Fae back.

They were vicious, savage. They wanted revenge and they took it. Even as comrades fell around them, the Fae pushed forward. Cries fell from their lips, screams of rage and pain. The clang of steel and crash of iron, the whinnied shrieks of horses, it all became a song. In the distance, Julius tore through their ranks like a charging bull, his guttural cries of rage echoing through the darkening skies.

From his steed, Valerio heaved a breath. "Let's end this."

Clay nodded at his cousin. He knew what he wanted, what he'd commanded Clay to do back in Covenglen but hadn't. But he'd do it now, or as much as the pulsing iron would allow him to. His hand lifted and the magic of blood stirred within his veins. He unleashed it as he closed his fist.

One by one, soldiers began falling as the blood was drained from their bodies. And even as it drained, Clay could feel it filling him. His heart beat faster as it tried to keep up with the excess liquid in his body. It burst past his eyes and down his nose. He tasted the copper of it on the back of his tongue, and when he spoke next, crimson stained his lips. "It is done."

The Fae watched as their enemies fell and stepped back. Except one. One female who sawed through the remains of human soldiers with a rage that rivaled hell. She screamed as her sword swung over her head, hacking up bodies. She pulled out pent-up rage, and the sight of it made Clay's chest tighten with something that had nothing to do with his magic.

Dawn. The figure was Dawn.

Valerio let her extract her vengeance. Her anger. He watched in silence as the Fae began to walk back towards their line.

It was done.

They'd won the battle.

But they still had yet to win the war.

From the other side of the battlefield, a single rider came into view. He came at a dizzying speed until he was twenty feet away from them. He wore the colors of Dana, and his eyes swept over the battle, of his felled soldiers, before he turned back to them with fear in his eyes.

"Seelie King," he greeted. Valerio didn't need to wear a crown for everyone to know who he was. He emanated the energy of the one who was in charge. "I bring a message from King Archibald and Princes Arthur and Tobias."

"Speak, human," Valerio replied in a droll tone.

"The King of Dana requests an audience with your party to discuss the terms of an agreement in regards to Princess Corvina and the young prince."

Just hearing this human filth say her name brought rage rising in Clay's chest. He leaned forward on his horse, flashing a hint of bloody canines. "You can tell your king that he can go fuck himself."

Fear smelt acrid, even among the death. The human turned back to Valerio, as if the Seelie King was the safer of the two. "He requests the meeting be on neutral ground. He wants a momentary truce to discuss how you should proceed. It will be a peaceful meeting. All Prince Tobias wants is his wife back."

Valerio was silent a moment, but Clay knew there was no way he would agree to it.

"Tell your king I accept meeting him to hear his terms."

"Valerio—"

"Silence, Clay!" Valerio snapped. Clay barely restrained his own growl of anger. "Name your neutral ground and we will be there tomorrow morning to discuss the terms."

After the human gave the location and rode away, Clay turned on his cousin, his body prepared and primed for a fight.

"I want to meet the king for myself," Valerio explained. "I want to see what he has to say for himself and what he thinks he has to offer us."

"It's a trap."

"Most likely. But I think he is surprised by the outcome today. He thought we would be easily felled and, if I am correct, wants this sit-down so we can gauge one another's mettle. We will hear him out. It could help us win the war if we do."

Clay's fingers tightened along the reins. "I won't give Corvina up. I won't do it."

"No one is asking you to, cousin. And I would not give her up, either. Having her on our side is vital in our survival. However, if you want to be the one to tell her..."

They couldn't keep this from her. This was her life they were playing with. It was everyone's lives and futures, but he swore he wouldn't be like Valerio, who held women against their will. Or Ryker who had pushed his mate away so often that the two had ended up hating one another. He would be honest. He would tell her what the king wanted.

"After all, perhaps there is some information that she can give that will give us the upper hand." Valerio pulled on the reins, turned his horse, and galloped away.

Things at the camp were chaos of bloody and broken bodies. He led his horse over to their makeshift stables, giving the bloody white steed a pat before he handed the responsibility over to a young Fae boy. Normally, Clay would have cleaned down his horse instead, but he had more pressing matters to see to first.

He spotted Corvina at the same time she saw him. She stood from a crouched position where she'd been hovering over an injured Fae and ran towards Clay. He waited for the impact of her body crushing against his, but it never came. She stopped herself at the last moment, breathing hard.

"Clay." Her bloody hands twisted against the folds of her skirts. Her eyes roamed over him, assessing. Something in him warmed at the fact that she was making sure he was okay.

"I am fine, my lady," he reassured, snapping her attention back up to him.

"I am glad. I—I was worried." It looked like it cost her to admit the words, which meant he appreciated them so much more.

"Are you alright, my lady?" She hadn't been in the battle, but she'd seen the aftermath of it and that was bad enough. He noted the way her hands shook and how she tried to keep it together.

"You can call me Corvina, you know," she whispered. "And I am fine. Can I check you for injuries?" She started forward and stopped herself before she could reach out and touch him.

"I promise you, I am not injured. But I *was* looking for you."

"Yes?" She blinked up at him. Her eyes wide, so shy, so innocent, and he couldn't fathom how anyone would want to hurt her. She was so small, almost fragile-looking.

"Corvina," he tested out her name, liking the way it tasted against his tongue. "We need to talk."

Corvina's legs threatened to give out beneath her. They buckled under her weight, and it was with great effort that she was even able to stand at all. White noise pounded through her ears as if she'd stuck her head beneath the water. Everything was muffled and she barely heard King Valerio's words as he spoke them.

"We agreed to meet him."

Her husband had requested a meeting with the Fae. He wanted to sit down in front of them and discuss the terms of her trade. Corvina and Basil in exchange for peace with the Fae. Perhaps that hadn't been specified, but she knew him. She and Basil were his most prized possessions. And he would stop at nothing until he had them back.

"He's lying." Her voice was a broken sound that fractured past her lips. Her eyes flicked up and she realized she'd interrupted the king. She didn't feel guilty about it, though. Not when there were more important things. "It's a trap."

King Valerio's grave expression softened. "That is what we're assuming."

Her mind whirred, turning in circles like the cogs in a machine. Tobias hadn't specifically requested her presence with them tomorrow, but if it was a trap, how could she let the Fae go without accompanying them? She wasn't stupid enough to believe that her presence would be enough to deter him from harming them, but for a second, guilt clouded her.

There was still a part of her that wanted to keep him happy, because keeping him happy, in whatever way she could do it, meant he would not be violent. He just wanted her back. If she went with him, then maybe...

No. It didn't matter what she did. If she gave herself up to him on a silver platter, he wouldn't spare them. He would kill them and make her watch out of spite.

She'd never be free of him, she realized. Not unless he was dead. Or she was.

But she couldn't die. In that cell, he'd broken her body and her spirit until she'd laid on the cold, musty ground and awaited her demise. He would not do that to her again because ever since she'd escaped his clutches, she realized she had a lot left to live for.

By no means did she think she was brave. Maybe a part of her would always be broken. Maybe a part of her would always be that fearful creature that he'd turned her into the moment they'd said their wedding vows. But something else lived inside of her, too. Something she'd forgotten existed until she'd come to this camp and had met the Fae. Had met Iona Wylde. Had met Shula Azzarh.

Shula had overcome her own trials. She had watched her parents get burned alive, and yet here she was, in camp, with a sword in hand. *Fighting.* She'd not wanted to at first, but she had. She *was.*

So Corvina would, too.

She swallowed past the emotions rising in her throat and looked King Valerio in the eye. "I am going with you."

That seemed to floor everyone that was in the king's tent. It just went to show how pitiful of a thing she'd been since she'd arrived. No more.

Her back straightened, the pride of her blood coursing through her veins. "I am going with you," she repeated with firmness.

"Corvina..." Clay reached out as if he meant to grab her but stopped himself, closing his hand into a fist. Had she become so pathetic that everyone had to measure their actions around her? That she'd earned their pity by flinching every time their hands lifted? This time, she didn't flinch. She reached out and grabbed his hand instead, threading their fingers together. He sucked in a breath. "You don't have to face him."

"Yes, I do."

"What if he sees you and—"

"I won't let it happen. Not this time." Her mind was on Shula and her magic. On how she could melt iron. Corvina would be that brave. She would be that fierce.

"If he tries anything..." He broke off on a growl, his grip tightening in hers a fraction. "I will protect you, Corvina. I swear it."

Their eyes held. In them, she saw a thousand emotions pass by like a rushing swirl of water. They crested and crashed over her body, enveloping her. She let it. This time, she let herself be swept away by what she saw in his gaze. Her heart gave a pang at everything she could see. Friendship and something that looked a lot like desire.

She reciprocated it. It hit her like the impact of a blow, oozing from her pores. Clay was so beautiful, so gentle. She imagined those lips roving over her body. She imagined his hands doing to her what Julius had done to Iona. Tearing at her clothes, giving control over to her as she slipped over his cock and rode his heat.

Clay's nostrils flared and she realized too late that he was Fae. Fae had better senses than humans. He could likely scent her arousal. Her cheeks heated at the thought, even though she didn't want to feel embarrassed.

"My lady," the king interrupted. "We need to ask you questions about your husband."

The word 'husband' was like being doused with a bucket of ice cold water. Clay's throat bobbed up and down before he slipped his hand from hers and stepped back. She watched the rise and fall of his chest as if he was struggling to compose himself. She finally tore her attention from him, her chest compressing uncomfortably to meet the Fae King.

"We need to know anything that could help us so we do not go in blind. Anything that could give us an advantage over him."

Corvina felt her mouth pull into an almost malicious smile. "Of course," she agreed. "Anything."

A Danarish Deal

They rode out to the neutral ground to find Tobias was already there. From atop a white steed, Corvina sucked in a breath as she caught sight of him. He sat on a mount next to his brother and a handful of guards. He looked regal in his Danarish regalia and the glimmering crown on his head. His expression was thunderous while Arthur's next to him was glinting with cautious amusement.

She could read the two of them so easily, she realized. It hadn't occurred to her until the night before when she'd gifted the King of Seelie their tells and secrets.

Their own party consisted of King Valerio, Uric, Julius, Iona, Clay, and a handful of guards. They came to a stop a ways away from the Danarish. Only then, did they begin to dismount.

Corvina's heart pounded and her hands trembled. She couldn't find the will to make her body move. Not when Tobias was glaring at her the same way he did seconds before he let his fists loose. She froze, wanting to cower away from what instinct told her was coming. From pain and cruelty.

Her breaths sawed out of her chest in shallow pants. Her vision started to tunnel, and Tobias smirked. Like he knew what his presence did to her. And he relished in it. She almost dropped from the horse and ran towards him out of habit. Because that's what that look wanted. He wanted her to submit. She gritted her teeth to resist.

"Corvina." A warm hand pressed against her own, jolting her from the instinctive urges trembling through her body. She sucked in a breath and looked away from Tobias. Clay was looking up at her with warm eyes. The promise he'd made shining in them.

I will protect you.

And she would protect herself.

Taking in a shuddering breath, she swung a leg over the side of the horse. Clay was there, his hands pressing to her waist and helping her down. They were pressed close together when her feet touched the ground. She could feel his breath fanning across the top of her head and she tilted her chin up, her hands still resting on Clay's shoulders.

For a moment, a single second, everything else faded away and it was just the two of them. She felt safe. With his hands on her and the connection buzzing through them, she felt safe. But that didn't last as they were forced to break away and she caught sight of Tobias once again.

He sneered at Corvina and Clay, his eyes flicking over every spot he'd touched. Fear made her knees shake. She was familiar with what he'd do to get the touch and scent of Clay off her body. He would chain her to the bed and force his way inside of her. Over and over again.

Remembering the cruel touch had her pulling away from Clay and walking at a safe distance near the Seelie King. There was already a space set up where they could sit as if this were an official meeting between kingdoms. Small tables with trays of food and wine.

"Don't eat the food," she'd warned the night before. If she knew her husband, than she figured he would try all he could to earn an advantage in any way he could, even on neutral ground. That meant using iron to weaken them or lacing food and wine with ashwood.

King Valerio eyed the food with a lifted tilt of his lip before pulling his attention back to Tobias and Arthur.

"King of the Seelie, I presume?" It was Arthur who spoke. He stepped forward with a careless swagger and bowed before Valerio with a smirk. Not once did he take his eyes off them, though. "I am Prince Arthur Wes, heir of Dana, firstborn of King Archibald Wes."

"Corvina!" Her name was snapped from Tobias' lips. He stepped forward in her direction and her whole body tensed, but Arthur stopped Tobias' trajectory with a hand to his brother's chest.

"My brother," Arthur introduced. "Prince Tobias Wes."

Tobias' worked his jaw before forcing his gaze away from Corvina and giving a stiff bow to the Fae king.

Valerio lifted a brow, almost with amusement. "King Valerio Ashera of Seelie." He jerked his chin towards Clay. "My cousin, High Lord Clay Valentino of the Sapphire Court." Neither of them bowed, something she was sure that Tobias and Arthur took notice of and likely found offensive.

"My father sends his regards and apologies for not being able to attend, but we are here to negotiate in his stead," Arthur continued, his voice smooth. "Please, have a seat and we can begin."

Valerio moved slowly and sat at one of the available chairs, his movements casual yet deadly. Uric stuck close to him, his black blade twirling through his pale fingers. Arthur and Tobias sat across from Valerio.

"Corvina," Tobias began again. "You look well."

And that likely pissed him off. He wanted her starved and weak. Easily bent to his will. She swallowed past the lump in her throat.

"I think we should begin and get rid of pleasantries, shall we?" Arthur smirked. "You look like someone who appreciates a direct approach."

"Hmm," was Valerio's reply.

Corvina had to hold back her smirk when she saw Arthur's lip twitch in annoyance. If there was one thing they hated, it was the lack of attention. Something she'd told the king the night before. It would hurt their egos if he gave noncommittal replies.

"The fact of the matter is, you stole something that doesn't belong to you."

At this, Clay snorted. "Something?"

Tobias' eyes blazed. He sneered at Clay. "You broke into a prince's castle and stole his property."

Hearing him talk about her in such a way made humiliation burn inside her stomach. But all Clay did was snort, like Tobias was beneath him.

The Danarish prince let out a low growl, but it was Arthur who kept speaking. "While what you did is cause for war, we are willing to negotiate and come up with a solution that benefits us all."

Valerio threw his arm around the back of the chair. "Do tell," he mused. "We are riveted to hear what *you* have to offer *us*."

Arthur smirked, the action cruel and familiar.

"I want my son back," Tobias said. "You can keep the bitch." He shot Corvina an open look of disgust. "Your High Lord looks like he already had a turn at her anyway. I don't want damaged property." Corvina let out a small gasp at the harsh words and Tobias turned from her. "But I want my son. My heir."

"Give my brother back his heir and we will let you and your armies walk free," Arthur drawled. "A fair trade, isn't it?"

Corvina couldn't keep silent any longer. She stood even though her legs trembled. "You're lying!" she accused, pointing a finger in their direction. "You will take us and kill them anyway. You don't want peace!"

Tobias lifted his lip in a sneer. "Shut up, cunt," he snarled. "The men are talking and you will be silent."

Up until this moment, Iona had been silent, watching the events unfold. At his words, she cackled, though the sound held no mirth. "Is this bitch-prince serious?" She lifted her elbow, placing it on Julius' shoulder in a casual move. She leaned forward, smirking. "*'The men are talking,'*" she mimicked. "Then I guess you should stay quiet too, because only a weak little bitch hits a woman. As far as I'm concerned, you're no man."

Tobias' face flushed an ugly shade of crimson, and Corvina felt a single moment of satisfaction. "How dare you, Fae bitch—"

"Careful how you speak to my soldiers," Valerio cut in, cool as ever. "Us Fae savages are so very hard to control. Anger them and you'll discover just how vicious we can be." This silenced Tobias. Valerio leaned forward, resting his elbows on his thighs. "I do believe you are being dishonest with me. I do not think the Danarish want peace. Skip the pleasantries, will you? You saw the decimation of your army and your king wants to avoid another massacre, does he not? Is he afraid that we will win? Is that why he sent you in his stead?"

Tobias' jaw worked and Arthur huffed a breath. "The Danarish do not fear a small army of crippled Fae. We have the might of our soldiers as well as the emperor's soldiers at are back. *We* are offering you a boon. *Dana*, not the empire of Illyk. *We* are offering you the freedom to leave our kingdom peacefully in exchange for a single child."

If Valerio agreed to this, if he handed her son over to Tobias, he would hurt him. He would take him to the Brotherhood and they would choke him on water that burned like they did to her. They would take away his goodness, make him suffer.

"Tobias," Corvina spoke again. "Why are you doing this? Why can't you just let us go?" But she knew the answer to it, even as she said the words.

"You think it's you I want?" her husband laughed. "You stupid bitch. You can do whatever you want. Go fuck this High Lord if you please. Whore yourself out to the entire camp if that's what you wish. I just want *my* son back."

His words hurt. They felt like a heavy weight pushing her down. "I'm his mother," she said. "He needs me."

"You're a Fae whore. And you didn't even want him in the first place. You'll recall you took rue to prevent pregnancy because you didn't want my child." Her whole body tensed and she felt like prey. Like he was a viper dancing circles around her, going in for the strike. "So you remember? How you fought me when I spilled myself inside you? I had to *force* you to have my heir. I had to hold you down with iron chains."

Her body trembled. Her face heated. The memories came back to her of that time. Of the pain she felt. And now, they would all hear. Clay would hear what had happened. They already knew she'd suffered and Tobias was only hammering down the evidence of what she'd gone through with that stupid smirk on his face.

She felt like she was going to be sick as he flayed her past open. What would they think of her, to know that she'd tried preventing pregnancy? Did it make her a hypocrite? She loved Basil with all that she was. She would put her own life on the line for him but his words still made her bleed.

"Reginald is *my* child," Tobias went on. "Mine. You didn't want him then and so you don't get to have him now." His gaze turned to Clay, who stood tense, unmoving. Tobias snorted at the High Lord. "Keep the whore if you want. She's tainted anyway, and more of a headache than she was worth. But you will bring me my son or our armies will decimate yours. No one will be spared. No woman, elder, or child. I will destroy your camp to get my son back. You have until morning to bring him here. If you do not, then prepare yourself, Fae. Prepare yourselves for war."

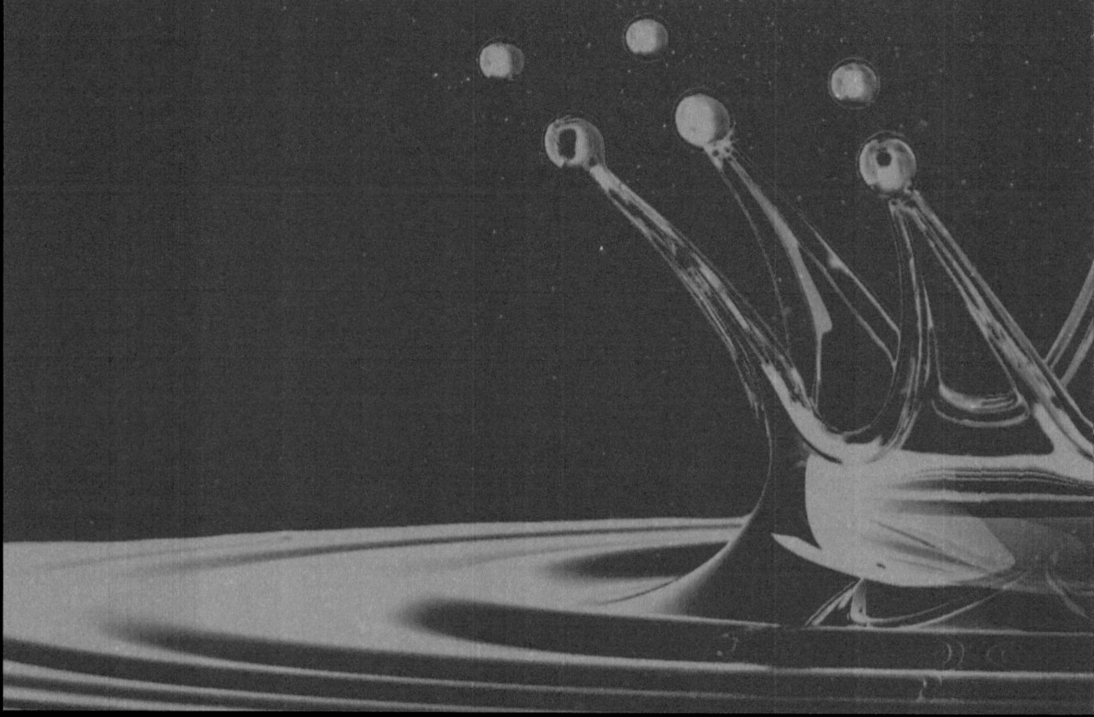

You Are Worth It

They left first. After he spit those words out at Corvina, they stood, meeting adjourned, and mounted their horses before thundering off, kicking up sand and grass behind them. The moment they were gone, Corvina turned and walked towards her own steed.

She couldn't stop and face the Fae. People she considered her friends. Not now that they knew the extent of her life. If she looked into their eyes, what would she see? She feared the answer. Her legs wobbled with each step she took. It felt like wading through honey. Every step felt weighted and painful. Her stomach heaved, her body trembled. And when she heard Clay cry out her name, she fell to the ground and vomited.

She retched and dry heaved like she could somehow expel the words her husband had pushed into her. But all that escaped her mouth were strings of saliva. And his words were still there, making her feel small. Worthless. All the power she'd professed to have, all that bravery she'd convinced herself lived within her like it lived within the Fire Dancer, dissipated into nothing. She was nothing, because Tobias said she was nothing. Made her feel like she was nothing.

His words were her haunting, and she knew she'd never be able to escape them.

"Corvina." Clay dropped to the ground next to her, his hand smoothing in circles along her back.

His touch hurt, so much that she shoved him away with a cry. "Don't!" she warned. "Don't touch me!"

His eyes flashed with hurt then worry. But she didn't deserve that. She didn't deserve his kindness. She'd been so convinced that she was strong, only to see him and have that fantasy come crumbling down around her once again.

"Corvina..."

"Clay, please don't." She sniffled, unaware that she'd even been crying in the first place. But now that she was aware, she couldn't hold the tears back any longer. They streamed down her face in rivers of emotion. "Don't comfort me. Not after that. Not after what he said."

He growled. "Fuck him and what he said."

She shook her head, her hair slipping from its coil to kiss her cheeks. "He's right, though." She turned her face and met the beauty of his own. It was like looking at the sun. Radiant, blinding, and she wanted to look away, but she tortured herself with the rays just a little bit longer. "I'm broken, Clay. I'm *tainted.*"

Something in his expression fractured, and she refused to believe it was for her. "You aren't." His voice was tight.

"I *am.* You heard what he said, you've heard and seen what he's done to me." She finally forced her gaze away, staring at the ground. At the pool of her vile weakness. "I can't be what you want. I am not the perfect woman. I'm broken, and I will always be broken. And you—you're *perfect,* and you deserve a mate as perfect as you are. Not *this.* Not me." Her fingers curled into the sand and grass. "So give me up, my lord. Give me up because I'm not worth it. I'm not—"

She didn't get to finish the rest of her tirade because Clay was gripping her by the waist and pulling her into his lap. He held her, caging her in with his arms. But she didn't feel afraid. Not with him. Never with him. Because she knew if she pulled away, he would let her go. He would give her the space she desired even if it killed him. Because that's just who he was. He had a goodness that lived in his soul, shining through every crevice like the bright beams of the sun.

His fingers pushed away her hair and he gripped her chin, forcing her to look into his eyes. What she saw floored her. It made her weak.

"I am not perfect, Corvina. No one is. In fact, we're all a little fucked up. We've all suffered, some more than most. That doesn't mean we are broken. It means we are strong. You're so fucking strong, and I admire you for all that you are." His palm smoothed across her cheek, pushing away her tears. "Don't ask me to give you up." His voice cracked. "Because I can't. I—*we* are your family. And we will never give you up. We will never give up on you, either, Corvina. Do you understand me?"

She didn't reply. She couldn't. Her tongue felt glued to the roof of her mouth, so she gave a single, slow nod. Every word seemed to brush away what Tobias had said. His voice was still there, her own insecurities eating away at her insides. But Clay was telling her she was worthy. And she wasn't sure if it was because they shared a bond or if it was something deeper even than Mana.

But for now, she would accept it.

She would accept *him.*

"We have to go now," he whispered gently. "It is time to plan this war."

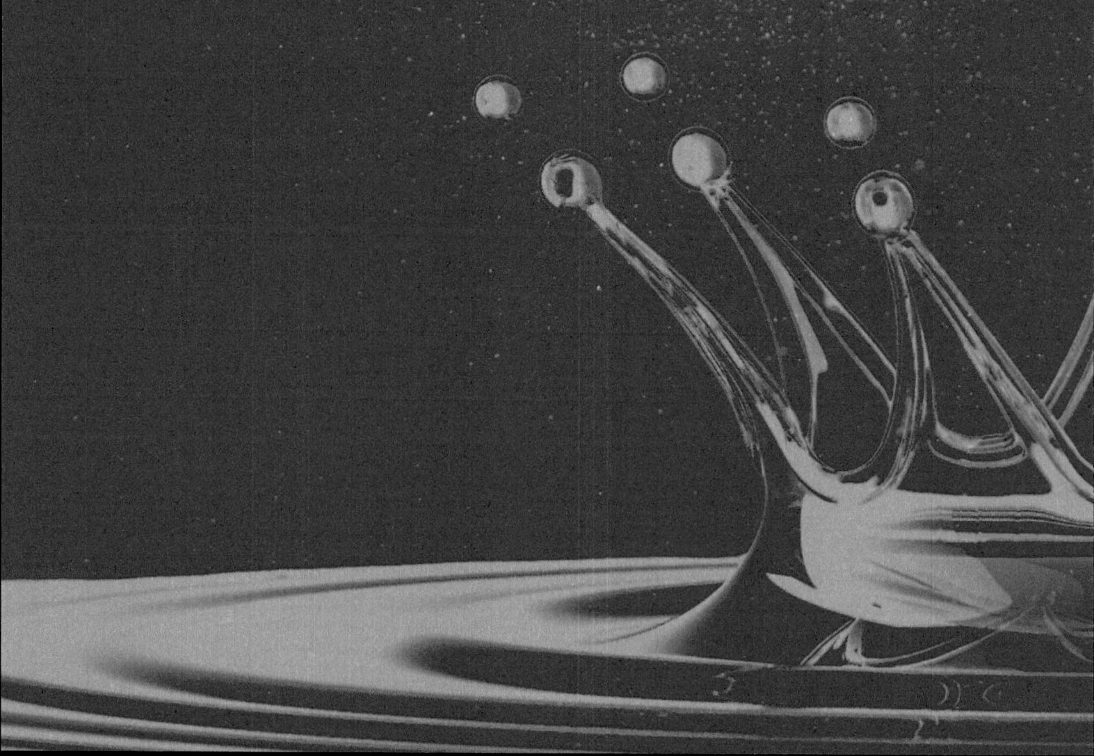

A Chilling Reunion

Shula worried at her bottom lip. Though her thoughts were miles away, she kept her attention on Basil as he waded through the water. There was a little stream a ways away from their camp where they'd been getting fresh water for their stews and to drink. Unable to take the melancholy of the camp, Shula had brought Basil here for a bath.

Ryker was tending to the injured, so she'd slipped away while he was engrossed in his work. The others that had stayed behind were helping patrol the area while Valerio, Julius, Iona, Clay, and Corvina went to meet the King of Dana.

She worried about that, about what seeing her abusers would do to Corvina. She tried not to think about it, because she saw a spark inside the water Fae. Corvina was strong, to have survived such terrible things. Of course, she hadn't wanted to take her son with her and because Basil seemed to enjoy Shula's company, she'd volunteered to watch over him.

The only kids Shula had ever been around had been those that had frequented the circus. A life of hiding never gave her a chance to explore relationships and she never thought about the future further than surviving the day. Needless to say, she'd never imagined a life of her own with children.

"Shula, look!"

She turned her attention to Basil. He was up to the knees in water, his pants rolled up to the thighs. His hands were held out and in his palms, he cupped a small seashell.

"That's so pretty."

"For you." He dropped the shell into her awaiting palm. "You can put it in your hair."

She smiled at the little boy and ruffled his curls. He was so adorable and whenever he looked at her with those round, innocent eyes, her heart clenched. Because he looked at her like she sometimes caught Corvina looking at her. Like she was worthy.

Then her thoughts took her down darker paths. Of his future, and what would become of him if they couldn't win this war. Of her own future, if she'd ever have children of her own. She'd never asked Ryker if he wanted them. Shula didn't. Not now with the world in shambles. Perhaps in the future, if they even had a future after this.

"You're so kind, Basil."

He beamed, his cheeks flushed from running in the sun. "My mommy says that, too."

"Your mommy is a smart woman." She tucked the shell into her pants pocket. The heat of the kingdom ensured that she was as scantily dressed as the young boy. In a pair of threadbare pants that clung to her hips and a flimsy shirt to let the breeze caress her sweaty skin. Her pants were rolled up at the knees and she was barefoot, careful to step over jagged rocks as she followed Basil in his journey through the water.

"My mommy is the best. But she's really sad. My daddy is always mean to her."

Shula felt floored. What was she supposed to say to that? She wasn't equipped to care for a small child, at least not when he started saying those things. She supposed, though, that all children wanted was honesty and to be spoken to like they had their own agency and intelligence. It's how her father had spoken to her, and how she'd speak to Basil.

"There are some people in this world who are very cruel." She thought of Fanny. How she'd elaborately tricked her just to turn her over to Captain Brannon. "But there are also people who are very kind." She thought of Des. Of the reverent way in which he stared deeply into Orna's eyes. The way in which he took her hand in his tenderly. Of Filomena and Imogen and the way they'd sacrificed themselves for the Fae. "Cruelty is wrong," she added. "Maybe mean people have their reasons for doing things, but it doesn't make it right."

He absorbed her words like a scrap of cloth and nodded his head. "I don't want to be mean like my daddy. He yells a lot. Sometimes I can hear him in my room hurting her. I like it here. Nobody yells at my mommy. And I like you, Shula."

Heat climbed up her cheeks at his declaration. It hadn't been a declaration of love. Mana's sake, the words had come from a child, but they felt like high praise indeed. It warmed her to know that he did. After so long of feeling like she didn't fit in, of hiding who she was, to find a group of people who accepted her... Even if it was a child and his mother.

"We should be getting back now, Basil." She held her hand out so he'd take it. Too late, she heard the whizzing sound through the air. Too late, she turned in time for the arrow to strike her shoulder. A surprised gasp left her lips as she fell backwards into the water. Pain sliced up her body and water soaked through her clothes.

Basil let out a cry, but before he could reach out for her, she sat up, slicing her palms against rocks. "Run!" she screamed.

But it was already too late.

She hadn't noticed them. Hadn't heard them creep up. But soldiers clamored out, kicking through the water. Basil was petrified, and the moment his feet moved to run, he was caught around the waist by a soldier and hauled up, a hand clamping around his mouth to muffle his shouts.

"Let him go, you bastard!" Shula pushed herself to her feet and staggered, her head dizzying. "W—what—?"

"An iron arrow coated in ashwood oil," a voice said. She spun, nearly falling, to face the familiar baritone. A cold spike of fear slid through her body as the man approached. A strange sense washed over her. Like she'd been here before in this exact same position, because she had been. Facing a nightmare brought to life.

He looked the same. Huge, with black and red armor, the colors of the emperor. His grave face flicked over hers with the same clinical disinterest they had the first time they'd met so many months ago at Piriguini's Circus. Except now, he seemed more menacing. It was in the eyes. They seemed to burn as bright and as hot as her own fire.

"Don't try to run, Fire Dancer," Captain Brannon said. "You will not get very far."

"You—" She stumbled and dropped to her knees, the impact shaking her skull. Fuck, how much oil had been coated along that arrow? Already her senses felt like they were dimming.

"Take the boy back to camp," the captain instructed. "The princes should still be distracting the Fae. We will use the boy to lure his mother out."

Her eyes widened and a strangled noise tripped from her throat. When Captain Brannon lowered himself in front of her, she couldn't bring herself to look up at him. As it was, his presence invoked memories of water that burned like fire. Of pain up her ribs. Of fear and betrayal.

His bare fingers pushed aside a long lock of hair, tucking it behind her ear. She couldn't even flinch away from him. Her body was too languid, her tongue too thick to even talk anymore. He invaded her space, his lips grazing the apple of her cheek. "I've been searching for you for months, Fire Dancer." His arms wrapped around her and then she felt herself being lifted up, up... "And this time, I'm not letting you go."

And then everything went black.

⋄⋄—•••—⋄⋄

They rode back into camp. The moment she pulled the reins to a stop, Corvina was slipping from her mount, calling out for Basil. She'd left him behind with Shula. Usually it would have been her maids who watched over her son, but he'd been practically glued to Shula's side. Thankfully, the fire Fae didn't mind. And Corvina trusted her implicitly to watch over her boy.

"Basil!" She walked over to her tent, pushing aside the flaps, but it was empty. Her heart beat fast in her chest. The meeting with Tobias and Arthur had left her rattled. Even though Clay's words had calmed her down significantly, she still felt shaken and didn't think it would ease until she had her boy in her arms. Until she held him and reassured herself he was safe. That Tobias would not get him just like Clay promised.

We will never give you up. That was the one thing that gave her confidence. She knew they protected her because she was a valuable member of their Resistance. Even if she had no particular skill when it came to fighting or bravery, she was still an Elemental. She knew they'd keep her safe and by extension, they'd keep Basil safe, too.

Her feet carried her away from her tent. She could feel Clay's presence at her back following her. Hovering. Making sure she was okay. She wouldn't lie. She wasn't. She needed Basil.

Usually, Shula could be found at Ryker's side tending to the wounded. She walked that way and ran when she caught sight of the big, scarred Fae male. He was helping an injured male drink sips of water. He straightened, set aside the jug of water, and turned to watch as Corvina stormed up to him.

Stopping a safe distance away from him, her breathing was erratic, her words jumbled. "Where are Shula and Basil?"

"She slipped away with him..." When Corvina whirled away from him to scream her son's name, she heard Ryker snarl, "What the fuck is going on?"

"Corvina..." Whatever reassurance Clay was going to give her was cut off by the sound of a horn sounding. Everyone snapped their attention to approaching soldiers. They were running and she knew they were supposed to be guarding the perimeter.

That meant something was wrong.

"King Valerio, my lady, my lord," one of the Fae huffed. "There's been a breach of the perimeter. We found soldiers dead at their stations. Iron arrows to their throats."

Her mind swirled like a thunderstorm.

"Have you seen Shula Azzarh and Basil?" Clay demanded.

"We haven't."

"Search the camp!"

Corvina's feet moved, faster than she'd ever run before. She tore through the camp, frightening her maids into helping as she screamed Basil's name over and over again. There was no reply. Pretty soon, everyone was searching until they made it to the little stream that bisected the camp.

"Shula and Basil are long gone."

Corvina's head snapped up to a nearby tree where she found Weylyn perched on a low branch. He held an orange in his hand, twirling it around and around on his finger like a child's toy.

"Weylyn, what the fuck?!" Clay shouted.

Weylyn's eyes glittered and he dropped the orange to the ground. A second later, he followed after the fruit, landing in a crouch. He straightened. "I searched," he said darkly. "Their consciousness is far away." He met Corvina's gaze almost apologetically. "They were both taken."

Her throat gave out a strangled noise of heartbreak. She struggled to keep her breath, but it was hard. She'd known Tobias was going to set a trap. But she hadn't seen it. She'd thought he'd take her or kill their companions. And she'd been so lost in her own mind and insecurities that she hadn't been able to think and realize that this had been his plan all along.

To take Basil by force.

And he'd taken Shula along with him...

Tears pricked at her eyes, but she forced them away.

"Corvina," Clay began. "We'll get them back."

In the distance, she heard a roar. Like a feral animal had been unleashed upon their camp. Moments later, Ryker appeared, his eyes wild, his breathing ragged. "Where is she?" he demanded. He swung his fists around empty air in a wide arc. He moved like a beast and looked like one with the scars and wild hair and beard.

He began pacing as if he'd been caged. She understood, because she felt a mirror of what he was feeling. Her skin began itching, like her magic wanted out. To be unleashed. Like it wanted revenge.

"Ryker," Clay tried to reason. "We will get her back."

The healer snarled a loud, vicious sound.

"We will get them back," Corvina said vehemently.

Everyone seemed to stop and stare at her as she marched forward towards a soldier. He startled backwards as she grabbed the pommel of his sword and yanked it from its sheathe. It was heavy, but she felt new strength surge through her. She turned, wielding it.

"We will get them back and we will kill them all. Every royal of Dana will die because *I* will kill every last one of them." Murderous intent burned through her. She was ready, like she'd never been ready before. To take them down. To fight for her son like she hadn't been able to fight for herself.

"How do we do that?" someone asked. She couldn't be sure who.

"Use me as bait." Corvina would give herself up for her son every time.

"Corvina, no." Clay grabbed her arm. "You can't. That's what the bastard wants. This was part of his trap."

"I don't care, Clay. That's my son."

"And Shula is my best friend." She lowered the sword and he slipped into her space, holding her tightly. She could feel the way his fingers shook against her skin. "I told you we wouldn't give up on you. Well, we won't give up on them either. We will find them. This I swear to you."

Her breath shook in and out of her chest, and she pressed her forehead to his. "We have to find them, Clay."

He breathed her in and she did the same. "We will."

When she came to, Shula's head was pounding. It didn't stop her from jolting up, despite the wincing behind her eyes. Her wrists felt heavy and she glanced down to find them clasped in iron manacles. The arrow was out of her shoulder, but she still felt a twinge of pain. She glanced down at it, finding it wrapped with gauze that bled through her still wet clothes.

She took a breath and surveyed her surroundings. When she saw Basil, she let out a breath of relief.

"Shula," he whined, tears spilling out of his big eyes.

"Basil, it's okay."

"I want my mommy!" He flung himself at Shula, burying his face in her wet shirt. It muffled the sound of his crying, but she could feel his fear like a tangible thing. All it did was bring heartbreak.

This was her fault. If she'd been paying attention. If she'd been fucking listening instead of lost in her thoughts. She'd been felled by that arrow, and thanks to the ashwood oil, she hadn't been able to use her magic to burn those soldiers alive. To burn Captain Brannon alive.

Captain Brannon.

Her breath stuttered.

She thought she'd rid herself of him that day he'd taken her to the Brotherhood. His haunting words made shivers break out across her skin.

"I've been searching for you for months."

She'd always known humans had been following them, but the thought of the captain following her specifically made her skin crawl. It felt like a violation. She recalled the press of his lips against her cheek, and in a moment of panic rubbed her cheek against her shoulder to rid herself of the lingering sensation. As if he was still there.

Once she took a breath, calm settled over her. She was fearful, yes, but she had to shove that aside in order to think rationally to be able to get out of this situation. *Sleight of hand.* She inhaled deeply.

"Basil," she said firmly, drawing his attention to her. "Are you hurt?"

He shook his head.

Relief was immediate. "We'll get out of this." She didn't know how, but they would. She'd gotten out of the camps, she'd escaped soldiers when she was twelve, escaped the Brotherhood, had melted iron, and learned to fight. She could fucking do this. "I promise, Basil."

Just then a door opened, causing Basil to flinch. He gripped her tightly as soldiers walked inside, among them Captain Brannon. With a single gesture of the captain's fingers, the soldiers started towards them. Shula snarled, jerking against her bonds but went ignored.

The soldiers bent and picked up Basil between them. The child kicked and screamed. "Shula! Don't let them take me! Shula!"

"Let him go!" She pulled against her bonds but fell short. The chain was hammered into the ground so she looked inside her well of magic for even a simmer of it, but it was dimmed. "You bastards, let him go!"

"I am afraid we can't do that." Captain Brannon gestured again and the soldiers took Basil away. "His father will want to see him, and it would be best if he weren't in the same room as you when he gets here."

Her chest rose and fell with her fury, but she tried to keep a level head. She wanted to get all the information out of him she could. "And where is here?"

Captain Brannon sighed and gave a look to the remaining soldiers. They obeyed without question, walking out and closing the door behind them. It wasn't until they were gone that he spoke. Shula tried to focus on the words, but it was difficult when she realized how close he was. How little space separated them.

"We're in a Danarish prison cell."

"At the castle?"

Captain Brannon observed her. It was unnerving, the way he could go completely still. It was like looking into the eyes of a Fae. It was preternatural.

"No," he answered. Then he was moving forward. Shula jerked back as far away as the chain would allow her. Too late, she realized her mistake. She ended up pressed against a wall and felt cornered as his huge frame towered over her. "You look different from the last time I saw you." It was odd how his voice was almost… reverent.

"So do you."

He looked more formidable. She hadn't been too afraid of him at Piriguini's Circus. Not in the same way she was now. Then, he'd been a mere soldier. Now, she feared him as a man. Because no longer did he look indifferent. He raked his eyes over her like he was searching for… something she couldn't place. His gaze stopped on her chest where the material of her shirt clung to her breasts. A chill raked over her body at the blatant admiration that flashed in his eyes before he hardened his expression.

"You are less… fearful," he mused, more to himself than to her. His hand reached out, capturing a chunk of her damp hair in his fingers. He rubbed at it, caressing it with a care that made unease grow in her stomach.

Come on, she thought to her magic. *Fucking work. Fucking do something.* There was nothing but silence.

He lifted her lock and sniffed it, and she fought back a gag. She wanted to suddenly chop off her hair, to get rid of anything he'd touched with his creepy fingers.

He lowered his fingers and rocked back on his heels. "Though I suppose that's to be expected. You've been with the Resistance for months. You've left quite the destruction in your wake. All those burned camps…" He *tsked* and it was followed by a chuckle. "I almost had you at that castle in Tuath and then you disappeared."

She tried not to show emotion but was afraid it bled through. "You were at Castle Aileach?" She looked at him up and down. "How? How did you find us?"

He seemed almost distracted with her, looking over her like she was a puzzle he wanted to solve. She knew he was curious about her ears, because he kept pushing away her hair to get a good look at the points of them. She hated how she didn't know what he was thinking, how it seemed so easy to hide his intent. It felt malicious and her gut was churning, instinct telling her that she needed to get far away from him.

"Finally," he whispered. "I finally found you. You are the first to escape me, but I vow this will be the last time. The Brothers were fools. But I am not. I secured your manacles myself and will post my most trusted guards at the doors. You will not escape me again, Fire Dancer." He stood up, his armor and swords clanking. "I *will* take you to the emperor. You will serve your purpose and afterwards…" He smiled, mirthless and cruel. "Well, we will see, won't we?"

A moment later he was gone, but Shula couldn't breathe her relief. Basil was gone, and she'd promised him she would protect him. Her magic felt dormant at the moment, but she would fucking force it out if she had to. Because she was strong. She would get out of this.

If it was the last thing she fucking did.

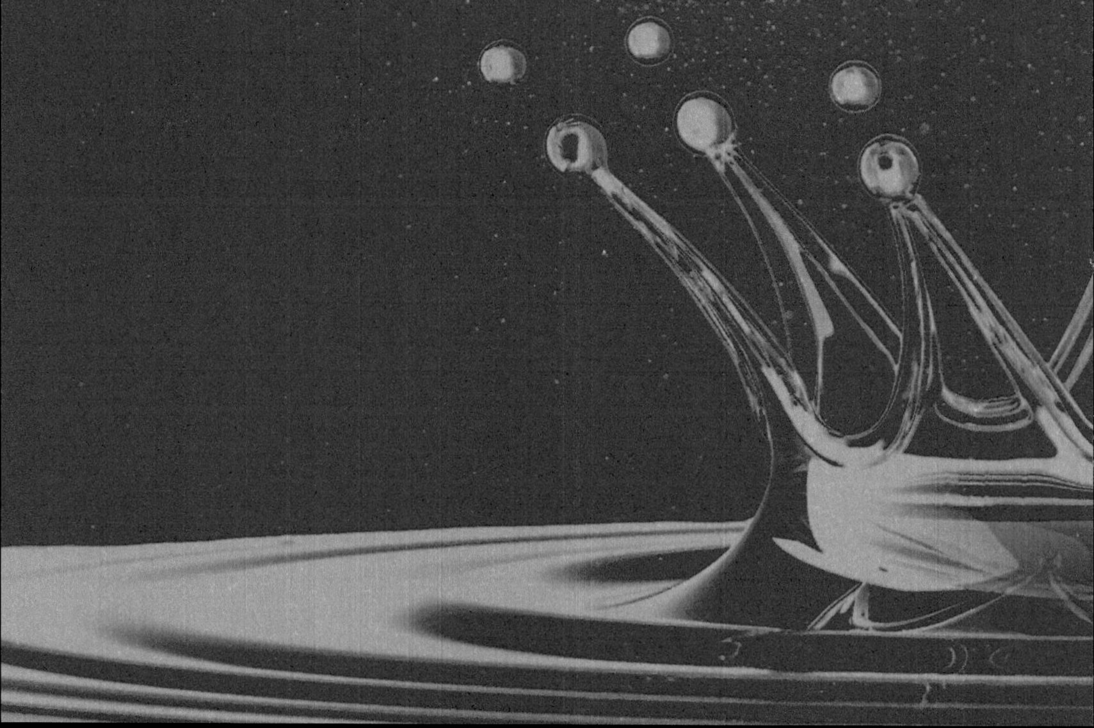

Of Waves and Death

Tobias was laughing when the portal opened and Corvina stepped through. He lounged against a throne, arrogant in his success, with his brother beside him. The sight was sickening. Arthur's pants were pulled down to his thighs and a Fae slave was between his legs, his hands tethered to her hair as he moved her up and down against him.

Bastards.

Both of them. So sure that they'd won just because they'd kidnapped her son and an innocent woman.

It took a moment before anyone noticed Corvina. All the soldiers were lazing about, taking in the show Arthur gave them. When they finally looked up, a series of shouts had attention snapping on her, one by one.

When Tobias' eyes finally lifted, the smirk fell off his face. His cheeks were flushed as he took her in. And the weapon she wielded.

Corvina lifted the sword and pointed it in her husband's direction. Lines of fury were etched on her face. She probably wasn't intimidating, what with her small stature and innocent face. But they should have been afraid.

"Corvina," Tobias all but purred. He pushed himself up to a standing position. "What are you wearing, wife?"

Armor. Snug pants and metal armor that overlapped like the scales on a fish. It was heavy, and it made her slow, but she'd wanted to make a point. That she was no longer the same woman he'd trapped into marriage. The same woman who he'd forced inside her body. She was no longer the meek little Danarish princess who ate what he told her to and dressed how he wanted. She was changed.

She was vengeance.

She was fury.

Beside him, Arthur pushed the Fae woman off of him and she fell back with a cry. Corvina didn't get a good look at her face. Arthur shoved his member back into his pants and stood up, grabbing for his own sheathe and sword while watching Corvina with both wariness and amusement.

"You took him from me," she accused.

Tobias snickered. "How else would I get you back? You both belong to me and it's time you came home."

"I am not your property, Tobias. And I want my son back. Now."

"Why don't you put down that weapon before you hurt yourself, Corvina? You'll see for yourself, you are outnumbered here and you didn't bring backup." He snickered as if she were dumb, petulant.

And Corvina was so very tired. Of it, of him, of being treated like shit.

The human camp had been only a few miles away from their own. She knew Basil wasn't here. He wouldn't have brought her son so close and risk losing him. Her son was likely back at his father's castle under heavy guard.

That's what she'd thought when she began concocting her plan. But then Weylyn told her he could feel their conscious thoughts and they were somewhere else. In a prison cell.

Her rage rose then.

He'd put her son in a cell. Like he'd done to her. Tobias didn't care about Basil at all. He didn't give a shit about his own son's wellbeing. All he wanted was to be feared, to be revered by his family, and he would use Corvina and Basil to achieve his goals, no matter what it did to them.

She was *done.*

"You have no idea what I've brought, Tobias." And then Corvina lifted her hand and her magic awoke.

It was like a puzzle piece sliding home, clicking into perfect place. She'd repressed it for far too long, only letting it out in small increments. Magic was not supposed to be contained. Not like that. Not like she'd been forced to do. You see, magic needed an outlet or else it festered and built, awaiting an explosion. And she had magic locked up within her in abundance.

The Lagnh Sea responded to her call. The same sea Dawn had wanted them to drown in. The same one she'd watched for years on end, wondering what would have happened had she listened. It was an old friend that heeded her needs and the waves lifted.

They rose...

And rose...

And rose...

And even miles away did not stop the screams as Corvina flooded the castles on those hills. As she let her magic and her water take over to kill the royals and courtiers of Dana. Their screams echoed, shrill like the cries of gulls. Then their drowning gurgles. First in Tobias' castle. Her prison. Her cage.

Tobias and Arthur paled and soldiers started towards her. She pointed her sword at their approach and magic gripped them, water choking through their lungs until they dropped to their knees and coughed it up, then died.

"Corvina, what the fuck are you doing?!" Tobias demanded.

She trained her sword on him. "My son, Tobias." The waves settled. "Give him to me or the humans of Dana will die."

Arthur visibly paled next to his brother, and she resisted a smirk. The Wes men were arrogant and cruel. Yet there was one thing she knew about them, and it was that they loved their people. They would do anything for them, even if it meant fucking over the Fae in the process.

"Corvina, stop this at once." Tobias started forward and in response, waves crested over the castle. The screams rose up once more. He froze.

"You are no longer my keeper," she spat. Her hands trembled, not from fear but from anger, rage. And he could see it. She made sure of that. "Give me back my son or your people will keep dying."

"Tobias, we should—"

"Shut up!" Tobias screamed at his brother. "Just shut the fuck up, Arthur."

Arthur's eyes narrowed. "Our people—"

"Fuck the people!" he screamed. "This is my wife and son."

"They are no more important than our citizens."

Tobias' eyes flashed. How he could change in a split second. How he could seem so normal and perfectly fine one moment and within the next, he was unhinged. His eyes flashed, his nostrils flared, and the hatred for his brother rose like the waves Corvina commanded.

"Stop telling me what to fucking do, brother," Tobias spat.

"Maybe if you weren't so fucking stupid—"

He didn't get the rest out. Tobias moved so fast, he was nearly a blur. There was just the sound of a sword sliding, and then a grunt.

And Corvina smelled the blood.

Tobias had stuck the blade in to the hilt and blood bloomed across his brother's chest. Arthur blinked down at the wound with surprise and then looked up into his brother's eyes. Corvina couldn't see his face, but she knew what she'd find there if she could.

Years of hatred finally poured over into a single act of violence. Madness. Craze. Desperation.

He yanked the sword from his brother, and Arthur's body crumbled to the ground. Around them, soldiers shuffled their feet. Murmurs rang out and Corvina wanted to scream at them.

Do you see now? She wanted to yell. *Do you see how fucked up your precious prince is?* But she didn't need to say anything to them when they were finally realizing the truth for themselves.

But it wasn't enough.

"I have had it with your insolence, you bitch!" Tobias turned that hatred towards her and started forward. The looming, threatening demeanor for a moment flashed her back towards what she had been and what he'd made her into. "You will come back with me or I will kill your fucking son and all of those Fae bastards you call friends. How about that?"

He reached for her and she flinched back. Her magic stuttered inside her, and she scrambled to grab a hold of it. His sword lifted and she let out a silent cry, the weight of it suddenly too much. It slipped from her grasp, falling to the ground.

Tobias advanced. He lunged, his own sword at the ready. Her magic rose, forming a shield of water in front of her, a wall that enveloped him. But in her brief moment of fear, it wasn't strong enough. He cut his way through it, drenched from head-to-toe, though not caring.

"You are *mine*, Corvina." He lifted his sword. The iron rings on his hands flashed and she flinched away, imagining them hitting against her flesh. The pain was a vivid memory. It always was. But then Basil flashed in her mind, and she straightened, taking a breath as he advanced.

When the sword swung in her direction, she lifted her arm, magic coalescing around her to form a thick shield. It didn't harden, but caught the sword within its depths, pulling within. Triumph gleamed in Corvina's eyes, but it didn't last. With a cry, Tobias wrenched the whole thing back and swiped his feet out at hers, cracking against her weak ankles.

With a cry she doubled to the ground. Her magic rained down into a pool on the ground. Then Tobias was falling on top of her, his thighs straddling her waist and pushing her down against the wet earth.

"Fucking pathetic!" The sword pressed against the edge of her neck. "You're right back where you should have been all along." He leaned forward, his teeth gleaming with manic pleasure. "Beneath me."

She swallowed, feeling the blade cut her skin. She was afraid. Her heart pounded, but she was determined not to cow beneath him again. "I could drown you right now," she said sweetly, her old self flaring to life. "I could use my magic to kill you here and now. I always could."

He blinked, as if surprised she had the audacity to talk back, before sneering. "Yet you never did. Because you're afraid. You're fucking weak, Corvina. Elemental or not. Fae or not. You don't belong in this armor, just like that sword never belonged in your hand."

"That's your problem, Tobias," she gasped. "You have no idea what the fuck I'm capable of."

Her magic blasted between them, pushing him away. He fell away from her with a cry, but not before slicing the sword out and cutting against her armor. As soon as he fell back, he stood up. When his soldiers rushed to help him, he snarled at them to keep back. Then he charged, volatile, angry. He didn't think before he ran towards her.

That's when the air beside her shimmered and a moment later, a body came hurtling out of a portal, intercepting Tobias in his lunge for her.

Steel met steel, surprising Tobias. The human soldiers grunted, but he shouted at them to stay back. The two bodies were a blur of fury and weaponry. They parried but the Fae man was stronger, shoving Tobias back.

That was his mistake. Seeing an opening, a human soldier lifted his bow and let loose an arrow. It soared through the sky, piercing the Fae's collarbone. He gasped and staggered, and Tobias jumped up. There was a grunt as steel met flesh. Tobias backed away and the man who'd protected her crumbled to his knees. And the blow, the pain? It hit her like it was her own.

"Clay!"

"Fuck your filthy lover," Tobias spat, laughter coating his words.

Corvina's head swam as she registered the blood. He'd jumped in front of her. He'd protected her. He'd taken the pain for her.

Tobias was still cackling; he didn't notice when a portal opened and several Fae stepped through to catch his soldiers by surprise. She barely noticed them either—even when all of this had been a part of their plan—when all she could focus on was the pain in Clay. In her friend. In her mate.

She exploded.

Magic tore out of her along with a screaming cry of rage. Water cracked out of her, forming a shield around Clay. Protecting him from Tobias.

"Get the fuck away from him!" Her hand blasted out and water emerged, snaking around like a coiling rope against Tobias' body. He screamed as it tightened, trying to swat it away. But it crawled, shoving into his open mouth and down his throat. His body convulsed. The sword dropped from his hand. She watched his body drop to the ground a moment later and she followed, crouching low. His eyes widened as he choked, and she smiled at him.

Years of enduring cruelty. Years of hatred and fear. Years of being degraded, used, and ashamed. It stopped then. It could have stopped years ago, but she'd been too afraid. She wasn't anymore, and she let him see that part of her. The birth of a new woman.

One who no longer feared, but who should be feared.

A woman who stood up for herself and had the strength to do what she hadn't been able to do before.

So with his eyes focused on her, Corvina smiled wider and willed her magic out harder, faster. And she didn't tear her gaze as she watched her husband choke...

...and die.

Arrogance is a Downfall

Shula sat with her eyes closed. The captain had left her alone, but she could sense other soldiers standing watch outside of her cell in that lone room. She leveled her breathing, letting the rise and fall of her chest lull her into a peaceful state while she waited... and waited...

She searched inside herself, and when the moment finally came, her eyes opened. Shula smiled and she *reached.* She pulled out her magic and it responded, stirring, fighting at first as it banged against the presence of iron. But she was a fucking Elemental and that was where Captain Brannon's arrogance failed him. They thought she was weak. He thought the iron would render her useless.

But she was a fucking survivor. She broke the bounds of magic and history. She was the first Fae in history to melt iron. And while the bonds on her wrists stung, they were no match for the rage she unleashed.

Fire flickered against her fingertips. It sputtered and she relaxed, calling it forth. It was second nature now. Instead of smothering it, she called for it, willing it to burn brighter, hotter. Her hands were set aflame and it only burned and burned, enveloping her entire body in glowing licks. She watched as the iron manacles slowly began melting until they slipped from her wrists.

She stood to her feet. She could feel her body glowing, set ablaze by the need inside her. She walked up to the door and held her hand up. Fire shot out, incinerating it until a hole was burned. She stepped through and met the blades of iron with her magic.

The humans on the other side cried out in fear, and she resisted the urge to smirk. They'd underestimated her. Everyone underestimated her, but she swore this would be the last time.

Their swords began melting down to their pommels, the heat pooling against their hands. They screamed as it went through their flesh. They dropped to their knees, looking in between their hands and Shula as her flickering figure stepped in front of them. Like they were taking in the reaper prepared to steal their lives.

"Where is the boy?" Her voice sounded far away, like it wasn't her own and was separate from her body. Ethereal. Magical.

They trembled, the stench of charred flesh prominent through the air, but she ignored it. And when they didn't answer fast enough, her hand lifted as if she meant to reach out for them. The glowing of it reflected in the humans' eyes, and they recoiled from her proximity.

"H-he's with Captain Brannon a floor above..."

Shula smiled then and the flames died. She bent towards them and the humans didn't move as she reached and plucked a set of keys from their sides. Fear lived in them. She could smell it. It gave her freedom to walk down the hall of the dungeon. Figures peeked at her from behind iron bars. When she passed, they shot back in their cells.

Her magic responded to this cruelty, shooting fire out to melt the iron keeping them confined. Only then did she toss the keys in their direction. "Free yourselves from your prison," she told them. "And rise up against Dana if that is what you wish." They weakly reached for the keys to freedom from their manacles. Shula smiled her encouragement before turning back to the way ahead. "The Resistance is here, and we are taking our lives back."

Fire trailed at her heels as she pounded up the steps. Iron melted in her wake and prisoners cried out their freedom. They tore from their cells, stealing the swords from guards and running them through their captors. They rallied together, and she could hear them piling out onto the streets. Pride swelled in her chest, but she pushed that aside as she tuned her senses into the sounds down the hall.

She heard Basil's muffled cries and followed, breaking down a door to find him. He was huddled in a corner and cried out when he saw her, and he wasn't afraid.

"Shula!"

She started forward, but the sound of a swinging sword had her ducking and rolling along the ground. The sword followed, but she dodged just as it struck the ground where her head had been. She hopped to her feet, magic burning her fingertips as she faced Captain Brannon.

The fury on his face was frightening, and surely if he had magical abilities, he would have killed her with that alone. Questions burned behind his eyes and she smirked in the face of it. He didn't know how she'd escaped, and if he left here alive today, he'd find out.

She couldn't let him leave here with his life.

"I cannot let you leave again," he said, his voice dripping with menace. "You will *not* leave. Not when the emperor wants you."

Sounds like he was just licking the emperor's asshole at this point. She wanted to say that aloud but was focused on his positioning and the sword in his hand. Memories of training with Julius and Iona overtook her body. It had already become instinct as much as her magic had. Fighting, learning the movements of her opponent. She was no expert, certainly not against the captain who had probably been fighting his whole life. But she had something he didn't.

Magic shot from the floor, enveloping him in a circle. He grunted from surprise and she thought she had time. To get Basil and leave before the flames claimed him and the building entirely.

But Captain Brannon burst through the flames with a cry, startling Shula. She slipped and started to fall backwards. Her ankle twisted as she gained her footing and she cried out. Magic and steel clashed. It shot out of her hands, scorching his blade, but he pushed through it.

His determination was a surprise that caught her off-guard. He gritted his teeth, feral as he pressed her back. She dodged and he parried. It was a dangerous dance between them. She gasped with every swing of his blade, rolling, dodging, whirling around him in a flare of fire and metallic sparks.

"You will not leave," he growled. "I am *not* letting you go." His words were an echo of what Ryker had said to her. They slipped through her uncomfortably, and she knew if she didn't get out of this soon he would take her and keep his promise.

From the corner of the room, Basil cried, his screams of fear growing louder.

They fueled her need to get through this. Brannon looked so sure in his victory. Like she was no match for him. Even after escaping, even after all she'd proved, he still doubted her. Maybe he always would.

She'd make him regret it.

The pommel of his sword hit her face and she fell backwards. Blood burst from her nose and she tasted the copper tang of it as it slid against her tongue. Her bottom hit the ground and Captain Brannon loomed over her, that same grin on his face. His sword pointed against the tip of her throat. Her breaths heaved, and with every inhalation the stinging press of iron against her skin made her flesh hiss.

"Got you." His smile widened, his teeth flashing.

"No," Shula whispered, despite the press of the weapon. "You don't."

Fire shot out, melting his sword. She'd fallen on purpose. *Sleight of hand.* Let him believe her weak. Let it be the last mistake Captain Brannon ever made.

She made it burn hotter as it incinerated his skin. He fell to the ground, writhing and screaming. The metal of his armor burned into his skin. His flesh bubbled and popped, charring him.

"Your arrogance was your downfall."

He screamed in response.

Shula stepped around his body, bending to Basil in the corner. His eyes were squeezed firmly shut, as though he were used to closing them against unpleasantries. Other than the tears streaking down his dirty cheeks, he looked otherwise unharmed.

"Basil," she said gently, even though the screaming rose and rose.

His eyes opened. "Shula..."

"Let's go." She opened her arms and he jumped into them. She held him tightly, his legs wrapping around her waist in a way that seemed to bring them both comfort. He buried his head into the crook of her neck, and once she had a good hold on him, she ran.

Smoke and chaos greeted them out on the streets. The battle had spilled outside. With Fae tearing off their collars and rising up. For a second, her steps faltered as she watched. They were taking up arms from within. And they hadn't known Shula, but all it had taken was a chance at freedom and whispered words of the Resistance to get them going.

To get them up and to get them fighting.

Such brave, brave people. Braver than she'd been. This just went to prove that they could be chained and degraded, used, abused, and broken but they would always rise from the ashes of what they used to be. Stronger. Fiercer.

And ready for vengeance.

Shula dove into the fray with Basil wrapped tightly around her. Her feet carried her. She wasn't sure where she ran, but through the melee, she kept hearing the same thing over and over again.

"Long live the Resistance!"

"Long live the Fae!"

She ran blindly, pushing through until she found herself near the king's castle. Fae swarmed through it, taking down soldiers. She stood, fascinated, watching as royals were pulled from the castle and out into the yard.

Among them, the King of Dana. His crown still sat firmly atop his head, even as Fae slaves yanked at his body, tugging and pulling. He screamed as he was forced to his knees.

"I am the king! You cannot touch me! Get your filthy hands off me, Fae bastards!"

"Look away Basil." Shula shoved his head into her neck, blinding him from the sight of the Fae taking a sword and swinging...

The king's head rolled towards the sand. Blood spurted in pools against the ground, and the Fae cheered as they bent and plucked the crown from the king's head. They lifted it and threw it.

"Long live the Resistance!" they screamed.

"Long live the Resistance!"

Long Live the Resistance

Ryker tore through Dana like he was controlled by some invisible bond of madness. He growled, searching for his lost mate in the chaos of battle. From within, the Fae who were enslaved to Dana had stood at arms. Fire rose from the prison she'd been at, but she was no longer there.

The thought of something happening to her crippled him. She'd already gotten dealt a shitty hand, what more did she have to go through in a sick twist of fate? She was good. Kind. Now she was being forced to face that bastard captain once again.

She didn't deserve that. She deserved better.

But she was strong. He knew she would get out of this alive. But even so, he couldn't control himself as he struck through soldiers of Dana and Illyk both. The emperor's and the king's alike.

Beside him, Corvina was vicious, as ferocious as he was in the search for her son. Her magic snapped like whips and walls. When arrows flew, she built up a massive shield of water, stopping their trajectory and swallowing them within the depths.

They rushed across Dana. Fae from within the kingdom were fighting, paving the way for them to make it to the castle. And when they arrived, Ryker's body calmed.

"Shula!"

She whipped around, her long hair whirling with her. In her arms she held the child and seeing them both unharmed nearly brought Ryker to his knees.

"Basil!"

The child wiggled out of Shula's arms, and the moment his feet touched the ground, he was turning and rushing towards his mother. She bent, holding her arms out to him, and he jumped into her embrace. Then Ryker was moving and so was Shula. They collided in the middle in a tangle of limbs.

They dropped to the ground, Ryker cradling his mate to his chest. There were no tears or sobs coming from her, but he held her tightly regardless. More to comfort himself rather than her. She wasn't trembling. Wasn't afraid.

"Ryker."

Their eyes met. Held. She must have seen the pain fractured in his gaze, because she cradled his scarred cheek with her hand. She held him reverently, stared at him the same way. Not like his scars were a thing of nightmares, like so many others stared at him, but like they were a testament of something greater.

"I thought I'd lost you," he whispered. In those moments when he'd found her gone, his whole world crumbled once again. Like seeing an arrow tear through her skin. Like seeing a camp without her presence. Twice now his beliefs had been put to the test. And in those two times he'd realized that it didn't matter how many Fae he saved in his lifetime.

If he didn't have Shula, he was lost.

"Shula, I—"

She smiled at him and leaned forward. Her lips silenced what it was he was about to say. As if she were telling him she knew.

As if she was telling him that she felt it, too.

The moment Basil jumped into her arms and wept into her shoulder, Corvina nearly lost her resolve to stay strong. The tears pricked at her eyelids, but she kept them at bay. She didn't want to give in to them. Not again. The time for crying was over.

She had her son back. Shula was unharmed and in her mate's arms. They were both okay.

She pulled away from Basil and looked him over. Aside from a dirty face, he was fine. "Basil," she breathed her sigh of relief. "Are you okay?"

"Shula protected me, mommy."

Just like Corvina knew she would. She owed the fire Fae everything. Everything.

"I am so sorry, Basil." She wrapped him in a hug. "I am so sorry you had to go through that."

His arms wrapped around her neck and held. Corvina couldn't look up until she heard her name whispered. Shula was above her, looking down with sorrowful eyes. Ryker stuck close to her side, his hands grazing over his mate like he was afraid of letting go.

"Corvina, I am so sorry." She dropped to her knees beside her. "I didn't hear them or sense them. They shot at me and I—"

"Are you okay, Shula?"

Shula blinked, as though surprised Corvina was even asking, as if surprised she wasn't reprimanding. "I—I'm fine."

"Thank Mana. I was so worried about the both of you."

"But I—"

"Protected my son. And for that, I owe you a debt." Her voice brokered no room for argument. Forcing Shula to take the words, to accept them. So Shula just nodded. And they embraced.

Then a portal opened in front of them and their companions stepped through; Weylyn with the black cat on his shoulder, Julius, Iona and her polar bear familiar, Valerio, and...

Clay.

Her eyes watched him wobble from the portal on unsteady feet. She'd left him, and he'd been the one to urge her to go.

"Find Basil," he'd insisted.

He hadn't attempted to hold her back. He hadn't put his own needs above hers or her son's. Even suffering and bleeding out due to a wound inflicted by her husband, he'd pushed her away because he'd known how important finding Basil was to her.

Blood still soaked through his clothes, and his skin had paled. But when their eyes met, he smirked, showing off the dimples on his cheeks and chin. Right before he dropped to his knees.

Ryker pulled away from Shula to kneel beside Clay. He let out a curse. "Fool," he spat. "You should have bound your wound."

Clay chuckled, though it sounded pained. "There are more important things."

Corvina's breath caught.

"Yes, well, I need to take you to the castle. I can't look over your wound here."

"It should be safe now," Shula said. "The Danarish King is dead."

"The Fae have successfully taken over the city," Iona added, a smirk in her voice as her hand reached for her familiar. The bear was coated in blood and ash. "The soldiers are scattering. The Fae slaves rose to take back their lives." She looked at Shula. "Did you happen to have anything to do with that?"

Shula looked sheepishly back at her friend. "Long live the Resistance?"

"Told you we were the Resistance." Clay chuckled, but it became a wheeze before he keeled over and fainted.

"Clay!" Corvina shot to her feet and rushed to him, but Ryker was already picking him up and carrying him away. Her heart dropped to her stomach at the sight of all the blood. At his pale, sweat-covered face. Wounds inflicted upon Fae with iron were harder to heal. They were fatal. She knew from experience. And the thought of losing him...

An ache built in her chest, one so painful it made her want to cry out. As if magic were responding to her distress, augmenting it. As if it were starting to break her heart.

But she couldn't lose Clay. She was finally free. She'd finally... taken herself back and she needed her friend at her side.

She needed her mate at her side.

Queen Regent

Corvina swiped a cold rag against Clay's forehead to bring the fever down. His body was working furiously at healing his wound. He hadn't woken up since he'd fainted. Not even when Ryker had cleansed and sewed up the wound. He tossed and turned on occasion, groaning and grunting his pain. It'd been for hours until he finally settled.

Ryker had left long ago, leaving Corvina to wipe away the fever. Her eyes were heavy with the need for sleep, but she couldn't bring herself to do so. Sitting vigil over Clay was far more important.

The door to the room opened and Corvina turned her gaze to the entrance. Dawn stood there, staring within. She wore Danarish armor and a smirk that was somehow mocking. Like she was trying to taint it by wearing it. Like she was mocking the kingdom itself.

"I would have taken the king's rooms," Dawn mused, looking around.

Corvina had thought about it, but couldn't bring herself to do it. She wanted nothing to do with the royal family. They were dead and couldn't hurt her any longer. Staying in one of those rooms would have only dredged up memories she otherwise wanted to keep away, so she'd taken a simple one meant for guests.

"These are more appropriate."

"Hmm. Indeed." Dawn stepped into the room. "How is the Sapphire Lord?"

"There has been no change."

"You should sleep, my lady," Dawn suggested. "At least for an hour."

She wanted to. Just the mention of sleep tugged at her eyelids, trying to force them to close. She pried them open. "I can't."

Dawn sighed. "Thought you might say that. Well, I've come to update you. Basil is with Wren, Gale, and Juniper. He is fine."

Corvina breathed her relief. She'd told him of his father's passing, and while he hadn't shed a tear, she'd worried how it would affect him. In the grand scheme of things, she should have known he was strong. He'd never really had a relationship with Tobias in the first place, so it was normal he not feel sorrow. Especially not for a cruel bastard, though she wondered if he would... later.

"Also, the Seelie King requests your presence in the throne room."

Corvina dropped the rag into the bowl of water. Nerves built their way at the base of her stomach. "Did he say what for?"

"He did not, my lady. But I will keep watch over the High Lord and alert you to any changes."

Covina sighed and offered her maid a kind smile. "Thank you, Dawn." She stood and started for the door after one last lingering look at Clay. As she made it to the door, Dawn's voice gave her pause.

"Do you wish you would have jumped now, my lady?"

Corvina sucked in a breath. She always ignored that question. Dawn would ask it of her whenever Corvina would visit with a particularly nasty bruise or wound covered with cosmetics. And every time, Corvina would turn away, shame heating her cheeks, before she gathered her wicker basket and left.

This time, she turned, head held high and pride shining in her eyes. "No," she answered truthfully. The same answer she should have given then. The same answer she'd wanted to give each time but had been too cowardly to do so. "I am glad we did not jump. Or else I'd not have my son." Her eyes flicked to Clay. "Or my mate."

"Corvina," King Valerio greeted.

She stepped into the throne room and curtsied. When she stood, Valerio was looking at her with warmth in his eyes. "You called for me, Your Majesty?"

"You do not have to call me that," he said. "And yes, we wanted to talk to you."

He wasn't alone in the throne room. Shula and Iona were there, as were Julius and Uric. She hadn't seen them since they came barreling into Dana, Ryker and Shula clashing in a tangle of limbs and kisses. She suspected the Fire Dancer's mate was tending to the wounded. As for the others, she wasn't sure.

"We wanted to talk about the future of Dana."

"What about it?" She stepped deeper into the room.

"With King Archibald and both princes dead, that makes you Queen Regent of Dana until Basil comes of age," he explained gently. "That means you are in charge of Dana."

She closed her eyes at his words. When she opened them again, she looked around the room. Gilded gold and glittering jewels were encrusted against pillars, floors, and walls. For so long these palaces and this kingdom had been little more than her cage. Her prison. She'd suffered here. But she'd also risen here, putting aside that suffering for something more.

And now she was in charge of it. After so long of being degraded and hurt, she was now the master of her own prison.

Everyone waited, but she didn't need to. She already knew what she wanted.

"I was given to Dana in exchange for the safety of the Gold Court." She thought her father had been doing the right thing at the time. That she was doing her own duty to her people. While she loved her father with everything in her heart, she also recognized he was foolish. A foolish old Fae afraid of the changes that were coming. He did what he thought he had to do, and it was the wrong decision.

But sometimes people acted cowardly in what they thought to be their best interests. Their people's best interests. It was why Corvina had stayed. It was why she'd taken Tobias' hands that day. It was why she'd suffered.

She believed it was for her people.

"Everything I suffered and did and held out for was for the Gold Court. And I thought you were all gone, my people destroyed." She thought of Weylyn and his glittering, golden eyes. His eerie silence and the simple act of kindness he'd showed by calling her his lady. "I don't want Dana," she said. "My place is with the Fae. With the Gold Court. Basil will be High Lord when all of this is over and the war is won."

"So you'll help us?" Iona asked. And in her dark eyes, something shone.

Something a lot like hope.

"I will," she said, and something *more* nestled its way in her chest. The same feeling she got when she stood up for herself. It felt good to take her power back. To feel like she'd found her voice again. Like she'd seen the light after so long in the dark. "I want to help." She made eye contact with Iona. With Shula. Magic zapped inside her friends, her new family.

The Elementals.

"I want to fight beside you. And I want to learn."

"We will teach you," Iona said firmly. "We will work together."

"Together," Shula agreed.

Corvina let loose a breath of relief. After so long of rejecting them, she'd been foolish enough to fear they would reject her in turn.

But they weren't like that. She should've known. Broken, bruised, and fixed again, they would accept her in any way or form. Because that's what friends and family did. They loved and cared unconditionally.

"Well, the soldiers have scattered once the Fae rose up. Humans have been thrown into dungeons. Not," Valerio added when Shula threw him a glare, "all of them. Fae have been freed and are celebrating through the streets. We have our stronghold." Valerio smiled. "We are one step closer to our goal."

He was right. They were closer than before. Perhaps it was not a huge victory. It was one small kingdom, the smallest in all of Illyk. But it was a victory for them just the same. And perhaps there were a hundred or even a thousand more steps they needed to take to rise up against the emperor, but this was the start.

And it felt good to win.

Clay groaned as he turned. His back met soft pillows and cushions, and the contrast from the usual hard cot and rocks that dug into his back made him jolt up in bed. He gasped as he felt licks of fire across his body.

"Careful there, Sapphire Lord," a voice purred. He turned slowly and met Dawn's smirking gaze. "You will open your wounds."

"Ah, fu—" He dropped his head back against the pillows. "What in Mana's name happened?" The last thing he remembered was jumping in front of a sword meant for Corvina. Her magic had exploded, enveloped him. He remembered her leaving, and then after that pain and darkness.

"You were shot at and then stabbed." Dawn flicked her fingers with disinterest, though a smile tilted her lips.

"Yeah, I think I got that, thanks." He winced. The pain in his side was piercing and he smelt like shit.

"We won the battle for Dana."

Clay blinked in surprise. "Some good news, at least. Is Corvina..." He trailed off. He caught a hint of her scent in the room. Water. Soothing water and lilting rain.

"Occupied at the moment. But I suppose my High Lady will be happy to know you are alive and well..."

He sat up slowly, breathing in through his nose so he could find the strength to throw his legs over the side of the bed. "I have to see her."

Dawn's nose wrinkled. "Looking like that?" She nodded and he looked down. He was in a dirty sweat-and-blood-soaked shirt. "You stink, my lord. And your wound is bleeding all over the place."

He sighed. She was right. And Clay was vain enough to want to look good—and clean—before going to find his mate.

"If you'd like, there are healing baths here at the king's castle," she continued.

"Healing baths?" He perked up.

Her smile widened. "I can take you there if you please, Sapphire Lord."

His thoughts raced. "I would like that very much, Lady Dawn."

Corvina rushed back to Clay's side after quickly checking in with Basil. He was fine playing with her maids. Though, she supposed, it was inappropriate to call them her maids. They were free now. She would be sad if they left her, because she'd grown fond of them the time they'd been with her. They were more than maids.

They were friends.

But if they left to seek their freedom, she would watch them go with happiness in her heart. They could be free from the confines of Dana like Corvina was. She'd never begrudge them that.

As she rounded down the hall, she almost ran into Dawn. Her feet skidded across the marble floors, and she pressed her fingers to her chest. "Dawn," she breathed. "Is everything alright? Is Clay okay?"

Dawn smirked. "The Sapphire Lord is fine, my lady. He is currently in the healing baths."

"Oh." Her chest rose and fell imagining it. She bit her lip, released it. "Then I suppose I should... wait..." In the room. Until he got out. Of the healing baths.

"Oooor, you could accompany him. He was in a rather bit of pain, and I think he needed assistance in washing his back." She leaned forward conspiratorially. "Between you and me, my lady, I think you deserve a bit of fun. You deserve to know what it feels like to have a real man between your legs." Her lips grazed Corvina's ear. "And from what I've heard, he is a man who knows how to please." She stepped away, her laughter trailing after her like the phantom of a ghost.

And Corvina just stood there, with her chest rising and falling, and a tingling spark of pleasure pooling between her legs.

Promise of Forever

The water was comforting. Clay could feel it infused with magic, something that felt similar to Ryker's, as the water enveloped his skin and healed his wounds and aches. The bruises were the first to go. The internal bleeding and stitches were harder to heal. After quickly washing, he laid back in the water, leaning his head against the side of the pool and closing his eyes.

He was surprised at the luxury of the healing baths. He shouldn't had been, given the fact that the royals of Dana were pieces of shit who valued riches over morality. But he had to say, he was impressed. Especially with the fact that the magical Fae who powered the waters were still in the castle. A pair of gentle healers who hid in the shadows.

There were several small pools for individual healing. Clay currently sat in what he assumed was the king's private baths. A waterfall fell from the ceiling and into the porcelain pool he was in. The water was warm and steam rose up from it.

It was a solitary, calm place.

So it was easy to place the footsteps that sounded across the floor and echoed through the cavern. He opened his eyes and swore on Mana. His breath faltered as he caught sight of the beauty before him.

Corvina stood at the edge of the pool, staring down at him. He'd never before seen her eyes look so intent, certainly not at him. He liked to think he listened and understood women. That he knew what went through their minds and knew what they wanted before they did sometimes.

With Corvina, things were different.

He couldn't read her, but what he could read was the desire in her eyes as she looked at his figure below the water. Not that she could see much with the bubbles from the falls rising around him. She could definitely see his pecs, and he would have flexed if his wound hadn't felt so tender still.

Slowly, so slowly he feared he almost imagined it, she toed off her shoes. She said nothing, but she held his gaze as she reached her hands behind her. He could hear the tell-tale sign of drawstrings being tugged, of each one being pulled through the loops at her back.

He bit back his groan as she shouldered off her top, dropping it into a puddle at her side. His eyes didn't know where to stay focused. Whether on the thin material of her shift and the contours of her breasts beneath, the small valleys poking against the material, or lower as she dipped her fingers into the waist of her skirt and pushed it down.

Corvina revealed her body to him in increments. It was somehow much more erotic to see her in nothing but a thin shift, where he could make out the highlight of her figure beneath, than to have witnessed her naked. This felt like a promise. And she stared at him unflinchingly. He'd never seen her look braver. Not even when she'd been wielding a sword and aiming it at her enemies, when she'd used her magic to drown those who had condemned her.

Her fingers danced along supple, creamy flesh. Rising along her arm and the ball of her shoulder, she slid the string of her shift off a shoulder, then moved to do the same with the other. He was entranced and his dick hardened beneath the water. Even with the steam rising around him to make him dizzy and the scent of soaps and scented oils, he could smell something much more heady beneath it.

Arousal.

She shimmied out of the shift and pushed it aside with her foot. Finally—*finally*—she was naked before him. With a single perusal of her body, he had her figure memorized. Her hair fell over her shoulders in thin wisps and she pushed it aside, giving him the perfect view of her pert breasts. Small enough to fit in his hands, with rosy tips that jutted out in the warm air.

She was still thin, though her body dipped into the slightest hint of curves, down to the flare of her hips. His gaze stopped between her legs and the patch of fine hairs there. He had the sudden desire to grasp her hips and tongue fuck her beautiful pussy. To tease her clit with his tongue until she screamed his name in ecstasy.

He wanted to give her everything.

Everything.

Corvina lowered herself into the water. It came up to her breasts, hiding them from his view. But if he looked into the soapy water, he could just make out her pebbled nipples. What would it be like, to take one between his teeth? To slide his dick between her breasts and worship them with his cock until he came against her mouth?

"Corvina." His voice sounded more like a groan.

She stopped approaching a foot away from him, but he could feel her. Even if she wasn't touching him, he could feel her heat, and it made his mind spin. It wasn't the warmth of the water. It was purely her. Purely this amazing, beautiful, strong, and powerful woman.

"What are you doing here?" he asked, his voice dropping low. From the scene pouring off her body in waves, he thought he had a pretty good idea. But he wasn't an ass. He wouldn't presume to ever know what a woman wanted. They were fascinating, marvelous creatures with minds and thoughts of their own. And whatever she wanted, it didn't matter. He would give it to her. If she wanted an orgasm, he would give it. If she wanted him to suck her clit, he'd do that too. If she wanted sex, a bond, he'd fucking give her everything and more.

"I—" Her arms lifted and crossed over her chest. Her cheeks flushed pink, and she suddenly looked shy.

He had the urge to pull her into his arms to get rid of that sensation. She was exquisite and had nothing to be shy about. It only reminded him how different they truly were. How inexperienced she was in comparison. She had only ever been with one man, and while he didn't know details—he'd commit murder if he did—he guessed it had not been a pleasant experience for her.

Would she even know what she liked?

She took a deep breath. "I thought I'd join you for a bath."

His eyebrow quirked. "Is that all?"

He wanted to hear her say it, if she dared. If not, he would back off, not tease her, wait until she was brave enough to ask and take what she wanted.

"I… I have no experience in this." She buried her reddening face in her palms. "I don't know what I'm doing."

"Hey." She lowered her hands to look at him. "I will only ever take it as far as you want me to go. Experience doesn't matter. I will do what you want me to do. Nothing more, nothing less. Do you understand? You have the power here."

She seemed to contemplate his words and that insecurity was replaced with the same determination she'd wielded when she was taking off her clothes. She wore it like armor, like a weapon. Or like someone who was just now learning just what type of power she held.

"Then if you would like, I would very much enjoy it if you touched me."

If *he* would like? Clay smirked and dropped the expression as he stepped towards her so they were but centimeters apart. His hand lifted, water dripping from his fingers, and when he settled them against the curve where her neck met her shoulder, the friction was slick, smooth, begging for more.

"Like this?" he purred low.

She leaned her head to the side, moaning as his thumb trailing circles against her skin. "Yes," she whispered breathlessly. Fuck if that sound didn't jolt straight down to his dick, making him twitch and ache beneath the water. "But I want more."

His other hand lifted to oblige, pressing against the opposite side of her neck. He began kneading and digging in, working at the knots of stress in her body. The groan she let out was positively erotic. He wondered if she could feel his erection. The tip of his dick swept up against the smooth skin of her stomach, just a graze that made her moan louder.

"More," she urged. "I want more."

He bent. "Tell me exactly what you want, my lady."

She stared at him for a heartbeat, biting her bottom lip. She released it with a sigh. "I want to be kissed by you."

Thank Mana.

He thought she'd never ask.

He dove for her mouth, and when their lips touched, it was like magic blasted through his entire body in a rapid-fire jolt of awareness. She felt it too, because she gasped and he took advantage of the fact to part her lips with his tongue. The action seemed to surprise her, so he pulled away a fraction.

"Is this okay?" He had to make sure he wasn't frightening her or going too fast.

"I—I really like that."

So did he. But he didn't say that. He bent down and kissed her again. This time she opened her mouth on her own, letting him inside. Their tongues tangled in a dance. It was slow, sensual. He took his time to explore her, to let her get used to the feel of him. It would give her time to learn what she liked and build up the anticipation. As it was, his dick was already screaming at him, demanding he plunge into her heat and ease the ache she'd caused since he'd met her. But he wasn't a selfish asshole. Had never been, and he wouldn't start now. He wanted to make this good for her. So he played, his tongue dragging against her own slowly, languorously.

She was panting against him, pressing closer with every stroke he gave until her body couldn't seem to stand it. She rubbed against him, the heat of her pussy grinding against his thigh. Her folds parted against his skin, and he bit back his own groan of pleasure even while hers tore through her mouth. Her clit rubbed against him. Her own hands rose while his stayed firmly clasped against her collarbones. Her nails explored his body like he was a map of treasure.

She broke off with a gasp. "Can you... can you touch me other places?" Her lips were swollen from his kisses. A marking that left some primal part of him satisfied. And her voice was a desperate whine. Like the pleasure she tried giving herself against him would never be enough.

"Where?"

Her face blushed.

"I want to hear you say it, my lady."

"All over. I need..." She grinded her center against his thigh, rubbing and easing the ache with a groan. "Please," she begged. "I want you to touch me. I want to feel you. I want your hands on me."

He gave in, sliding one hand down her back and over the curve of her ass. She gasped at the gentle firmness of his touch. The other hand slipped between them, going slowly down her stomach and lower still until he reached her heat. They both groaned the moment his palm cupped her there.

"That feels so good," she whimpered.

"I'm just getting started," he promised.

His finger slid between her folds, from the bottom all the way up to pause against her clit. He pressed down against it. She jolted against him, her hips jerking on his hand. "Oh, Mana," she breathed. "That..." Her big bright eyes found his. "Can you do that again? And kiss me some more."

"I can do whatever you want me to do." He bent and kissed her, all while stroking her folds. He didn't penetrate, but teased, occasionally grazing her clit to drive her wilder with every touch. She began jerking against him, looking for friction to ease her desire.

"I've never felt this before," she breathed, riding and chasing her orgasm. "I don't—"

"Just let it happen." He pulled his hand away to turn her, pressing her against the edge of the pool. "I can make you feel better, if you'd let me. With more than just my hands."

Her lashes swept low against her cheekbones. "I want to experience it all. Everything you have to give me."

His eyes closed against such a declaration. When he opened them again, he was surprised by the trust shining in her eyes. "You're sure?"

She nodded vigorously. "I... I trust you."

She may as well have declared her love for him, with how much those words meant to him.

"I will give you anything, Corvina, but I want to know what makes you uncomfortable. What don't you want me to do? I don't want to ruin the moment for you or make you upset in any way."

She thought about what he said, and he was glad she wasn't jumping in, telling him to do whatever he wanted. That could go wrong in so many ways, and he cared about her pleasure more than his own. He could easily learn her body based on sighs and moans. But there was nothing like teaching a woman what she loved, or knowing a woman who was vocal about what she wanted.

It was the same with dislikes. What some women sought desperately, others avoided. He wasn't ashamed that he had slept with many females in his time.

He was old, had sought companionship. More than that, he'd sought to make women happy in any way they wanted.

He would do the same for Corvina.

"I want you to kiss me as often as you can," she said.

He made note of that. "What else?"

"Don't say mean things."

He bit back the growl that rose in his chest.

That piece of shit. He wished he could bring him back from the dead just to kill him all over again.

"I would never insult you, Corvina. Never degrade you."

There were women who liked that. Women who liked to be called names during sex. He'd done it with others and had taken great care with them after. There was always vulnerability before, during, and after sex. He was being trusted with something precious. And he would never break his mate's trust.

"Please don't choke me."

"I won't."

"Or get too rough, hit me, or wear jasmine oils. Ever."

His palms landed on her hips and hoisted her up, sitting her on the edge of the pool. He pushed himself between her legs, his hands meandering across her skin in lazy strokes. This close, he knew she could feel the head of his cock press against her folds, but he didn't push forward. Not yet.

"I will be gentle, and I will only go harder at your insistence."

She let out the breath she'd been holding. "Thank you."

She didn't have to thank him for being a decent person. It was respect she was owed. Respect that asshole should have given her. But he had no space between them. There was no room for him in her mind or in this moment.

Clay dropped his voice to a husky whisper. "Feel," he ordered. "And enjoy." Then he was kissing her again, building up the desire they'd momentarily lost in their chat. She reached for him, scraping her nails down his back. She moved softly, timidly, but he didn't mind. She'd learn what he liked soon enough. He trailed kisses down her chin and her head dropped back, giving him access to her neck.

His tongue found a pathway that had her moaning and urging him on as she tangled her fingers through his hair. When he reached her breasts, he let out a sound that was animalistic at best. Then he was lapping at her nipples, tugging the sweet buds into his mouth and licking the water from them. He gave them attention in equal measure, alternating between one and the other until her breathing was little more than a rasp. Until her hips began rolling, seeking friction and pressure.

His hands pressed her hips firmly against the marble. Firm enough to keep her from moving, but not enough to make her feel like she was trapped. He began lowering himself in the water, bending his head over her thighs. He pressed kisses against her body, licking every contour, mole, and freckle he could find. Her thighs trembled around his ears. He massaged up her calves, pressing down and lingering on places that made her sigh and groan.

His lashes flickered as he stared up at her. She was a beauty with her head thrown back and her bottom lip taken between her teeth. He leaned forward then, breathing against the center of her pussy. She groaned, her hips jerking as if seeking his mouth.

And when he leaned forward to press a kiss to her center, he groaned and swore he saw Mana.

This was torture in the most delicious of ways. All Corvina had ever known was cruelty. With Clay, she felt fulfillment for the first time in her life. It zapped through her body. Everywhere he touched, he left a trail of wanting behind. Like fire pressing across her skin, and she craved to follow the trail of it.

Her breaths came out in shudders and pants every time his tongue and lips grazed across her skin. She whimpered with each touch, wanting more but unsure how to convey it. Her hips sought him. His touch, his hand. If only to chase that feeling she had earlier. One that balanced her on a delicate precipice.

Then she felt his tongue press against her folds. She jumped up, crying out in surprise and yearning as he licked her slowly, like one would lick melting chocolate from their fingers. He lapped her up like she was a delicacy he couldn't get enough of. His tongue flicked slowly against her inner walls, while his hands kneaded and massaged her thighs. She trembled and whimpered around him, and it was then she realized her hips were moving of their own volition against his face.

It was wanton and erotic. She didn't know what to expect. She was chasing something. Longing she had in abundance, but it was like her body was searching for more. For something that felt just slightly out of reach. She wanted it, and she almost got it when Clay pressed the flat of his tongue against her clit.

She bowed off the marble, not caring that it was cold and wet beneath her naked body. All she cared about was the feeling coursing through her. His tongue teasing and nipping, wrenching desire out of her like she was attached to a hook. He pulled and she could do nothing but follow as the sensation crested...

There was an explosion of feeling throughout her body. She gasped, her scream of surprise echoing through the bath house. She couldn't hold back the sounds just like she couldn't stop the movement of her hips as they went wild against his mouth, bucking and seeking more, more...

Her body felt languid and she melted against the marble as Clay pressed a final kiss against her clit. He prowled up her body, water sloshing over her skin as he held himself over her, his arms on either side of her head. Healing water dripped against her face, and she tasted it against her lips.

Clay smiled down at her, the action radiant. She always thought him beautiful. Now was no exception, but somehow he looked even more so. He brightened any room he entered with little more than a smile and his positivity. He was kind and caring, and Corvina's chest ached with the reality of what he was.

Her mate.

He was the mate she'd always dreamed of, and one she thought she didn't deserve for so long.

Tears prickled behind her eyelids, but she pushed them away and reached a hand up to his chest. This close, she could smell herself—her desire—on his breath. It was erotic. She pushed against him, startling him as she switched their positions, shoving him down against the marble so she was straddling his waist on top.

She felt breathless, like the little glimpse of pleasure he'd given her had just been the beginning. Was she greedy for wanting more?

"Is this okay?" she asked, gesturing at the new position.

His smile widened, making the dimples on his cheeks that much more prominent. "I am yours to ride and do with as you please."

Her face heated. The thought that she'd have the power... Her mind flashed back to Iona and Julius. How the female had commanded him like she was commanding a legion. And he would have gotten down on his knees for her. He would have torn the world down if she asked it of him.

To have that in her own grasp...

She experimented by slipping her hand between them and wrapping it around the hilt of his cock where his girth met his balls. He let out a groan that she couldn't interpret and loosened her hold.

"Is this okay?" She didn't want to hurt him.

"Mana..." His nostrils flared. "It's more than fucking okay."

She smiled shyly at him, a perfect contrast to the sudden boldness of her strokes. She gripped him tighter and moved her wrist, sliding up and down. She watched his member with fascination. She was no stranger to them, but she certainly was a stranger to one this beautiful. He was long and thin, hard when she squeezed, but with soft skin that she teased with her touch. She pulled the skin back from the head of his dick. It was bright red, and a pebble of clear liquid beaded against the tip.

Her mouth watered with the sudden urge to taste it.

So she did exactly that.

She sat back on his thighs and wiggled forward. Her hair swept over her shoulder, nearly shielding him from her view. She groaned a complaint a second before his hand reached up and gathered a fistful of hair in his hand. He did it so gently that she didn't even flinch.

Corvina's tongue darted out now that she could see him, licking and swirling around his head. The taste of musk and salt and something far headier exploded on her tongue. It was like taking his scent, his essence, and it coming to life in her mouth. That cider-y, bubbly, intoxicating scent of him. She inhaled it, sucked it onto her tongue. She played, her mouth moving up and down his length. She'd never done this before willingly, and this felt sloppy, but she never realized just how arousing it could be.

"Fuck, Corvina," Clay cursed. "That's so—Ngnr—"

She pulled off his length with a pop and smiled. "Do you like that?"

A growl rumbled in his chest that turned into a purr. "Do I fucking like it?" He chuckled. "I loved it. Everything you do... Fuck, it feels like Mana."

She smiled. To know that she was bringing him pleasure, that she controlled it for them both? She scooted up his thighs again so she straddled his waist perfectly. It felt comfortable, to have his dick rubbing against her slit, pressing against her clit.

Their wet skin was slick against each other and warm. Her palms spread across his chest. His form was perfection. Naturally, a lot of Fae were more attractive than humans. At least, the High Fae were. They were perfect with strong bodies. Clay was no exception. Ridges bumped down along his abdomen and she ran her hand over every curve. He wasn't as strong or bulky as the other Fae in their party, but his body was exceptionally beautiful just like his face.

"You're perfect," she whispered.

"I can assure you, my lady, I am not."

She pressed her knees down against the marble and lifted herself. She wanted to play around a little longer, to be brought to the heights of pleasure with his tongue and hands, but she also wanted to take the pleasure for herself.

So she gripped him at the base of his dick and positioned his tip up against her folds. He gasped, his hands grasping at the sides of marble. Not touching, because she hadn't asked it of him yet. She smiled.

"Touch me," she pleaded. "Grab my hips."

He obliged immediately, blunt nails digging into her skin. He didn't yank her against him, just touched, and the heat of his skin against hers gave her the courage to slowly slide herself against him. He stretched her body, his length pushing through her tight channel. It felt like she slid down on him for miles, until her bottom finally touched his thighs and he was fully sheathed within her.

She felt so full, so incredibly full. But she still felt like something was missing. Like she needed more.

"Fuck, Corvina, you're so beautiful. You're like a vision on top of me. I never thought this would happen."

His words were like breaking a dam and pushing water forward. Her magic seemed to respond, and without meaning to, water began falling in a sprinkle from the ceiling. It coated their skin like a second layer, slickening them even more. And she moved against him, driven by some wild instinct to find her pleasure and give it to him as well. She moved, rolling her hips experimentally and finding a rhythm. She tried slowly at first, leaning her palms against his chest as she rolled her hips forward. When their skin met, he groaned. She was learning what she liked, and she liked meeting him in the middle. So she moved faster. Faster.

Harder. She ground herself down, and his hands stayed firmly on her hips. But she wanted more. She wanted him to move with her.

"Clay," she gasped. "Move with me."

His hips thrust up, hitting something inside her that made her throw her head back and scream. Her magic lashed out, water from the pool rising and whipping around them. She controlled it unconsciously as he took over the movements, holding her hips and pulling her down against his length. She tried to keep up with his quick pace, rolling her hips to match his movements. He bounced her up and down his cock and her breasts moved with the rapid pace he set, up and down.

Around them, water rose in tendrils, snaking around their bodies like hands caressing their skin. "Ah fuck!" Clay shouted as a tendril slid over his chest and around his throat. "Fuck, that feels so good." His cock seemed to swell inside her so she focused, controlling her magic. Tendrils snaked around him as if they were her hands, caressing, touching. Water slipped through his hair like fingers from one end and from the other; she let them snake around his legs and thighs, then higher until the water pressed between their joined bodies and wrapped around his balls.

"Oh, fuck, fuck, fuck, Corvina." Clay howled to the ceiling, jerking, his hips stuttering from the magic she pressed against him. She almost thought he would release then, but he stopped moving, holding her firm. His eyes opened and he pierced her with a smoldering look that she felt down to her core. "I am not going to cum inside you like a fucking untried youth," he growled. "I want you to enjoy this."

She smirked. "I am enjoying it." She accentuated her words with a press of her magic around his cock.

His brows rose as he bit back his groan. "That's how it's going to be? You want to bring magic into this?"

Her eyes widened. His words felt like they were laced with a threat and—well, fuck—she wanted everything he had to offer and more. Her eyes must have said that, because he lifted his hips, pushing her up and pulling out of her. She felt surprisingly empty without him and gasped as he set her against his thighs.

"I can play dirty too, lady mine," he growled. "And maybe you want to see just what it is that makes the women go crazy."

A feral growl rose in her chest that she couldn't stop at the mention of other ladies. She knew he'd been with more, but she felt suddenly possessive of him. Maybe she didn't have the right to feel that way, but she'd be lying if she said she didn't want to know what he'd given them. She wanted that and more. She wanted to be the only woman on his mind.

"Yes," she gasped. "Yes, please, I want that."

His eyes narrowed on her. There was a beat of silence and nothing happened. She almost believed that nothing would happen, but then she felt flushed. Her face heated, like all the blood in her body had rushed to her face, and that sensation traveled in small increments all across her body. It felt like hands were pressing against her. Not just any hands, but Clay's hands. Like he was inciting pleasure when he wasn't even touching her. It was in the flow of her blood as it heated beneath her skin, hotter and hotter, rushing across every inch of her. From her nipples to the curves of her breasts. It went lower and she felt herself growing wet, leaking liquid desire against Clay's skin that should have embarrassed her, but she was too busy feeling to think about that.

Then the blood rushed straight to her core. It made her moan aloud and her eyes zeroed in on Clay. On the way he was biting his lip and staring at her figure. Slowly, blood began to leak from one nostril. She wanted to reach out and wipe at it, but she couldn't. Not when the pleasure was becoming so crippling, she could scarcely move.

And then the blood rush was at her clit. A throbbing incessant need that built and built until it finally erupted. He wasn't even touching her and she exploded, her orgasm overtaking every inch of her body, her soul. It went on, the pressure against her clit never stopping. It only rained down harder, drawing out her orgasm. She grinded against his body but felt no friction and still it came. Over and over again, the pleasure invaded her body until she lost count. Until she couldn't take it any longer.

"Please," she begged. Her magic flailed around her as she tried to grasp for a semblance of control. She nearly fell backwards, but somehow managed to keep herself upright on shaky arms. When her eyes opened, she stared at Clay's smirking face, his teeth stained with blood.

"W-what the fuck did you just do?"

His smile widened, likely at the shakiness of her voice. "I don't think I've ever heard you say 'fuck'."

"Clay..." she groaned.

"When a female orgasm's," he began, "blood rushes towards her clit." He pressed his thumb against that part of her body and she grunted, jolting against him. "After a great amount of foreplay, the skin feels sensitive, the blood heats, and it all rushes down to one place to prepare your body for orgasm. I happen to have blood magic, and I can make a female come with nothing more than a thought." He blinked and an orgasm slammed into her body once more. Her nails dug into his thighs as she gritted her teeth through it, gasping and writhing. When it ebbed, she opened her eyes. "I make the blood in your body rush and heat, and I pool it towards that one spot to wrench pleasure out of you. I don't even have to be touching you to make you lose yourself."

Her breath came out in pants. She felt exhausted, wrung out, but how was it possible that she *still* wanted more?

"No wonder they all sang your praises." She collapsed against his chest. "And still I want more."

"I can oblige, if you want me to do all the work."

Her limbs felt too weak to move. It was different from being immobile, from being chained in iron. She wasn't helpless, and he would stop if she asked. She just felt weak with everything he pulled out of her. She'd never had this before and within the span of a few minutes, he was making her feel so much.

"Yes," she whispered against his skin. "I would like that very much."

"I'll go slow," he promised as he took her hips in his hands and aligned himself with her. She waited with bated breath as he lifted his hips and pushed his way inside of her. She felt so sensitive, that her body clenched tightly around him, pulling him in deeper. He groaned as he slid all the way inside to the hilt.

Then he began to move. His movements were languid, lazy, and she didn't have to move with him because he took over, holding her hips firmly in his hands as he rolled his up to meet hers. With every slide of his dick against her insides, she groaned. She wasn't sure if she was capable of much more, but he proved her wrong. Not with magic this time, but by the things he whispered against her skin.

"Beautiful." He pushed her locks away and kissed her neck. "Perfect." His tongue grazed across her collarbone. "*Mine.*" He captured her lips in a kiss that left her reeling. It made her head spin and he jerked against her, his cock swelling. That seemed to set her off in a final orgasm that he met with his own. Their bodies shuddered together, both of them holding tightly to one another as they rode the waves of something new. Of this, whatever it was.

And she was so lost in bliss, she knew she never wanted it to end.

Clay's fingers massaged her scalp as he rinsed the soap out of her hair. It'd been a strange sensation, she thought, the fact that he wanted to take care of her after what they'd shared. She was so used to being used and discarded that when he'd gently pulled out of her and cradled her body to his chest, slipping them both into the water, she nearly swooned.

Then he began lathering her body with soap. Every movement was gentle against her sensitive skin, and there was a certain vulnerability to be found as he took care of her, that tears slipped from her eyes. This was new and foreign, and yet she relished in every moment of it.

"This feels nice." She sighed.

Clay rinsed the rest of the suds from her hair and turned her slowly so she was facing him. He pushed aside her wet locks, his fingers hovering over her collarbone. That spot felt especially sensitive and she couldn't be sure why.

"I will always take care of you," he vowed. "Of you and Basil. Anything you need, it's yours."

Her breath caught and her eyes closed. The tears slipped and he caught them with his thumbs.

"Sometimes this feels like a dream," she confessed. "And I fear I'll wake up."

"It's very real." His fingers danced along her collarbone, tapping lightly. He was staring at the spot contemplatively. "We are perfect for each other. Not just because Mana claims it so, but because you're my match." He smiled warmly. "I've never met someone as kind or as fierce as you, Corvina. You have this light inside you that I'm drawn to. Even when you thought you didn't, I could see it." He bent forward and pressed a kiss to her skin. She felt the lightest graze of his teeth and when he pulled back, she saw his canines were elongated. They didn't make him intimidating. In fact, they made him even more beautiful. "Corvina," he whispered. "Can I bond you?"

The question caught her off guard. She jolted, blinking at him. He wanted to bond her? To... to bite her and accept the ties that Mana had tethered around them? It was an almost surreal question. For so long, she'd dreamed of this. Then despaired for she thought she'd never have it.

She'd been broken, torn down, and had risen up to become who she thought she wanted to be. And Clay was offering her something she'd always wanted.

Vividly, she could picture that future. A future where they were bonded by magic and something more. Something fiercer, stronger.

And she longed for it. She wanted it like she'd never wanted anything else in her life, and that scared her. She'd risen from a terrible situation and she deserved happiness. She deserved someone who revered her like Clay seemed to. But she also knew that she was still lost.

One victory did not equate to being healed. Parts of her still felt broken, bruised. And Clay could offer to fix them all he wanted, but she knew that in the end, it was up to her to heal the broken parts of herself. She couldn't rely on anyone to do the work for her. She had to stop thinking like a victim. Learn to stop flinching every time someone raised their hands. It wouldn't be easy, and perhaps a part of what Tobias had made her into would always live in her. She would always be that broken Fae who had become shy and sad. But instead of cowering in the dark corners of her mind, this new self could embrace the broken version of herself. She could wrap broken Corvina in a hug and whisper the words she'd never believed before.

"You are brave."

But she knew she wasn't quite there yet. She wasn't quite who she wanted to be. She'd only taken the first step, just like the Resistance had. And there was still a long way to go.

She took a breath and answered, "No."

His face looked crestfallen for a moment, but he didn't pull away. Didn't react in anger or irritation. He smiled, even if it was a little sad.

"At least, not yet," she added. His eyes lit up at that. "I feel strongly for you, Clay. You are everything I ever dreamed I'd have, but I can't bond with you just yet. If only because I want to be worthy of you."

He blinked, surprise coloring his features. "You *are* worthy of me, Corvina."

"Then I want to be worthy of myself."

And those words nestled inside her like a truth. Perhaps she was already worthy of him, but she still wasn't as strong as she wanted to be. She wanted to find herself again. Be what she knew she could be. Discover all she had to discover.

She wanted to bond Clay. She really did. And one day, they would. If he would still have her in the future. But right now, she wanted to focus on herself. She just hoped he understood that.

Again, Clay surprised her. "Alright," he conceded. "Take your time. Do what you need to do, do what is best for you. But know this: I will wait. However long it takes, I will wait for you."

Her heart nearly cracked at those words.

"What if it takes forever?" she asked timidly.

"Then forever will I wait. I will wait until the sun bleeds out and the moon's light extinguishes. Until the stars in the sky die and the oceans run dry. Until mountains can be brought to their knees, until Mana becomes little more than a legend and a whisper of ancient magic. I will wait for you always. Until the end of time."

Tears fell again and she cupped his cheek, leaning forward to press a soft kiss against his lips. "Thank you," she whispered.

He smiled against her mouth. "Always," he vowed. "Always."

And the magic of their bond strengthened. Though they hadn't officiated it, though they hadn't marked one another, it grew, and they both felt it in that instant. As it wrapped around their bodies, sealing around them.

Like the whispered promise of forever.

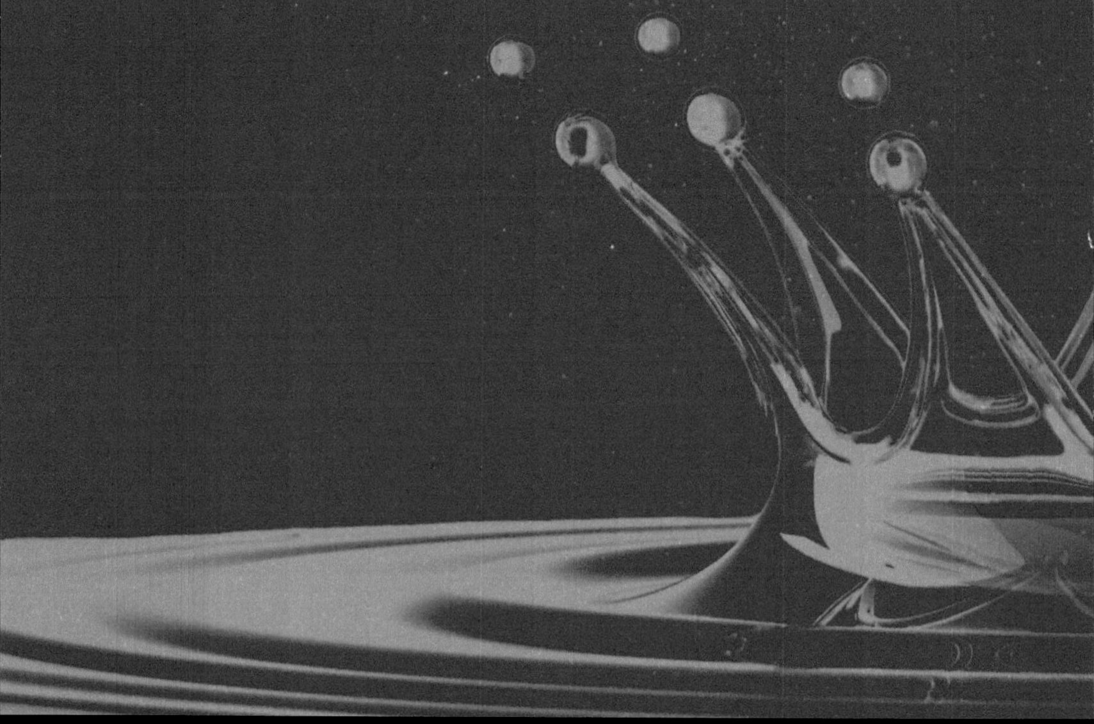

A King and a Crow

With her damp hair braided over her shoulder, Corvina stepped into the throne room, hand-in-hand with Clay. Their fingers were entwined and firm. Confident. United. Eyes turned in their direction, and she felt her cheeks heat as the Fae took in their joined hands just before their eyes flicked up to zero in on her neck and then his.

Surprise colored their features. Perhaps they were expecting to see the mating bond and both of them wearing it proudly. She wondered in a brief flash of insecurity if Clay was embarrassed. They knew they were mates, and when they were near the presence of Shula and Ryker, Iona and Julius, she wondered if he felt regrets.

But those thoughts blew from her mind as he pulled her closer, wrapping their joined hands around her shoulder. He let out a laugh that seemed to break the tension in the room.

"I know I'm beautiful, but you don't have to stare. Perhaps you can commission a portrait instead."

Julius cackled and Iona and Shula both snorted. Valerio rolled his eyes. "Now that we are all present and accounted for," he drawled, "there is still the matter of deciding who will rule over Dana."

They all sat in a series of cushioned chairs in a circle. Corvina found it odd that Valerio hadn't take the king's throne for himself. Instead he sat with his friends like an equal. It made her admire him much more. There were two empty chairs there already for the two of them and Clay led her towards them, waiting until she took her seat before he extricated himself and sat in his next to her.

"Dana is ours now," Valerio said once they were all seated. "We need to keep it protected. I have no doubt that the emperor's soldiers will come to take it back, and we need someone in charge who can see them coming."

Julius stroked his ginger beard in throat. "I can give you a list of my strongest men."

"Why not one of you?" Corvina suggested. When attention drew to her, she lifted her chin. She was trying not to blush every time she felt the pressure of their gazes, but some things were hard to unlearn.

"I trust everyone in this room implicitly," Valerio said, though she saw as his eyes flicked sideways to where Weylyn lounged lazily in his chair. The golden Fae smirked, as if he knew where the king's thoughts had strayed. "I would trust no one else to come with us in our search for the fourth Elemental. I cannot spare any of you."

The fourth Elemental. Being a part of them, of the Resistance, meant searching for them. For others like her and Shula and Iona. And if the fourth Elemental was anything like Corvina or in a situation similar to hers... Determination gripped her. She wanted to go with them and find the Elemental. To protect them. To bring them into their fold.

The Resistance had saved her life. They would save the others as well.

"The Fae have proven loyal to us," Valerio continued. "They will protect Dana now that they are free." He smiled. "We finally have an army of our own."

Julius clapped his hands together. "And the humans won't know what fuckin' hit 'em."

Shula shifted in her seat, the action almost uncomfortable. Ryker reached a hand out and settled the scarred limb over her own, squeezing. The action made her relax a fraction into the chair. She chewed her lip but said nothing. No one seemed to notice it, but Corvina had. She made a note to ask her about that later. Perhaps she would want to talk with Corvina.

And Corvina admitted she wanted to talk to the fire Fae as well. About training and... everything else.

"Now, I think—"

Valerio's words were interrupted by the startling sight of Weylyn's eyes rolling to the back of his head until only the whites of them were visible. His lazy posture slackened and he slid down on the floor, hanging half-on the chair.

Corvina shot to her feet, staring down at her fellow Gold Court Fae, her heart beating. "What's happening to him?"

Clay's touch against her arm and his words calmed her down. "It's fine," he whispered. "It's the price of his magic."

How could that be the price of his magic? To be immobile. It didn't even look like he was breathing. She had the urge to drop beside him and feel for a pulse, but no one else rushed to help him either, so perhaps it really was his magic. They all stared. Waited.

It felt like she held her breath for five minutes straight before his eyes blinked and from his position half-on the floor, he smirked. "Open a portal," he said to Uric, though his body still didn't move, even though his eyes were now focused. "There is someone who wants to see us." His eyes flickered again and Corvina stared between him and Uric. The silver Fae's eyes widened, as if he could hear or see what Weylyn was.

A moment later, Uric's magic stirred in the air. The surface of the air shimmered like an illusion coming to life. It hardened until a tall and wide mirror appeared in the middle of the throne room.

Corvina stared at it, watching with bated breath as a figure pushed his way through the surface and emerged, tall and proud, before them.

He was a Fae, tall and formidable with dark hair and a braided beard. His severe expression flicked around them, the sharp angles of his face intimidating. He wore a simple traveler's cloak and worn clothes and boots. And perched on his shoulder was a black crow.

The crow cawed.

Valerio stood from his seat slowly, stepping towards the figure, his jaw slack and his eyes wide with surprise.

"Father?"

In his surprise, Valerio couldn't bring himself to drop to his knee and bow before his father. It felt like a ghost had materialized into the room before him. A ghost he'd hunted and held hope for day and night until the day that hope ended and Valerio had given up his father for dead.

But the King of Seelie stood before him, the resemblance between father and son striking. The king was bulkier and bled arrogance. Valerio could barely spare the crow on his shoulder a glance, because he felt like he was looking at a phantom. Like his world had once again tilted and fell. What was one truth became another.

His father was alive.

"Father," he repeated. It was the only word he felt he could say in his shock. Their eyes held, and his father smirked. Usually, that look was accompanied by something malicious. By harsh words and a whipping with magic. But his father surprised him.

The king stepped forward and opened his arms, jostling the crow on his shoulder to take flight and find perch somewhere else in the room.

"My son," the king said. And he wrapped Valerio in his arms.

The king felt solid, strong. Real. It snapped Valerio out of his stupor. This was real. His father was alive! His arms lifted and wrapped around the king. They never showed this much affection, but for the moment he relished in it like he was a starving man fighting for a scrap of food. It wouldn't last, so he took what he could.

And when his father pulled away, he knew the niceties were over. Thick brows pulled into a disapproving line. “You disobeyed me,” the king said sternly. “I told you to find the Elementals.”

Valerio’s jaw locked. Of course, he would not see the fact that he had taken a whole kingdom for the Fae. He would focus on the one thing to prove that Valerio was as worthless as he thought him to be.

“We found her.” He turned and gestured at Corvina.

His father followed to where she stood next to Clay. His nostrils flared as he took her in, seeming unimpressed with the thin scrap of a woman. He dismissed her just as easily to turn back to Valerio. “A single Fae. You could have had at least two by now had you not been gallivanting around Illyk assuming my title.” He stepped deeper into the throne room and looked around, distaste evident on his features. When he caught sight of the throne, he climbed up the steps towards it and took a seat.

As soon as he did, the crow cawed and flocked to him, sitting once more on his shoulder.

“We needed an army,” Valerio argued. He hated how everyone was here to witness his father’s words. He knew the king was doing this on purpose. To humiliate him. To bring him down. Because it had not mattered that Valerio thought him to be dead. He knew his father thought him a would-be usurper. He thought that Valerio had been trying to purposefully take his crown, his position. When that was not the case at all.

“We need the Elementals,” the king countered. “And you have wasted enough time playing at king.”

“Your Majesty, I procured you a kingdom.”

The king’s fingers flicked with disinterest. “One which I will rule over while you and your companions continue to find the Elementals like I ordered you to do.” He reached his fingers out and the crow flapped its wings, dropping to perch against the king’s hand. “You seemed to have forgotten, son of mine, that I have eyes everywhere.” He smirked. “Even within the emperor’s own ranks.”

Valerio wanted to scoff. “And who is your informant?”

The king pierced him with a glare. “All in good time. Now go. Find out where the next Elemental is and get out of my sight. Take a small party with you.” He chuckled. “War is coming... and we need to be prepared.”

To Ielwyn

"So what do we do?" Corvina sat cross-legged on the ground, staring at the crumpled map on the floor between them.

The three Elementals sat in a circle around it. Iona's fingers solidified to ice before melting. Shula juggled stones in her hands. The men hovered around them. Julius at his mate's back and Ryker at his. Clay was at Corvina's back, her son perched on his shoulders. The rest, at least, gave them the illusion of space.

She didn't like feeling trapped, even around people, but she calmed her breathing. Her hands shook so she clasped them tightly in her lap. She thought that she was nervous from the presence of the Seelie King. The *real* Seelie King.

For weeks, she'd given that position to Valerio, but now that his father was back, she would have to grow accustomed to calling him Prince Valerio. She didn't feel like he should have that title. He was more a king than his own father.

She'd heard stories of the Seelie King, but they'd been of grandeur. Not of the cruel man she'd met earlier. And Corvina was familiar enough with the cruelties of men to know that something evil dwelled within the king's eyes.

And what must it have been like for Valerio, to think his father dead only to have him come back and take over everything he'd worked so hard to achieve?

"It is for the good of the Fae," he'd said, though the words had sounded stiff. And before they'd left, he'd asked his father one last, lingering question. "How did you evade Weylyn's detection?"

The king seemed loathed to admit what had happened. His nails dug into the arm of the Danarish King's throne. "I was fatally wounded and comatose," he said dismissively. "Now get out of my sight."

They'd reconvened in a separate room together where Shula had promptly pulled out a map and smoothed it out on the floor then taken six stones in her hands.

"We hold the stones together and drop them on the map," Iona supplied with a smile. "Nothing to it, really."

"You have to think about the magic inside you," Shula added, throwing an exasperated look at Iona for her minimal description. "Imagine what makes you an Elemental and reach for it. You feel the power when the three of us are together..."

"I do." Even now it was humming and vibrating down the line between them.

"Reach for that and then we will drop the stones."

"I still don't see why Weylyn over here doesn't just use his own magic to creep on our fourth Elemental," Clay grumbled.

Weylyn chuckled. "I told you, it does not always work that way."

"You found Corvina easily enough."

She turned to watch them and found Weylyn's golden gaze on her. "That is because Corvina and I share a connection."

Clay's warning growl ripped through the space. Surprisingly she didn't feel afraid of that display of jealousy, but she found herself placating him anyway. "He means because we are both from the Gold Court."

Weylyn flashed a smile that was all teeth. "Sure," he said. "That's what I meant."

"Let's just do this," Iona snapped before an argument could break out. "You heard the king. He wants us gone as soon as possible."

"Hands out."

Corvina obeyed Shula's command, placing her hands over the map, palms up. The other two Elementals did the same, and as one they clasped their hands together. Just touching made a surge of magic flow through her body. It felt powerful, like having an electric current zapping between them, just following one after another.

"Reach for it," Shula said.

And Corvina did. She reached for her magic, thinking of what it meant to be an Elemental. It was unity. It was power. It was friendship and hope and the ability to make or break an entire race.

"Let go."

Their hands separated and the stones fell against the map. Corvina watched them clunk, all on separate spots. Her eyes widened and a gasp tore from her mouth. Three stones fell into place on the spot that marked Port Bay, Dana. The others scattered around.

Ielwyn.

Vellm.

And the last bounced around. Not in one place, but in several.

Lights interconnected the stones like rivers of color spreading on the map, buzzing softly and beckoning.

"Amazing, isn't it?" Iona asked.

"Incredible."

"I still don't see it," Julius said.

"So, where to next, ladies?" Clay bent to stare at the map. "Please don't say Valley of the Dead."

"Will you shut up with that already?" Shula teased.

"It's the fucking Valley of the Dead! No one who goes there survives. It's where they dump monsters and criminals."

Corvina barely listened to their argument. Her gaze was riveted on the map before them. On the bouncing stone that hopped from place to place. It paused in certain locations for a few minutes before bouncing again. It flicked from Teg to Orknie to Dana.

"Here!" Shula slammed her finger down on the map. "This is where we're going next."

"Ielwyn?" Valerio had crouched down to see. "You are sure?"

"Positive."

"Then to Ielwyn we will go." He stood.

"Time to place bets," Clay began, sliding Basil off of his back. Corvina's son scrambled into her arms, laughing. "Who is the next Elemental and who's mate will she or he be?"

Valerio rolled his eyes. "This is not a game, Clay."

"Earth Elemental," Julius said, mischief glowing in his eyes. "Paired with the prince."

Valerio jolted at that and froze. For a split second, Corvina caught a glimpse of something in his eyes. Something a lot like longing.

"Spirit Elemental," Clay countered. "Paired with Uric."

Iona laughed as she pushed her way to her feet. "Both of you are wrong. It's the air Elemental."

They froze for a second, cocking their heads in her direction. "Can you tell what Elemental it is by looking at the map?"

Iona just flashed them a feral smile that made them groan. She laughed and shook her head. "We can't, but I want in on this bet. Air Elemental paired with..." Her gaze went over the line of men. "Uric."

Uric growled in response, his fingers deftly pushing his black dagger around in a dance. "Fuck that. I do not want or need a mate."

Iona teased him and the others laughed. Corvina watched as she held her son close. Never before had she felt such a feeling of contentment.

Never before had she felt home.

She stood with Basil in her arms. "Earth Elemental," she joined in. "Paired with Weylyn."

"Noooo!" Everyone cried at once, staring at her with abject horror.

"What?"

"Weylyn, love, really?" Clay asked gently.

"It's rude to talk about him as if he's not in the room."

Weylyn just smirked. "Worry not, my lady Corvina. I am used to the disdain." Something flashed in his eyes before he schooled his expression and turned away from the group. She watched him go. He'd been right when he said they had a connection. She felt protective of him, like she would a friend or her son. She couldn't explain it and wasn't sure if she wanted to.

"Valerio deserves a mate," Julius went on boisterously, pulling her back into the conversation. "If anyone deserves a mate, it is him."

Valerio chuckled. "I appreciate that, my friend. But I doubt it very much."

"Well, you never know. Mates are always hiding in the damndest of places." Shula placed her hand on his shoulder a single second before pulling away. "I've no doubt you will find them."

Valerio stared at the Fire Dancer in silence, and that longing burned so deeply it made Corvina's chest ache. It was gone though as quickly as it came.

"Thank you, Fire Dancer," he whispered. "Thank you."

Pain awoke him and his mouth dropped open in a silent scream that wouldn't come. Agony seared over his face and body. He trembled in shock and made an attempt to move his limbs, but nothing responded.

Never before had he lost control of his functions. Never before had he fucking *lost.* And the pain of that was even worse than knowing what wounds crawled across his body.

The fire had eaten away at his skin on half of his body. It had crawled up in dangerous licks to kiss his face and destroy him.

That fucking Fire Dancer.

That fucking bitch.

At least his cock still functioned enough to get hard at the thought of her betrayal. Treacherous thing. He tried to move and when he failed, a flash of laughter shook in the back of his mind along with a voice.

"Your own arrogance will be your downfall. And that which you have hunted your entire life will be the death of you."

That fucking witch of a Fae. Davina. He wished he could go back in time and grasp her neck in his hands and pull the life from her himself. Instead, he'd been forced to be lenient. To take her to the Emperor of Illyk and let him deal with her.

Now he would die without having killed the bitch. He would die without having delivered the fire Elemental to the emperor. And the shouting cries of "Long Live the Resistance!" in the streets let him know that they had lost.

Fuck.

He wished he would just die already instead of having to listen to that bullshit. It was almost as bad as hearing the Brotherhood preach their nonsense.

At least he had his swords strapped to his waist. He just hoped that if someone happened upon him, they would be intelligent enough to take them both. To know who he was, if he wasn't so disfigured, and know that they could use the weapons to track the Fae down.

Footsteps alerted him to someone's arrival. He tried to pry his eyes open, but even that was agony. Besides, all he saw was a blurred figure looming over him. A flash of black and red, and a flash of purple.

"You're alive," the voice whispered. A very feminine voice.

He groaned in response.

"Don't worry, soldier. I'll get you out of here." The figure bent, and when she grabbed him beneath his arms, he blacked out for a second from the pain. When he came to, he felt his body being dragged through ash and dead bodies, and the soft grunting of the female as she moved him.

He groaned his pain with every step.

"We'll find you a healer," the female assured. He swore he heard the word "Portal" whispered beneath her breath. But he couldn't see it. He did feel it, though. How his body pushed through a honey-like surface. A second later, the scent of ash and death disappeared, though remnants of it still clung to his own body. "You are safe now from the Resistance," the female said. "Long live the emperor."

And before Captain Brannon closed his eyes to sleep, somewhere in the distance, he could hear a crow caw.

Acknowledgements

I have to be honest. A Shield of Water has been the most difficult book I have ever written. There were times I didn't think I was going to finish it, times when it was so hard to get through that I just wanted to give up on the series altogether. I can't particularly pinpoint a reason as to why this one was harder than the others. I think it's because this was Clay and Corvina's book, and as you may have seen, they are vastly different from Ryker and Shula or Julius and Iona.

Each book, I add bits and pieces of myself, of my experiences, of my own flaws and my own life, and it makes every single book that much more personal to me. Readers always ask how I get my inspiration for certain characters, and easily enough to answer... I find myself in a lot of my book babies. Especially within the Elementals.

Shula Azzarh is such a personal character to me because I breathed all of my own flaws into her. The insecurities she feels, while I noticed some readers and reviewers have called her annoying, have stemmed from my own deepest fears. My fears of not being accepted for who I am. My bad habit of comparing myself to others and feeling like I won't measure up. My fear of speaking out... A lot of her flaws live in myself because, well, quite simply, Shula Azzarh is me. The ugliest parts of me, at least.

Iona Wylde was also someone I deeply connected with. While I don't have her sense of speaking out and fighting spirit, I do have her anxiety and her anxious habits. The finger tapping? I do that when my anxiety gets really bad. I have to drum my fingers or else my hands shake, or else I can't breathe. I know a lot of anxious people do something, whether that be move their legs, their hands, bite their nails, etc. We all deal with things in our own way. I also have a touch of Iona's impulsive ways. Especially in the way her and Julius came together. It reminded me a lot of my husband and I. We knew each other a week before we got together. Then seven or eight months later, we started a family. Seven years later we got married. We kind of rushed our lives together, much like Iona and Julius rushed their relationship. I've read reviews and readers have said to me that it was fast, or that they didn't get a chance to get to know Iona and Julius like they did Shula and Ryker, but I disagree. See, with Julius, what you see is what you get. He doesn't have secrets. He has overcome his childhood traumas. Would I say he's a completely functioning adult? Maybe. He does have a bit of a drinking habit, and that might be how he copes. I know he's not angsty like Ryker or Valerio and so that might not make him interesting in others' eyes, but Julius is a breath of fresh air to me. That's why I love his character. He is fun, boisterous, and he's what I need when I sit to write this kind of content.

Now, the real reason this all came up...

Corvina Rhian.

This might be the reason this book was so difficult for me to write and I may not have even realized it at the time. When I sat to write, I had a goal to finish months before I actually did. That's because I took a month-long break to gather my thoughts. I felt like this book just wasn't coming together. It was an arduous process that was killing me slowly.

I felt like I couldn't connect with Corvina like I could Shula and Iona because I realized I just hadn't lived the same trials that she had. It's difficult trying to dive into the mind of someone you feel like you can't relate with or someone you don't understand. But guess what? After going over this book, I realized I do understand. See, I reached out to those who knew what Corvina was living. To the strongest women of us all who have lived through domestic violence. Who have explained to me in detail what's happened to them. How they coped. How they're doing *now.*

It opened my eyes to a lot.

So I want to thank Alexis, Nikki, and Lisa for opening up to me about your own stories. Thank you for helping clear the spots that were dark in this book. Thank you for being you. I am in awe of you and I am in awe of every woman who has had to deal with something like this in their lives. For those who have dealt with it, who are dealing with it, who will deal with it. My heart goes out to you. And don't ever forget...

You are not weak. You are not broken.

You are strong. You are perfect.

You are us.